WITH

THE
DEVIL'S BAG MAN

THE
DEVIL'S
BAG MAN

ADAM MANSBACH

HARPER Voyager
An Imprint of HarperCollins Publishers

THE DEVIL'S BAG MAN. Copyright © 2015 by Adam Mansbach. All rights reserved. Printed in the United States of America. No part of this book may be used or reproduced in any manner whatsoever without written permission except in the case of brief quotations embodied in critical articles and reviews. For information address HarperCollins Publishers, 195 Broadway, New York, NY 10007.

HarperCollins books may be purchased for educational, business, or sales promotional use. For information please e-mail the Special Markets Department at SPsales@harpercollins.com.

Harper Voyager and design are trademarks of HCP LLC.

FIRST EDITION

Designed by Shannon Plunkett

Library of Congress Cataloging-in-Publication Data has been applied for.

ISBN 978-0-06-219968-3 (hardcover)
ISBN 978-0-06-243372-5 (international edition)

15 16 17 18 19   OV/RRD   10 9 8 7 6 5 4 3 2 1

For Healy, I guess. Whatever.

THE
DEVIL'S BAG MAN

CHAPTER 1

Izel Notchi Icnoyotl stood atop the sweep of glimmering quartz stairs that fronted the great golden temple of Tezcatlipoca and gazed down at a thousand of the empire's most prosperous souls.

He could get used to this.

He *would* get used to this.

The guests were warriors and politicians, merchants and traders—all of them gathered to witness the minting of a new dynasty, to celebrate a consolidation of wealth and power that foretold the lessening of their own prospects and promised to nudge them further from the innermost circles of influence.

But to *not* be present would be even worse.

Izel breathed in their discomfort. It was intoxicating. The sun blazed overhead, fiery and huge, as if the celestial body itself sought a closer view of the union.

And why not? The prize of an empire was about to be bestowed upon its favorite son, in a perfect wedding of beauty and power, flesh and spirit.

His oldest sister, and his oldest friend.

New money, and ancient power.

It was a day for which Izel's family had waited decades—though *waited* was a euphemism, a nicety; a truer word would have been *plotted*, or *strategized*.

Murdered would not have been inaccurate, either.

But all that would fade away now, the history rewritten by the winners. And besides, the machinations might have been unsavory, but they sullied neither the bride nor the groom; that young radiant pair was oblivious to the low-toned musings and raised-eyebrow speculations of their fathers. Neither was ignorant of politics—on the contrary, Izel's sister was his father's right hand in matters of business, and Cualli had been raised from birth to wield the full power of the Line of Priests—but their relationship's prehistory, its convenience, did not concern them.

Cualli loved Chacanza with a fierceness so pronounced it was like a force of nature, and he had for as long as Izel could remember. Sometimes he marveled at the way Cualli's will operated on the world, the force of it so intense that you could almost see mind and matter bend in accordance with the holy man's desires.

Or perhaps Izel had it backward, and it was Cualli's love for Chacanza that had shaped *him*. Perhaps through his devotion, the priest had grown into worthiness, become the very man she wanted.

It was impossible to say which of them was the sunflower and which the sun, and when it came down to it, Izel didn't care.

His victory had already been secured.

Cualli had made him an initiate, ushered Izel and his sons and theirs into the House of Priests. It would not have happened if Cualli had not been negotiating for Chacanza's hand, but in many ways the bond superseded marriage, was stronger, more sacred. And though Izel's appointment warranted no grand display, it was just as magnificent a coup for the family.

He would never have Cualli's power, but Izel would always have his ear.

And perhaps, in a few years, his younger sister.

Not bad for the grandson of a provincial spice merchant.

Izel's dark eyes flicked away from the throng and settled on the couple, arrayed on a raised platform, their jeweled feet at the level of his waist. Normally, a priest would have performed the ceremony, but it was unthinkable to suggest that any man might be closer to the gods than the groom himself, so Cualli played both roles.

Marry himself, as it were.

Chacanza must have felt her brother's eyes; she turned and treated him to an enormous smile, emerald eyes flashing, and Izel's heart filled with happiness. She was dazzling, resplendent in a saffron dress, the jewels of her necklace throwing sunlight back at the heavens.

She deserved this.

Cualli's attention followed his beloved's, and as she looked away, Izel locked eyes with the priest.

In an instant, the happiness drained from his heart, and a cold, nameless dread descended. The sun might as well have vanished in a puff of smoke.

Something was wrong. Had he not known Cualli so well, Izel never would have seen it. But behind the smile, the healthy glow of his skin, the proud straight back, his friend's dark eyes were like two bottomless pits. Cualli was somewhere else—somewhere this moment of triumph could not touch.

Where that might be Izel could not fathom and feared to know.

But to serve Tezcatlipoca was to know terror, just as it was to know power.

The terror of power.

The power of terror.

One did not exist without the other.

The serpent ate its tail.

The sun had returned to the world—it resided inside Izel's chest now, pulsing with unbearable heat. Sweat burst from his pores, and Izel dropped his gaze, unable to bear the depths of Cualli's eyes a moment longer.

Instead, he found himself staring at his friend's hands. One was intertwined with his sister's, their long, elegant fingers perfectly matched just like everything else about them.

The other, Cualli held behind his back, curled like a talon. His nails dug into the soft flesh of his palm, as if the priest hoped to redirect all the violence of the universe inward, visit it upon himself.

Izel startled as Cualli's clear, resonant baritone boomed over the waiting crowd, reciting the first words of the matrimonial blessing.

Only Izel saw the fat droplet of blood fall from the priest's hand and splatter into a vivid crimson blotch on the pristine white quartz below.

CHAPTER 2

The laws of the universe were simple, Domingo Valentine thought, as he folded his crisp white shirt into a precise square and placed it carefully atop a low stone table positioned close to the bathtub.

Power—real power, brutal and awesome, the kind most people didn't know existed and could not have fathomed even if they'd come face-to-face with it—did not simply disappear. It might change shape, abandon one form for another, but it did not cease to be.

None knew this so well as Domingo, for none had stood as close to power. For six years, he had provided Cucuy—the Great One, the Ancient One, the Timeless One—with the only form of sustenance he required. He had watched Cucuy devour the beating hearts of countless virgin girls, *the vessel of the gods,* and desired nothing more than to remain at the right hand of the master forever.

Domingo stepped out of his trousers and added them to the neat piles of garments. Candlelight grotesqued his shadow, threw an elongated, flickering version of himself across the earthen walls.

A dim memory, dormant for years, flitted through his brain, like a piece of paper animated by a sudden breeze. Domingo was seven years old, sitting with his grandfather by the sea. It was a time before time—before the fire and the city, before the brothel in which his mother worked became his home, before his own induction into the business of selling female flesh. And long before he'd been thrown in jail to rot and instead found his true calling, here in the bowels of Ojos Negros Prison, in service to the Timeless One.

Domingo's abuelo had pointed at the water and whispered into his grandson's ear. *All the water in the world has been here since the beginning of time. And since the beginning of time, not a single drop has been lost. It's in our bodies, our oceans, our sky. It never stops moving, but it's always the same. How's that for magic, mijo?*

If water didn't disappear, then how could power?

Yes, two months ago he had discovered Cucuy's body, lying in a chamber adjacent to this one in an advanced state of putrefaction, the flesh melting from the bones, the heavy amulets sinking into a murky stew of organs.

This despite the fact that he had been alive no more than a few hours earlier—alive, and making grand plans to abandon his five-hundred-year-old body for another. A pure, still-beating heart imbued with all his power was en route to Texas, where Cucuy's son Aaron Seth would consume it and be consumed.

At least, that had been the plan.

But Cucuy had not returned. In Seth's body or any other.

Hence this desperate attempt to communicate.

Domingo removed his underwear, raised his leg over the side of the tub, and paused for a moment, foot poised inches from the surface of the bath.

The candlelight did no justice to the color, made the blood that filled the deep basin appear dull and rusty instead of bright and thick and—well, if not alive, then *vital*. Brimming with the stuff of life, like some primal stew just waiting for lightning to strike. Domingo could feel the heat rising off it, in the cool damp air; it was exactly the temperature of a living body.

Had to be, or the communion he was attempting would surely fail.

It would probably fail anyway, he told himself, tamping down expectations as he eased his leg beneath the surface, inch by precious inch, acutely aware of the young lives that had been forfeited so that this tub might be filled.

Domingo was no initiate. No priest. Nothing holy flowed through his veins. But desperate times anointed men. Demanded that they become other than they were.

For better, or worse.

As the Great One's procurer, Domingo had supplied him with far more than a steady flow of young girls. His expertise had expanded with his responsibilities, until he provided all that Cucuy's vast, unknowable plans required: guns, drugs, men to move them both. As his devotion to his master grew, the outside world faded like an old photograph, withered to the size of a chessboard, with Cucuy looming over all.

Domingo's eyes and soul had adjusted to the darkness; candles replaced the sun, and the old religion overtook the new. Erased it, like a mistaken calculation scribbled on a scrap of paper.

That part had been easy. Effortless, even. Domingo had always been a creature of logic—and if man had been created in God's image, as the priests of his youth insisted, then how ridiculous was the lame on the cross, suffering gladly for the sins of his own creation? Or his holy mother, sacred of cunt, a perversion of every elemental truth?

Domingo knew how a mirror worked. If man was a reflection of God, it was a god like the Ancient One—cruel and ruthless, straining against the confines of the body, the strictures of the world. *That* was an image he could believe he had been made in.

He, and everybody else he'd ever met.

And now, perhaps inevitably, Cucuy had escaped those confines, cast off his mortal coil the way a snake shed skin.

Perhaps Cucuy had never been alive to start with—at least, not in the narrow, mortal sense of the word.

In which case, he certainly could not be dead.

Domingo's line of reasoning had bent itself into a circle those first days. He'd paced that track endlessly, looking foolishly for an exit.

Finally, he'd shaken himself free of the impulse to understand and turned back to the practical matters at which he excelled, the skill set that had made him indispensable to his master to begin with—and asked himself the only question he might hope to answer.

Where was Cucuy now?

It ran through Domingo's head on a loop, as he struggled to maintain the illusion of normalcy, hold together the sprawling, fractious empire the Timeless One had left behind. Perhaps his role was simply to hold down the fort, wait for Cucuy to reestablish contact from whatever realm he now inhabited, whatever vessel now contained his multitudes.

Soon, though, Domingo had tired of waiting. It was not his way; he was a doer, a man who made things happen.

So he'd made things happen.

In the library was a book the Terrible One had read and reread ceaselessly, seeming always to glean new knowledge, excavate old memories. Perhaps, Domingo mused, some explanation of what had happened might be found there—or better yet, some method of communication. And so the procurer had extended his long arms, reached into corners of the world that had never before concerned him. But it was all the same.

There was always a price.

Either you paid it, or they did.

He brought in a translator, an esteemed professor of religion and antiquity said to be one of the few who could decipher the language contained within the ancient scrolls. Munoz was his name: a nebbish-looking man, long faced and crooked toothed. The blindfold he'd been forced to don before stepping into the armored car didn't seem to worry as much as excite him.

But after fifteen minutes in the Ancient One's cavernous, domed library, carved from the bedrock of the earth, discretion had given way to stronger emotions. The professor's hands shook as he turned the gold-leafed pages, traced the ornate handwritten script. Sweat beaded on his brow; every few seconds he dabbed it with a handkerchief, lest he sully the volume splayed open on his lap.

This is unbelievable, he had stammered as he looked up wide eyed at Domingo, standing at the room's threshold with his arms folded across his chest.

Do—do you understand what this means? If this is authentic, it, it— well, it rewrites everything we know about the Aztec Empire.

Munoz jabbed a bony finger at the page, and Domingo felt an unexpected stab of disgust, as this peon's digit made contact with the sacred, burgundy handwriting.

Right here—right here!—is the story of how the cult of Tezcatlipoca began! The historical community knows almost nothing of this cult. Even its existence has never been proven! And now . . .

Domingo had turned on his heel and stalked off down the corridor. He was a man who hated mistakes, and the instant he realized he had made one, he sought to eradicate all traces of it. It was a compulsion that threatened to trump even his pragmatism, and he knew himself well enough to avoid the temptation to indulge it. Munoz's passion meant he could never be trusted, never be allowed to leave. The realization set Domingo's body vibrating, made it sing with the urge to kill.

Where he came from, problems were best handled swiftly, directly, and brutally; to let a resentment fester or an uncertainty unfold was to invite worse trouble tomorrow. That impulse had served him well on the outside. There was even a certain blunt honor in it. But in the Timeless One's employ, Domingo had begun to learn more artful methods—to look beyond both today and tomorrow, and to find pleasure in subterfuge.

The honor in dishonor.

And so he had stepped into the chamber that served as his office and summoned the guard who'd fetched the professor.

"Sí, jefe?"

Domingo looked the heavyset minion up and down, searching for some sign that he suspected. He did not. None did. Why would he? A man might serve Cucuy for years and never see his face. Most of them prayed not to. They were used to taking orders from Domingo.

"Tell our friend he's looking for anything about communication," he said, voice low and level, forcing himself to keep his eyes buried in the ledger lying open on his desk. "Ancient ways of making contact across long distances. Comprendes?"

"Sí, jefe."

"If he finds something, he writes it down. When he's done, he calls you. You take him out of the library and shoot him in the head."

"Sí, jefe."

Domingo glanced up and nodded in dismissal. The guard swiped a hand over his bushy mustache, as if patrolling for crumbs, then turned and lumbered away. From his carriage, he might just as well have been on his way to retrieve a lunch order. Domingo appreciated that in these men: they questioned nothing, and they didn't spook.

Then again, once you'd seen the devil, what else was there to be scared of?

It was a question that seemed particularly poignant now, as Domingo Valentine took a deep breath and sank the rest of the way into the tub, letting the warm viscous liquid fill his ears.

He was no priest, and he was no monster. He had taken no pleasure in the hundreds of deaths he'd arranged. But nor was he a sentimentalist. The butcher did not mourn the cow. He recognized that it gave up its life for a higher cause, and in his own way he honored that.

Just as Domingo honored the girls he had procured on the Great One's behalf.

And the girls whose blood was the medium that might allow him to reach out now, across the cosmos.

Domingo closed his eyes, and waited.

You must clear your mind, Munoz's notes had said.

He did his damnedest.

Nothing happened.

He became acutely aware of an itch on his left ankle. He scratched it with his right foot, tried not to disturb the surface of the bath, the profound and unexpected heaviness of the blood against his chest and stomach. But his movement caused a slight ripple, and the taste was in his mouth now, hot and metallic. A slight burn to it, even, perhaps generated by Domingo's imagination.

He resettled. This ritual, like every other Munoz had revealed before his passing, was only to be undertaken by the Line of Priests. What exactly that meant, Domingo did not know. Except that the line was broken—that much was for sure. And the way he figured, that meant all bets were off, and anything was worth trying.

He was no priest, but he was the only one left.

That ought to count for something.

He tried to focus on the Great One's spirit and thus summon him.

Imagined Cucuy's voice slithering through the inside of his skull, as it once had. But the taste would not fade from Domingo's mouth—if anything, it was growing stronger. And the weight, the warmth, the failure, the oppressive way the blood seemed to coat his skin—it was all too much.

He sat bolt upright, his chest heaving.

He had been wrong to play at priesthood.

This wasn't in his nature, and it wasn't going to work.

But something would.

Domingo stepped out of the tub, exalted in the cool air as the blood slid down his thighs in thin rivulets.

He had been going about this wrong. He was a man of the world. A fixer. A procurer. A deal maker. Nothing under the sun was beyond his reach, if he willed himself toward it.

And all that he could reach, Domingo Valentine could reap.

CHAPTER 3

Sheriff Bob Nichols rambled his cruiser over the dirt service road, one hand on the wheel and the other between his legs. He couldn't help playing with it, teasing himself. It was bad, he knew, but he was granting himself a lot of leeway these days, treating himself with kid gloves, and the flask wedged between his thighs served as a kind of security blanket.

Knowing it was there calmed him down—presented a challenge he knew he could meet at a time when Nichols was sure of very little, trusted the world about as far as he could throw it. The flask was a sober man's dumb-ass attempt to dramatize a state of utter, brain-melting confusion.

The discipline not to get shithoused.

You're a real winner, huh, Nichols?

On paper, everything should have been fine. Better than fine. For the first time since the ink had dried on his divorce, he was in a solid and loving relationship, something that might conceivably come equipped with a future. He'd met Ruth Cantwell less than three months back, when he'd been called out to investigate the kidnapping of a local girl named Sherry Richards. Ruth was the family's therapist, had helped pry them free of a cult leader to whom the mother had been in thrall.

One Aaron Seth, currently deceased.

Courtesy Jess Galvan, father of the girl in question.

Sherry's mother was dead now too. Murdered that very same day by Marshall Buchanan, a massive, fire-scarred thug in Seth's employ. It was Sherry who'd discovered the body—and Sherry who'd pushed a knife into the belly of the killer a few hours later.

She was living with Nichols and Cantwell now, since her mother was too dead to take care of her and her father too fucked up. A real sweet kid, even if traumatized beyond belief. They all were on some level, he supposed. Made for an interesting household dynamic. Hell of a way to kick-start a romance, too.

Nichols thrummed his fingers against the flask again and reminded himself that everything was fine. Hell, even the traditionally under-funded, overworked Del Verde County Sheriff's Department was less fucked up than usual. Nichols had managed to flip a modest surplus and a pair of useless, overpaid, verge-of-retirement ass-clowns into one promising rookie cop.

Sometimes he could get through half a day on all that, blot the rest out of his mind, feel like the guy he'd always been. The sure-handed, eagle-eyed kid who'd led the Del Verde Vipers back from a three-touchdown deficit in the state semis twenty-five years back and rode the long local memory of his teenage heroism to the unbelievable glamour of his current station.

Methodical and unflappable, that had been Nichols. Keep everybody locked in, move the ball down the field one play at a time. It had been the same drill in Iraq, give or take a few improvised explosive devices. You either lost your cool, or you didn't. The guys who didn't were the ones everybody else wanted to be around, in case it was contagious.

Sometimes it was.

If only Nichols could find a guy like that now. Instead, he had a head full of memories that called into question everything he'd ever believed.

And everything he'd refused to.

Sure, at election time he'd bullshitted the Bible-humping voters of

Del Verde County into thinking he was down with Team JC, but until ten weeks ago? Nichols had been agnostic to the core, a firm believer that what you saw was all there was. That anybody who claimed otherwise was fooling himself, building castles in the air.

Then he'd watched physics take a holiday.

Though maybe *holiday* was the wrong word. It was more like Nichols had watched physics huff a gallon of paint, take a dump in a urinal, make out with its own sister, black out behind the wheel of a big rig, and broadside a fireworks factory.

The images were seared indelibly into his mind. When he tried to sleep, there they were, playing in lurid Technicolor.

Jess Galvan's hacked-off forearm regenerating right before his eyes, tendrils of sinew and muscle wrapping themselves around pure-white bone, skin pouring itself over the form, tiny hairs sprouting like spring shoots from new-made pores.

A soft red lump of muscle twitching in a box, miles from the body it had once animated—miles Galvan had been forced to carry it, across a desert pocked with creatures who had once been girls. Who sensed its presence, climbed out of the ground, and tried to take it for themselves.

White-robed men standing still as cacti, waiting for a new world to be born, an old god to return.

An involuntary shudder passed through Nichols despite the autumn heat, the dun-brown uniform shirt sweat-pasted to his back. The fact was, the visuals were the least of it. He'd *felt* the presence of something ancient and monstrous that night, and it had hit him with the force of revelation. He'd *fully believed* that a banished deity might be sprung from cosmic jail and reclaim the earth as his domain.

And then *bam*, it was as if the house lights had come back up, and life just as he'd always known it had resumed. Coffee and pay stubs, cheeseburgers and TV shows and trying to keep a woman happy.

To call it a mindfuck didn't even come close.

And then there was Jess Galvan, who had eaten that heart himself instead of handing it over to Aaron Seth, killed everybody who needed killing, and promptly exiled himself to the fringes of society.

Whose beat-to-shit trailer half a mile from the end of the service road was just coming into sight.

Nichols checked his Timex. It was seven on the dot; the sun nearly kissed the horizon, the mountaintops outlined in orange. He pulled into the patch of dirt that passed for a front yard, gratified to see Galvan's wood-paneled station wagon, the pride of 1982 Detroit, parked a few feet off. That had to mean he was home—there was nowhere to walk from here, that was for sure—and Nichols's trek hadn't been in vain. Galvan's cell had been going straight to voice mail for a day and a half, so this little visit was both overdue and unexpected.

Nichols unfolded himself from the squad car, knees unlocking with a satisfying pop, ambled up three rusted-out front steps, and rapped on the trailer's busted-and-duct-taped screen door.

Nothing.

"Galvan? It's me, Bob. You in there?"

He peered inside, took stock. A jumble of sheets on the narrow bed, a stack of dirty dishes piled next to the sink. A flannel shirt and a cowboy-style one on plastic hangers in the tiny, jacked-open closet. A bedside minifridge doubling as a night table, strewn with newspapers. Nichols recognized a Sunday section three or four weeks old.

No Galvan.

But no heads on stakes, either.

That was a plus.

Nichols stepped outside and eased himself onto the top stair, figured he might as well watch the sunset, maybe rehearse what he would say. Jess couldn't have gone far.

As soon as he thought it, Nichols winced in self-censure. What Jess could and couldn't do was not something he oughta make assumptions about. For all he knew, the dude had taken a nice long running start and jumped onto the goddamn moon.

A few minutes passed, and then a large-animal rustle someplace nearby brought Nichols to his feet, hand dropping instinctively to the butt of his service revolver. There were mountain lions out here, and those things didn't play. He peered into the twilit underbrush, but the rustling was coming from someplace else—from behind the trailer, it seemed, though pinning down directionality in all this open space was surprisingly tricky. Nichols took a tentative step down and cocked his ears.

Something was definitely coming closer—heavily and steadily—and Nichols didn't like what that might imply. A jag of movement swept across his left periphery; the sheriff spun toward it and found himself face-to-face with Jess Galvan.

He was shirtless from the waist up.

Unless the dead mountain lion slung across his shoulders counted as clothing.

"Sheriff," he said, with a crisp, weirdly formal nod.

"Hercules."

Nichols returned the nod. "Whatchu, uh, got there?"

"Action kinda keeps me sane," Galvan said, and turned sideways to give Nichols a look at the lion. It was a full-grown male, a hundred and forty pounds of coiled muscle; front incisors protruded from the mouth like daggers. The massive head lolled backward, the animal's neck broken.

Nichols pretended to examine the beast and instead took stock of Jess. An inch-long gash on his right forearm oozed blood, and a broad smear of red painted his chest. He was clad in cutoffs and cross-trainers; there was no possible place he might have been carrying a gun, or even a knife.

"You killed this thing bare-handed?"

Galvan shrugged. "I've got a good fifty pounds on him."

"Yeah, but you *chased him down*." A beat of silence, the heat coming off Galvan in waves, Nichols wondering just how far to push this.

Fuck it, he decided.

As he often did.

"Look, I'll pretend that's normal if you want me to. But, I mean, come on." Nichols spread his arms, tilted his head to the side. "I'm guessing you weren't doing shit like this say, oh, three months ago."

Jess's eyes flickered up to meet his, and Nichols could feel his friend straining within himself; the sheriff had the uncanny feeling that if only he could figure out the secret knock, Galvan would open up.

The moment passed. Galvan sloughed his bounty to the ground with a small grunt, dropped his hands to his hips as the dust kicked up around them.

"I'll get us a couple beers," he said and disappeared into the trailer.

He reemerged with two generic supermarket cans, tossed one at Nichols, and shrugged on the flannel from the closet.

"Oughta be a lawn chair over there," he said, pointing. Nichols unfolded it, metal grinding against the grit worked into the joints, and made himself semicomfortable.

Galvan popped the tab and knocked back half the beer in two swallows. Nichols waited for him to take a seat on the stairs, but he stayed put, legs spread shoulders' width apart, staring into the desert and the darkness like he didn't want to miss what happened next out there.

Nichols felt strange sitting, so he stood too.

It didn't help much.

"Your phone's been off," he said after a while. Galvan didn't respond, so Nichols pressed.

"Is everything . . . okay?"

Galvan finally looked over. "You fuckin' kidding me? Yeah. Sure, Bob. Everything's just hunky-dory."

"Well, do you wanna talk ab—"

Galvan turned, heaved open the screen door. It slammed against the trailer's exterior and stayed that way.

Nice going, Nichols. You're off to a great start.

An instant later Galvan was back, a second round of brews in his hand. Nichols was only two sips into the first. It was the shittiest beer he'd ever tasted. He turned the can in his hand, looking for the ingredient list, wondered if weasel piss was on it.

Galvan threw his empty can at the sky. Try as he might, Nichols couldn't hear it land. Imagined it attaining escape velocity, rocketing into the next solar system.

"I moved in with Ruth," he heard himself say. "We're gonna try and make a go of it."

"Congratulations."

Nichols grimaced. "We'll see what happens. They say when you've been through a traumatic experience with someone, it either bonds you, or tears you apart, so . . ." He flashed on his marriage to Kat, the prolonged struggle to conceive. It had certainly seemed traumatic then, but the goddamn bar on trauma had come up a ways since.

The velvet blackness had engulfed them now, the moon late to rise.

"That's good," Galvan said at long last. "For Sherry too. Having a man in the house."

"She misses you," Nichols said quickly. "Last thing I wanna do here's step on your toes."

"And I miss her." Galvan said it without inflection or conviction. "But I can't do it right now. I mean, look at me, Nichols. I can barely . . ."

He sighed and tipped the new can to his mouth. Nichols waited. There was only so much beer in there.

Galvan crushed this one before he pitched it. Not much of an environmentalist, thought Nichols. Though the farmers would certainly applaud his dedication to wildlife control.

"You know why I live like this, Nichols?"

"Because you're broke."

"Because I'm broken."

He finally sat down.

"I don't trust myself around people, man. That shit took too much out of me."

That shit. That night. What happened. Nichols wished he could cut through all the euphemisms, get to what was real: *You ate that goddamn heart and grew an arm and threw Seth thirty feet as if he were a fucking Beanie Baby. You wrestle mountain lions. You're a goddamn superhero, and you're paying the price—I don't know what that price is, but I know there's no such thing as a free lunch.*

"It took a lot out of us all, Jess. Including your daughter. I'm just gonna come right out and say it, man—you're breaking her heart. She's in a bad way, and she needs you. Whatever you've got to give, even if it's not a lot."

Galvan furrowed his brow, stared down at the ground like he was trying to burn a hole through it.

Hell, maybe he could.

"I went by the ice cream shop a couple days ago," he said. "She seemed okay."

"Because she doesn't want to worry you. And that wasn't a couple days ago, Jess. Sherry told me this morning she hasn't seen you in two weeks. Going on three."

Galvan pressed the heels of his hands against his eyes. "I lose track," he said quietly.

"You can talk to me, you know," Nichols blurted. "Shit, Jess, I was there. Whatever you're dealing with, maybe I can help."

Galvan dropped his hands. Blinked, shook his head, blinked again. Finally, he looked over at Nichols, and the sheriff felt his face redden beneath the heat of Galvan's scrutiny, his heart race in anticipation.

Here it came.

The Unburdening.

"You're already helping me. With Sherry. The rest of this shit, I gotta figure out myself." He raised up, brushed his palms against his shorts. "I should grab myself a shower."

Don't quit your day job, Nichols.

Galvan extended a hand.

"I'll see you soon."

"There's something else."

Galvan crossed his arms, and Nichols noticed that the cut had stopped bleeding.

"Kurt Knowles got picked up a few days ago in Ardmore, Oklahoma."

"Who's he again?"

"The biker? President of the True Natives? If I'm not mistaken, he and his gang held you down while that corrupt Mexican Federale took a machete to your arm."

"Oh yeah. Him."

Galvan twisted at the waist, peered into the trailer. For a second, Nichols half expected him to pretend he'd heard his mother calling him home for dinner.

"I just got word today," Nichols went on. "But I'm gonna do everything I can to make sure they throw his ass underneath the fuckin' jail until the end of time. I don't know what he's been charged with so far, but with my testimony plus yours—"

Galvan shook his head. "Forget it. I'm keeping my head down. Supposed to be in a Mexican prison right now, in case you forgot."

It was Nichols's turn to shake his head. "Nah, I looked into it. Your record's clean. Nobody ever filed anything with Texas. Hell, you could probably apply for food stamps if you wanted to."

Galvan's voice darkened. "I'm off the grid, Nichols." And then, for no apparent reason, his whole face squeezed tight—contorted into a mask of agony or anticipated agony, like a little kid bracing for a flu shot.

"You okay there, Jess?"

Galvan exhaled—a short sharp breath, like he was fighting it off. Gradually, his face relaxed.

"Been getting these migraines," he muttered.

"You oughta see a doctor. I'm sure Ruth can—"

Galvan spun toward him, all the pain replaced with rage, and a bolt of fear shot through Nichols, adrenaline overruling intellect, fight-or-flight synapses decussating wildly.

As if this weren't a disagreement with a friend, but a wild animal about to pounce.

It was all he could do to stand his ground.

"No fucking doctors!" Galvan roared, jabbing a finger in his chest. "No courtrooms, no shrinks—and if I gave a shit about that Knowles cocksucker, I'd have killed him already. You got it?"

"Sure, Jess. Sure."

Galvan seemed to deflate then, to pull back into himself.

"Sorry," he mumbled, eventually.

"Yeah," Nichols replied. "I'll see you later."

He dropped his half-empty beer, watched it topple sideways. A weak stream of amber pisswater leaked out, and the parched earth swallowed it greedily.

He strolled back to the cruiser, threw his arm out the window, revved the engine. Jess was still watching him. Perhaps it was a trick of the light, or perhaps the helplessness, the misery on his face was real.

"Maybe you're right," Nichols heard himself say. "Maybe it is best if you keep away from Sherry for the time being."

Galvan's head dropped to his chest. Nichols couldn't be sure if it was a response or not. For all he knew, Galvan's mind was drifting again, and he hadn't even heard.

Nichols wedged the flask between his thighs and drove into the night.

CHAPTER 4

Galvan picked himself up, staggered into the trailer, and collapsed onto the bed. The strain of interacting with Nichols had sapped his mental resources utterly, and when he was weak, he was vulnerable.

He was always vulnerable.

The monster knew him so well now.

But no better than he knew it.

Theirs was an intimacy that defied description. An abomination beyond words.

Galvan knew how he must look to others. To Nichols, or Sherry. To Cantwell especially, with her psych degree and diagnostic skills.

Like a textbook psychotic dissociative case—that was how. Flat affect, prone to fits of rage and spells of isolation. Just another lost soul, unable to tune out the voices in his head.

Except for one thing.

You don't understand, Doctor—I'm different!

The voice in Galvan's head was real.

The one telling him to kill, insisting that the subjugation of inferior men was his birthright and destiny. The one forever probing and testing, attacking and seducing, cajoling and terrorizing. Relentlessly widening the corridor of its influence by scraping away at the bedrock of Galvan's humanity. And always seeking the same thing.

Control.

Two souls, one body.

The math was a bitch.

It was a battle Galvan suspected he could not win. He was a man, and Cucuy was something else—a debased god, a self-made demon, a being whose very existence had so violated the natural order that perhaps no word existed to describe him. He would have obliterated Aaron Seth had Seth eaten that heart—the cult leader had been bred for just that purpose. And Galvan had expected to be destroyed himself—to consume the vessel and have his soul and body torn asunder, find himself banished to the purgatorial realm of the Dominio Gris.

But life was chock-full of fuckin' surprises. A thin genetic filament connected Cucuy to Galvan, and so here they were instead.

Roommates.

Galvan felt himself go drowsy and scrabbled to his feet. He didn't need to pass out yet, would not give in to the urge. Cucuy was winning the war for his subconscious, and so Galvan parried by learning to steer clear of that dark neighborhood, get by on two or three hours of sleep as many times a week.

That was the irony of this infestation, this tumor, this virus: even as it sought to subsume him, to take over his body and eradicate his mind, it imbued him with certain gifts that he could use to fight back.

Strength and speed. Endurance and reflexes. Pain barely registered; wounds mended quickly. It was a loophole of sorts: Cucuy could not insinuate himself into the folds of Galvan's soul without giving off his powers. And if Galvan could maintain the precarious limbo state in which he dwelled, using those powers to stave off their master . . .

Well, then maybe he could buy himself a few more hunted, hellish months. Stumble on to a plan, or somebody who had one.

Or a land mine.

He stepped back into the cool night air and felt his senses flicker and flare, like a fire finding oxygen. When they were fully engaged—when he was running, hunting, sweating, fighting—Cucuy receded, drew back his tentacles and waited.

Yet another irony—Galvan's fucking life brimming with them—respite in violence.

Not a good thing for the mountain lions of Texas.

He unbuttoned his shirt, sloughed it to the ground, and walked around the trailer. He had a fire pit in the back—an excuse to chop wood, really.

Ax, block, tree chunk.

Lift, swing, *thunk,* stoop, toss. Repeat.

A few hours of this would do him good. Then, a nice long run into town. By the time he got there, the bars would be closing, which meant drunken shitheads looking for the same thing he was.

Trouble.

Ax, block, tree chunk.

You only postpone the inevitable, Cucuy said.

Thought.

Transmitted.

Whatever the fuck he did.

"Fuck you," Galvan replied. He'd taken to that recently, speaking to the monster aloud as a way of refusing to acknowledge and thus strengthen their oneness, their inextricability.

It was probably useless.

It didn't make Galvan look any saner, either.

The blood of holy men runs through your veins, my son. Weakly, it is true. You are a mongrel. A bastard's bastard's bastard. You would have been put to death in the days when I was a man. But today, in this diminished world, where the spark of greatness flickers so dimly, you could be a king. A god. If you only knew the power I could give you, you would end this foolish resistance and join with me. Before you are destroyed.

"Yeah, well, if you're so fuckin' powerful, how come I'm still standing here?"

Lift. Swing. *Thunk.*

Only because—

"Besides, I don't want your kind of power. Murdering innocent girls ain't very godlike in my book."

Galvan could feel Cucuy's sneer curling up within him, like the edges of a burning piece of paper; it was a physical sensation, everywhere and nowhere at once, and he braced for the jab it heralded.

Your understanding is as pathetic as your precious morality. There is nothing more godly than sacrifice. Man's purpose, his entire reason for being, is to die for his god. You people have perverted that, with your childish fables, your martyr gods—hidden from it any way you could think to, because your ego is a plague that has swept across the world. But you cannot hide forever. What has always been shall always be.

"Then I guess you'll always be a fuckbag," Galvan grunted.

Lift, swing, *thunk.*

Not his wittiest comeback—downright idiotic, actually, but he didn't feel like debating theology with the monster just now. He was too ragged around the edges; he might let something slip, give Cucuy new ammunition to use against him or reveal some element of his own embryonic strategy.

An image flashed through Galvan's mind.

The woman in yellow, beckoning in secret from his dreams.

Cucuy didn't know about that. Had never mentioned her. Some firewall in Galvan's mind separated them, and if there was freedom to be had, she was involved. Somehow. She had to be. Her will was set against Cucuy's. That much, Galvan knew.

The enemy of my enemy is my friend. . . .

Ax, block, tree chunk.

Lift, swing, *thunk.*

The bloodlust is in you, Jess Galvan. I can feel it. How long can you sate yourself on animals? On meaningless skirmishes with weak men?

"I got a better question, dickwad. How come you always refer to me by my full name? Seems a little formal, considering that you're squatting in my fuckin' body, don't you think?"

Galvan shouldered the ax and allowed himself a smile. It was Cucuy who had revealed something: he had not divined the reason for all Galvan's exertion—was too firmly locked in the prison of his own mind to realize that it was not bloodlust that drove Galvan at all. He thought the appetite for violence signaled the erosion of resistance, when really it was resistance itself.

Good.

All violence was not the same—Galvan had always known that. The distinctions might not have meant anything to the monster, or even to the law, but they comprised Galvan's personal code, and he'd lived by it long before Cucuy had yanked him from the hell of Ojos Negros, dropped him into a deeper and darker one, handed him a beating heart, and dubbed him a Righteous Messenger.

The devil's bag man was more like it.

That code of honor had kept him alive in the desert, afforded him safe passage through a minefield of undead virgin girls—and when he'd forsaken it in a moment of fury and levied punishment on a pair of child-trafficking scumbags, safety had returned the favor.

But Galvan was a Righteous Messenger still. He'd carried evil then, and he carried it now—cradled it deep inside, and there wasn't a damn thing he could do about that. Hell, maybe everybody did, and this was just a starker, higher-stakes dramatization of the universal human condition.

More likely, that was a load of poetic horseshit.

But the fact remained—maybe *fact* was a little strong; Galvan's *impression* was—that evil multiplied evil. When he did something bad, departed from the code, Cucuy gained a toehold in the cold war they were waging. A little more of Galvan's soul dissipated, the cigarette burning down toward the filter.

Smoke 'em if you got 'em.

What exactly "bad" meant—and this was a mindfuck, the kind of circular, pound-your-head-against-the-wall shit that a guy like Galvan, who'd built himself a life of flesh and blood, brick and mortar, actions and consequences, absolutely couldn't stand—well, that seemed to be somewhat subjective.

No, not subjective. It was ironclad, a clear line in the sand. Step over it and pay the price.

The word he was looking for was *internal*. Or *self-generated*. It was Galvan himself who'd made these rules, erected this moral framework, and it was Galvan who suffered the consequences. When he did shit he knew was wrong—and especially when he drew on the glowing, clenched nexus of power that Cucuy's presence afforded him in order to do wrong—the monster surged and swelled and Galvan could feel himself getting sucked away, as if his soul were a puddle of water somebody had sicced a vacuum cleaner on.

His soul. Most of the time—and Galvan did spend most of his time contemplating his soul, its strength and shape and qualities—he pictured it as a color-saturated version of that Ojos Negros labyrinth, a subterranean warren of corridors and rooms the deep red of a human heart.

Cucuy might be hiding in any one of them.

Galvan's job was to cordon them off, brick them up, trap the monster inside.

He was getting good at it.

But the monster always escaped.

And there was always another room.

The soul being fuckin' infinite and all.

Cucuy had fallen quiet, Galvan realized. It happened. Sometimes his mind cleared and quieted—as if the monster had other business to attend to, hung up a BACK IN FIVE MINUTES sign, and disappeared. The lacuna was welcome but eerie, a respite Galvan could never enjoy, the other shoe always about to drop, the fear that Cucuy was off improving his position dominating what should have been an out-breath of peace.

Galvan tossed the ax aside, sat heavily on the chopping stump, and replayed the encounter with Nichols in his mind, now that he had the bandwidth to analyze it.

The impotence he felt at knowing Sherry was in free fall and he couldn't do shit to help her was staggering. For years, the desire to protect her was all that kept him alive. To be this close and yet this far away—to know that the greatest threat to her safety was him—that knowledge threatened to break him faster than the monster.

Galvan wiped the cooled sweat from his brow and stood. He bent double, picked up the ax, and ran his thumb across the edge of the blade, swiping off the pungent sap with which his frenetic activity had left it coated. The blood of trees.

He was a fighter. He wasn't done yet.

Not by a damn sight.

There was still too much he loved in this world.

CHAPTER 5

There's something unique about everybody, Kurt Knowles's mother had told him, on a damn-near daily basis, back when he was just a skinny little knees-and-elbows bastard, riding his cousin's hand-me-down Big Wheel around in the chicken-beshitted dust outside their double-wide.

For years, he'd tried to figure out just what that could be. What separated him from everybody else he'd ever met. Sure, he'd grown up bigger than most, and maybe better with his hands. He could outdrink and outdrug many a man, and he didn't fear the law. People listened to him, heeded what he had to say—other hard-drinking, rock-fisted, speed-freak lawless sons of bitches, anyway, if not the folks he'd by then come to think of as *civilians*. But none of that quite cleared the bar on unique.

Then he'd met Aaron Seth, a great man if ever there was one, and started opening up his eyes to the various and sundry ways the deck was stacked against regular old hardworking natural-born American white men like himself. Started speaking out on the need to keep the country free and pure, the beaners on their side of the fence and American jobs on ours. Started doing whatever Seth said was necessary and improving his own prospects in the bargain. Learned discipline. Found out what it was to have a father.

You had to shake your head at that. Knowles, a grown-ass man, discovering for the first time what it meant to have somebody in your life whose authority you didn't question. It was amazing how completely that could put you at ease, how much sharper your focus became. Seth had turned him into a goddamn laser beam of intention, filled him with purpose and confidence. Made him a part of something.

The Prophet's Sergeant at Arms. That was the private title he'd given himself and worn like a mantle of honor.

Now all that was gone. Destroyed. And what did Kurt Knowles have left? What made him unique now that Seth was a corpse and his followers had scattered like roaches when the kitchen light turns on?

Well, there was one thing.

He was the only son of a bitch he'd ever met or heard of who liked prison food. Didn't just tolerate it but found it delicious.

As of about forty-eight hours ago that fact had become mighty handy, Knowles reflected, and crammed the rest of his cheese sandwich down his gullet.

He'd been at loose ends since Seth died—Seth, and the better part of Knowles's charter, his brothers in arms, his fucking *family*—and the only surprise was that he hadn't seen the inside of a cell earlier.

He barely recognized himself; worse yet, he recognized himself as the shithead he had been at twenty-five. Pissing around on his bike, meandering from one sad-sack town to the next, fucking with civilians, daring them to step up. Stealing goddamn burritos from gas stations just to watch the pimply-faced countermen gulp and turn away. Staying tooled up on booze and shitty crank. Banging the sleaziest hookers he could find. Passing out over a campfire and a bottle of Jack, a few hundred feet off the road. Waking up the next morning and doing it all over again.

They'd pinched him for vagrancy, run him through the system, and hit the jackpot. Fucking Ardmore, Oklahoma. If the world had an asshole, this town was the little shitberry dangling from the longest hair. The jail was a glorified drunk tank, a fifteen-by-fifteen holding pen down the hall from the front door, the patrol desks. Open toilet, fluorescent glare, couple of lice-ridden mattresses.

All the comforts of home.

He currently shared it with a hammered old Mexican day laborer and a terrified teenage shoplifter.

That meant two more sandwiches for Knowles. They tasted even better when they were stolen.

He was looking at a transfer to Texas tomorrow or the next, according to the cop who'd booked him. A supermax facility. Bad sign. Guy couldn't or wouldn't tell him what the charges were—he looked about two years past his senior prom, the little pencil-dicked fucker—but Knowles figured the worst of what he'd done couldn't possibly be in play. He'd seen the dead climb out of the goddamn ground and walk, but unless they'd learned to testify in a court of law, he wasn't gonna burn for human trafficking or murder. Nobody saw shit and lived: that had been the True Natives' policy for as long as Knowles had held the gavel.

An all-business female voice, fall-apple crisp, jarred him out of his reverie.

"Good evening, Officer. Adrissa Coleridge. I understand you have a Mr. Kurt Knowles in custody. Is that right?"

He strode to the front corner of the cage and tried to catch a glimpse of her. A thin vertical strip of high heel, black nylon, and dark knee-length trench coat were all he could make out.

What new fuckery was this?

"I'm sorry, ma'am, we, uh, we don't have visiting hours here." The fluster in the young cop's voice suggested that she was something to look at.

"Quite all right, Officer. I'm not here to visit. Let me explain how this is going to work."

Knowles saw her lift the briefcase, heard the clasp click open, the soft thump as she laid it flat across his desk.

"Mr. Knowles will be leaving with me, Officer Blanton. We can—"

Knowles heard him stand, the desk chair toppling over backward with a clatter.

"The hell you say, lady. What the—"

Her voice cut through his like a garrote through a neck.

"We can do it the fun way, or we can do it the ugly way."

"Listen, lady, I—"

"Either you take this briefcase and cook up a nice little escape story, or I press a button on my phone. If I do that, we'll have about twelve seconds to make conversation, and then four men with automatic weapons will walk in the door and put your brains all over that wall."

Knowles pressed himself against the bars, all his senses strained toward the scene playing out around the corner. He could feel the electricity in the air, smell the cop's panic as the sweat burst from his pores. He braced himself for the kid's response, realized he was pulling for the hard way.

Roast that fuckin' pig, lady.

Whoever you are.

And whatever the hell you want with me.

Knowles was a realistic man. He didn't imagine she was his guardian angel. However much money was in that briefcase, it was more than anybody he knew had.

Even if it was stocked with rolls of pennies.

A little clicking sound echoed through the corridor. At first, Knowles thought it was a gun. Then he realized it was the cop's mouth, popping open.

"Fun way," he stammered.

"Excellent choice. Your keys, please."

A jangle like sleigh bells, as he fumbled them off his belt, handed them over. And then the rhythmic clop of high heels as Adrissa Coleridge strutted his way.

She was a sight for sore eyes, all right. Looked like a rock video chick, before she takes off her glasses and undoes the bun in her hair and starts whipping it around.

Somehow, Knowles doubted any of that was gonna happen.

Before he could open his mouth, she'd reached through the bars and pressed a manicured fingertip to his chapped lips.

"I'm going to unlock this cage, and then you're going to follow me outside and get in the car. There's no need for us to speak. Got it?"

"Got it," he said, and grinned against her finger.

She spun away, inserted the key into the lock. A moment later, the door swung wide. Kurt looked over his shoulder, treated the shoplifter to a shit-eating grin and a two-fingered wave.

Adrissa was already striding down the hall, apparently unconcerned with reestablishing the cell's integrity. Kurt took a moment to appreciate her muscular little ass, snug inside its business suit, then followed her toward freedom.

Or whatever it was that lay outside.

He caught up to Coleridge at the door. The light beyond was pinkish, glowing, and for a moment Knowles couldn't remember whether it was dusk or dawn, had to count backward to the last time he'd slept. The cop sat motionless behind his desk, the briefcase open before him, eyes flitting up and down like he wasn't sure where he was allowed to look.

"Pleasure doing business with you, Officer Blanton," Coleridge said. "And please, give your sister Katie-Ann my regards. And her twin daughters, too. Are they still at 12 Pine Bottom Lane?"

His face went even paler than it had been, and Coleridge smiled.

"That's right, Danny. We know all about you, so play it smart. That's a nice chunk of change for a kid like you. Enough to maybe get out of public service, go into business for yourself. But hey, that's just my advice. Take it or leave it."

She pushed open the door, and a gust of good clean desert air swept through.

"Adios, pig," Knowles spat, mostly to irritate the broad, show her he'd speak whenever he damn well pleased. And he treated Blanton to the same little bye-bye wave he'd thrown his cellmate.

"Lead the way, Counselor," he told Coleridge, and he cupped her left ass cheek with his big, florid hand, gave it a good hard squeeze.

"Hey!" She sprang away from him, pure reflex, stumbled out into the muggy twilight. Spun toward him, fury flashing in her eyes.

He loved an angry woman. The reddened cheeks. The animal musk. A chick about to take a swing at you looked uncannily like a woman you'd just fucked.

This one recomposed herself in the blink of an eye, the professionalism trumping the ire. Knowles wasn't worth getting upset over; the decision might as well be written on her face. The color died down, and she pursed her lips, exhaled through her nose.

It made him feel disrespected—obscurely, but intensely. Knowles felt his half-hard dick stand down, and his self-confidence shrivel. Now *he* wanted to take a swing at *her*.

"Get in the car."

There were two. A late-model Beemer and a Lincoln town car, the latter fully murdered out, windows tinted so dark you could barely see where they began or ended. Knowles goggled dumbly at it for a moment, his own wide meaty reflection staring back from inside the high-gloss paint.

Coleridge had the Beemer's door open by the time he snapped out of it.

"Where's the guys?" he heard himself ask. "With the, the guns?"

"There's no guys." She slid behind the wheel, reached for the door. "Get in the car."

"Where's it taking me?"

"I'm sure I don't care," Adrissa Coleridge said and slammed the door. The engine growled to life and she peeled out, dust swirling up as high as Knowles's waist, then floating silently back down to the ground.

The town car just sat there, sleek and solid and indifferent. Knowles considered walking away, just to see what happened. He realized he had no idea where his bike was. Impounded, no doubt. The one thing he owned free and clear was history. And he was a fugitive now, a jail-breaker.

So that was that.

The town car continued to sit there, patiently waiting for him to arrive at what should have been a foregone conclusion and climb in.

He did.

The driver's partition was tinted the same impenetrable color as the windows. The leather felt cool to the touch. Two bottles of water sat in the cup holders. Knowles cracked one, guzzled.

"Where we going?" he asked the plane of Plexiglas before him.

The car banked out of the parking lot, onto the road. "Who the hell sent you?" Knowles demanded, but at this point he was only talking to himself.

CHAPTER 6

Knowles woke gasping from a restless, terror-speckled sleep—the only kind he knew, unless he drank himself into a stupor. No such luck in the back of the town car, which had shrunk from spacious and luxurious to cramped and miserable over the course of the last ten hours. They'd stopped only for gas, and the invisible chauffeur had ignored his demand for a bathroom break. The two water bottles were full of piss now, Aaron Seth's frequent admonishments about befouling the nest turned literal in the great void of his absence.

Knowles reverting back to his animal nature.

It was dawn, give or take, the tinted windows leaching the color from the spectacle, repainting the picture in frigid hues.

Knowles wouldn't have enjoyed it anyway.

Before him loomed a great high concrete wall, coils of razor wire rimming the top like salt on a margarita glass. Three slim towers jutted from within the compound. Those were crowned by rifle-toting men, their silhouettes backlit by the rising sun. There was nothing else around, probably for miles. This wasn't the only show in town.

This *was* the town.

Knowles's heart sank, the subconscious hopes he'd been nurturing revealing themselves only at the moment of their demise.

Sprung from jail and delivered to prison.

It didn't make a goddamn lick of sense.

The locks on the car doors clicked open, offering Knowles a freedom that had lost a good deal of its luster. He stepped out anyway, squinted against the assault of the light. The Lincoln wasted no time in roaring away.

Knowles shaded his brow with the flat of his hand and waited for something to happen.

Hopefully breakfast.

Instead, with an ear-piercing metallic whine, a heretofore invisible door swung open, and a man in a guard's uniform strode toward him, eyes cloaked behind black aviators, gun holstered at his waist. The swing of his arms bespoke confidence—the kind of unearned, cocksure swagger that came with authority, with wearing a gun on your hip and telling a bunch of convicts what to do. A quick appraisal told Knowles he had six inches and sixty pounds on the dude, and he liked his chances of getting the weapon away from him.

And then what? Shoot a hole in the earth to escape through?

"Señor Knowles," the guard said, halting a few paces away and dropping his hands to his hips. "Sígueme, por favor."

Knowles scowled at him. "The fuck you talkin' Mexican for?"

A twitchy little smile blossomed across his thin lips, and Knowles felt the sap rise in him. "Because this is Mexico, shithead. Follow me."

The guard turned and walked back the way he'd come.

Damn. No wonder this place seemed familiar.

Ojos Negros. The end of the line for Aaron Seth's pussy parade. He and the club had made this run dozens of times, picking up young pious girls from Seth's compound and delivering them here, but Knowles had never been inside—never even been face-to-face with the front door. The Natives had done their business a quarter mile away, surrounded by scrub brush and sand—a bulkhead opened like a service entrance and a couple guards ambled out into the sunlight. Money and product changed hands, and that was that.

Clean girls for dirty money.

Lifeblood of the club.

One more thing to mourn.

The guard vanished from sight, and once again, Kurt Knowles found himself faced with a choice that really wasn't one.

Once again, he did what he was told.

AT WHAT POINT, Domingo Valentine asked himself as he waited for his guest to be shown in, did the steward stop waiting for the king to return?

A better question—more pressing, certainly—was at what point did the king's subjects begin to take note of his absence and whisper revolt? They'd sworn no fealty to the steward. His word meant nothing if he did not speak on the king's behalf. Command the king's army.

And for all Domingo knew, the whispering had already begun.

Cucuy's empire—the portion Domingo knew of, at least, and not for a second did he doubt that there was more—rested on the Ancient One's ability to calibrate and profit from a never-ending, low-grade war. On the subtle machinations by which he pitted one cartel against the other, tipped the balance left and right and left again. The cross-continental drug trade was a ship forever listing on a sea of blood.

It was not a performance Domingo could hope to duplicate. Cucuy saw the whole chessboard, every past configuration and future contingency. Domingo was lucky to understand how his next move would ramify it. He'd never been privy to Cucuy's long-term plans; the latest collision course on which he'd set Barrio Azteca and Federacíon Sinaloa would explode into conflagration in a matter of weeks, or even days, and Domingo had no idea how to prevent or resolve or exploit it. Was one organization to be reduced, by means of a controlled burn, a concentrated bloodletting? Was the profit to be made in guns? In drugs? On the political side of the sprawling equation, with which Domingo was barely even acquainted? Was it a test of the leadership? A diversion, while some greater plan unfolded?

The procurer leaned back in his chair, interlaced his hands behind his head, and sighed. He was overdue to catch a break, and with any luck, Kurt Knowles would provide it. Quite a waste of resources, if he couldn't. Adrissa Coleridge wore Armani suits, and she charged Armani prices.

A moment later, the biker sat across from him, deposited roughly in the room's only other chair by a pair of corrections officers who lingered by the room's threshold until Domingo dismissed them with a flick of his eyes.

Knowles seemed to spill out of the chair in all directions: a massive, florid man, his limbs like overstuffed pillows, his face underlaid with broken blood vessels, his clothes stinking of campfire smoke and cheap liquor, sunbaked sweat and jail.

Domingo regarded him for a moment. The biker shifted in his chair, eyes darting around the room as he tried to get his bearings. Domingo had instructed the guards to bring him in through the yard, so that Knowles might get a fuller sense of the prison, contemplate what an indefinite stay as an unaffiliated gringo might feel like.

Looking at him now, Domingo realized that had been a waste of time. This wasn't a man who buckled under fear. Or, for that matter, one unduly concerned with envisioning the future.

Your options were limited with a man like this.

But there was no reason to think he and Kurt Knowles were not on the same side.

You didn't play the hand. You played the man.

"We've never met, Mr. Knowles. I'm Domingo Valentine. I manage operations here, you might say. The wares your club delivered, for instance, I received. Now. Can I get you anything." He kept the inflection flat, the question mark out of it. "Something to drink. Something to eat."

Domingo's voice had been his first weapon in life. It was as smooth as high-grade motor oil, could betray nothing or lay everything bare.

Knowles grunted, rearranged himself again, tugged at his dick through his denim. "You got some whiskey or somethin'?"

"Certainly." He rapped his knuckles on his desk, the sound echoing through the chamber, and a guard appeared.

"Whiskey for Mr. Knowles. And for me," he added, not wanting to affront the man by making him drink alone. Not that Knowles was likely to give a shit.

"So," Domingo said, leaning forward and interlacing his fingers on the desk. "I hope your trip was comfortable."

Knowles just stared, his eyes bloodshot and mean.

Domingo gave him a close-lipped smile. "I'll come to the point. I am trying to determine the circumstances of our friend Aaron Seth's demise, and locating witnesses has proven quite difficult."

The whiskey arrived: a half-full bottle of a rotgut brand. Domingo stifled the urge to break it across the jaw of the guard who'd delivered it. But they didn't keep a stock of alcohol on hand; he'd probably gone upstairs, borrowed it from some cartel chief's cabinet.

Knowles kept his eye on the bottle as Domingo poured them each three fingers of the pungent brown liquor. It disappeared into his mitt when Domingo handed the glass over, and then straight down his gullet.

Glass back on the desk. Domingo poured a refill, watched the biker chase the first drink with the second.

"Why the hell should I tell you anything?" he asked at last.

"Our interests are aligned, Mr. Knowles."

The outlaw, impatient with the service, leaned forward and grabbed the bottle by the neck.

"Yeah, how you figure that?"

"You worked for Aaron Seth. I work for his father."

Knowles paused, the bottle cocked just short of a pouring angle.

"His father," he repeated.

"That's correct."

Third whiskey, down the hatch.

"Forget it," he said. "I ain't goin' nowhere near that fuckin' . . . if that's what you think, you got the wrong guy, I'll tell you that right now."

He reached for the bottle again, but Domingo snatched it away.

"What are you talking about, Mr. Knowles?"

"The guy who killed Seth. Galvan. Look, I want revenge so bad it makes my dick hard. But I'm not tanglin' with him."

Domingo relinquished the whiskey, crossed his legs. "And why is that?"

"'Cause that son of a bitch ain't *human*. I watched him snap Seth's neck like a fuckin' twig. Hell, we hacked his goddamn arm off, and bam—he grows a new one." Knowles gave an involuntary shudder.

Domingo's heart was racing. He filled the biker's glass. "Go on, Mr. Knowles. Tell me exactly what happened."

Knowles narrowed his eyes and drained his glass. "You know, I'm a fugitive thanks to you, Valentine. How 'bout we talk money?"

Domingo swiped a palm over his lips, as if spot-checking his poker face. "An interesting perspective. One might also say that you're a free man thanks to me, Mr. Knowles."

The biker took that in—that, and a fifth slug of whiskey. Domingo watched, placid, mind sprinting to keep up with his heartbeat.

It was the Great One. It had to be. These were not acts of man Kurt Knowles described, but acts of god. Cucuy had cast off one form, taken up another. Domingo's faith had been rewarded.

Man had died for god, just as he always had. But why had this Galvan been the Ancient One's instrument, and not Aaron Seth?

And why had he not come home to reclaim his throne, his kingdom? Was all this useless to him now?

Or was something, someone, somehow holding him back?

Domingo would find out. His will surged toward knowing, compressed itself into a single arrow point of purpose.

"Tell me all you know of this Galvan," Domingo demanded, his voice a razor now, cutting through Knowles's games and the sweet haze of the whiskey. "What did you see? Where can I find him?"

Knowles grinned at him from behind the glass. "Let's talk money, Valentine. I could be a real good—"

"Do not overplay your hand," the procurer snapped, rising to his feet.

Cucuy was out there: the knowledge had annihilated what patience Domingo might otherwise have had with this hulking moron.

"Everything you know. Right now. Or you can spend the rest of your life in this prison. Do we understand each other?"

"Loud and clear, boss," the biker drawled, raising his palms in mock surrender. "Like you said, same team here."

He looked up at Domingo, grim and unfazed, and Domingo had the sense that it was he who'd overplayed. He was not Cucuy, from whom a threat could never be perceived as a sign of weakness. Domingo was vulnerable, and he had to be cautious. A man like Kurt smelled frailty. There was no percentage in making him an enemy.

Domingo smoothed his shirt, found his seat and his manners. "From what you say, this Galvan is too dangerous to go after directly, Mr. Knowles."

Especially with my resources tapped, my legal protections evaporating, my loyal subjects gossiping at the palace gates.

"We need a pressure point," Domingo went on. "Something to leverage. Something he cares about. Someone he loves."

Kurt Knowles nodded and cracked the knuckles of his right hand with the heel of his left. "That's easy," he said. "Cocksucker's got a daughter."

CHAPTER 7

Sherry Richards swept through her room—"her" room, in "her" house, where she somehow *lived*, was somehow *alive*, was somehow expected to pick up the pieces, the fucking shrapnel, and soldier on like everything was hunky-dory, like she hadn't lost her mother and her faith and maybe, no, *probably* her father and her mind as well.

She was filling her purse with everything she'd need to make it through eight stultifying hours at work.

Celebrity gossip magazine. She wouldn't even open it, couldn't care less about the couplings and baby pictures of these anointed, oblivious fools. She bought them by rote because she could now, because her mother wasn't here to call them idolatrous. Because it kept Melinda's memory alive, in some perverse and distant way.

Enamel one-hitter, painted to look like a cigarette, snug in its slim wooden holder with the spring-loaded release. A gift from Eric—or, rather, a memento of their time together. Sherry had broken up with him a month ago and questioned the decision every day since, his cell-phone number forever tingling on her fingertips. Eric was the sweetest guy in the world, no doubt about it. But looking at him brought back the horror, overwhelmed the fragile dams Sherry had erected inside. A normal conversation with Eric had never stopped feeling like a charade, and the effort of talking around what lay between them, huge and unmovable, was exhausting. He'd been there, too, after all. Seen her mother's headless body moments after she had. Been thrown, flailing, into that same fetid car trunk. Run from the same monsters. How did you talk about anything else? How did you stop reliving those moments, or want to feel anything besides numbness?

For a while they'd tried not talking—taken all their succor from each other's bodies. And in truth, that was really what Sherry yearned for. To hold him close, to find release and relief and silence. But it wasn't enough. You had to talk eventually.

Sherry needed new beginnings.

If those actually existed.

A week ago, she'd started to think maybe they did.

Maybe they strolled right into your stupid ice cream parlor, flashed you a boyish grin, and asked if by any chance you had a flavor called vanilla.

Don't get your hopes up, Sherry told herself sternly, for the millionth time. *He doesn't know anything about you.*

The thought of unburdening herself was terrifying, a burden in itself. And the thought of *not,* of letting him go on believing she was a normal girl, unmarked by tragedy and worse, felt dishonest. Like she was peddling shoddy merchandise, selling him a bucket with an invisible hole in it or something.

For now, though, Sherry was having fun. When she was with Alex, she thought of nothing else—not Marshall Buchanan's breath in her face as he tried to pry her legs apart, not how fucking good it had felt to push the knife into his gut and watch his eyes go wide and glassy, not why her father had gone through hell to save her only to abandon her again, not the worms slithering through her mother's cold dead flesh.

With Alex, she got to live in the present. That was all she could ask for, and probably more than she deserved.

Certainly, she thought with a pang of guilt, it was more than she ever had when her mother was alive. Melinda's piety was like a chain around Sherry's neck, forever tightening with stricter rules about what she could do and say and wear. The only thing worse was the lapses, those dreaded days when Sherry would come home from school and find Melinda taking a vacation from the Lord with a pint of whiskey for a traveling companion.

She twisted the stopper, and the one-hitter jumped into her hand, bringing the waft of singed weed with it. She used the light on her phone to check the long, narrow stash chamber, make sure she had what she needed. Rolled the hitter between two fingers, wished she could blaze right now and feel that sweet gauzy sense of vagueness descend on her like a transparent cloak, mellowing everything out, giving her the strength to accept the world as it was. To find the beauty in the pain.

And man shall have dominion over all the plants of the earth . . .

Thank God for that.

"Sherry! It's quarter of, honey! Don't you have work?"

Ruth, calling from the kitchen, chipper to the point of near mania after two espressos.

Her own time-honored morning head rush.

Sherry sighed, pretending it was a plume of smoke instead of a cloud of exasperation.

"I'm on my way," she replied, voice conversational, a little passive-aggressive reminder to Ruth that the house didn't require so much volume.

As they both well knew.

The relationship was weird—not unpleasant but unsettled, under construction.

Guardian and ward?

Big sister and little?

Roomies?

Whichever it was, they'd definitely heard each other have sex more than a few times.

Sherry jammed the one-hitter deep into her purse, checked to make sure she had a lighter, and set off down the hall.

"Good morning," Ruth greeted her, turning from the counter. "How about some eggs?"

"Morning," Sherry said. "No thanks. Hey, Nichols."

She headed for the fridge, the orange juice.

"Howdy." He was scrutinizing the newspaper, legs outstretched, mug steaming in his hand. They were a two-coffeemaker couple: one stainless steel Italia, one plastic piece of crap, the white yellowed with age. Ruth had tried to sell him on Americanos, as a compromise, but no dice. Nichols stood by his sludge.

Sherry respected that.

"What are you doing after work?" Ruth asked, her tone a tad too cavalier, and Sherry felt her throat tighten.

Here we go.

"I don't know." Long swallow of juice, eyes furtive behind the mask of the glass. "Nothing, really."

She hadn't told them about Alex. There was no reason to. They'd only raise their eyebrows at the fact that he was a few years older, or question whether she should be spending so much time with him so soon. Besides, Ruth and Nichols had barely tried to mask their disappointment when she'd broken up with Eric. As if the move called their own relationship, forged in the fires of that same horrible day, into doubt.

Or maybe they just worried about her. It wasn't like Sherry had any other friends, after all.

"I was thinking we could go shopping," Ruth said, deliberately casual, wiping her hands on a dishrag and then smoothing down her skirt. "Pick up a few things for—"

"I'm not *going* to school. Please, do we have to have this conversation again?"

Ruth looked at Nichols before plunging in.

Oh, great. They'd *discussed* this. Sherry braced for battle, acutely aware even as she did so of how bad she felt for them—bad, and guilty, and ashamed. Who wanted to be saddled with a shell-shocked teenage refugee when you were trying to start a relationship? God, could there *be* a worse handicap, a bigger albatross than her?

"Listen, Sherry, I understand—"

"We both do," Nichols chimed in, looking like he'd rather be anywhere else.

"—that you're not ready. That's fine. But there's got to be a plan, honey. A timetable. Something. I mean, you're not just going to scoop ice cream all your life."

No, maybe I'll run away with Alex. Get as far away from Texas as the road will take me.

He drove a '66 GTO convertible, burgundy over tan. Sherry didn't know a thing about cars, but she knew Alex's front seat was her favorite place in the world: that when she slid in, she felt like anything was possible, like the world hadn't collapsed on itself.

The car was no sixteenth birthday present from Dad, either. Alex was a man. Nineteen, and out on his own. Seeing the world, paying his own way by flipping vintage finds on eBay, records and books and clothing for which hipsters in Japan coughed up top dollar. He was beholden to nothing and nobody—his past firmly behind him and his future an open vista, a picture still being painted.

Maybe there was room in the frame for Sherry.

She imagined walking out of hers and into his, then tore herself free of the fantasy, snapped back to the present. The promise of a different life, a reset button, filled her with new recklessness.

"Look, if it's a problem, I can always move in with my dad."

It was meant to bring silence crashing down around their shoulders, and it did. The specter of Jess Galvan haunted them all. He wasn't quite Melinda's precious Christ on a cross, hadn't died for their sins exactly, but he'd saved them and he'd paid a price.

Given up a piece of his soul, maybe. Sometimes Sherry thought of it like that.

Not that she hadn't lost something, too.

The father she'd always waited for, snatched away the second he'd come back.

Maybe she had no right to be furious—and for sure, the last thing Sherry needed in her life was anger. Anger had better take a number, if it wanted a seat in the psych ward that was her mind, and she was trying very hard not to feel that way. She knew her father loved her, would do anything for her. Already had. If he was staying away, he had his reasons.

Guess what, bitch? Everything isn't always about you.

If only she could help him. She wasn't a kid anymore—whatever she was, she wasn't that. It was time she manned up, or whatever you wanted to call it, though *woman up* definitely sounded stupid. Maybe the way to get some stable ground under her feet was to be useful. To give back, instead of running away.

After all, who else did her father have?

Ruth and Nichols were still staring at her, as if maybe they could wait out the mention of Jess.

Nice try.

"I'm serious. Tell me where to find him."

Nichols folded his paper, dropped it on the table. "For the last time, Sherry. He and I agree, it's better for now if—"

"I'm his daughter."

Nichols picked up the paper again. "It's not a good idea." And pretended to read.

Sherry looked at Ruth, saw that she was about to cry, and felt her own tear ducts fill. She willed the water to stay where it was and swung her bag onto her shoulder.

"Yeah, well, neither is school."

She stalked out the door, left them frozen in their weary little tableau, and made it to the corner before the first tear fell.

Her hands shook as she lifted the one-hitter to her lips, the orange flame to the tip. She felt her chest expand as she inhaled, the smoke filling her lungs. Another greedy pull, the one-hitter really a two-and-a-half-hitter, Sherry turning the good local greens her coworker Meghan's older brother had sold her into fine gray ash.

Her head lightened deliciously, and her heart went along for the ride. She ground the hitter in its compartment, refilled it, suddenly proud of herself for not breaking stride, playing it so cool, just a girl smoking a cigarette, nothing to see here.

I'm a survivor, she thought suddenly. It was Ruth's phrase, therapy-speak, everybody a survivor of something in the doctor's book, the syntax tortured and awkward—like, if your mother got murdered, that made you a *murder survivor,* which sounded about as retarded as *woman up.*

Supposed to be empowering, probably.

It had never done shit for Sherry—but now, in the exultant blush of her high, she felt the word swelling with new meaning. Felt it pulling her spine straight, squaring her shoulders. Goddamn right, she had survived. And then some. She flashed on the knife in her hand, sliding into Marshall Buchanan's gut. She'd do it again. Do it every day of her life, if she had to, and never lose a moment's sleep.

I am my father's daughter.

Before she knew it, Dreamery Ice Creamery loomed before her, the universe settling into perfect harmony with Sherry's immediate needs: to consume tiny pink-plastic sample spoons' worth of at least twelve flavors of premium hand-packed small-batch ice cream and sit in an air-conditioned room with Meghan, who had opened today and was sure to be baked as well, trading occasional stony remarks but mostly just listening to random crappy inoffensive pop music on Meghan's iPod, plugged into the Dreamery house system, and not causing each other any drama.

In an hour Sherry would be bored stupid, but right now everything felt right.

And at four, she'd walk out the door and into Alex's car, with the whole night stretched out in front of them like an endless red carpet.

Maybe I'll never come back.

CHAPTER 8

Galvan broke wood until he broke dawn. He broke six eggs into a dirty glass and let them slide into his stomach, then broke three more and chased the first batch. He could feel the fatigue weighing down his muscles, knew he was about to round the corner into the asleep-on-your-feet exhaustion he craved—and also that, weirdness among weirdnesses, he'd be good as new after three hours of sleep, like a cell phone in need of charging.

But there was nothing easy about sleep. Nothing restful.

Galvan never knew whose dreams he'd have.

He'd seen glimpses of a life he assumed was Cucuy's, been enfolded into a consciousness he knew was not his own. He'd occupied a distant past, filled with grandeur and brutality: eaten roasted meats from golden platters while men fought to the death for his amusement; walked through a stone palace bathed in remarkable quantities of sunlight as a retinue of servants trailed behind; prostrated himself before a mammoth altar in a darkened room and brought fire to a fragrant herb of some kind, sending the smoke billowing toward the heavens. And he'd dreamed of darker times: strode across battlefields strewn with the dead and the dying, a bloody spear in each hand. He'd sat in grim judgment, hearing pleas of fealty from his ruined enemies and demanding their lands, their gold, their daughters in tribute.

He'd received those daughters. Ripped their hearts from their chests with his bare hands, and taken them into his own body, fresh and warm—the vessel of the gods, the sustenance of the accursed.

The hell of it was, such dreams were the least of Galvan's problems; the past was the past, at least until further notice. He didn't know whether he saw the things he did because Cucuy wished him to, the monster orchestrating the show, or because Cucuy was helpless to prevent Galvan's incursion into his own psyche here in this altered, passive state.

Whichever it was, Galvan's dreams of the future were far worse.

Or perhaps they were Cucuy's dreams.

Or perhaps they weren't the future; perhaps they were a sales pitch.

Galvan, all-powerful.

Striding through the world like a god.

His will supreme, his strength boundless, his dominion unopposed. All of creation reduced to subservience, worship.

The dream never evolved, never whittled itself down into specificity, never revealed itself in scenes. It was an abstraction. A feeling.

Intoxicating, though that word did it no justice. *Endless fucking orgasm* was more like it. Only crueler, sharper, the ecstasy without the release, the high without the comedown.

A state no mortal could maintain.

Godhood.

Galvan awoke from those dreams in a lather of sweat and terror and arousal. The sense of omnipotence lingered for minutes, and most frightening of all was that Cucuy stayed silent and let Galvan ride it out—as if he knew the feeling was more seductive than anything he could say. And yet, in these frantic silent interludes Galvan had to triple-check each thought, each impulse, before he could be sure it was his own.

How the feeling faded, how the violence flooding his brain drained, Galvan couldn't say. But it did—that was the important part. He met the challenge. Chopped his wood. Ran down his prey. Kept the prison cell inside him locked down.

Galvan's reward was the other dream.

The *other* other dream.

If he was lucky, he thought, collapsing on the thin, sweat-redolent cot, she'd come to him tonight—or rather today; the sun had climbed high enough to fill the trailer's windows with light, and Galvan covered his eyes with a pillow, rolled onto his side, and tried to conjure her without Cucuy knowing. It was a new trick he'd been working on, a way of thinking one thought for cover while another ran underneath, undetected. The way a TV news story took up almost the whole screen, but that little crawl of words kept scrolling across the bottom, nice and quiet.

Who knew if it worked. Who knew if it was necessary. Who knew anything.

Fuck it.

Galvan let the woman in yellow fill his mind. Maybe if he fell asleep that way, the dream would come.

It was the closest thing he had to intimacy these days, and she hadn't laid a finger on him. The seduction was agonizingly slow, governed by a rhythm Galvan didn't understand but couldn't question. It was as if she were probing the dark contours of his soul, stretching him out flat and smooth so she could see and know and feel every inch. She moved like a cat, circling him, engulfing, her emerald eyes flashing and bottomless at once. He didn't move a muscle, but every fiber of his being sang out for her. The sun pounded down on them, and on the featureless, glassine desert in which the encounter always took place.

There was a resonance there, some echo of the familiar. Galvan had been trying to put his finger on it ever since the dream began, and all of a sudden, as he teetered on the brink of sleep, it hit him and he almost threw up.

Of course.

The woman in yellow looked at him exactly like the Virgin Army did, back when he was a Righteous Messenger and those first young blameless undead girls had sensed the heart he carried and emerged to take his measure, the bylaws of their charter, or whatever the fuck, rendering Galvan upstanding enough to be untouchable.

For a while, anyway.

It was the same energy. The same paralyzing, probing feminine lust.

I don't know what to do with that, Galvan thought. And then, at long last, he passed out.

It was a sleep without dreams, pure and black, restorative, heaven sent.

Until it wasn't.

Galvan floated up from that dark, silent place, like a diver breaching the surface of a lake, and found himself staring down at the twinkling lights of a town he didn't recognize. The sky was blue black, mottled with stars, like a mirror doubling the windows below. The air was warm, pleasant, spiced with sage.

And Galvan was Galvan. He contained no multitudes, possessed no powers.

It was glorious.

The scene was coming into focus now. He was on a bluff, a scenic overlook, the kind that drew sunset enthusiasts and teenage couples. And sure enough, a handful of cars were scattered across the broad hilltop, pointed at the early-evening view.

Galvan's attention lasered in on a convertible muscle car, parked at a rakish angle to the bluff. Two moonlit heads inside, parked at rakish angles to each other.

One of them was Sherry. He knew, somehow, and started toward her.

Or tried to.

It wasn't that kind of dream. Galvan couldn't move. He was incorporeal—an observer, a ghost. As Cucuy was to Galvan, Galvan was to the world of the dream.

An orange glow lit the blackness like a firefly, inches from his baby girl's mouth. A cigarette. No—a joint. Galvan could smell the rich, fruity smoke. He clenched his fists, felt a bead of sweat roll down the inside of his arm.

She took another draw, then offered it to her companion, fingers bunched around the base as if the joint were a tiny torch.

He shifted on the bench seat, their merged silhouette separating, and Galvan saw his face in profile, the handsome jut of his forehead, nose, and chin. His lips separated to take the joint.

No—to lean forward into the empty space and kiss Sherry full on the mouth.

She leaned back against the passenger door, left hand cradling the back of his head, pulling him on top of her. The glowing tip of the joint streaked across the blackness, and then it and Sherry and the boy all disappeared below Galvan's sight line.

He stood rooted to his spot, vibrating with intention. He felt it in his bones: something was wrong here.

Something was not as it appeared.

Shadowed body parts rose into view. His daughter's left leg, from the knee down, thrown over the upholstery. The boy's back arched, then hunched. The top of his dark head bobbed down the length of her body—and then, suddenly, he was visible from the waist up, brushing back his hair, stripping off his overshirt to reveal a threadbare orange tee. The kid's mouth cleaved into a smile as he said something to Sherry, sprawled beneath him, and Galvan saw her wriggle, the leg disappearing, knew she was shrugging her jeans down past her hips, that in a moment they would be a rumpled afterthought on the floor.

And then the boy lurched into the backseat and lifted a backpack. Galvan cringed inwardly, expecting to see him extract a small square foil package from the bag, *please don't make me watch this dude put on a condom,* but what the kid took out was worse.

Far worse.

A Ziploc bag, with a piece of fabric inside. His body was twisted away from Sherry's; she couldn't see what he was doing.

But Galvan saw. Galvan understood.

Galvan, the paralytic.

The ghost.

And then he was on top of her—invisible, but Galvan knew exactly what was happening.

The weight of his body pressing Sherry down.

His forearm locked across her windpipe as she bucked and kicked, reflexes tamped down by the weed, the shock, the confusion.

The rag pressed to her nose and mouth, Sherry twisted her head left and right to escape the fumes.

Her eyes saucered as the chloroform took effect, then rolled back into her skull. Her head lolled and she went ragdoll limp.

The whole thing was over in fifteen seconds.

Galvan couldn't even scream.

The brake lights glowed, and the kid slammed the shift into reverse, threw his arm across the top of the seat, and twisted to look behind him as he backed out.

For a moment, they were face-to-face, the car coming within a few feet of where Galvan stood—long enough for him to commit the boy's features to memory: the thick black hair, the widow's peak, the Cupid's bow lips, the steely, emotionless eyes.

He spun the wheel, put the car in drive, and rambled down the hill, taking it nice and easy. Just a sweet young kid taking his sleepy girlfriend home. Galvan watched them disappear around the bend, swallowed by the moonlit night.

And finally, he screamed. A full-throated bellow of agony and impotence that turned the night sky bright, curled back the edges of the universe like burning paper.

The sound of his own voice woke him, and Galvan squinted in the midmorning sunlight, his chest heaving, his hands clenched into fists.

He leaped up, scrabbled through the bedside mess for his cell phone, pressed On and waited for it to find a satellite, his breath coming fast and ragged. The goddamn thing barely worked out here, got two bars at the best of times, was basically a glorified answering machine.

The screen pulsed once, coming in range, and Galvan pressed Talk. The only number he'd ever dialed was Sherry's.

One ring. Two.

His heart felt like it would explode. Galvan could sprint for miles at a time and it barely jackhammered, but this was something else again.

You cannot defend her without me, Cucuy said, in his head. *As long as you resist, she will never be safe.*

"Shut the fuck up."

Three rings. Four.

"Dad?"

There was fear in her voice. Galvan stood, snatched up a shirt, made for the door.

"Sherry. Sweetheart. Are you okay?"

"Uh . . . I guess."

Her voice quivered. It was a lie. There was a knife at her throat. A gun to her head. Adrenaline coursed through him.

"Is someone there? Does he have a weapon on you?"

A pause like a sob. Galvan halted at the doorway, spun and searched the trailer for his boots.

"I'm at work, Dad. What are you talking about?"

Galvan froze, boots dangling from his hand.

You will tear yourself apart, Jess Galvan, and for what?

"Sherry, listen to me. If someone's there, give me some kind of signal—"

"No one's here, Dad. Just calm down."

Another pause. He could hear music playing in the background. Galvan dropped the boots, closed his eyes, massaged them with a thumb and forefinger.

"Are *you* okay?" his daughter asked. "Where are you? You sound really weird."

"Sherry, listen to me." He heard the choke in his voice, tried to swallow it down. Imagined her leaning over the ice cream counter, rolling her eyes. "Are you seeing somebody right now? A boy?"

Another pause, as if the words had to travel some fantastic distance in order to reach her. Perhaps, in some sense, they did.

When she finally spoke, her voice was rimmed with a chill he'd never heard. She sounded like her mother.

"We don't speak for weeks, and *that's* what you want to know? How about 'How are you, Sherry? How's life *completely on your own* with *no parents.*'"

Galvan sighed, the breath shuddering out of him. "I'm sorry, baby. I'm just scared is all. I-I had a dream, a nightmare, that something happened to you—"

"Yeah, well, something *did.*"

The conversation was getting away from him. Galvan shook his head to clear it.

Fat chance.

"Look, it was just a dream, okay, Dad?"

"Sherry—"

"I've got a customer. I gotta go. And no, for your information, I'm not seeing anybody."

The line went dead, and Galvan sank to his knees, alone with his demons again.

Which wasn't really alone at all.

CHAPTER 9

It had to be some kind of self-hate thing, Nichols thought, his interior monologue dappled with Cantwell's psycho-speak these days. Either that or a macho thing: Nichols playing the stoic, the man who could take a licking and not start bitching.

Why else—now that the department had both a pot to piss in and a window to throw it out of—would he refuse to get himself a goddamn working air conditioner?

The twelve-to-eight shift fit better with Ruth's schedule, meant he could linger at the breakfast table the way she liked—weekend breakfasts had been marathon affairs in Cantwell's house growing up, apparently, and for her domestic bliss started with re-creating the ritual.

And it meant he could be privy to shit shows like this morning's, play stepdad to the bundle of nerves and hormones that was Sherry Richards—and hey, Nichols wasn't complaining, was happy to do his part, had been an equal partner in the decision to take her in. A no-brainer, considering the lack of options the girl had.

But still, Jesus Christ. He wasn't qualified for this. And two women in one house? Nichols was no goon, women were his equals and his betters—but goddamn, that was a lot of estrogen whipping around, a lot of emotional updrafts and downswings. More than he could keep track of, for sure.

He parked the cruiser in his reserved space, made for the front door. He swung it open and tamped down the irrational, guilty feeling that he was sneaking in late. Starting at noon just *felt* wrong. It threw off his rhythms, made him feel like he was playing catch-up all day. Robbed him of his morning rituals.

Like feeling his office heat up. By this time of day, it had already completed the transformation into a sweltering, fetid armpit. Where was the sport in that?

And when the hell were you supposed to eat lunch on a noon to eight? An hour after you got to work? At three? Were you supposed to eat two meals on the clock? Starve yourself, then strap on the feedbag for an early dinner?

First-world problems, Nichols.

Use 'em to block out what's underneath, long as you can.

He grabbed the stack of paperwork waiting for him on the department secretary's desk—Maggie was already out to lunch herself, no fool she—walked into the Armpit, and turned on the Eisenhower-administration fan. He'd stopped for an iced Dunkins on the way, despite the pot of coffee he'd already poured down his throat at home. Sheer force of habit. He plunked it down on the desk with a reproachful glance, unable to even take a sip, and took a baleful look around.

This room, and the job he did in it, represented the only continuity Nichols had left.

Sure, you've got a brand-new house and a brand-new lady friend and a brand-new sense of existential dread, but hey, at least the wood paneling and the smell of mold remain the same.

Talk about cold comfort.

At least something was cold.

He drummed his fingers atop the paperwork, not ready to slog through it yet, and felt a familiar restlessness creep though his muscles, a desire to move just for the sake of moving, the desk like a ball and chain around his leg.

Get out there and do some good—that was the self-exculpating, rah-rah version.

Went down a lot easier than *I can't sit here with myself or I'll go nuts.* Protect and Serve, motherfuckers.

He called the rookie's name, hoping maybe something had happened out in the world that required sheriffly attention. Anything major, and he'd have gotten a call; the deputies weren't shy about interrupting Nichols's off-time, passing the buck to the buck-stopper. But a man could dream, couldn't he?

"Boggs."

"Yessir?" Boggs called back, from his cubicle in the big room, not even standing up.

What was it with these kids, and their willingness to conduct a conversation through multiple walls? Sherry was the same way. Nichols ran the numbers, realized that Russell Boggs was probably six years older than her and nearly two dozen younger than himself.

The fact that it keeps surprising you how old you are, you know what that is?

Proof of how fucking old you are.

"C'mere, dammit!"

Boggs appeared at the threshold a few seconds later, a rangy kid with curly brown hair and arms 25 percent longer than seemed necessary. He was a little doofy, but he had the makings of a solid cop—*good bones,* as they always said about a house they were about to gut-renovate on those design shows Cantwell sometimes watched.

Nichols shook his head, playing at fatherly rebuke. "What do you think, I wanna talk to you across the whole office?"

"Sorry."

"Don't be sorry. What's new? All quiet this morning?"

Boggs shrugged, helped himself to a seat across the desk. "Pretty much. Had a B&E call over on the east side around seven. Lady woke up and found her kitchen door pried open—with a screwdriver, it looked like—and some cash and small electronics gone. But her son's a methhead, and she kicked him out last week, so . . ." He shrugged again. "All in the family, probably."

"Fair enough. You want this iced coffee? Fresh from Dunkins. I haven't touched it."

Boggs raised his eyebrows, nodded. Nichols handed it over and leaned back. The deputy's smooth cheeks went concave as he drew on the straw.

"Oh, and Oklahoma put out an APB on that Knowles guy. Apparently, he escaped from the lockup in Ardmore a few days ago."

Nichols sat bolt upright. "What? How? And they're just putting it out now?"

Boggs turned red. "Um, no. Actually, I just kind of forgot to tell you. It came in right at the end of my shift, and then I had to—"

"Goddamn it, Boggs."

"Sorry, Sheriff. I—"

Nichols took a deep breath, let it out through his nose. "Don't be sorry. I obviously didn't make clear to you how important this son of a bitch is to me. We've got . . . history."

Escaped. The word chimed in Nichols's head, abrasive and off-key. This wasn't the Wild West. Nobody escaped these days—not without a whole lot of help, or some very willing incompetence. Which came down to the same thing, really.

Who the fuck would expend that kind of energy on a scumbag like Knowles? His club was tattered and scattered, those once-ubiquitous convoys of True Natives absent from the local landscape since the Night. Aaron Seth's organization had shown no signs of rising from the ashes either; cut the head off the charismatic leader, and a cult usually folded.

A man always stepped out of jail with a sense of purpose. And if he was a fugitive, the clock ticking down on his freedom, every day quite possibly his last?

There were only a couple of things a man like that might have on his mind.

Settling scores, or disappearing.

Or both.

Putting whoever he blamed in a world of hurt, and then making for the border.

Whoever he blamed.

That'd be Nichols, and everyone he loved.

Before he knew it, he was brushing past the deputy and heading for the door, cell phone out in front of him like a compass, stone-faced and scrolling through the numbers.

Boggs raised up, stepped into his wake.

"Boss?"

"I'll be back."

"Anything I can—"

"No."

He jumped into his car, the seat back still warm from the journey over, the cell wedged between his ear and shoulder now, the home phone on its tenth ring.

Where the fuck was Ruth?

He hung up, tried her mobile. Twice. Nothing.

Her office, even though she wasn't scheduled to work today. Straight to voice mail, the answering service telling him that if he was having a medical emergency, he should hang up and dial 911.

Nichols felt the sweat ooze through his pores. He gripped the wheel tighter.

It made no sense to panic. The old Nichols—the Nichols of three months ago—would not have.

The new one was downright prone to it.

Calm down, he told himself. *Knowles was on the loose for months before this, and he didn't beat a path to your door.* Hell, he'd busted out nearly a week ago, and it had been all quiet on the Western front.

There's no need to do eighty in a thirty-five, Nichols. She's probably in the shower or something.

He hung up, held the phone at arm's length to search for another number, phone inches from the windshield, Nichols's bifocals still lying on his desk. *Get it together, you fucking dinosaur.*

Three rings.

"Hello?"

"Sherry! Are you okay? Is everything all right?"

A desultory sigh. "Why is everybody asking me that today?"

Nichols felt his throat constrict. "What do you mean?"

"My dad called. He sounded, like, freaked out. Is something going on?"

Without meaning to, Nichols accelerated. "What did he say?"

"He had some dream or something." A pause. "What's happening, Nichols?"

Should he say anything? Infect her with his own panic, or be the rock Sherry needed?

The quivering, terrified rock.

"It's nothing. Just . . . be careful. I'll see you later on, okay?"

"Yeah, I guess. You be careful too, or whatever. And Nichols?"

"Yeah?"

"I'm not going back to school."

Click.

Nichols banged a right, tires screeching. Two blocks from home.

He lifted his phone again, wondered if he should call Jess, give him a heads-up. But Knowles would never be able to find him anyway—and if he did, well, best of luck. Galvan would see the biker coming a mile away. Probably rip off his head and punt it into the fucking stratosphere.

It was Ruth whose name was in the phone book, who'd liberated Sherry and her mother from Seth's compound, gone after the cult leader so relentlessly he'd filed a restraining order against her.

Nichols skidded to a halt in front of the house, and what he saw kicked the panic into a higher gear.

Ruth's red Audi, parked in the driveway, the driver's door jacked open, the car beeping insistently.

Her gym bag, lying on the ground.

"Ruth!" He raced toward the house, found the front door standing open, tore inside.

"Ruth! Baby, where are you?" The front hall, the kitchen. Empty.

Only then did Nichols think to draw his gun.

He spun into the living room, weapon first, swept left to right.

Nothing.

"Ruth!"

From the back of the house, a tiny, breathless cry. "In here."

He found her in the bathroom, curled around the toilet.

Nichols holstered his gun and felt the adrenaline flow out of him, leaving him weak, deflated as an old balloon. He slid down the wall and reached out to touch her hair, sweat-plastered to her forehead.

"Baby," he breathed. "What's wrong?"

She gave him a weak smile. "What are you doing here?"

"I was worried about you," Nichols said. "You weren't answering your phone, and then . . . your car was . . . I . . ." He smiled at her— helpless, ridiculous, not caring, his limbs rubbery with relief.

"What's wrong?" he asked again.

She blinked rapidly, then wiped a phantom tear from her cheek.

"I didn't want to say anything yet," she started, and Nichols's heart surged.

She read the joy on his face and smiled broader. "It's only been eight weeks. But . . ." She reached out, grabbed his warm meaty hand in her thin clammy one, and pressed it to her belly.

Nichols didn't realize he was crying until the first tear hit his knee.

"I know what it did to you and Kat," she whispered. "Trying for so long. I wanted to wait until I was little further along, in case . . ."

But Ruth was glowing like she didn't believe a word.

"I know the timing is kind of crazy." She caught his eye, held it, squeezed his hand between both of hers. "But you want this, right?"

"More than anything in the world," he said, and Ruth pitched forward into his arms.

Nichols pressed his cheek to the top of her head, closed his eyes, and tried to figure out what it was he felt. A soaring sense of hope, for sure. Of possibility. The searing burn of love, for Ruth and for their baby.

And also a pounding trepidation, like a drum inside his stomach.

How do you bring new life into a world you don't even recognize?

For reasons that were beyond him, the phrase *no free lunch* popped into Nichols's head, and once it was there it wouldn't leave.

CHAPTER 10

The late-afternoon rush was crazy, one youth soccer team after the next, the place filled up with the high-pitched laughter of seven- and eight- and nine-year-olds, kids too young to practice proper cone management, the ice cream sliding down their elbows in white and brown and peppermint-green rivulets, their parents giving duck-walk chase with wadded-up paper napkins while their own scoops went melty in their Dixie cups.

Sherry could watch kids be kids forever, as long as they were somebody else's responsibility. Had she ever been that young, that carefree? The joy she took in them was cut with heartache: How long could their innocence last? What would happen when they found out there was no Santa Claus, that their parents were mortal, that tragedy was inevitable and nobody—nobody—would be spared?

God, Sherry thought later, as she wiped down the sticky tables after the rush, *I sound like some ancient crone. Some one-eyed witch from a Greek myth, sitting in my cave, shaking my head at the coming doom.* She glanced over at Meghan, using a waffle cone as a microphone as she crooned along to some tacky love song, and gave her a tick of a smile.

How were they the same age? How was that even possible?

Hey, Megs, guess what? I used to live in a cult, but then we left, and so they cut my mom's head off and kidnapped me, but then my dad broke out of prison and ate like this magic human heart and fucking killed every-body—oh, except for the psychotic rapist who kidnapped me; I stabbed him to death myself. Yeah, it was awesome. So, like, how was your summer?

Fuck. My. Life.

"I'm taking a smoke break," Sherry called. Meghan gave her a thumbs-up without breaking character, arching her back as she hit the song's pièce de résistance high note. Sherry grabbed her purse from her locker, then stepped past the storage freezer and through the back door, into the heat and quiet. There was nothing back here but Dumpsters, nothing to hear but muted traffic and the low thrum of refrigeration.

She pulled out her kit, ground the hitter until the tip was packed, lifted it to her lips. Sparked the herb and inhaled with all her strength, wanting to fill her lungs and feel the world lose focus.

Aaaaah. She closed her eyes, savored the float.

"And just what do you think *you're* doing, miss?"

Oh, *fuck*.

Her eyes popped open, and Sherry grinned. Alex was walking toward her, hands jammed into the front pockets of his slim-cut jeans, orange T-shirt fluttering in the slight breeze, gravel crunching beneath his per-fectly worn cowboy boots. God, he was beautiful. The way he moved: a careless, confident, unspeakably masculine saunter. The way one thick lock of black hair broke free of the short ponytail and framed his face. The two days of stubble on his cheeks, the light in his brown eyes, the glow of his olive skin.

He didn't say anything more, just came straight up and kissed her like Sherry was the only thing that mattered in the world. His hands slid over her waist, up her forearms, back down. And then Alex was unfurl-ing her palm, finding the hitter and the lighter stashed there. When his lips left hers, they locked around the pipe. He flicked the lighter, pulled until the load was ash, exhaled out the side of his mouth.

"Hi, baby," he said.

"Hello." She wanted to kiss him again, taste the smoke on his tongue. "Nice entrance."

She took the hitter, packed it again, and handed it back. "How's your day going?"

He smiled, the lighter frozen halfway to his mouth. "My day started the second I saw you."

By the time they cashed the load, Sherry was soaring and work was a distant thing, a virtual impossibility.

"Going back in there right now seems like a form of torture," she said, leaning back against the warm metal fire door.

Listen to me, she thought suddenly, the epiphany blooming like a flower. *Torture. I've* been *tortured. And here I am applying the word to scooping ice cream. If I wasn't me, I'd be fucking offended. But I guess we all just go on. Maybe that's a beautiful thing. Maybe that's, like, the human condition.*

Wow, I'm really freaking baked right now.

"So don't," said Alex, snapping Sherry out of her reverie.

"Huh?"

"Don't go back." He took her hand. "Let's get out of here. Go watch the sunset. What do you say?"

She goggled at him. "I'll get fired."

He waved her off. "Aaah, Meghan will cover for you. It's only a couple hours. You want me to sweet-talk her for you?" He waggled his eyebrows, and Sherry laughed.

"No way. I'm not letting you flirt with her. I'll ask her myself."

Five minutes later they were in his car, the town shrinking behind them and the open road ahead.

"Where are we going?" Sherry asked idly, as the sagebrush flew by, a light green blur, and the deepening blue sky held steady above. A slivery, silvery moon had already snuck out, ahead of the sunset.

"One of my favorite spots. You'll see."

That was enough for Sherry. Alex lay his hand on the seat between them, palm up, and she dropped hers atop it, interlaced their fingers.

"As far as I'm concerned, we don't ever have to come back."

He glanced over sharply, and Sherry felt a stab of panic. Too much? Too needy/clingy/desperate?

But all he said was, "Why don't you tell your parents you're staying over at a friend's tonight?"

Sherry felt her face flush—at the suggestion and at the word *parents,* a reminder of just how little Alex knew about her, how completely new and fresh and unbesmirched she was with him.

"Okay." She slipped her phone from her bag, texted Ruth, and then switched the thing off, in case the reply wasn't to her liking.

"I'm all yours," she said, and slid toward him. Alex lifted his arm, and she snuggled in beneath.

"This car is so awesome. I feel like we're about to go to a drive-in movie, or a, I dunno, like a sock hop or something. Like we're living in simpler times. Is that stupid?"

"Not at all, baby. That's why I bought it," Alex said. "It's a classic."

He spun the wheel, and they banked left, up a snaky little road Sherry never would have noticed and into the hills.

"What is a sock hop, anyway?" she asked.

"You got me."

The climb was long and steady, and before Sherry knew it, they were cresting the top of the mountain—or hill, rather; it was more like a really tall hill—and looking down at the sumptuous view below: the glittering lights of the town, as sunset descended upon it in concentric bands of orange, pink, and blue.

Theirs was the only car, though the dirt lot had room for eight or ten. Alex pulled right up to the edge, so close to the sloping hillside that Sherry clutched at his forearm in half-manufactured fear.

"This is the best way," he explained, cutting the engine and rolling up his window against the slight chill. "It feels almost like we're floating above it, right?"

"Totally. You want some more of this?" She rolled up her window and waved the one-hitter at him.

"I'll roll us a proper joint. That's what they smoke at the sock hops, I'm pretty sure."

He slid a pack of Zig-Zags from his pocket, flipped them across his knuckles, and in about twenty seconds, the pinner was ready to smoke. He handed it to Sherry, and she stared at it with trepidation for a moment, already plenty high.

Fuck it. You could always get higher. And anyway, Alex would take care of her. For the first time she could remember, she felt cocooned, safe. There was something about him—a calm, a confidence, a *manner*—that put her at ease, made her want to relinquish control. Maybe she needed to feel that way so badly she was projecting those qualities on him—but no, that was the old Sherry's way of thinking, the scarred, scared Sherry, the one she refused to be anymore. Alex was real. This was real.

This was her life, and it was just beginning.

She took a pull, passed, then leaned back against the door to watch his pillowy lips pinch tight around the joint.

Instead, Alex parked it between his scissored fingers and leaned in for a kiss. Sherry pulled him to her, sliding down until her head rested on the seat and she had a clear view of the stars.

"Hey there," he murmured, kissing his way down her neck. Sherry arched her back and ran her fingers through his hair, feeling all her concerns evaporate like sweat from skin and float off toward the new night stars.

The sound of shattering glass put an end to that. They scrambled away, Alex shielding her body with his own, pressing her against the passenger door.

A hulking man stood by the driver's door, fist webbed in blood, face cloaked in shadow. What was left of the window collapsed into diamond-sized bits and fell like sand in the wind.

Oh, shit.

"What the fuck, Dad?"

He's lost it, was her first thought. *He's lost it, and he's capable of anything. Stay calm, Sherry. He loves you. Find his eyes. Talk him down.*

"Dad, this is my *boyfriend*. His name is Alex. I'm *fine*. Nothing is wrong."

"Get out of the car, Sherry." He spoke low, through gritted teeth.

She threw an arm around Alex, pulled him to her. "No, Dad. *You* get out of here. You're acting crazy right now."

Her father lunged forward, his arm like a python, grabbed Alex by the ankle, and pulled him halfway out of the car.

"Get out right now, Sherry, or I'll break his neck. Do it!"

"Okay—okay! Just take it easy." She threw her weight against the door and stepped into the cool night air, onto legs like melting Popsicles.

"I'm out. I'm out. Just—" Words failed her, and she lifted both palms in a *steady, steady* sign.

"Come here," he demanded, pointing at the ground beside his feet.

"Not until you let him go." They eyed each other for a moment across the car, and then Alex found his voice.

"Hey, look, this is obviously some kind of misunderstanding, okay? Can we just— Mr. Galvan, sir, can we just talk?"

Sherry's father tightened his vise hold on Alex's ankle, and he howled in pain.

"You told him my last name?" he demanded, eyes darting back to Sherry as Alex continued to thrash. "Huh? Why would you?"

He turned his attention back to Alex. "How the fuck do you know my name? Who sent you, motherfucker?"

"Stop it!" Sherry screamed, at the top of her lungs. "You're fucking paranoid! Just stop!"

Alex was scrabbling at the seat, trying to pull himself up. He bent double, got a hand on Jess's, tried to break the grip.

Bad move. Jess swatted him across the face with an open hand, and the top half of Alex's body disappeared beneath the seat.

"Alex!" Sherry's legs had come back into focus now, and she ran at her father.

The sound of a gunshot brought her up short.

It came from inside the car. Alex had pulled a revolver from the glove box, it seemed like. Fired a warning shot into the air.

Or else—

No. Warning shot. It had to be.

Sherry's father was nowhere to be seen. He'd dropped flat, probably, at the sight of the gun.

"Alex!" she shouted. "Dad! Both of you, st—"

She never finished the thought.

Her father was on his feet, he was in back of the car, he was bending, grabbing at the bumper, the undercarriage, the muscles of his neck and thighs and biceps straining against his clothes—

"No!"

She was too late. The burgundy-over-tan GTO flipped through the air and down the hillside. The rear bumper landed first, a hundred and eighty degrees later, with a sickening, metallic crash, and the vehicle only picked up speed from there—became a blur, a series of horrible crunching noises.

Became wreckage.

Became fire.

Became death.

Sherry crumpled to the ground, her body racked with sobs, the world gone black around her. For a moment, she couldn't breathe—and then all she could do was breathe, fast and ragged, and then she was on her feet, flying at Galvan, a frenzy of punches and kicks, saltwater and fury.

She might as well have been attacking a brick wall. He stood perfectly still, and took it—but no, he didn't *take it*. Her father didn't even seem to notice.

"You monster!" she screamed, clawing at his face, nails drawing blood from his cheek. "You insane fucking psychopath!"

He said nothing. Did nothing. His eyes were unfocused, vacant.

She stepped back, panting, scared for her own life now. This man was no one's father, no one's son, nobody's friend. He was a shell, a ghoul, something to fear and loathe. He—

"Shut the fuck up!" Galvan bellowed, fists clenched, head lifted to the night sky. "Just shut the fuck up!"

And then he looked at her, and he was Jess Galvan again. Desperate, haunted, confused Jess Galvan, who would do anything for her, who already had, who needed her to understand why he'd done this.

But no.

Just no.

"Sherry—"

He opened his arms, body already pleading before his brain had found the words.

"Stay away from me!" She scrambled farther away, down into the underbrush. Where she could see the flames, licking at the carcass of the car.

"He was going to hurt you. It was all some kind of—"

"Stop it!" The tears were hot, so hot they burned. "You're a fucking murderer! Stay the fuck away!"

He fell silent, and Sherry took another step backward, the brambles biting at her thighs.

Her bag was still slung over her shoulder. She felt around inside, closed her hand around her phone, turned it on and stared into the glow. Dialed Nichols's cell and brought it to her ear and locked eyes with her father as it rang.

"What are you doing?" he said. "Put it away, Sherry. Just give me one minute to explain. That's all I ask."

Nichols picked up. "Sherry? Where are you?"

"Something's happened," she heard herself say. "My father, he— my boyfriend's dead. You've got to get over here."

Galvan held her gaze a moment longer, his face contorted in pure misery, and for a split second Sherry doubted all she'd seen.

Then her father turned and ran.

CHAPTER 11

At the height of the empire, when Izel Notchi Icnoyotl had lived in light and splendor, men said there was a special place in hell reserved for those who offered false counsel. And while he had not intended to betray Cualli, Izel's words had wrought ruin—of the man and the world, and perhaps the universe—and he had no doubt that when this life concluded, damnation would be his reward.

If anybody was minding the store, anyway. If the thirteen heavens, the nine underworlds, had not simply ceased to be. Or perhaps they stood abandoned, forsaken like the toy blocks of a child called to dinner, and of no greater importance.

There was very little evidence to suggest that the gods had not done exactly as they'd said they would and left the world to destroy itself at its own pace. They were someplace else now—some other dimension, distant, invisible and unknowable—fucking one another and playing some new sadistic game on some new terrestrial board.

Could Izel have prevented calamity? Would Cualli have listened if Izel had found the courage to tell the priest to turn his back on the god he'd pledged to serve?

On madness?

On duty?

On power?

On divinity?

Perhaps not. But the opportunity had been his, and his alone, and he had failed to seize it.

Failed them all.

At the very least, Izel was complicit in the Great Disordering, the casting off of grace and glory and the birth of an Age of Chaos from which the world had not recovered.

That day was seared into his memory, undimmed by the centuries he'd spent reflecting on it.

The blazing sunlight. The temple's endless chiseled quartz. The plaza, brimming with the empire's elite, gathered to witness the birth of a dynasty.

The ceremony had ended, and Cualli and Chacanza had descended the steps, arm in arm, husband and wife, to accept benedictions and blessings, sincere and otherwise.

Izel followed in their wake, troubled by the dread he'd seen in his friend's eyes, the drop of blood Cualli's nails had drawn from his own palm. Something was amiss, and he resolved to stay close, to give the priest every chance to confide the problem. Nothing should trouble him on this day—and certainly, whatever it was must not be permitted to vex Chacanza. Her mind and body must be preserved in a state of perfect tranquility, absolute equilibrium, so that her womb would welcome and nurture new life later tonight.

That, too, was part of the ceremony. An immediate pregnancy would confirm the favor of the gods, the auspicious nature of the union. And it was well known that a woman who conceived on the night of her wedding brought forth a male heir.

Izel's chance came an hour later, the banquet under way, the guests lazy with opulence, sun, copious draughts of the liquor known as pulque.

Cualli's skin looked papery and gray, and he had scarcely eaten. The goblet in his hand never met his lips.

He rose from his seat, kissed his bride, and strode toward the temple's lowest entrance—a pauper's door intended for supplicants and slaves. Izel found him just inside, crouched against the cool stone wall, elbows resting on his knees, head bowed.

Izel knelt beside the priest.

You are troubled, my brother. What is wrong?

Cualli looked up, and Izel blanched at the sight of him. Tears ran freely down a face that had never known them. The priest's eyes were hooded, veined with red. He spoke in a harsh whisper, as if his throat were made of sun-parched leather.

Tezcatlipoca has visited me in a dream, brother. But not a dream—a nightmare.

Our god is to be banished, Cualli went on. *His brothers and sisters fear his strength and say that he has taught his priests too much. He is to be imprisoned in a realm wrought solely for that purpose, and all that he has given us shall be taken away.*

He rose slowly to his feet—Cualli's great height unfolding, his regal back straightening until it was rigid as steel.

But it need not be so.

Izel looked up at him and felt his breath quicken.

What must we do? he asked.

He commands me to keep his power for him, until he can return. It must pass through the sacred vessel of the gods, and into me.

The heart of a pure woman. The seat of her soul.

All at once, Izel understood.

He asks you to—

He choked, unable to say it.

Cualli's eyes closed, then opened again.

Yes, Izel. He asks me to sacrifice that which I love most, so that his power and his wisdom are not lost to us forever. So that all we have built is not destroyed. He and Cualli locked eyes, and Izel understood that the priest was asking for his counsel.

His permission.

Or perhaps he hoped Izel would stop him.

Tell him this was madness.

Save his sister.

I can't do it, Cualli said. *I won't. I love her. I'd rather die.*

Izel had never seen weakness in his friend before and found that it sickened him. By this man's grace, Izel had become a priest; by following this man's example he had been ushered into the mysteries and miseries of Tezcatlipoca, come to understand the sacred obligation of man to god.

One did not renounce such things lightly. One did not spurn the gods, nor see the work of centuries undone for the sake of sentiment.

It was the hardest decision he had ever had to make, but Izel made it. He was swift; he did not waver. A surge of grief filled him, terrible and consuming, and then his heart hardened and his jaw stiffened and he knew that he was doing the right thing.

He took Cualli by the shoulders, pressed him to the wall.

Man dies for god, Cualli. It is the way of things. It is an honor. You know it, and my sister knows it. He who is called must answer. We will mourn later, and honor her forever. But now, my brother, you must do as you are told.

Izel stood back, so that he might measure the impact of his words. There was no doubt: they had found their mark. Perhaps Cualli had merely needed the inescapability of this doom confirmed. Regardless, there was no doubt in his eyes now.

No doubt, and no life.

The priest seemed to shrink into himself. When he spoke, his words sounded distant and hollow, as if emanating from a cave.

I do not know what I will become, Izel. What man can contain the power of a god?

Izel could not answer, had neither words nor voice. It was one thing to die for a god—but to live for one? Cualli was right; it was unfathomable. He left the priest there, wreathed in shadows, lost in darkness. Izel had to see his sister, say his silent good-bye.

The banquet was to reach a crescendo when the full moon rose; custom dictated that the couple bid their guests a raucous farewell and retire to a sacred subterranean chamber, and the pleasure that awaited them there. The celebration would continue, in a lower key, until sunrise, when the couple returned triumphant, adorned in crimson outfits, the color a symbol of their union's consummation.

By the time the moon crested the horizon, red and swollen, Izel was so drunk he could hardly bring the serving vessel to his lips. He'd grabbed all the pulque he could carry, staggered into the bowels of the temple, and sequestered himself in the ancient catacombs where the first priests were buried. The smell of dry decay filled the air, and Izel sprawled beside the dead and venerated, the progenitors of his line, and drank as if he sought to join them.

The liquor was eye-wateringly strong, ordinarily served in a diluted form. Izel opened his throat, guzzled, and felt his muscles loosen, his stomach swell.

It is the only way, he told himself, as his sister's smiling face floated before him in the dark cave. He shook his head clear, refused to let himself consider what was about to happen, the desecration she would endure—but no, not desecration. Honor. She would embody the god; his holy essence would impregnate her. Yes.

It was a thing to celebrate, if only one could think in euphemism. In abstraction.

If only one could refrain from imagining Cualli thrusting himself inside her, and then lunging for the knife.

And if one could not, there was pulque for that.

My family will never accept this, he thought, as his eyes fluttered shut and oblivion closed in. *The outrage will spread like wildfire. The empire will be engulfed by war.*

Izel fell into a dreamless stupor, beside the skeletons.

He awakened to a nightmare.

Head throbbing. Stomach rebelling. The torments of the body synchronized with the foreboding that filled his mind.

Izel stood slowly, and moved on unsure legs, stopping more than once to let a torrent of bile spew from his mouth and splash against the timeworn stone.

At long last, sunlight began to penetrate the tunnel through which he hobbled. He squinted and moved toward the plaza, the banquet, the shattered future that was now the past—and froze, beneath the arched entranceway, totally unprepared for the sight that confronted him.

The carnage was absolute. Unfathomable.

They had been executed in their feasting seats, throats slashed from ear to ear.

Cut down as they fled, spears still protruding from their backs like gruesome flags, the territory of their bodies claimed by a new power.

Corpses had been heaped in the center of the square and set aflame—a giant bonfire carrying the scent of human flesh to the heavens even as rivers of blood leaked from the base, as if trying to escape.

The empire's entire ruling class, obliterated from the earth in one fell swoop. Slaughtered like animals. Sacrificed.

To a god, or *by* a god?

There would be no outrage. There could be no war. All those who might have raised a voice, or a spear, lay dead.

Their remains disposed of without thought or honor.

Such savagery.

And yet, such efficiency.

Such genius.

A dozen soldiers strode through the wreckage, swords in hand. They were tidying up, tying loose ends. Killing the almost dead. Feeding the fire. Their faces betrayed nothing; they might as well have been digging ditches, or splitting logs. They had followed orders; that was what they had been trained to do from birth. An enemy was an enemy. It did not matter if he had once been a guest, a benefactor, a brother.

Izel flattened himself against the tunnel wall, his body melting into the shadows. There was no reason to believe he was safe.

There was no reason to believe anything.

The smoke burning my eyes. That is my family.

I've got to get out of here.

But he couldn't bring himself to move. Some force held him—it was physical, magnetic; it compelled him to look upon the face of the man who had wrought this.

If anything of that man remained.

Izel inched forward, sought an angle, a sight line on the temple steps. Cualli was there; Izel could feel him. He summoned all his courage, leaned forward the final inch.

And there he was, inches from where he had wed mere hours before, presiding over the mangled bodies of everyone he'd ever known, ever cared about.

Almost everyone.

Izel watched, transfixed, as the entity that had once been his fellow priest raised its arms, inch by inch, until their span seemed to encompass all the world.

His body glowed from within, as if lit by some internal sun, and the blackness of his eyes was absolute. It was impossible to say what he saw, whether his vision took in what was before him or transcended material reality entirely, bored through matter and peered into some other realm.

The power that radiated from him was like a gust of wind, a sonic boom. Like some perversion of a sunbeam.

He raised his head to the sky and opened his mouth. The sound that emanated from it seemed to exist in every register at once—to fill the air, silence the birds, blot out the sun. It was not Cualli's voice, but Cualli's voice was contained within its multitudes.

He spoke the tongue of the gods. The language Tezcatlipoca had taught the Line of Priests, the language in which they had transcribed his dictates with their own blood.

To speak it was forbidden to man; its sound was entirely unknown.

And yet, Izel understood perfectly.

I will never give this back.

With all the strength that remained in him, Izel turned away and backed into the tunnel.

The darkness.

It was time to disappear.

CHAPTER 12

Nichols kept Sherry on the phone until his battery ticked down to its last 10 percent; he didn't want her sitting out there alone with the shock and grief, the goddamn boomeranging PTSD—and besides, he was hoping that if she calmed down enough, she might remember something about where the hell she was. Sherry hadn't been paying attention to the drive, just the driver. Didn't know which highway they'd been on, whether it led north or east or west.

Nichols ran through a mental list of scenic overviews and make-out spots he remembered from high school, matched them against the size of the town Sherry said she was staring down at, the amount of time she guessed it had taken to get there. And for once in his life, Nichols was smart enough to get lucky, or lucky enough to look smart: he found Sherry in the first place he looked, pulled on to the scene a mere thirty-three minutes after his phone rang.

Larry Bird's jersey number. Or Jesus's life span, if you preferred. Nichols did not.

This was gonna be a shit show, he thought as the cruiser powered up the final incline. He shouldn't even be here—this was a textbook recuse-yourself situation if there ever was one, but who the fuck was Nichols going to send in his stead?

And besides, it was a little late to play anything by the book where Jess Galvan was concerned.

Nichols wasn't proud of it, but he felt calm and strong right now, like he owned the moment. A crime scene always did that: you spun yellow tape around it, cordoned it, gave it parameters. And then you went to work. You brought logic to bear, you comforted survivors, questioned witnesses and imposed order on chaos, stabilized the world right before the eyes of the traumatized. You made them feel that whatever horrible thing had just happened, it was only an aberration. A blip. A tiny blemish on the smooth skin of civilization.

Sometimes you made yourself believe it, too.

Nichols was pretty goddamn sure this wasn't one of those times.

The car crested the hilltop, and there was Sherry, caught in the high beams, turning toward him, her face tear streaked, hugging herself for comfort or warmth. She ran toward him without uncrossing her arms, and Nichols cut the engine, stepped out just in time to enfold her against his chest.

Sherry's sobs were huge, convulsive.

"It's okay," he murmured, splaying a hand across her back and rubbing. "It's all right."

The things we say for no damn reason at all.

He shut his trap and let the sadness run its course. Everybody stopped crying eventually, and if you tried to rush them through, the tears just welled back up, interrupted the conversation you'd been so impatient to have.

It took Sherry a couple of minutes to compose herself. That wasn't much bounce-back time; the bar on tragedy had been set pretty fucking high for the poor girl. She stepped away, wiped her face with her palms, and blinked up at him, expectant.

"You cold?" Nichols asked. "You wanna warm up in the car, while I have a look around?"

She shook her head, crossed her arms again, gave an involuntary shudder. "I'm okay."

He reached into the backseat and handed her his jacket. She slipped into it, the size of the thing transforming her instantly into a little girl.

"Look," he said, leaning back against the driver's door. "I'm not here to judge you. I'm here to help. This is Nichols the sheriff, not Nichols the guy sitting around watching baseball in his bathrobe, okay?"

That got the grudging tick of a smile he'd been hoping for.

"Okay. So. Who was he, and how long had you been seeing him?" *And why didn't you tell us?*

Sherry sniffled, swallowed, gazed off into the darkness.

"Not long. His name was Alex."

"And he was from here? He went to your school?"

She shook her head. "He was from all over." She looked him in the eye. "He was nineteen. Just passing through. And now—"

Her voice caught in her throat, and Sherry shook her head. Covered her mouth with both hands to trap the sob.

"Walk me through it again," Nichols said after a moment. "When you're ready. Everything that happened. You were in the car . . ."

But Sherry was staring off now, in the direction of the cliff, the wreckage down below. Nichols had glimpsed it on a switchback—not close, but close enough to know it was gruesome.

"He's still *in* there," she said, the tears leaking with the words. "Shouldn't you— I mean, what if—"

"We'll get to that," Nichols assured her. "My backup is on the way. Right now, I need to understand what happened. Why your father . . . did what you say he did."

"I don't know." She shook her head, slowly at first, then faster and faster. "We were just sitting in the car, watching the sun set. And then out of nowhere, the window shattered, and there's my— there's Galvan. He must've followed me from work."

"And how did he seem?"

"How did he *seem*? He seemed crazy. He's out of his fucking mind." She let out a shuddery sigh. "He grabbed Alex and started asking all this crazy stuff—who sent him, how he knew his name—"

"How Alex knew your father's name?"

"Yeah. He called him Mr. Galvan."

"And *did* you tell him your father's last name?"

Sherry scowled and shrugged further into the jacket. "I guess I must have."

Nichols felt his cop brain whirring to life, like a computer booting.

"Are you absolutely sure, Sherry? How would it come up—and if it had, wouldn't you remember? And why would *he* remember, when he's sitting there scared to death?"

Nichols dropped his hands to his hips. "Look, Sherry. I'm gonna level with you. I owe you that, after everything we've been through. And because I love you. Okay?"

She looked scared, but she nodded.

"Okay. Your father is real fucked up right now, just like the rest of us and probably more so. But I don't think he's crazy. And I don't think he'd have done this without a solid reason. Or what he considered one."

She threw him a look so cold Nichols actually shivered, and when Sherry spoke, her voice was just as frosty.

"A reason. To kill my boyfriend. Who he's never even met."

Nichols held her gaze. "Like keeping you safe."

"Bullshit. Fuck him, and fuck you too."

"I know it's hard to hear. But come on, Sherry. You barely knew this—"

"I barely knew this guy, so *what*? He deserves to be *murdered*, because my father has a bad *dream*?" She spun on her heel, stalked a few paces, and turned back. "I can't believe this. Aren't you supposed to be, like, *the law*?"

"He had a gun," Nichols reminded her, filing that bit about the dream away for later. "Right? You said on the phone that he grabbed a gun from the glove compartment, or from somewhere, and fired a shot. Any idea why he had that gun, Sherry?"

She threw up her hands. "Because this is fucking Texas, Nichols."

A car was approaching, and they both fell silent, squinting as the high beams found them.

It was Boggs. Nichols raised a hand in greeting, waited as the kid cut his engine and trotted over.

"Deputy Boggs, Sherry Richards. I want you to take her home, and keep watch on the house until I get there. You understand?"

"Yes, sir."

"Where are *you* going?" Sherry demanded.

"To investigate."

"Investigate *what*? Why don't you go arrest my father?"

Nichols sighed. "I'd have to find him first, wouldn't I? And since all you can tell me is that he ran off into the woods, that might take a little time. The important thing is to keep you safe while we figure this out, Sherry."

Her eyes narrowed to slits. "Safe from who? Because the most dangerous person *I* can think of is the one *you* don't seem to have any interest in finding."

"Just safe," he said, and started to turn away.

Sherry reached out and grabbed his hand.

"He was the only good thing in my life, Nichols," she said in a fierce whisper. "I've got nothing now."

He studied her for a second, not sure whether she'd accept an embrace or kick him in the balls for trying.

"I'm sorry," Nichols said at last, softly. And then, "Do you know if he had any family? Anyone we should notify?"

She shook her head, and her gaze dropped to the ground. "He didn't. There's no one. We just had each other."

The anger had burned itself out, at least for now, and Nichols decided to glean what he could before it flared back up.

"Where was he staying?"

"Some motel."

"You been there?"

She shook her head. "He said it was gross."

Nichols clasped her hand between both of his, and the two of them stood that way for a moment before she let Boggs guide her to his cruiser.

Nichols watched him get her settled in the backseat, then ushered the deputy back.

"I'll call the coroner's office when I'm done here," he said. "For the time being, this goes on the record as a car accident, you understand?"

"Whatever you say, Sheriff."

Nichols pointed a finger at him. "Don't let her or Ruth out of your sight for so much as a minute until I get back. I don't care if aliens invade."

Boggs yessed his head and took off. Nichols made his way down the hill, toward the smoldering remains of the car.

He'd seen his share of automotive disasters in his time on the force, scraped plenty of drunk teenagers and text-happy businessmen off the pavement, but this one took first place by a country mile. The car was top-down, smashed into the hillside like the forefinger of God had reached down and pressed.

The fire had burned out, the metal charred black, the air acrid, the tall brush littered with tiny glinting bits of windshield glass. No sign of the kid's body; it was trapped beneath the mangled carcass of the car, and the extrication wasn't going to be easy or pretty; he'd probably been squashed flat on impact and then burned to a crisp.

Nichols paced a wide perimeter around the crash site and finally found what he'd been hoping for: the license plate, wedged in among a stand of low-growing cacti. He slipped it under his arm, circled again in case the gun or any of the kid's personal artifacts had managed to wing their way free, and then climbed his ass back to the overview, grabbing on to strong weeds to ease the way.

He threw himself behind the steering wheel, fired up the radio, and asked Gloria, the desk jockey who'd been working the night shift slathered in bright red lipstick since time immemorial, to run the plate.

She clicked and clacked as Nichols waited.

"It's registered to a rental company. Guillermo's Classic Cars, in Dallas," Gloria reported, through the buzz of static. "You want a phone number?"

"Yeah." He was down to 6 percent on his phone battery, and he hadn't called Ruth yet, which meant she was going to be blindsided when Sherry showed up bleary eyed and inconsolable in Boggs's car.

"Wait—no. Give me, uh . . . dammit, what's that cop's name in Dallas? The guy we worked with on that trafficking thing a couple years ago?"

Gloria didn't even pretend to think, just waited to see if Nichols could dredge it up.

He snapped his fingers. "Sullinger. Edward Sullinger. It's on my office Rolodex."

Five percent left, by the time Sullinger picked up his cell, sounding halfway in the bag. Four by the time Nichols sweet-talked him into calling Guillermo's Classic Cars, local heat always the warmest, telling them they had a piece of inventory smithereened five hundred miles south, and finding out whose name was on the rental.

Nichols was halfway home when Sullinger buzzed him with the info, straight from Guillermo himself. Nichols pulled over, flipped open his notepad, and scribbled down the name and billing address.

Lalo Albarra, twenty-five, of Fort Worth. Or so said his license.

If nothing else, the kid was a liar.

Nichols radioed Gloria, had her run the name.

It came back dirty as a motherfucker.

Lalo Albarra had spent half his short adult life in prison. Transporting minors across state lines. Coercion to prostitution. Possession of a type-A controlled substance. Domestic abuse.

It was the résumé of a pimp, a jackal, a pretty-boy hustler. Preying on young girls, filling their heads and hearts with dreams and promises and then turning them out.

Somebody had put him in motion, sent him after Sherry. That someone was still out there.

And so was Galvan.

Nichols floored the gas pedal. He wasn't sure where he was going, but he knew he had to get there fast.

CHAPTER 13

He was known, by allies and enemies alike, as El Cortador. The cutter. Most would have been surprised to learn that the nickname did not bespeak violence. He was, in fact, good with a blade, but Herman Rubacalo's true skill was in cutting to the heart of a matter. Excising incompetence from his organization with surgical precision; hacking new trails like a bushwhacker with a machete. His blade might be broad or slim, might saw or stab or merely flash. But it was always sharp.

Most men in Herman's business were born into poverty and rose from disposability to prominence through a combination of ruthlessness and animal cunning, loyalty, and luck. They moved up the cartel's ranks, accumulating bodies and profits and avoiding gunfire, stepping into vacancies that opened up when others' nerves or brains or reflexes failed. Eventually, prison claimed most. The rhythms of their rise and fall were as predictable as respiration.

Herman was the exception. He had been born into the trade and groomed to run it—his mind a precious commodity, his father a shrewd investor determined to extract maximum profit. Herman's education had not been in the streets, but rather the halls of privilege; he had studied alongside the sons and daughters of tycoons and aristocrats, rubbed up against money so old it had succumbed to dementia and couldn't remember where it came from anymore.

Trace that money back through time, and all of it was covered in blood, just like his own. That was the history of capitalism, of prosperity. It didn't mean you couldn't run your organization like a professional and aspire to something better.

The whole messy business was, in truth, a means to an end. Herman had a deeper purpose, an agenda that swallowed the drug trade whole.

That, too, had been in his family for generations. They were strategists, long-term thinkers.

Connoisseurs of irony.

An urgent mission, carried out over centuries.

As a child, Herman had read a science fiction story in which aliens, who exist in a dramatically sped-up version of time, arrive on Earth. From their perspective, only the movement of plants is discernible, and so they conclude that only the plants are intelligent. The flickering lives of humans do not register at all, and so mankind is annihilated without a thought. Herman couldn't remember the title or the author, but the idea had stayed with him all these years.

Slow and steady wins the race.

El Cortador sipped from a bottle of mineral water as his three-vehicle convoy—the armored limousine in which he rode, the gun-turreted Hummer that trailed it, and the military helicopter hovering above them both—approached Ojos Negros Prison, after a three-hour drive.

The display of force and power was customary. Perfunctory, at this point, like the handmade Italian suits Herman wore, the Philippe Patek timepiece on his wrist, the charity galas his family foundation hosted on a quarterly basis, their surname forever gracing another hospital wing or university building.

If a quarter century atop the cartel throne had taught him anything, it was that appearances were paramount. One never knew who was watching, and the perception of weakness got you killed faster than weakness itself.

By the same token, the illusion of strength could tide a hobbled man over until real potency returned.

Today's gambit was all about appearances.

Not his own, but his adversary's.

Sometimes you had to play a hunch.

The gates opened, and the cars entered. The chopper veered off, having chaperoned Herman to his destination. It would disappear now, or seem to. In actuality, Herman's security detail would maintain surreptitious contact with the pilot and alert him if air support was necessary—in the event that Herman had to make a quick exit and needed the prison's rooftop snipers neutralized. It was unlikely but not impossible, and better to have your contingencies covered than to leave anything to chance.

The limousine drew up beside the entrance, and Herman took a final sip from his bottle. He could not remember the last time he'd felt nervous. Before his final undergraduate exams, perhaps.

This would be an entirely different kind of test, he thought—and then hastened to remind himself that it was he who would be asking the questions. This meeting was a concession in itself, an admission that reassurances had to be made. Never before had Herman or any of his predecessors—nor any of his rivals, for that matter—been granted an audience with El Cucuy. The Ancient One had always preferred to have them look upon his works and not his face. To maintain the mystery of his existence.

That he had agreed to meet bespoke a house in disarray.

Maybe.

A guard led Herman and his entourage through a warren of tunnels, heavy with the musk of decrepitude. The thought that hundreds of men who worked for him were housed in the tiered cell blocks above—men who would spend their lives trying and failing to serve him well enough to earn notice and reward—flitted through Herman's mind, and then the passage widened, became a room with walls of dark stone, lit by torches. A slablike table, fashioned from the same stone as the walls but stained unmistakably with a burgundy wash of blood, dominated the space.

Seated behind it was a man, his legs crossed at the knee. Small-boned, clean-shaven, handsome.

"Welcome, Mr. Rubacalo," the man said, rising and stepping around the table to extend a hand. "Domingo Valentine."

El Cortador ignored it—stepped closer, forcing Valentine to drop his hand, and drew himself up to his full height. At six four, he dwarfed this peon—Herman's stature a point of pride, an ever-present reminder that his family's history stretched back into the mists of time, before miscegenation and migration and debasement, when men walked tall and the gods looked on them with favor and delight.

"Your name is of no interest to me. I have come to see your master."

Valentine retreated. Stepped behind his chair and tried to reestablish authority.

"I'm afraid that is not possible. He has been called away on other business."

El Cortador narrowed his eyes, as his brain calculated furiously. His security detail appraised Valentine's, both sides immobile and discreet, standing recessed in the room's plentiful shadows.

"There is no *away* for him," Herman said slowly, dialing back the menace for now, replacing it with a pointed deliberateness. "And no business more important than mine."

Valentine met his gaze, and Herman could see the tectonic plates shifting below the surface of the man as he considered his response.

"I do not speak of a physical absence," he said at last. "The Ancient One is a being of . . . of spirit. And meaning no insult to you, Mr. Rubacalo, he is in a state of meditation that no earthly business could disturb. You and I—all of us—we exist on a single plane of being. The Great One—"

"I didn't drive three hours for a lecture on metaphysics, Valentine. Revenues are down. Conflicts are going unresolved. Business is suffering."

"I will convey your concerns, Mr. Rubacalo."

Herman unbuttoned his suit jacket, sat down, and crossed his legs, enjoying the stricken look on Valentine's face as he contemplated the move. Haltingly, Valentine sat as well.

"My sources tell me that no girls, no virgins, have been delivered to this prison for several months," El Cortador said, in a voice so airy he might have been discussing the weather. "Perhaps you imagine that the

Great One's habits, his patterns, are unknown to us. I assure you, Mr. Valentine, that is not the case. As a businessman, it behooves me to keep tabs on the health of my partners."

He let that hang in the air, watched Valentine's Adam's apple bob up and down in his throat.

"I assure you—"

"No, Mr. Valentine, you don't."

Cucuy's man blinked at the insult, but he recovered quickly, his face hardening into a mask.

"You have never been graced with his presence before, Mr. Rubacalo, and you are not owed it now. If you have business to discuss, discuss it with me."

Herman stifled a smile. Valentine's sudden aggression had confirmed all his suspicions. There was no doubt about it: something had shifted. Perhaps Cucuy's time was running short, and self-preservation was his only concern. Or perhaps his time had already run out, and this bantamweight usurper had stepped into the void, scavenged the keys to the kingdom from the body.

Was it really possible that the Great One's reign had ended, after all this time, with a whimper and a puppet show?

Had Herman's sacred oath been fulfilled, rendered null and void? Was the chain of centuries broken? Was he free to lead his life, to leave this odious business and this shadowy vigil behind?

He tried to read Valentine's face, found it weak but inscrutable.

Power does not disappear. It only changes hands.

Or bodies.

Time would tell. The Enemy would emerge with strength anew, or he would not.

In the meantime, Herman Rubacalo would fortify his own position. Turn chaos into opportunity. Eliminate the competition.

That would flush Cucuy out, if anything would. To see his fragile ecosystem torn asunder, his chessboard overturned.

"Rosales," Herman said. It was a conversational pivot toward the tangible, the flesh and blood.

Valentine's relief was palpable. "Rosales," he repeated, as if hearing the word for the first time—a distinct possibility. "What about it?"

Herman made a show of sighing. "What about it. Are you a lover of poetry, Mr. Valentine?"

"I—"

"To paraphrase Mr. Frost, two roads converged in a wood. And the name of that wood, Mr. Valentine, is Rosales."

He crossed his legs, in subtle mimicry, and waited for Cucuy's servant to say something. Then he tired of waiting.

"I need that town—my distribution chain endures great hardship without it. And so, apparently, does Sinaloa's; the government's new enforcement protocols have cut down both our options. Do you follow?"

The slight man gave a slight nod. He was playing it close to the vest. Herman wasn't quite sure how to read that; from a man squatting on a vacant throne, he'd have expected obsequience, or a show of force—desperation in one direction or the other. But not stoicism.

Don't grasp at conclusions, he reprimanded himself. *Just gather information. That's all you've got to do.*

"This is the kind of situation Cucuy has always refereed," Herman went on. "If he won't, or he can't, then as far as I'm concerned his time is over. Barrio Azteca will take its business elsewhere."

"Is that a threat?" Valentine asked, voice low and serpentine. As if he was coiling himself up. Preparing, in slow motion, to strike.

Herman rose from his seat. "Certainly not. It is a plea for the Great One's attention, in the fervent hope that our relationship might continue to flourish for many years to come."

He buttoned his jacket and smiled. "Believe me, Mr. Valentine: if I were to threaten you, no explanation would be required."

He turned on his heel and strode toward the door, security detail massing into a phalanx behind him.

El Cortador strolled slowly down the corridor, the decorum of his departure belying a desire for fresh air so pronounced it was all he could do not to sprint toward the light.

Five hundred years, he thought. The words echoed in his head, syncopated to the rhythm of his footfalls.

Five hundred years.

CHAPTER 14

E l Chango.

Galvan had never dreamed he'd see the inside of this bar again.

This bar, on the Mexican side of the border, where the strippers eyed the patrons like they were thinking about forgoing the usual tits-for-tips exchange and just robbing them blind. Where guns got checked at the front door, backrooms were for losing your shirt in poker games, and the walk-in storage locker probably housed the local health inspector's corpse.

This bar, where everything had started. Where a moment's compassion for a girl his daughter's age—drunk, vulnerable, about to become the victim of men twice her age and half her worth—had bought Galvan a blackout beatdown and an eight-by-ten cell.

Pick the underdog, and you died by the odds.

He'd run all night to get here. Ran until the sun was hot on his back and then hot above his head. Ran without stopping, except to swim. His clothes dried on his back, the moisture lifting away as if by magic. His body was like an arrow shot from a crossbow, cleaving a path through space that was sure and true, unalterable.

Fleeing one country for another had been much harder the last time he'd had to do it.

What he was hoping to accomplish here, Galvan wasn't sure. It was as if the coordinates had been programmed into him without his knowing. Like a reboot. A fail-safe.

If everything goes to shit and you murder your daughter's boyfriend in cold blood right in front of her, head for the scummiest bar in Mexico.

He sure needed a drink, though.

Cucuy had been quiet the whole way down. Maybe because the exertion muzzled him, or maybe because things were going exactly as the monster wanted, and he was content to sit back, throw his vehicle on cruise control, and watch it charge straight into his own country.

Take him home.

Hell, Galvan realized, the thought like a punch in the gut, maybe the dream had been Cucuy's. A false vision he'd smuggled into Galvan's subconscious to trick him into killing an innocent kid. Into letting that much more of his humanity crumble and blow away, like ash in the wind.

Who could be sure? The previous night was like a dream. All Galvan could remember clearly was the look of hatred on his daughter's face.

Something told him he'd never forget that.

"Otra vez?" the bartender asked, jutting his chin at Galvan's empty glass. The dude's face rang a bell: the hairnet, the lazy eye. Galvan nodded, and cheap whiskey splashed into the vessel. He'd slapped a twenty on the bar when he'd staggered in, an hour earlier. It was the only money he had, and if he hadn't drunk his way through it by now, he couldn't be far off.

This wasn't the kind of joint that encouraged you to drink on credit.

The barman lingered, watched him pour the liquor down his throat. "You look familiar," he said, cocking his head to jog his memory.

"Well, I ain't," Galvan grunted, and he punctuated the remark by plunking the glass down on the bar.

The dude raised his palms in a practiced none-of-my-business gesture and turned away.

"I am looking for work, though," Galvan informed his back, drunker than he must have thought, the sentiment sliding from his brain to his mouth with zero friction, the whiskey turning Galvan into a waterslide.

The bartender shrugged his shoulders, grabbed the towel off his shoulder, and polished some grime into a shot glass.

"You seen the pit out front," he said, sizing Galvan up. "Might make some money that way, if you don't mind a little risk."

It had been empty when he'd entered, but Galvan remembered from last time: roosters kitted out with razor blades, clawing one another to death, the money flowing as the warm blood sprayed.

"I don't know shit about picking a winning bird."

The barman shook his head. "Weekdays, it's cockfighting. Weekends, that pit's for men. Ultimate fighting style, carnal. You look like maybe you could kick some ass, ey?"

Galvan took that in and sighed.

"You got a fuckin' sign-up sheet or something?"

Three whiskeys and thirty minutes later, he was in the ring, shirtless, facing off against a three-hundred-pound Mexican with arms like Christmas hams. Drunken gaming enthusiasts surrounded them on all sides, leaning over the barbed wire that marked off the arena, shouting and waving fans of currency.

Kill him, Cucuy crooned. *Snap his neck like you did Seth's. The door to your old life has closed. You are a fugitive. Dead to your daughter. Dead to them all. Become what you are meant to be. It begins right now.*

They were more than words. Galvan could feel the monster's strength, pulsing through his muscles like bursts of electricity. It merged with the flow of his adrenaline, the cocktail dizzying.

Why the fuck not? he thought, as the enormous luchador-looking cocksucker stampeded toward him and the crowd roared, drunk on the promise of blood, the possibility of money.

What have I got to lose?

Why fight it?

I've been a loser. I know what that's like. Been a moralist too.

Maybe he's right. Maybe we don't understand shit. Maybe we're all just ants. Maybe our only purpose is to die for God.

So why not be a god, then?

The man was almost upon him. At the last possible instant—well after it, if your neurological frame of reference was the human male, and more so if it was the human male after seven whiskeys—Galvan darted out of his path. Raised an arm to crucifix position and let the dude run straight into that instead.

It might as well have been a brick wall, the way he went down—broad back slamming against the hard-packed dirt a fraction of a second before his skull landed, lessening the impact and allowing him to maintain consciousness. He slurped for breath, the intake riotously loud against the throng's stunned silence.

Galvan's knee was on his throat before the guy could exhale. His hands clamped around the luchador's wrists, as inescapable as the steel shackles he'd found himself wearing when he first awakened in Cucuy's dungeon beneath the prison, three months and an entire lifetime ago.

Finish him. You are a god.

A flash of crimson obscured his vision, and Galvan shook his head. He could not extricate his thoughts from Cucuy's, did not know whether the man below him was supposed to live or die or why or whether such a thing as why existed anymore. He jerked his head and felt a shooting pain, then looked into the man's eyes, found them wide with surrender. He pulled his knee back, sprang to his feet, offered him a hand up. Yanked the luchador vertical and turned to address the audience.

"So. Who's next?"

We call that mercy, motherfucker. It's what makes us human.

Silence. Both inside and out.

The win netted Galvan a C-note, plus all the whiskey he could stomach. Its speed and flawlessness prevented him from earning any more; the patrons of El Chango might have been desperados, but they weren't stupid.

The fight earned Galvan a new buddy, too: Bebo, his conquered foe. He'd insisted on buying the first round, regardless of the fact that it was supposed to be on the house. Turned out he'd held the crown for two or three months—easy enough to believe; the motherfucker was built like a brick shithouse, probably hadn't been knocked off his feet since he was knee high to a duck. His friendliness seemed to stem from a mixture of awe that Galvan has bested him so easily, gratitude that he hadn't taken the opportunity to pound Bebo senseless once he was down, as most would have, and relief that Galvan was just passing through town and thus Bebo would be the odds-on favorite again come tomorrow.

"So where you headed?" the dude asked. He and Galvan were hunched over the bar, and roughnecks clamored for beers on either side of them, the handful of big winners who'd bet on Galvan engaged in the time-honored tradition of giving the money right back.

"Dunno. South." He shrugged. "Gun for hire. Just looking for work."

Bebo arched his eyebrows, jowled his cheeks, nodded. "Just steer clear of Rosales. Trust me, no amount of money is worth getting caught up in that."

A guy with his back to them perked up his ears at the mention of Rosales and turned toward the conversation. He was tall and poker-faced, the poker having hit him just beneath the cheekbone, the gash poorly stitched, the scar a livid red.

"Don't listen to this pendejo," he said, throwing a play punch at Bebo's meaty shoulder. "He's a family man. In Rosales, any vato willing to get his hands dirty can make three, four times the normal rates."

"Sure," said Bebo darkly. "Just enough to cover your own funeral."

"I wanna be where the action is," said Galvan, glancing at one and then the other. He rapped a fist against his skull. "Keeps me sane. What's in Rosales? *Where* is Rosales? I never even heard of it."

"That's cuz it's a little godforsaken fishing village in the middle of nowhere," said Pokerface.

Bebo drained his drink, beckoned for more. "It was. Until that big-ass cell-phone company decided to build its corporate headquarters in Gómez Palacio and brought in an army's worth of private security to drive out Barrio Azteca. Now Rosales is the only place with a seaport and a highway for a hundred miles."

"Which is why Federacíon Sinaloa was set up there to begin with," Pokerface finished.

"So it's war," said Galvan. This was sounding better and better. Keep the ol' brain and body occupied, maybe even do some kind of good in the world.

Or at least do some bad to some bad guys, if he had to do some bad. Which it seemed like maybe he did.

Bebo affixed him with a wet-eyed look, full of a pleading affection that belied the thirty-seven minutes they'd known each other. "Don't do it, man. Hell, stay here and kick my ass once a week instead."

Galvan clapped him on the back. "I wish I could. How far's this village?"

Pokerface calculated. "About two hundred miles southeast," he said.

"All right, then." Galvan slammed his drink, beckoned to the bartender. "You got gallon jugs back there? Yeah? Fill two of 'em with your finest water, would ya?"

Bebo blinked at him. "You're not leaving *now*."

"Sure am."

"Where to?"

He already knew, so Galvan didn't tell him.

Bebo swiped a hand across his face. "You're not *walking*."

Galvan shrugged. "Probably run most of the way, and walk the rest. I'm a, whaddayou call it—an endurance athlete. This kinda shit is fun for me."

Bebo stared at him. "You're not kidding, are you?"

He knew the answer to that one too, so Galvan kept it zipped.

"There are easier ways to kill yourself, cabrón. Shit, wait till tomorrow and I'll drive you there myself."

"Thanks anyway," he said. "You're all right, Bebo."

Galvan dug into the pocket of his jeans, pulled out the damp, folded wad of bills he'd won and pressed them into the dude's hand. "Here. I'm gonna be raking in the big bucks in a few days anyway."

Bebo tried to give it back.

"I can't take this."

"Buy your kids something," Galvan said. He grabbed the water jugs from the bartender and headed for the door.

"At least sober up first!" Bebo called, behind him. "You've had like fifteen drinks."

"That's what the water's for," Galvan replied and stepped out into the sunlight.

Here it comes. Here it comes. He braced himself.

You cannot outrun me, Jess Galvan. You cannot outrun your destiny.

A sharp pain flashed through his head, his chest—like the electrical bursts he'd felt in his muscles, before the fight, but different.

Weaponized.

A lash. A slavemaster's whip.

"Fuck you," he said.

And Galvan ran.

CHAPTER 15

When the sun disappeared, Galvan slowed to a walk and kept on trucking. He had yet to locate the limit of his endurance; he knew how to tire himself enough to sleep, but he'd never pushed past what the weightlifting magazines of his youth referred to as *muscle failure.* That last rep you just couldn't power through, that wind sprint your body insisted you abort.

He was determined to do it now. He'd move until he couldn't. Drop where he stood. The tank had to empty out sometime.

But when the pink blush of dawn came, he was still putting one foot in front of the other. Just as remarkable, he had one full jug of water left, slung across his back in what had once been his best shirt—best and second-worst—and was now a makeshift bandolier.

The early morning desert stretched out in front of him, an endless gold-lit vista of scrub brush and cacti, rolling hills and shallow valleys and big sky. He'd been charting a rough southeastern path, keeping well off anything that resembled a road and tacking wide anytime he saw so much as the distant glimmer of lights.

Every once in a while, the breeze shifted and he caught a waft of salt air, but whether he was anywhere near Rosales, or the ocean, was strictly a matter of conjecture.

Sooner or later, he'd have to roll through civilization, ask somebody for directions. Find a meal.

It wasn't a thought he relished.

Cucuy seemed determined to match Galvan's feat of endurance with one of his own. There had been no silence on this journey, no respite. The narrative unspooling from the monster's mind was wide-ranging, part history lesson and part enticement, part threat and part theology.

He discoursed on the Line of Priests: the farmer who had been its progenitor, how he'd seen a vision and wandered the desert for weeks, growing weaker and purer, the veil between the worlds lifting, lifting, as he searched for the *great spear cast from the heavens into the earth* so that he might *mortify his flesh upon it, and come to know the mysteries of the Divine Sorcerer.*

How Tezcatlipoca, Most Fearsome and Beloved, had taken an interest in man that far surpassed that of his fellow gods and molded the world like clay, through the Holy Instrument of his priests. How his dictates had caused the scales to fall from the eyes of man, so that Tezcatlipoca came also to be known and worshipped as the Bringer of Glory.

Galvan knew he should shut it out. Shut it down.

But it was fascinating.

So he listened.

And he walked.

Cucuy told him of the great betrayal of Tezcatlipoca by the goddess Omecihuatl: how she seduced him, then bound him to a magical bed as he slept. He awakened to find the greatest of the gods assembled before him, a celestial tribunal eager to judge and sentence him.

Tezcatlipoca's crime, they said, had been to teach his acolytes too much. To love mankind with too hot a passion.

Tezcatlipoca argued that the spark he lit within his priests was meant to illuminate the ways of the universe. So that they could more fully understand, more skillfully serve the majesty of the gods.

This explanation was deemed irrelevant. But then, the crime of which he was accused was not the real reason he was on trial. That would go unspoken.

The gods conferred at length about his punishment. Tezcatlipoca had grown to be among the most powerful of them. His sorcery, his spellcraft, was unmatched—and these were arts he had invented and perfected, not attributes endowed to him upon creation.

This, according to Cucuy, was the real reason the others sought to be rid of him: in Tezcatlipoca's diligence, his enterprise, they saw their own demise foretold. He alone possessed the capacity for change, for growth, and they found it terrifying. His very existence had become a threat.

And yet, he could not be destroyed. For the gods to raise arms against one of their number would bring about calamity, unmake the universe.

Instead, they expanded it. Called into being a new realm, a dimension beyond all knowledge, for the sole purpose of imprisoning their brother. Then, in hatred and jealousy, they cast him into that gray place.

But Tezcatlipoca was not entirely without defenses.

Nor was the gods' fear misplaced.

Had they not conspired to strike first, the Divine Sorcerer would soon have forced a reckoning. His mastery of his arts had grown apace with his disdain for the natural order, the fixity of power. And in the fervor of his boundless exploration he had discovered a method of rending that order, that fixity.

He meant to increase his power by leaching it from others—to render those who dared to challenge him impotent, victims of their own refusal to embrace the principle of change.

Of evolution.

Now, instead, he would teach his priest—a lowly mortal, a halting supplicant—to do to Tezcatlipoca exactly what he had schemed to do to them.

There was no other way. It was either that, or allow his very essence to be obliterated. Sheared from him the instant Tezcatlipoca stepped into the great void of the Dominio Gris.

But along with all that was great and potent, Tezcatlipoca decided, the priest must also inherit his god's pain.

He must know heartbreak.

Betrayal.

If he was to become more than a man, he must first become less.

Empty himself utterly, so that he might be filled anew.

The vassal would become a vessel.

And the Dominio Gris would perhaps not be so barren as Tezcatlipoca's enemies intended.

If he must serve out eternity in hell, the god would make of it a kingdom. Shape it to his needs.

And what he needed most was company.

Galvan jerked his head sharply, at the word. "Whaddayou mean, *company?*"

You're having a conversation with him, Galvan reprimanded himself. *Like he's a friend. Stop it.*

The monster within paused, almost as if it pained him to explain.

Don't assign him human attributes. He's only got one purpose.

And then Cucuy's answer filled Galvan's mind, the way a candle did a cave.

When the soul and the body are severed from each other in a manner that is unnatural . . .

He trailed off, and Galvan finished the thought aloud.

"The soul goes there. To the Dominio Gris. While the body . . . stays behind."

That is correct. In a manner of speaking.

A few minutes of silence, Galvan picking up the pace, matching body to mind as he parsed the ramifications.

Keep it to yourself, Galvan. There's no fuckin' reason to tell him what you think. He ain't gonna give you a gold star for being such a smart boy and figuring it out. Just—

But he was already talking. Apparently, the art of ignoring Cucuy had deadened his ability to listen to his own advice, too.

"Tezcatlipoca didn't just take away your wife. He *took* your wife. For himself."

Cucuy was silent. Galvan felt a chill run down his spine, as if an inky cloud had passed over the mounting face of the sun.

Another thought hit him, and Galvan stopped dead in his tracks.

"But not just her. All of them. It's like the goddamn—the Muslim heaven for martyrs, where everybody gets, what is it, seventy-two virgins to fuck around with."

I do not know what it is like, Cucuy said, the words icy and sharp.

For the first time he could remember, Galvan grinned. "Boy, ol' Tez-catlipoca sure did all right for himself, didn't he? Talk about making the prison experience comfortable. These cartel bosses got nothing on T-Cat, lemme tell you."

On the contrary, his separation from the divine is an agony you cannot begin to fathom.

"And here you are, his sworn enemy for what he made you do—"

I am no such thing. I am him. All that he was, and more.

"Yeah, no, that's bullshit. You hate him. But what do you do? You keep on sending over girls. It'd be fucking hilarious, if it weren't so tragic. He played you like an all-day sucker, and you know it."

Cucuy fulminated, and Galvan grinned wider. Those cheek muscles were gonna be sore tomorrow.

"Five hundred years is a long time to be pissed off, man. Maybe you oughta just let it go, find some new hobbies. Do a little yoga, learn to yodel—"

Enough! Your insolence grows tiresome. But understand, Jess Galvan: if I depart this world, Tezcatlipoca will return. The Dominio Gris is no longer his prison—I am. You are. The other gods have withdrawn from this realm—

"Because they couldn't stomach *you*, from what I heard."

What he made me was an abomination in their eyes, yes. But if you believe nothing else I say, believe this. Tezcatlipoca's return would doom mankind.

"I thought he was this big-time friend of man. Wasn't that the whole problem to begin with? You're not making a whole lot of sense here."

Galvan shook his head—and then narrowed his eyes at a small, jerky movement just short of the horizon line.

Something was out there, and it wasn't an animal.

"I don't buy it," he went on. "Your doom, maybe. Yours and mine. But you know what? I'm good with that. I'm *great* with that."

You do not understand. There is nothing left here that can match his power.

"Funny, I seem to remember you telling me the same thing about yourself. All that 'rise up, embrace your destiny, kill people for the hell of it' shit—and now, what, you want me to believe that you're the lesser of two evils? I've *seen* you, motherfucker. I *know* what you do."

You—

"Shh." Galvan raised an arm. Like Cucuy could see it. "There's something out here. We're being watched."

He squinted, scanned. Maybe it had been a mirage, a trick of the light. He had been walking for damn near twenty-four hours, after all, without more than a piss break.

But no.

There.

A rustling in his periphery, a football field away. Galvan spun left, pinpointed the sound, and sprinted toward it.

What a relief it was, to run at something instead of away from everything.

The movement stopped, abruptly—the quarry, realizing the jig was up, dropping and playing dead. Too late for that. Galvan was there in a flash, sweeping back the brush.

Huddled beneath, face buried in the crooks of his arms, knees tight against his chest, was a scrap of a man, clad in scraps of clothing—his filthy, billowing pants tied with a rope belt, his T-shirt Swiss cheesed, more holes than fabric, the soles of his mismatched shoes flapping at the heel and toe.

"Get up," Galvan ordered. "Let me see your face."

Slowly, the man withdrew his bony arms, raised himself into a sitting position, opened his cracked lips to bare his scattered, rotten teeth.

Galvan's stomach curdled. He knew the guy. What's more, a part of him had been waiting for the motherfucker to turn up again.

He was a skulker, a denizen of the desert.

A walker in two worlds, his soul severed from his body—a Righteous Messenger who had turned on his employer, eaten the heart with which he'd been entrusted, and banished himself to the Dominio Gris.

"Gum," said Galvan. "You sorry son of a bitch." And extended a hand.

Gum looked up at it and shuffled back a pace, as if Galvan had thrust a live snake at him.

"Suit yourself," said Galvan, dropping it to his side. "But why follow me, if you don't wanna say hi? 'Cuz it's just me now. Nobody around for you to turn against me anymore. Nobody to convince I oughta die. Just me and you and a whole lotta open space, pendejo. So you might as well state your business, or move the fuck on."

Gum stood and filled the distance between them with a filthy, tremoring, outstretched arm. His eyes were red-rimmed dinner plates, his voice a weak rasp, a knife dull with rust.

When Galvan heard the creature's words, he didn't know whether to feel terror or relief.

"I know what you are."

CHAPTER 16

So what are you trying to say?" Sherry demanded, holding her bathrobe closed with one hand and flinging the other in Nichols's face. "That he was *right*?"

Welcome to the Lockdown Show, Day Three.

In today's episode, tempers flare when a harried but well-meaning sheriff tries to protect his pregnant lady friend and traumatized teenage ward from unknown dangers by keeping them home, under police protection.

Nichols clenched his jaw, ground his molars together, and headed for the refrigerator, where the beers tended to congregate.

Count to ten. Calm down. Take a swig before you answer.

Remember you've gotta go to work in ten minutes. Put the beer back in the fridge. Lament the decarbonation of a perfectly good beverage.

"For the last time, I didn't say he was *right*. But he wasn't wrong, either. He wasn't *incorrect*."

He sighed and raised his eyebrows at her. "You wanna see Albarra's rap sheet again? Look, Sherry, I know it hurts, but you've got to accept it. He was a fraud, and he was out to hurt you."

She crossed her arms. "I thought your job was to arrest people who break the law. You know, like *murderers*."

Nichols rubbed his weary eyes with a thumb and forefinger and tried to pretend this conversation wasn't making his blood boil.

"Was he a murderer when he killed Aaron Seth? How about when you stuck a knife in Marshall Buchanan? Should I arrest you for that? Let you explain it to a jury?"

"Both of you, stop it." Cantwell tottered into the room, faintly green of face, and went straight for the teabags. They both gave her a wide berth, as if pregnancy might be contagious.

Sherry complied, only to open up a new front a few seconds later. Her anger was untethered, floating through the air in search of something, anything, to latch on to. Nichols felt for the kid, but Jesus Christ, was she becoming unbearable.

"So how long are we in jail?" she asked, fake-casual.

"You're not in jail," Nichols heard himself respond by rote, wondering why he bothered.

"If you can't leave, it's jail," Sherry retorted, sounding pleased with her logic.

"Fine. Have it your way. You're in jail until I figure out who sent Albarra, and why. And how your father knew. And where he is."

Oh, and how the fuck Kurt Knowles managed to walk out of a county lockup and vanish into the night.

Nichols kept that part to himself. Ruth and Sherry were frazzled enough already. And it didn't make a difference, as far as the security; that was already ramped up as high as it could go.

Besides which, keeping it to himself made Nichols feel like he was protecting his women from something, even if that was goddamn idiotic. Shielding people from the truth and shielding them from a bomb were two entirely different things.

Get it. The Fuck. Together.

"So, basically never," Sherry shot back.

Nichols grabbed his holstered weapon, shades, and newspaper off the kitchen table. "I gotta go. Boggs will be out front. Let him know if you need anything." He kissed Cantwell on the forehead, rubbed the small of her back. "Think of it as a vacation. A shitty, shitty vacation."

He threw Boggs a nod as he left the house, stifling a pang of guilt for ordering the deputy to babysit—especially since it served the secondary purpose of keeping the kid sidelined, questions to himself, while Nichols continued to treat the Albarra incident as a blameless death.

And investigated it off the books, on department time, while neglecting the rest of his duties.

The apartment in Fort Worth had been a send-off; the old lady who lived there had never heard of any Lalo Albarra. She'd served coffee and Danish to the cop Nichols sweet-talked into running the address down, let him poke around to his heart's content. Nothing.

The trail hadn't gone cold; the trail simply didn't exist. Albarra's last prison stint had been two years at Beaumont; he'd checked in with his PO once, then disappeared. Not a blip on the radar in the two years since, which probably meant the kid had linked up with somebody who'd bumped him up a notch, taken him off the street.

Or that he'd crossed the border and become someone else's problem.

Or maybe he'd seen the error of his ways, found Jesus and a quiet life of service.

Hardy fuckin' har.

Bottom line, Nichols had spent the past three days with his dick in his hand, unable to scavenge so much as a lead on a lead. At first, he'd held on to the hope that Jess would reach out. Or that he'd go back home, continue living his life of psychotic drunken isolation as if nothing had happened; that seemed crazy enough to fit.

No, and no. The trailer showed no signs of occupation. Not the first night, not the second. By the third, a family of raccoons had moved in. They seemed to be in the process of tidying up, so Nichols left them to it.

Jess was gone. And around these parts, a man on the run only headed in one direction.

That meant it was time to call Miguel Fuentes.

Love him or hate him or a little of both, he was the best friend Nichols had south of the border. And the gambit he'd roped the sheriff into on that fateful fucking day three months ago had gone over like gangbusters with the brass—Fuentes had managed to spin the whole revenge-fueled, seat-of-the-pants shit show as an impeccably executed, long-in-the-making joint operation, gotten his contacts in the press to spill an ocean of laudatory ink, and surfed his way to a plum job a few rungs up the ladder, supervising intelligence operations. All that Last Honest Cop horseshit he'd been blathering about for years had come to fruition; he was now the man who'd brought down a corrupt Federale, Luis de La Mar, and it was either celebrate Fuentes's relentless, self-sacrificing thirst for justice, or admit that de La Mar was not the exception but the rule, and take a long, close look at the whole bureau.

Nobody wanted to do that.

So.

Welcome to your new office, Señor Fuentes. We're honored to have you.

The guy owed Nichols a lifetime's worth of favors, but calling them in was low on the list of things Nichols wanted to do. Fuentes hadn't seen Galvan's grand finale, had missed all the brain-melting shit; to him, the world was the same disgusting and corrupt and predictable place it always had been. There was a gulf between them, and Nichols had avoided reaching out because it only widened that gulf.

Oh, and because Fuentes had revealed himself as manipulative, untrustworthy, and far too comfortable turning judge, jury, and executioner into a one-man show.

But hey, nobody was perfect.

And Nichols needed eyes and ears in Mexico, land of Jess Galvan and Kurt Knowles and who the fuck knew what else. As soon as he rolled into the office, he asked Maggie to get his old friend on the phone.

"Line two," she called a moment later. Nichols lifted the receiver, passed it from one hand to the other, steeled himself for the usual juvenile banter.

"Señor Fuentes. Long time no speak. I hear your dick's about three feet long now, eh?"

"You heard right, cabrón. I been using it to club rats to death."

"Now there's a lovely image. Listen, I need a favor."

"Of course. Anything I can do, just ask."

Nichols pictured him leaning back in his chair, cowboy boots up on the desk, hands interlaced behind his head. Fuentes, the benevolent.

"I assume you remember Jess Galvan."

"Every night in my prayers, hermano. How is that crazy bastard?"

"Missing."

"Missing kidnapped? Missing on the run?"

"Missing off the record. This is for your ears only. My own people don't even know."

Nichols stood up, phone in hand, and walked to the door. He opened it a crack, peered out, and made sure no one was within earshot, well aware of the precaution's utter pointlessness. A slave to his compulsions.

"He killed somebody. But I'm pretty sure he had his reasons."

"Sounds like Galvan. So . . . what? Be on the lookout for a one-armed gringo who doesn't give a fuck?"

"Actually," said Nichols, resisting the urge to smack himself for failing to think this through ahead of time, "he's got two arms now. Or, I mean, a really good prosthetic. You can't even tell."

"Kind of like your prosthetic dick, ey?"

"I'm glad to see that power hasn't changed you, Fuentes. Very inspiring."

"The man makes the money, Nichols. The money don't make the man. So who did Galvan kill? Anybody I know?"

"That was gonna be my next question. The victim was a kid named Lalo Albarra. One of yours. Twenty-five, ex-con, general scumbag. But he jumped parole a couple years back, disappeared off our radar. You got anything on him?"

"Give me a second and I'll tell you."

The clicking of a keyboard, as Fuentes typed the name into whatever sleek machine was perched on his desktop.

"Let's see . . . the only Albarra I have is at Ojos Negros, doing three-to-five for trafficking underage girls."

Nichols heart thudded against his ribs.

"Same prison Galvan was in. That's him—that's my guy."

"Except that your guy's dead over there, not locked up over here."

"Send somebody to his cell. I'll bet you a steak dinner it's empty."

"I'll make a call. So he and Galvan had some kind of personal beef, you think?"

"That wouldn't explain how he waltzed out of prison without anybody noticing," said Nichols, the gears of his mind turning. "Somebody sent him on a mission. And it wasn't Jess he went after—it was Jess's daughter. Who really runs that prison?"

But even as he asked, the answer crashed against Nichols's skull, like a wave against a levy.

Cucuy.

That was who.

The dark power that lurked belowground. The defiler of girls. The bogeyman who had brought Aaron Seth into the world and set Galvan on his gruesome quest.

He was still alive.

"I'll look into it," Fuentes promised. "Barrio Azteca, I think. But Sinaloa is strong there, too. Like everywhere. The usual song and dance. But listen, what about Galvan? Where could he be headed?"

An image of Jess flashed before his eyes: naked to the waist and smeared in blood, the still-warm corpse of a mountain lion draped over his shoulders like a scarf.

"He'd be looking for action," Nichols said, with sudden conviction.

"Well, we got plenty of that. Don't get me started, cabrón. I got cartel drama on my hands so crazy I can't even send in my guys. All we can do is lie back and wait for it to burn itself out, know what I mean?"

"That sounds just about his speed," said Nichols. "Where's it at? Wanna meet me there? I'll bring a picnic lunch."

"You're crazy, Nichols. He could be anywhere. It's a big country, tu sabes?"

"Call it a hunch. I gotta try. Besides, isn't this kind of thing your job?"

"Not even a little bit, cabrón."

Fuentes sighed, and Nichols knew he had the bastard. Miguel was a loyal son of a bitch, when it came right down to it.

"Look," he went on, "I don't like red in my ledger. If I roll down to Rosales with you, we're square. Debt's paid in full."

"Absolutely," Nichols agreed. "I'll owe *you*, even."

"I can't be coming heavy, either. Just the two of us. No uniforms or any shit like that. We take a quick look around for Galvan, and then haul ass out of there before we end up with our heads on stakes."

"Sure. Definitely. Thank you."

"And one more thing, pendejo."

"What's that?"

"You better be serious about that lunch."

CHAPTER 17

O h yeah?" Galvan spread his arms to crucifix height. "What am I?"

Kill him, Cucuy hissed. *He is a body without a soul. You will be doing him a favor.*

Gum's blistered bird-chest shuddered with tremors like a ragdoll shaken by an invisible hand. "You're *him,*" he whispered. "He's in you. I feel him, man. I *know.*"

Galvan cocked his head and lowered his arms. The fact that he was having his first honest conversation in three months was hard enough to process. That it was with a man who'd tried to kill him—a failed Righteous Messenger who'd eaten the heart he'd been tasked with carrying and become a ghoul, a scheming, wandering wastrel—made it even weirder.

"Yeah? So what are *you,* then?" Galvan asked, practically screaming the question in order to hear himself over the jackhammer blare of Cucuy's monologue.

I remember this one. A drug addict. American, like you. Raped and beaten every day in prison, until he tried to take his own life. The guards brought him before me, and I promised him a new one. I gave him strength. Protection. Made him a Messenger. He repaid me with betrayal. This is his reward. He does not eat. He does not drink. There is no death for him, unless by force. Ten years, this torment. It is enough.

End it.

Gum sniffled wetly, his red-rimmed eyes darting up and down, an animal confronted by a predator.

"You know what I am," he managed, the words shaky as shadows in candlelight.

Slowly, haltingly, he lifted the tatters of his shirt, so Galvan could see the crosshatched scars covering his torso—the imprint of the baling wire that had attached the box, the heart, to him. They were deep, seared into the flesh. Galvan's own skin tingled at the sight, the memory.

He must have carried it for weeks, thought Galvan. Escaped the harness only when he grew so emaciated he could wriggle his way free.

"You ate it too," Gum said, meeting Galvan's eyes now. "Like me. Only you ain't where I am. Something different happened." His nose twitched, like a rabbit's—as if he were culling information from the wind, the scents on the air. "What are you?" he said at last.

"Thought you knew, shitbag."

Galvan swung his arms, fake nonchalant. He was feeling suddenly, perversely giddy.

The truth shall set you free, or whatever the fuck.

"I'm a prison," he told the creature, bouncing on the balls of his feet. Cucuy hated it, recoiled inside him like a cat from water. "Turns out me and Cucuy are distant relatives or some shit, so now I get to share my body with his fucking spirit. Pretty awesome, lemme tell you. Like having a secret best buddy you can talk to any time."

Gum swallowed twice before he got the next question out, Adam's apple bobbing in his dessicated throat like a drowning man in the ocean.

"What's he . . . saying about me?"

"That I should kill you. Which is why I ain't gonna." Gum stared beyond him at the nothingness.

"Yeah, you're welcome," growled Galvan. "We done here? I got places to be."

Gum stood there, vacant as a parking space, so Galvan put his head down, made to brush past.

"I sleep," the wastrel blurted, bringing Galvan up short. "I dream. I see the other place. My other . . ."

He trailed off.

"Your other what? The fuck you talking about?"

"I'm here, but I'm there," Gum said in a fierce whisper and jammed his hand down the front of his raggedy pants. Whether he was scratching or squeezing, Galvan couldn't tell, and he hated himself for even wondering.

His dreams unite his body and his soul, Cucuy said, voice strained with what sounded like excitement. *He has seen the Dominio Gris. Seen Tezcatlipoca.*

"And why am I supposed to care?" Galvan shot back, not entirely sure which one of them he was even addressing.

"I can help you. We can figure out how to kill him. I know shit, man. I seen shit."

"Yeah, you got it all figured out. You really wanna help me, tell me how to get to Rosales. I got business there."

Gum scrambled to his side. "I'll show you, boss. I know exactly where it is."

"Just point me in the right direction. You ain't gonna be able to keep up."

Gum acted like he hadn't heard. "This way," he said. "I know these roads like the back of my hand."

"There are no roads," Galvan grunted.

"To me there are."

"Shut the fuck up and walk, then."

IT WAS TWILIGHT when the smells and sounds of civilization began to infiltrate Galvan's sun-dulled senses. He'd have made it there by noon without Gum, but then again, he might never have found it at all.

The time, the world, had gone blurry; the desert had insinuated itself into Galvan's mind, a blinding haze of sand and sun that bleached away all else. Gum's chatter barely registered, and when it did, Galvan responded with the phrase that had become a mantra: *shut the fuck up and walk.*

Cucuy's voice was equally distant, as if the unchanging, oppressive landscape and the sheer, dumb monotony of putting one foot in front of the other had turned down the volume on all other stimuli. Galvan was in a place beyond exhaustion—not past it, but adjacent to it. Half of him wished he could linger there forever. It was the closest he'd been to peace in a long time.

But Galvan hadn't come here for peace.

Not by a damn sight.

Somebody was roasting a chicken.

That person was a genius and a saint.

The aroma wafted past, and Galvan's senses reawakened. A churning hunger in the pit of his stomach led the charge.

Columns of smoke rose in the southern distance—from homes, hearths, grills. He could see low buildings, barns and houses, their outlines framed against the crisp night sky. Farmland: neat ordered rows of earth, unruly bean plants wound their way up stakes, proud cornstalks stood at attention, the low foliage of strawberries. And beyond, through a scrim of trees—fucking trees!—the distant, jeweled glint of the ocean.

"That's it," he said to himself, to Gum, to nobody, and stepped toward it—onto a proper two-lane asphalt road.

The highway. Hugging the coastline, save for this narrow buffer of a town.

"We should stay off the road," Gum advised, scuffling along at his side.

"Shut the fuck up and walk."

Ahead of them the road veered sharply, bent toward the town at something like a right angle. Galvan followed it.

Where the curve resolved into a straightaway, a huge black military Jeep was parked across both lanes, kitted out with floodlights and a weapons mount. Three men loitered in front, the tips of their cigarettes glowing orange in the darkness, assault rifles slung over their shoulders.

They were too busy trading swigs from a bottle of mezcal and casting aspersions on each other's manhood to notice Galvan's approach.

He stopped a few feet from them, planted his feet, and cleared his throat.

They scrambled to raise their guns, a three-part harmony of rote aggression.

"Who's there?" one of them called, stepping closer.

"Name's Jess. And this here's my fuckin' personal assistant—" He looked left and right, but Gum had vanished.

Fair enough.

Galvan shrugged.

"Guess he took a coffee break."

The lead man stepped closer, both hands on his gun, the butt pressed to his shoulder.

"Who you with?" he demanded, nostrils flaring. Galvan took his measure. Kid probably hadn't seen his twenty-first birthday, and the odds weren't looking good.

He seemed like he might know how to shoot a gun, though.

"You wanna be careful where you point that thing," Galvan told him, taking a sideways step. The kid swung the barrel after him, kept Galvan between the crosshairs.

"Who you with?" he asked again.

"I ain't with nobody, junior. Just me, myself, and I."

And just like that, a goddamn De La Soul song started boogalooing through his cranium, taking up valuable real estate.

Dunt-dunt-dunt-dunt-dunt-dah. . .

The kid scrunched up his face. "This road's restricted, fucker. If you ain't with us, you gotta step the fuck off."

Galvan cracked the knuckles of one hand against the palm of the other and shot him an inquisitive look. "Who's 'we' again, junior?"

The kid furrowed his brow, took another step forward. The gun was nearly poking Galvan in the chest now. If the little shitstain had any real training, he would know better. The whole point of a weapon like that was the way it let you keep your target at a distance.

At this range, what was to prevent your antagonist from grabbing the barrel, jerking it out of your hands, duffing you in the face with the butt, then pointing the business end at your stunned friends and splattering them all over their fancy Jeep before they could get off so much as a shot?

Nothing.

So that was exactly what Galvan did.

The kid on the ground was hyperventilating now, one hand cupped around his broken nose as he tried to shuffle away from Galvan, knees bending and straightening, a comically inept quasi escape.

Galvan rested the rifle on his shoulder.

"I didn't catch that, junior. One more time: who's 'we'?"

The blood from the kid's nose was dribbling down his lips, making its way into his mouth as he heaved for breath.

Galvan stepped toward him. "Take your time, boss."

"Azteca!" the kid finally spat, with admirable bravado for a dude crab-walking backward as he spoke. "Azteca, maricón!"

"Azteca Maricón, huh? Never heard of it. Are y'all affiliated with Barrio Azteca? Like a subdivision or something?"

The kid didn't find it as funny as Galvan did.

"Enough with the crawling shit. Stand up."

The kid did as he was told, then snuck a backward glance at the carnage and nearly buckled.

"You got a light?" Galvan asked, and the kid twisted at the waist to look at him, the soft features of his face locked in a death mask, the space between them filling up with the pungent smell of boozy urine as his bladder released.

It took a moment for the question to register, another for the kid to fumble through the pockets of his jeans and draw out a cheap white Bic.

He thrust it at Galvan, with considerably less force than he had the gun.

Jess shook his head. "No. Light yourself a cigarette. You got a cigarette?"

The kid just stared.

"A cigarette. Un cigarillo."

A shaking hand produced a rumpled, generic soft pack. Somehow, the kid got it lit. He never took his eyes off Galvan. Was probably still expecting to die any minute.

"Good. Now go over there, open up the gas tank, throw the cigarette inside, and run. Get the hell out of here, and tell your whole squad there's a new fucking monster in town. Comprendes?"

The kid nodded. Walked over to the Jeep like he still expected a bullet in the back and stepped gingerly over the corpses of his friends. Had the presence of mind to pull hard on the cancer stick before he tossed it in, so that the ember was good and strong.

Gold star for that one.

He was out of sight by the time the fire spread from the fuel line to the gas tank. Missed the spectacle of the oversized vehicle catching air as it caught fire, chunks of fiery automotive shrapnel flying through the sky as the blaze roared.

Galvan took it in alone, grinning like a maniac and feeling recklessly, gloriously alive.

CHAPTER 18

Izel fled first to his family's compound; exile would be easier if he was well provisioned. And there were the children to think of—his nieces and nephews, too young to attend the wedding feast. They had to be hidden, delivered into the hands of servants to be raised in secrecy.

Cualli would think of that. Of them. Of all who might swear vengeance against him. He would snuff them out before they grew strong enough to—

To what?

How did you stop a god?

Izel took back roads, detoured through the teeming slums of the capital and then the verdant plains of the lowlands. He ran until his lungs felt ready to burst, climbing the hill that led to the sprawling, magnificent home of his father at midday.

It was ablaze. Flames licking at the sky. A thick cloud of black smoke billowing from the foundation.

Izel watched as the roof collapsed.

In the distance, through air wavy with heat, he saw more fires.

Cualli had wasted no time. Izel pictured his troops, flowing out from the capital like blood leaving the heart. There was no shortage of them, no limit to the destruction they could wreak. Izel fell to his knees, tears springing from his eyes as he thought about the fate of his brother's children, and his own grandmother.

This house was their tomb. Their pyre.

"Uncle!"

He turned, just as his youngest nephew, Yaretzi, threw himself on Izel's neck. The child was covered in soot, smeared with blood, his small heart pounding so hard Izel could feel it when he splayed his palm over the boy's back.

Izel stood, and the boy wrapped his legs around his uncle's torso as if he had renounced the ground entirely.

"Your brother?" Izel said, in his ear. "Your sister? Anyone?"

Yaretzi shook his head and hugged Izel's neck tighter.

They made camp that night a quarter mile upwind from the smoldering wreckage. Izel figured it was safest to remain where the earth was already scorched. When the child was asleep and the moon showed its face, he knelt and began to pray for the dead, then realized it was impossible. To whom would he supplicate himself if Tezcatlipoca was gone? What could prayer even mean?

In that instant, Izel realized what he must do. He roused the somnolent boy, whose rest was fragile and shallow, broken frequently by cries of anguish, and hefted him onto his back. Yaretzi settled wordlessly, and Izel began to walk.

The temples had fallen by now, he was sure. With the priests and their closest acolytes already dead, those holy sites would be defenseless and spiritually unprepared. And there was no doubt that Cualli would seek to erase all access to any memory of the other gods; resistance to his reign would be predicated on their intercession.

Indeed, it was Izel's only hope. Cualli might unmake the temples hewn by man, but he could not bring down the places made sacred by the gods themselves.

On the contrary, Izel thought with a start, he might well seek them out himself. Feed upon the power that resided there, until they were unmade.

Izel's resolve hardened. *I must get there first.*

The temple was the seat of his worship, but the Rock of Tezcatlipoca was his most hallowed and mystical ground: the place where the first priest had been anointed, and to which all who had followed were obliged to journey. It was where the god spoke directly to man, where the dictates were given and Book of Knowledge was written in the blood of priests.

Izel had never been there.

But then again, neither had Cualli. Only after a man had an heir was he permitted to undergo that journey.

It was said to be grueling.

But those who said so had never lived through times as dark as these.

Izel set off into the desert. He would find the site and hope its holiness amplified his entreaties even in the absence of the divinity who had claimed it. He would call upon any and every god he could name, implore them to unmake this abomination whose very existence blasphemed the world they had created.

They walked by night and slept by day, to conserve their strength. With nothing more than a knife, Izel managed to keep them both alive; he knew how to relieve a cactus of its precious store of water, how to flush a prairie dog from its hole. With each passing hour, Yaretzi seemed to withdraw further into the cocoon of his grief, but there was nothing to be done about that except go on living.

One way or another, the boy's pain would soon come to an end.

On the third day, they reached the jagged quartz pillar, and Izel swallowed the other gift his knife had reaped: the fruit of a desert plant that induced a powerful trance state, opened the mind to the cosmos. Its use was ubiquitous among the priests of the gods.

Had been ubiquitous.

Before their slaughter.

Whatever happens, whatever you see or hear, do not be frightened, he told the boy. *Watch me, but do not speak. Do not interfere.*

Yaretzi's dark eyes grew large, and he nodded.

Izel lay down atop the sacred altar, and let the vision come. Soon new hues, sharper and brighter, suffused the landscape, turning the cacti a more vivid green and the earth a richer brown, filling the vault of the sky with subtle, shifting patterns. It was as if everything was coming into focus, revealing its deeper nature, its higher energetic self.

This, Izel thought, *is how the gods must see the earth.* He focused on his breath, realized it was synchronized perfectly with that of the cosmos—that creation pulsed in the same rhythm, that all were one and one was all, the majesty of the moon mirrored in each and every grain of sand, every speck of animal matter.

And in the fullness of that understanding, the great ecstasy of it, Izel cried out across the void.

A creature of terrible purpose violates the beauty you have wrought, oh Great Ones. He wields a power that is yours and yours alone. Your priests lie dead. Your worship is at an end, if you do not stop him.

The blackness faded from the sky, until it was a parched white the likes of which Izel had never seen—not the white of cloud cover, but a white as pure and pale as death.

He sensed that he was not alone and scrambled to his feet.

Indeed, striding toward him across a landscape that suddenly appeared as cold and lifeless as the moon was a being of such luminescence that Izel averted his eyes. The light that emanated from her filled his eyes, his brain—to wash his insides clean, purge all impurity away. There was no color to it, and no warmth.

And yet, it burned. Burned cold.

Her form was human, but this being was not of matter, not of earth.

She was light. She was spirit.

She was a fraction of her true self, as unglorious as she could make herself appear, so human eyes and ears could perceive her at all. So that a human soul could withstand her presence, even for a moment.

Izel felt as if he were floating. He wanted nothing more than to be subsumed by her light. Pulled into that vortex and obliterated.

He closed his eyes.

It made no difference. There she was.

The goddess of fertility. Of life and death. Of rebirth.

Chimalma.

Izel's heart pounded in his ears. Yes. This was perfect. Who among the Great Ones could be more offended than she by the sorcery of Tezcatlipoca, the sin that was Cualli?

Surely, she would set things right.

I have heard you, Izel, Priest of the Sorcerer. Your words have reached me, across the Great Vale.

Her voice was everywhere at once, cold, beautiful, a voice like a thousand flutes.

I beg your help, Chimalma, Shepherdess of Life, he said, and fell to his knees before her.

There is no help to give. I am the last to withdraw from this world, but withdraw I shall. For the abomination our brother has brought into being so affronts the gods that we renounce this world and leave it to its doom.

But . . . Izel stammered. *But . . . you cannot!*

I am sorry, Priest. Already, our dear brother Tezcatlipoca is lost to us. I assure you, worlds have been renounced for less.

Please, Most Exalted One. If he so offends you, tell me how to stop him.

I cannot.

Chimalma's light began to fade.

No! Izel felt madness set in, felt the world flicker and move, before his eyes and beneath his feet, as the glow of the goddess diminished.

In a moment, it would depart this world forever.

What is hell? Cualli has once asked him.

Izel had fumbled for a response, and the priest had interrupted.

The answer is simple, Izel. Hell is merely the absence of the divine.

He cast wildly around, a primal scream emanating from the depths of him as the darkness spun up to engulf Izel, engulf everything.

Yaretzi ran toward him, a look of terror on his face.

Izel rose, grabbed the boy by the neck, and threw him down upon the altar. The knife flashed in his fist; he pressed the blade to his nephew's neck and bellowed into the abyss the goddess trailed in her wake.

Beloved Shepherdess of Life and Death, do not forsake us yet! I offer you that which is most precious to me!

It was the oldest of all oaths—the most powerful, the most reviled. A primitive enticement, from a time when the gods were understood only as elemental abstractions, bringers of calamity who fed on human misery.

It was the oath that rendered Tezcatlipoca's need of Chacanza legible. Perhaps, Izel thought, as the sweat poured off him and the knife drew its first drop of crimson from the boy's soft neck, it was the only oath that had ever meant anything between the gods and their creations.

God does not die for man.

Man dies for god.

The light of Chimalma flared bright.

In an instant her potency, her presence, filled the world again.

Release the child. That which is most precious to you has already been surrendered.

Izel's knife clattered to the ground.

Thank you, Most Honored One.

Her light grew so intense Izel feared he might be incinerated, reduced to a small pile of fine white ash. He clenched his fists, squeezed shut his eyes.

Chimalma was everywhere.

And not just now.

Not just her.

The gods were present in everything and everyone. He had always known this, and yet had never realized it until this very moment.

Soon they would be gone, beyond the reach of all mankind. Forever.

Perhaps he should die now.

Do not thank me until you have heard what I shall say. This abomination will multiply, until the world is overrun by the unholy, and nature is utterly perverted. So, too, shall the means of his unmaking be unholy . . .

Izel retrieved his knife. And like each priest of his line since time immemorial, he flayed open a vein and began to write the words of a god in the blood of a man.

CHAPTER 19

The blaze had died down to a smolder when Galvan realized he was being watched. The fire made the night impenetrable, but he could still feel eyes.

Not like that was unexpected, after the entrance he'd made.

"That was quick," he said into the blackness. "You bring marshmallows?"

They'd come at him hard, and the smart play, the obvious play, would be to stay hidden, and open up on him from where they stood. Except that when their muzzles strobed the night, they'd light up their locations for him.

It wasn't the kind of thing a shooter fretted over, unless the target could dodge automatic motherfucking gunfire.

Luckily for Galvan, he was pretty sure he could.

A sound of footfalls, coming closer, and then into the light stepped a sun-wizened man sporting a John Deere hat and denim overalls. A rifle dangled from his right hand, barrel pointed lazily at the ground.

He toed the edge of the road and looked Galvan square in the eye.

"You ain't who I expected," Galvan said dumbly, the adrenaline tucking tail and trudging back the way it had come.

"Same to you."

In the flickering firelight, the topography of the man's face was remarkable. Deep furrows like dry riverbeds lined his cheeks, surrounding two eyes like deep shimmering wells. He might have been eighty and spry, or sixty and not.

He was no cartel fuckboy, though. That much was clear.

"Name's Jess." He twisted at the waist, jammed a thumb in the direction of the wreckage. "Those guys friends of yours?"

The man narrowed his eyes, reached up and adjusted the brim of his cap. "This is my farm," he said, sweeping his arm in the direction from which he'd come. "They are no friends of mine."

"Oh. Well." Galvan shrugged his shoulders. "Happy to help."

The man beckoned. "You must come with me. They will return."

Galvan ran a hand against the grain of his stubble. "That's kinda what I was waiting for," he said.

The farmer shook his head. "First you need food, and rest." He extended his hand. "I am Louis. Please. If you have come to help us, then my prayers have been answered. But this is not the way."

He took Galvan by the elbow, and Jess allowed himself to be led off the road, steered across a broad, wild field, and into a storage building that smelled of motor oil and chicken shit. Before he knew it, he was reclining on a thin mattress, atop a bale of hay. After two days on his feet, it might as well have been the fucking Waldorf Astoria.

"I am sorry it is not more comfortable," Louis said in a loud whisper. "But you will be safe here. And out of sight. My sons . . ."

He sighed.

"Better they not see you. The men you killed, their friends will offer money for you. And some of our boys here . . . it is seductive to them, this life. They fly toward it like moths to a flame. You understand?"

Galvan nodded. "I do. You're a good man, Louis. Thank you."

He patted Jess on the arm. "I'll bring you some supper. And tomorrow, we will discuss the trouble you have come to make."

Galvan nodded groggily and watched him putter off. The new battle was going to be staying awake long enough to eat, and he had a feeling it was a lost cause.

Sure enough.

Head. Pillow. Gone.

And there she was.

It felt like coming home.

If this was Cucuy's dream or memory or fantasy, so be it. Galvan didn't care. He just wanted to touch her. To look into those eyes.

Come for me, she purred.

I'm here.

No. This is not real.

She traced a finger down his chest, and Galvan shuddered with pleasure, closed his eyes and lifted his face to the sun, watched the mandalas kaleidoscoping on his inner eyelids.

How can I find you? he murmured. *What do you want?*

I want you to give yourself to me.

She pushed him to the ground, swung a leg over his torso, straddled him, leaned low.

Heart and mind. Body and soul.

Galvan woke bathed in sweat, the vision dissipating, the feel of her lingering on his fingertips. The barn was pitch-black, but he could smell the food Louis had left, and one form of lust quickly supplanted the other as Galvan tore into a greasy, cold, delicious piece of roast chicken, and a heaping mound of rice and beans.

It was only ten or eleven, but there would be no more sleep tonight— the woman in yellow wasn't coming back, and he would not risk night-mares, and besides, Galvan felt fully recharged. He stood, bent at the waist, and felt a row of vertebrae pop into place.

Time to do some exploring, he decided. Check out the town, get the lay of the land, figure out where his attackers would come from.

What will you do when there are no more animals to kill, Jess Galvan?

"There will always be animals," Galvan shot back and headed for the door.

Fifteen minutes of walking brought him to the silent center of town. A church, a bar, a market, and a café eyed one another across a wide plaza. All of them looked, even in the moonlight, like they could use a fresh coat of paint. Or maybe a wrecking ball.

He sat on the cold stone steps of the church, his will to explore suddenly drained. Louis was right; if he was going to be of any use to this town, he had to have a plan. A strategy.

The old catch-22.

Can't act without thinking.

Can't think without acting.

Let me tell you about freedom, Cucuy whispered, apropos of nothing, the words slithery, the monster in seduction mode. *Freedom from fear. From death. From judgment. Once you have tasted its sweetness, all else is like ash upon your tongue.*

"You're a real fuckin' poet, you know that?"

The hum of an engine in low gear commanded Galvan's attention. He looked up to see a dust-covered sedan motoring toward him, headlights doused, at about five miles an hour.

The car came to a stop in the exact middle of the plaza, and two guys stepped out: midtwenties, buzz cuts, rhinestone-bedecked T-shirts over black jeans. The trunk yawed open and they stepped to it and bent low, precise and perfunctory in their movements, like men working on an assembly line.

When they straightened, they were holding a dead man at the knees and armpits. His arms lolled loose; there was a dark gash across his neck and a dried gush of blood painted across the chest of his work shirt.

And affixed to that shirt, duct-taped in place, was a square of cardboard, with words scrawled on it in black marker. Galvan couldn't read it from his vantage, didn't want to risk moving and be seen.

Not just yet, anyway.

They laid him on the ground delicately—a perverse mockery of the way a parent lays a sleeping child in her bed, Galvan's heart panging suddenly for Sherry, remembering better times and sweeter nights.

The men arranged the corpse: spread his arms and his legs until he resembled that Da Vinci drawing, Vesuvius Man or whatever, and then tilted his head back until the wound gaped open: a pair of macabre chefs, plating a grisly entrée.

They backed away slowly, as if afraid to disturb his rest, and examined him from a distance. Decided they were satisfied and turned toward the car.

Galvan waited until their asses rested on upholstery and they were reaching for the doors before making himself known.

"Hey, there. What's that say?"

They were on their feet in a flash, the driver crooking his arm toward the handgun at the small of his back. Galvan paid him no mind, strolled toward the body with an exaggerated, arm-swinging jauntiness he figured would read as absurd gringo obliviousness or outright insanity, throw them off balance a bit.

The driver's gun was trained on him now, both hands wrapped around the barrel, knees bent, advancing slowly—a textbook approach, no flashy gangster-movie flex to him. Galvan feigned tunnel vision, bent at the waist, furrowed his brow.

" 'Fuck with Sinaloa and die,' " he read, sounding out the words like a first grader, then straightened. "Who's Sinaloa? You? Or you?" He pointed at the corpse and continued spouting rapid-fire inanity.

"Who's he? Looks like a farmer to me. Was he a farmer? Or a fisherman? Heck, everybody around here's pretty much a farmer or a fisherman, am I right? How 'bout you guys? You like to fish?"

The driver lowered his gun a quarter inch. "You got three seconds to get your crazy gringo ass the fuck out of here."

Galvan grinned, spread his arms, and sauntered toward him.

Playing the maniac was surprisingly fun. And disturbingly easy.

"Leave? Hell, I just got here." He looked from one to the other. "So which one of you is Sinaloa?"

The dude cocked back the hammer. "Federación Sinaloa, pendejo. We own this town." His raised the pistol to Galvan's temple—which brought his arm well above his own head, given the six inches Jess had on him.

"You don't own shit," Galvan said. "Pull the trigger. See what happens."

Dude didn't need any more convincing. He got the shot off, but not before Galvan's arm shot out, corralled his wrist, snapped it backward like a twig, and slammed him to the ground. The pistol's report echoed through the empty square, overlaid with the sound of the shooter's bellow. The pistol clattered across the flagstone, came to a rest against the dead man's leg.

Galvan glanced up at the other man, saw the sweat on his brow and the trajectory of his gaze. He was clocking a run for the weapon, wondering if he could skirt Galvan, reach it, spin and take him down.

"Jump, if you're feeling froggy," Galvan said, stepping back. "But one of you is gonna die, and the other's gonna drive me to your little Sinaloa clubhouse. You're in the lead for chauffeur right now, but it makes no difference to me." He turned toward the gun, made a show of appraising the distance.

"Matter fact," he told the guy, "go ahead. Walk over there and pick it up. We might as well make this interesting."

The Sinaloan didn't move.

"I mean it. Here's what we're gonna do. I'll stand right here. You get the gun, and you shoot one of us. Me or him. You hit me, then hey, it's all good, the both of you go home. That's if you hit me. But I'ma tell you something, and maybe you'll believe it and maybe you won't. You *can't* hit me, because I'm too fast. Bullet looks like a fucking badminton thing-amajig to me, whaddayou call it—a shuttlecock. And if you miss, I'm gonna rip your head off, tear a couple trees out of the ground, build me some goalposts, and punt your skull through 'em from sixty yards away."

You are enjoying this, said the voice in his head, with a kind of curdled satisfaction, and it took Galvan a moment to understand that it was not Cucuy.

It was him.

The would-be gunman didn't move. His partner was still writhing, quieter now, cognizant of the way ownership of his fate had changed hands.

"Shoot this crazy son of a bitch," he yelled. "Put a fucking bullet in his brain."

Galvan raised his eyebrows. "Pretty much what you'd expect him to say. All right, let's go, we don't have all night here."

Haltingly, the Sinaloan walked over, crouched, picked up the gun. He was ten feet from Galvan, from the driver. Galvan had to give it to him: from the look on his face, he had absolutely no idea what the dude had decided.

"No man is faster than a bullet!" the guy with the broken wrist screamed, and then the crack of the gunshot tore through the air.

CHAPTER 20

The slug caught the driver in the chest and he fell silent forever. His boy squeezed off another three to be sure, the shots tightly clustered, a downright respectable bit of marksmanship, stopping only when the gun clicked.

He dropped his arm and let the pistol fall from his hand. It thunked onto the stone, a low-key punctuation mark.

"Smart man," said Galvan.

The shooter shrugged. "I only met him Tuesday. He seemed like a prick." He turned a steady gaze on Galvan. "So now what?"

"First, pick up that gun before some little kid finds it."

Galvan watched as he complied, contemplating the absurdity of his own words. There was a pair of murdered men lying in the middle of the plaza, and he was worried about an empty handgun?

The kid straightened, jammed the gun into his pants.

"Okay. So?"

"Like I said. Wherever you're staying, take me there."

"So you can . . ." He didn't break eye contact but couldn't finish the sentence.

"Have a frank exchange of views. You got a problem with that, Bosco?"

Bosco thought about it, or pretended to.

Or wondered why he'd been dubbed Bosco, which was certainly a legitimate question.

"Can you get me a job with Azteca, then?"

Galvan goggled at him. "Excuse me?"

"Tell them I helped you or whatever. I got four kids to support, carnal."

"I don't work for Azteca. I don't work for anybody."

Now it was Bosco's turn to goggle.

"So what the fuck, then?" he asked, after a moment.

"I'm on the Rosales Beautification Committee. Get in the car."

Bosco shook his head. "I gotta get paid, man. One way or another, you feel me?"

Galvan walked over, came face-to-face with him. Bosco's cheeks were pockmarked with acne scars, his hairline mottled with pimples. He looked like he ought to be worrying about who to ask to the junior semiformal, not working as a hired gun in the middle of a war zone.

"You wanna do right by your kids, find another line of work. Your life expectancy's like *this*." He snapped his fingers. "Now get in the car. You don't have to get out. Just drop me at the front door, and you're done."

"What—"

"I'm not asking, chief."

Bosco didn't press it. He retrieved the keys from his ex-partner's pocket, slid into the driver's seat. The engine turned over, and he swept the car around in a wide U-turn, navigating carefully around both bodies.

Soon they were on a narrow dirt road, winding through forest thick enough to stanch the seep of moonlight.

Bosco drove with his hands at ten and two, his posture rigid. Like Galvan was his driver's ed teacher or some shit.

After a dozen forks, the forest thinned and the ocean came into view, surreal in its sudden expansive rolling grandeur. Bosco jabbed the brake pedal with a heavy foot, and the car lurched to a stop.

"There's no point, you know," he said. "They'll just replace 'em with new guys."

"Then the replacements are gonna need replacing. I ain't got shit else to do, homes."

Bosco shook his head. "Whatever. At the end of this road, look to your left and you'll see an old hotel, a hundred yards up the beach. They're gonna have sentries posted."

"How many?"

"Maybe three, four. I never did it yet, so I'm not sure."

"And how many men inside?"

He shrugged. "Like thirty."

"All right, get outta here. And don't let me see you again."

Bosco nodded, fast and tight. Galvan heaved a sigh, climbed out of the sedan, shut the door softly. He watched Bosco bang out a three-point turn and tear off down the road, three times faster than they'd come.

He trudged up the path; at its head a dozen vehicles were parked, from beat-up Toyotas to murdered-out Jeeps like the one he'd barbecued.

Galvan tried a couple of doors, thinking there might be a cache of weapons he could liberate, but everything was locked down tight. He weighed smashing a window and stuck a pin in the idea—no use drawing out the sentries before he'd gotten the lay of the land.

He strode up the path, onto the sand. To his left, as promised, was a ramshackle three-story hotel. It sat on stilts at the edge of the woods, a hundred feet from the water. The windows were dark, half of them broken. The paint had peeled off long ago. The whole thing looked slapped together from driftwood, maybe by shipwrecked carpenters delirious from sunstroke.

Galvan walked to the shoreline and let the ocean lap gently at the toes of his cross-trainers.

The temptation to throw himself into the water was unexpected, and tremendous.

Galvan resisted.

Resisting, after all, was what he did.

He'd take a swim later. When he'd earned one.

Bathe in their blood, my son. Show them what real strength looks like.

He saw a cigarette flare, on the porch of the hotel, and then another. The crash of tiny waves made it impossible to hear the men from here, but they'd hear him if he made a sufficiently hellacious amount of noise—flip a fucking car over, and they'd come running.

He ran the movie in his mind, saw himself waiting in the woods as they tried to figure out how the fuck a Jeep had done a backflip then springing at them, a human sandstorm of violence, taking down the sentries, grabbing their weapons, and tiptoeing toward the house.

Eh.

It seemed needlessly elaborate. Plus, the sound would be hard to calibrate, might be loud enough to wake the soldiers slumbering on their dirty mattresses and bring everybody rushing outside.

Galvan clocked the men a moment longer, dim shapes lounging on plastic chairs, their rifles resting against the broken railing.

Vigilant was not the first word that popped into his head. More like *ass-clowns*.

The shortest distance between two points was a straight line.

Works for me, he thought, and ran toward them—footfalls silent in the sand, body gathering speed, a perfect blank clarity filling his mind. He vaulted the porch and came down between them: two guys in T-shirts and cutoffs, exclamations frozen in their throats, weapons out of reach.

Time up.

He snapped the first one's neck between his palms, spun away from him, grabbed the other by the arm and tossed him off the porch. The two sentries landed simultaneously, one crumpling lifeless and the other landing shoulder-first in the sound-muffling sand. Galvan leaped after him, foot connecting with the side of the sentry's face as he tried to stand and knocking him flat. Galvan grabbed a handful of hair, yanked the head backward until he heard a crack.

Two down.

Galvan froze, ears cocked for any hint of movement from inside the house. Nothing.

Go time.

He crept back onto the porch, glanced at the rifles. They might as well have been alarm clocks, for all the racket they would make. Galvan walked past them and through the front door.

He looked left: a dining room, stacked high with broken chairs.

Right: check-in desk, two couches, two dudes asleep beneath thin blankets.

Galvan stared down at them, hands flexing at his sides, hypnotized by the syncopated rhythm of their breath, and felt all the resolve drain from him.

They are no less guilty asleep than awake, Cucuy hissed. *Give them what they deserve.*

Galvan clenched his jaw and shook his head. *Not like this.*

More false morality, the monster sneered. *A man lives because he sleeps and dies because he wakes? Understand, Jess Galvan: there need be no reason. No law but your own.*

He shook his head again, heart beating faster now than it had in the thick of combat.

A shout from outside broke the stalemate. Galvan whipped toward it just as the report of a rifle split the air like lightning.

An alarm clock after all.

This was about to get interesting.

He dove off the porch and found a third sentry standing over the body in the sand, firing rounds into the air.

For a dude pounding a panic button, he wasn't very attuned to the presence of danger. Galvan hit the ground three feet in front of him, rolled, stood, and as the guy scrambled to lower the barrel of his rifle, Jess plowed into him, shoulder to gut, a nice clean football hit. The rifle flew from his hands as the guy went down and Galvan snatched it in midair, momentum carrying him forward; he pump-loaded the next round single-handed and shot the guy in the sternum.

You didn't have to be a sniper at that range.

The first window to light up was on the top floor. Galvan beelined for it, *be the last place they're expecting.*

A standing leap, and he was back on the porch railing; another, and his hands gripped the ledge of a second-story balcony. He swung himself up, leaped again, *fucking King Kong shit,* and by the time a shirtless torso leaned out that lit window, right arm terminating in a pistol, Galvan was propelling himself upward again. He grabbed the dude's arm like a gymnast on the uneven bars, and a couple heartbeats later Galvan was standing where the guy had been, holding his gun, and the guy was facedown in the sand below.

Four rooms on the top floor, two men per room. Galvan cleared them all in less than thirty seconds—head shots until the clip was empty, these dudes clumsy-stumbling from their beds, half of them too confused to shoot straight and the other half too far from their guns to even do that much.

He ran out of bullets, dodged a knife, heard it thwang into the door frame beside him, pulled it out, returned it to sender. Found the last dude, roommate of the first, cowering in the bathroom, a porno mag still spread across his lap, and kicked him backward through the clapboard wall, taking out half the toilet in the bargain.

Footfalls on the stairs, a clatter of them like a sudden monsoon. Whatever confusion there might have been about the attacker's location had burned off; the twelve or fifteen Sinaloans left were ready for a fight.

Might as well keep 'em guessing.

Galvan swung himself out a window, made a lateral jump onto an aluminum drainpipe, and shimmied down to the first floor.

The rifles were right where he'd left them. Galvan grabbed one in each hand, set up shop behind the welcome desk, and trained his sights on the staircase. Sure enough, the herd reversed direction a few moments later.

Might've sounded like buffalo, but they were sitting ducks.

He picked off ten without moving more than his trigger finger, the bodies logjamming the stairs and the final gaggle of soldiers tripping over the fallen, some reversing course and others planting their feet, making a last stand, jockeying for a sight line, finding nothing to aim at but a banquette.

Galvan pressed himself flat, crept around the far side of the desk, and was back on the porch before they'd even noticed he was gone. He sprinted around the back of the hotel, nabbing a pistol along the way, courtesy of the dude he'd tossed from the window.

They were still arrayed along the staircase, firing at the desk; he could see them clearly through a busted window. He wondered how long they'd do that. Decided to find out.

Until they ran out of bullets, was the answer.

And then, the silence was deafening. Smoke, blood, terror filled the air. Somebody'd shit himself, too. There was also that.

Galvan closed one eye, lined up a head shot, squeezed. The man fell over the staircase railing, head over heels, and the last four broke in all directions: upstairs left, upstairs right, downstairs left, downstairs right. It would have looked choreographed, if it weren't so ugly.

Galvan watched them go. He'd made his point. And somebody had to tell the Sinaloa higher-ups what had happened. Might as well let them sing the story in four-part harmony.

He turned on his heel, figuring he'd grab a Jeep and find his way back to Louis's in style, and found himself face-to-face with one of the runners, a young kid with a busted nose.

Both their eyes went wide, and then the kid threw it in reverse, twisted an ankle in the sand, and landed on his ass.

Galvan shot him a grim look and started to walk away. But wait.

He'd seen this kid before.

The busted nose.

He'd done that.

Who's we, junior?

Azteca, maricón.

Bosco, you sly motherfucker.

Galvan trudged toward him, until his body bathed the kid in shadow.

He raised a hand, thrust it up into the space between them, shook it frantically.

"I told them, man. Just like you said to. 'There's a new monster in town.' I said it just like that."

Galvan sighed and threw Bosco a grudging imaginary head nod of respect.

Well played, pendejo. Hope you took my advice and went home to your kids, because if I see you again I'm gonna rip off your head and feed it to your asshole.

Good thing Galvan didn't give a fuck which cartel he'd just slaughtered.

Six of one, half dozen of the other.

He looked down at the kid. "Well, junior, I guess you'd better tell somebody a little higher up the food chain, me entiendes?"

CHAPTER 21

Sherry sank onto the couch, a pint of ice cream in one hand, a spoon in the other. She wasn't even hungry. Just bored. No wonder everybody in this country was fat. They sat in their stupid houses watching moronic shit on television and shoveling garbage into their faces. It anesthetized them to the tragic pointlessness of their own lives somehow, this endless parade of girls who didn't know which tattooed loser had knocked them up and wanted to find out before a live studio audience, and then fight the guy's wife.

Cooking. Home renovation. Hillbilly shitheads. The same five news stories. The same five baseball highlights. Click. Click. Click. It was amazing how fast your will seeped out of you and into the cushions.

The weight of everything Sherry tried not to think about was like a roiling storm cloud, and she expended tremendous energy shooing it away—keeping the horrific, the unfathomable at arm's length, the death and loss at bay.

Ruth had work to make the house bearable. She brewed her coffee, poured it into a travel mug—that was rich—carried it to her home office, fifteen feet away, and shut the door. Sherry could hear her in there, the tapping of her fingers on the computer keyboard almost as loud as her voice on the phone. She broke for lunch, slapped together sandwiches for them both, then went right back to it. Evenings were better. Normal-ish. Nichols brought home groceries. The three of them would collaborate on dinner, maybe watch a movie together. But now that he was gone—for what he promised would only be forty-eight hours, though Sherry had her doubts—the nights would be an extension of the days. The same stale air circulating between them without so much as a hint of a breeze.

Sherry had begun the morning with a resolution to read, marched over to the bookshelf and picked out a proper hardcover novel. But she couldn't focus, didn't have the attention span to get through chapter two. She'd tossed the book aside by eleven, scooped up the remote. Her phone lay beside her, and she checked it reflexively every few minutes for messages, even though the volume was on.

Closest she'd come to exercise.

Yesterday, Eric sent her one of his periodic puppy-dog-hopeful, poorly punctuated texts—*hey I'm here if you wanna talk we can still be friends at least right?*—and her heart soared at the mere prospect of human contact. All the reasons she'd stopped seeing him seemed shortsighted and childish now; who else but Eric would ever, in a million years, understand even a fraction of what she'd gone through?

Sherry had been about to invite him over when she caught herself. What could she tell that sweet boy? That her life continued to be a rollercoaster ride through shit fields? That she was about to be a fucking high school dropout? That it wasn't safe to leave her house, between the kidnappers, the mysterious plots, her psycho father? That she needed him to bring over some weed, because she was all out and couldn't cope without it?

At some point even gentle, loyal Eric would have to conclude that Sherry *attracted* drama, just like these gross fucking women on TV.

At some point, she'd have to conclude the same.

Let's grab coffee next week? she'd texted back at last, some fourteen hours later, figuring that by next week things would have either calmed down or she'd be willing to risk her life to leave the house.

Midafternoon, Ruth sashayed out of her office, all fucking radiant.

This pregnancy thing was a real trip: wake up looking like a seasick crackhead, progress to glowy earth goddess by noon, pass out at eight thirty, repeat.

"Do some yoga with me," she said, flashing a *Prenatal Poses* DVD in her hand and heading for the TV.

"No thanks. I'm prenatal by, I dunno, about ten to fifteen years."

"Ah, who cares? It's good to move a little."

The doorbell rang, as if to signal the end of round one, and both their faces lit up. It had come to that: Boggs letting them know that he was clocking out and Hildebrand was taking over had become the highlight of their day.

Sherry beelined for it, with Ruth a pace behind, pulling her hair out of its ponytail so Boggs could fully appreciate its new bun-in-the-oven luster.

"Check the peephole first, Sher," she cautioned.

"Yeah, yeah." Sherry peered through it, saw the uniform, Boggs's back turned to them, the cruiser parked curbside like always, the whole tableau fish-eyed, distorted.

Just like her life.

She flicked the first lock, undid the chain on the second, and pulled the door wide.

"Hey, Russell."

Right away, even before he turned, Sherry knew it wasn't Boggs. Or Hildebrand.

And she knew something was very wrong.

She tried to slam the door, but he was too quick: boot to the jamb, the big slab of wood shuddering on its hinges.

And then his fat red face and massive body filled the threshold, blotted out the world beyond.

"Hello, Sherry. You remember me."

She did.

All too well.

Kurt Knowles threw his shoulder against the door and forced his way inside. Slammed it behind him and stood looking at them both, hands hipped, grin wide, teeth like jagged gravestones in his enormous mouth.

"Howdy, Doc."

The chest of his uniform shirt was soaked with blood, and there was a two-inch rip in the fabric stretched across his barrel chest.

He followed her eyes to it. "Don't worry, sweetheart. That ain't mine."

He jerked his thumb toward the street, the car. Toward Boggs.

"That's his."

He took another swaggering step into the living room and tapped his hand against the knife strapped to his thigh, the blade still red with blood.

"I'm not here to hurt y'all," he said. "But I am allowed to, if you don't cooperate."

Sherry looked at Ruth, found her frozen in place, the color drained from her face, both hands splayed protectively, unconsciously, over her stomach. She wasn't going to be doing any fighting; there was too much at stake for her, too much to lose.

Sherry, on the other hand, really didn't give a fuck anymore.

And this was on her. She was the one he'd come for.

"What do you want?" she blurted.

"The three of us are gonna take a little drive."

"Where are we going?" Sherry asked, mind racing. "Do I need my passport?" There was a gun in a box in the bedroom closet. Nichols kept it loaded. If she could get to it, she wouldn't hesitate.

"You'll see when we get there. Now let's go." He grabbed her by the elbow, yanked her toward the door.

She yanked back, wrenched her arm free. "Just take me," she said. "I'm the one you came for, right?"

Knowles cackled—whether at the defiance or the question, Sherry wasn't sure—and a toxic bouquet of blood, sweat, and motor oil billowed toward her.

"What, are you fuckin' kidding me? Me and the doc go way back. Ain't that right, Doc?"

"Get the fuck out of my house!" Ruth snarled. *She looked like a cornered dog,* Sherry thought, and then *No, like a mother dog, defending her young.*

Sherry had been wrong—a hundred and eighty degrees wrong. Ruth had too much to lose *not* to fight.

No sooner had she thought it than Ruth turned and dashed from the room.

She's going for the gun, Sherry thought. But no. The bathroom; she heard the door slam, the lock click into place.

"I'm calling the police!" she screamed.

Sherry felt a drop of sweat slide down the inside of her arm as she braced to run: in an instant Knowles would make a move, storm over there and kick in the door, and when he did she'd break for the bedroom, grab the gun—

But no.

This wasn't his first rodeo, and Knowles wasn't about to let her out of his sight. He grabbed Sherry by the back of the neck, his arm like a steel cuff, and half dragged her over to the bathroom. Slammed her up against the door and called to Ruth.

"Put it down or I start breakin' bones, Doc. That what you want?"

He twisted Sherry's arm behind her back until pain shot through it, hot and sharp, and she screamed.

Ruth opened the door, face blank with fear, cell phone in hand.

Knowles grabbed it and released Sherry. She crumpled into a pile on the floor, cradling one arm in the other, and cursed herself for being weak. Fragile.

So fucking human.

"Hey, asshole," she said, blinking back stars.

Knowles looked down at her, and Sherry lifted her face, threw everything she had into the biggest shit-eating grin she could muster.

"You know my father's gonna kill you, right?"

Knowles shoved the phone into his pocket. "Your father's already dead. Now stand the fuck up." He grabbed her by the arm he hadn't just nearly snapped and pulled her to her feet.

And then, for the first time in days, Sherry was outside, squinting in the sunlight as Knowles paced them toward the cruiser, hands manacled around each of their wrists.

Sherry cast around for anybody who might help—a neighbor, a passerby, a landscaping crew, a fucking dog—but the block was empty of all life. Folks were at work, or they were someplace air-conditioned. She got off half a scream anyway, *Hel*— before Knowles shoved them both into the backseat and the locks clicked shut.

He opened the driver's door and rolled Russell Boggs's shirtless, bludgeoned body into the gutter.

Sherry gasped, the sound huge in the hermetic, airless car.

Knowles fired up the engine and pulled away from the curb.

The cruiser cruised. Down the block, full stop at the sign, two-second pause, left onto Edmund, right on Bristol. The police radio babbled anodyne mundanities, no big action in Del Verde County this afternoon.

Ruth grabbed her hand, squeezed. Whether she was the beneficiary of comfort or its dispenser, Sherry was not sure.

Except, neither.

"You know, Doc," Knowles said after a few blocks, half turning toward the grated metal partition that separated the backseat from the front, the criminals from the cops, "Aaron Seth was like a father to me. And my club, well, they were like my brothers."

He put the monologue on hold and made a looping left onto Old Ranch Boulevard. They were coming up on the highway.

"What would you do if somebody took away your family, Doc?"

All Sherry could see of him were huge fists, choking the black leather steering wheel.

"If I've done something to hurt your family, I'm sorry," Ruth said, and Sherry could tell she was trying to keep the quaver out of her voice, inject the therapist into it. "That was never my intention."

"Don't you fuckin' lie to me. Mr. Seth told me all about you, Doc. You're a meddling little cunt. He'd be alive, it wasn't for you. Well, guess what?"

"You're a fucking psychopath," said Sherry, for no better reason than the fact that it was true.

Knowles cackled. "Guess again."

He turned far enough to look them both in the eye. "Give up? Well, Doc, you got a real special treat coming. Seeing as how you spent so much time up Mr. Seth's ass about what was happening to all them girls, you're gonna get to find out for yourself where they ended up."

He turned back toward the road.

"This here, Doc? This is what we call a pussy run."

With that, Kurt Knowles merged onto the highway, headed south. Sherry heard an earth-shaking rumble behind her, and then another. She twisted in her seat, in time to see four True Natives pull off the shoulder, the chrome pipes of their Harleys gleaming in the afternoon sun, and settle into formation around the car.

CHAPTER 22

"I gotta say, Fuentes," Nichols offered as the scenery sped past, "power agrees with you. You musta dropped what, forty pounds?"

The Mexican laughed and flipped the toothpick in his mouth, end over end, without taking his hands off the steering wheel.

"Thanks, cabrón. What can I say? I'm a stress eater. I'm feeling more relaxed these days."

They were a hundred and twenty, hundred and thirty miles south of the border, zipping along an empty two-lane road in Fuentes's brand-new Prius, past farmland and scattered shacks, the occasional huddled town.

"That's good," Nichols said. "I mean, I don't think ten times more responsibility would chill me out, but hey, whatever works."

Fuentes chuckled, flipped his mouth lumber again. He'd been worrying the thing for half an hour. Disgusting fucking habit.

"Well, don't get me wrong. The narcos and the politicians are still jacking each other off, and I still don't have the resources to be more than an inconvenience to any of these hijos de putas. But the view from twenty thousand feet is better than the view from ground zero, tu sabes?

At least now, I feel like I can see the whole chessboard. Know who the players are."

"Guess that counts for something," Nichols grunted, half sorry he'd gotten Fuentes going. A hard man to shut up, once he got on a roll. Then again, as long as he was ruminating aloud, Fuentes wouldn't be cranking the *Ennio Morricone's Greatest Western Movie Themes* CD waiting in the deck. That stuff worked fine behind a shot of Eastwood lighting a cigarillo, but Nichols couldn't think of another context in which he'd choose to hear it.

"I hate to say it, amigo," Fuentes went on, "but the position I'm in now? I'm learning to see the gray areas. Lesser of two evils, enemy of my enemy, shit like that."

He shook his head, shifted his hands to twelve and six. "It's like those old questions they used to ask us in school—you know, you're driving a train, and ahead of you on the track are four kids playing, and if you do nothing, you're gonna hit 'em. But on the only other track you can switch onto, there's two kids. So do you make a move and kill fewer kids, or do nothing and kill the four?"

Nichols scowled out the window. "The fuck kinda school you go to?"

Fuentes laughed. "A shitty one, carnal. Ay, you thirsty? Let's get something to wet our whistles in the next town, yeah?"

"Why not? Gotta be coming up on happy hour by now." He stretched his legs—as best he could, anyway—and then his arms. Loosed a savage yawn, closed his eyes, and opened his big fat mouth.

"Moral relativism's really not a good look for you. I think I liked Fat Fuentes better."

He tried not to crack a smile. Failed.

Fuentes cackled. "I got your Fat Fuentes right here." Nichols didn't have to unshutter his eyeballs to know the cop was grabbing his crotch.

Nichols drifted off, awakened only when the lulling hum of rubber rolling over road cut out from underneath. They were in a parking lot, the neon CERVEZA sign in the bar's front window glowing the same electric blue as the evening sky.

"Vámonos, gringo." Fuentes got out and slammed the driver's door, sauntered toward the entrance.

Nichols unfolded himself, knuckled the crust out of his eyes, and had a look around. Something was off, but he couldn't pinpoint what it was. Maybe just his postnap grogginess, or a touch of the off-balance feeling he got in Mexico sometimes, everything the same but slightly different, a Coke not quite a Coke.

The Cokes were better, actually. Real cane sugar, not that corn syrup crap. That was now a *thing,* apparently—you could get Mexican Coke in all the hipster bars in Austin. Kat had told him on the phone, though for the life of him he couldn't imagine how he and his ex got on the subject. Maybe because they'd honeymooned in Mexico, discovered Mexicoke together. Whatever. They were friends now. That was okay. You could be friends with your ex. Especially if she was a lesbian.

Your mind is wandering, old man. Pull it together.

Suddenly, it hit him.

Theirs was the only car in the lot.

"You sure this joint is open?" he called to Fuentes.

"It's open," he called back, without turning. And sure enough, a moment later the newly svelte cop slipped through the smoked-glass door. Nichols ambled after him, sufficiently awake now to relish the thought of an ice cold beer.

He strode into the long dim roadhouse, still mulling over the vacant lot. Maybe they were near a factory or something, and everybody walked here to drink.

Or maybe it was a roach-infested pisshole the locals stayed away from in droves.

"Fuentes?" he called, smiling at the thirtyish woman standing behind the bar, acting like he was invisible or she was out of booze.

"In here, cabrón."

Nichols walked toward the sound of his voice, figured the barkeep had steered Fuentes toward the back room. They probably consolidated the afternoon crowd there or something.

Sawdust and peanut shells blanketed the floor, glued in place by spilled beer and crisscrossed with the muddy treads of shitkickers.

Lotta charm, lotta charm.

"Just 'cause I'm buying doesn't mean—" Nichols was saying, when the sight of what lay through the open door brought him up short.

Fuentes sat at a four-top, eyes fixed on Nichols, jittery as a speed freak.

Next to him sat a man Nichols had only seen in photographs—grainy black-and-whites snapped from a distance as he strode from nightclub to chauffeured car or chauffeured car to mansion, ensconced within a phalanx of security.

Speaking of which.

"Arms up, please."

Nichols obliged, as a young man sporting a high-and-tight crew cut and a Kevlar vest approached him. Another stood behind the table; they were a matched set, and Nichols guessed a few more were floating around. Out back by the car, probably.

Car or the goddamn helicopter.

"Lemme save you the trouble," he said. "Gun on the waist, and a Bowie knife strapped to my ankle, if that type of thing's of interest."

The kid nodded, palmed the gun, and bent to pat him down anyway. Did it with a certain respect, which Nichols would have appreciated if he wasn't busy being perplexed and furious.

"Wanna tell me what the fuck is going on here?" he demanded, when the search was over.

The seated man rose. He was deeply tanned, impeccably dressed, and towered over Nichols.

"I apologize for all of this," he began, spreading his arms to take in the surroundings, and then extended a hand. A large square jewel on his pinkie finger caught the light.

It was a goddamn Harvard University class ring. The balls on this asshole.

"My name is Herman Rubacalo. Please, be so kind as to sit down."

"I know who the fuck you are," Nichols snapped. He glared at Fuentes. "This what you mean by the lesser of two evils, you slimy son of a bitch?"

Fuentes raised his palms, showed them to Nichols in a calm-down gesture. "Hear him out, my friend." And then he narrowed his eyes, shot Nichols a look rich in the ferocity of its intention.

I had no choice, it said.

For whatever that was worth.

Rubacalo beckoned toward the chair, his voice a low, solicitous rumble. "Please, Sheriff Nichols, let us talk." He cupped his hand to his heart. "I am not what I appear to be."

He turned up his lips to leaven the cliché and then sat down. Leaned forward, dropped his elbows onto the table, and used his left palm to cover his right fist.

"Alonzo, Gabriel, get us some beers." The guards vanished quickly and quietly from the room.

Nichols relented, yanked out a chair, plopped himself into it.

"Say what you gotta say. I'm not here on vacation."

"Indeed you are not," the drug lord agreed. "You are here to find Jess Galvan."

Nichols lobbed a murderous grimace at Fuentes, then turned back to Rubacalo. "You're very well informed, Cortador."

"Please, call me Herman. That name, Cortador, it's for the tabloids. And yes, Sheriff. I am."

He leaned back, caught Nichols's eyes in the tractor beam of his own steely gaze. "I may even be able to give you some answers, where right now there is only confusion."

"What the hell is that supposed to mean?"

The goons returned, deposited three sweating bottles of beer on the table. Nichols wondered if it would be giving in to drink.

Then he drank.

Fuentes and Rubacalo raised their bottles, too.

"You have seen things you cannot explain, Sheriff. This man Galvan has caused you to call everything you thought you knew into question. Yes?"

He was fishing, Nichols thought, and stayed quiet.

"I'm going to tell you a story," the cartel chief declared, crossing his legs and settling deeper into his chair. "It begins five hundred years ago, with a man named Izel Notchi Icnoyotl, a low-ranking priest in the Aztec Empire's most powerful cult, the Temple of Tezcatlipoca."

He paused, waiting for some sign of recognition. Nichols maintained his poker face.

"Tezcatlipoca was a sorcerer. And a warrior. Over the course of many generations, his priests' influence came to transcend religion. They held sway over the politicians. Controlled the military."

"Like the pope," Fuentes interjected.

"Precisely. The head priest was a man named Cualli. You now know him as Cucuy." He paused, gave Nichols another look of appraisal. "You have heard this name, Sheriff?"

"Rings a bell."

"And what do you know of him?"

"That he gave Jess Galvan a heart in a box to take to his son. Seth was supposed to eat it, and . . ."

He trailed off. Saying this shit out loud still made him feel like a fucking lunatic.

"And what?" Rubacalo prodded.

Nichols took a deep breath and exhaled a gust of words. "And get all Cucuy's powers. But instead, Galvan ate it and his fucking severed arm grew back and he's basically been a psychotic superhero ever since."

Rubacalo was silent for a moment.

"Then it is as I have feared," he said at last.

"And why's that, Herman? Don't you have a fuckin' international drug cartel to run?"

They stared at each other until Rubacalo blinked. He took a long swallow of beer, then hunkered low over the table.

"Izel could have stopped Cualli from becoming a monster. Instead, he gave his blessing. Allowed his sister to be sacrificed."

"That ain't what I asked you."

"The power of Tezcatlipoca was too much. Cualli became a monster. He sustained himself on the hearts of virgins; his madness and his power knew no bounds. The gods themselves turned their backs on the world. And as the centuries passed, he faded into the shadows, conned the world into forgetting he was real. Made himself into a myth. His body weakened, and he began to look for another. Now it appears he has found one."

"Whoa, whoa, hold on a second there—"

"Jess Galvan is not Jess Galvan anymore, Sheriff." He cocked his head, spoke softly. "But you already know this."

Nichols shook his head. "That's impossible."

"Are you still so quick to think you know what's possible?"

"No, I mean—I've talked to him. I *know* him. He's not the same, but he's—he's still him. Last three months, he's been living out in the sticks, because he doesn't trust himself around people. He hunts, he chops wood. He drinks beer. That sound like Cucuy to you?"

"But he's not chopping wood and drinking beer anymore, is he, Sheriff?"

Nichols closed his eyes and massaged his temples.

"No," he heard himself say. "He's not."

"On the contrary, he's murdered thirty-one of my men in the last twenty-four hours. And some number of my competition, as well."

Nichols' head snapped up. "*What?*"

"He seems to have taken a liking to a village called Rosales. As you surmised."

Nichols nodded, stupefied, and waited for him to go on.

"Rosales is a violent place, just now. Ironically, it was Cualli who maintained whatever balance there can be in a business as erratic as my own. With him gone, there is nothing to prevent me from crushing my competition." He smiled. "Or them from attempting to crush me."

"And why would Cucuy want to defend some random village against the cartels?" Nichols demanded. "How does that make any sense at all?"

Rubacalo raised an eyebrow, gave a sideways nod. "On the surface of things, it does not. But it has been prophesied that when the Ancient One reemerges, he will disguise himself as a defender of the weak, a bringer of justice. Until his cruelties reveal him."

"Yeah, well, Galvan has pretty much made a career out of defending the weak. Besides, why would Cucuy piss around for months impersonating some isolated weirdo? That doesn't lead to world domination, usually."

"Allow me to finish," Rubacalo said, and tapped the table with a splayed hand. "There are two possibilities. What's for certain: Galvan and Cualli are related. They share blood. A lineage. If they did not, eating the heart would have destroyed him."

He paused, stared past Nichols and into space. "But it may be that Galvan has not been subsumed. The genetic link may be too weak. He may be . . . fighting it."

Nichols picked up his bottle and fleetingly considered how inadequate a beverage it was for this conversation. He needed tequila. Or maybe a nice warm glass of bleach.

"*That* sounds like Galvan," he said.

The silence welled around them as Rubacalo mulled that over.

"You still haven't told me how the fuck you figure in," Nichols said at last.

Rubacalo trickled some beer down his throat.

"Izel is my forebearer, Sheriff. For five hundred years, my family has sought to stop Cualli. The rest is just a means to an end. A base of power from which to operate. A way to get close to him."

"You're the biggest narcotics trafficker in Mexico."

"I'm afraid so, yes."

"You're directly responsible for thousands of deaths."

"You're absolutely right, Sheriff." Rubacalo leaned forward, his eyes wide. "And I'm the good guy."

CHAPTER 23

So what do you want from me?" Nichols asked.

"Your help. Cualli *will* destroy Galvan, if he has not already. It is only a matter of time. And if that happens—"

"Let me guess: we're fucked."

"In so many words. Even in his decrepitude, unable to leave his lair, Cualli has held organized crime by the balls for the last hundred years."

"Now there's an image." Nichols glanced over at Fuentes. "You're pretty quiet over there, Miguel."

"Just taking it all in, cabrón. Who's ready for another beer?" He stood, grabbed their empty bottles off the table, and strode toward the bar.

"So, what?" Nichols asked. "You think Galvan's gonna listen to me, is that it? Assuming he's still Galvan?"

"That's what I'm hoping, yes."

"And I'm telling him . . . what, that the jig is up and we know Cucuy's in there, so . . ."

Nichols threw up his hands, at a loss to complete the sentence.

"You are telling him there's only one scenario that does not result in utter catastrophe."

"You want him to kill himself."

"Yes and no."

"Yes and no," Nichols repeated, craning his head, suddenly eager for another beer.

"If Galvan kills himself, Cualli will die with him. But Tezcatlipoca's power will not. It will be restored to the god. And he will return from his exile, to a world where none remain who can oppose him."

"That's bad?"

"That's bad."

"We don't want a psycho Aztec god rampaging through the world, is what you're saying."

"You catch on fast, Sheriff."

"Always been a quick study, Cortador."

Maybe a second beer wasn't a good idea after all. Nichols was feeling drunk enough already.

Right on cue, Fuentes returned, balancing three Pacificos and three brimming shot glasses on a tray.

"I thought we could use these," he said, distributing the tequila.

Nichols tossed his back straightaway, to avoid finding out how clinking glasses with a crime lord would make him feel.

"But he would die, though," he said, as the liquor blazed a path down his throat. "Galvan."

"There is a ritual. A way of excising Cualli from the world—unmaking him, as it were. But it will not be easy. And it must be undertaken willingly."

Nichols chased the liquor with beer, felt the icy trickle reach his stomach, and wondered when he'd last eaten.

"Believe me, Sheriff. At this point, there is no coming back for your friend."

That struck him as true, and Nichols sighed.

"Well," he said slowly, "he was willing to die before. To save his daughter. When he ate that heart."

He fell silent, felt Rubacalo's eyes bore into him.

"Maybe it's time for him to finish what he started," Nichols said quietly.

Rubacalo nodded. "Destroying Cualli."

Nichols looked up at him. "No. Dying."

Fuentes hadn't touched his tequila. Nichols reached over, grabbed the glass, and gave the liquor a nice warm home.

"You got a fucking plan?" he asked his new buddy the drug lord.

GALVAN FOUND HIS way back from the beach by sunup and was promptly caught reentering the barn by Louis's eldest boy, Manuel.

Take out a hotel full of heavily armed goons? No problem.

Sneak into a barn? Epic fail.

The fact that he was covered in sweat and blood—the former his own, the latter mostly not—didn't make Galvan's presence any easier to explain. The kid was eighteen or twenty, short and stocky like his old man but with hard, beady eyes, where Louis's were gentle and wise. It took him all of three seconds to figure out who Galvan was.

Jess could see him sizing up the situation. He was up early to milk the cows, sure—but he still smelled like last night's beer, still had on last night's clothes, and it was a good bet that his head still buzzed with last night's gossip.

Galvan had a pretty good idea what that was.

New monster in town, yadda yadda yadda.

He was in no mood for finesse, so Galvan cut right to the chase. It would be the last thing the kid expected, and maybe it would throw him off his game, hit the reset button on whatever scheme he was hatching.

"So how much is the price on my head? 'Cause you're looking at me with dollar signs in your eyes, Manuel."

Quaking in his boots wasn't just a metaphor after all. This kid was actually doing it. Looked as if he were experiencing his own highly localized earthquake.

"I'm just asking, Manuel. You ain't gotta be scared. No harm, no foul."

The earthquake gave way to aftershocks. "Ten thousand from Sinaloa," the farmer's son managed. "And twenty-five from Azteca."

Galvan squinted in appraisal. "Huh. Seems kinda low. If I was you, I'd wait a few days. The way I'm going, I'm a lock to get it up to fifty by the weekend."

Manuel was having trouble getting the words out. "I-I-I . . ."

"Relax, kid. I'm pretty sure you know better. Now. Tell me what I can do to help around here. You need some hay baled or some shit like that? I like to keep busy."

"I see you two have met."

It was Louis, walking across the field with a steaming mug in each hand. Even in broad daylight, the dude was a fucking master of stealth.

He handed one to Galvan, looked him up and down.

"Interesting night?"

Jess shrugged and took a sip of the strong, rich brew. "Pretty quiet. Just, you know, took a stroll around town, made a few new friends."

"More than a few, the way I heard it," Louis replied, over the lip of his raised mug. Galvan must have looked surprised, because the farmer added, "It's a small town. Word travels fast." He slurped his coffee, lowered the mug to waist height. "Couldn't wait, huh?"

Galvan shrugged. "Just kind of happened."

The blend of affection, bemusement, and disappointment with which Louis regarded him made Galvan feel like nothing so much as the man's son. It was wholly unexpected, strangely comforting.

Cucuy had a different interpretation.

The rush of sentimentality you feel is the last of your humanity, ebbing out of you like blood from a wound. You are to be reborn in blood, Jess Galvan. The course is set. That you believe you are resisting only makes you more mine.

Not until he opened his eyes and found Louis staring at him with concern did Galvan realize he had squeezed them shut.

"Are you feeling all right?" the farmer asked. "You disappeared for a second, there."

Galvan shook his head clear. "Yeah, no, I get these headaches sometimes. They come on real suddenly."

"I see," the farmer said, his tone shading toward resignation. "Well, there's no point in hiding you out here anymore. You might as well come inside and have some breakfast. Meet the rest of the family."

"I could eat," Galvan agreed and followed him toward the house.

The smell of bacon filled the kitchen. Louis introduced his wife, Concepción; she turned from the stove to greet him and her smile lit up the room. Something about the woman reminded Galvan uncannily of his own abuela: the mirth in her delicately wrinkle-filigreed cheeks, the way she'd doted on him as a child. A moment later two more boys, Alberto and Carlos, stumbled down the stairs, half asleep. Their eyes widened at the sight of Galvan, but they were gracious, welcoming, their father's sons.

Louis put a hand on Galvan's shoulder, steered him to the bathroom, handed him a towel and a bar of soap. Galvan took a thorough rock-and-roll shower, face and arms, pits and hands, and when he opened the door he found a clean white T-shirt dangling from a hanger. He pulled it on and found to his surprise that it fit, which probably meant the boys' preferences ran toward oversized and baggy.

He ambled back to the kitchen, found the family seated around a table laden with eggs, bacon, fresh milk, cereal. They'd waited for him, and now, as he sat down, they joined hands and bowed their heads. Galvan found himself holding Concepción's dry, smooth palm in his left hand, delicate as a baby bird, and sixteen-year-old Alberto's farm-calloused mitt in his right.

"We thank you for the bounty of your grace, Lord. And for the help you have sent us, in our time of trouble. We ask that you protect him and allow him to serve your justice upon the wicked. Amen."

"Amen," the family chorused. Galvan tried to eat, found he had to force the food past a lump in his throat. When the meal was over, he followed Louis and the boys into the fields, waited until the kids had embarked on their tasks, then buttonholed the old man.

"Look, I'm no avenging angel, Louis. I'm not heaven-sent."

He smiled. "You don't have to know you are sent by heaven to be sent by heaven. You are his instrument, Jess, whether you know it or not."

You are his instrument, Cucuy repeated, with a brittle cackle.

"It's a nice thought, Louis, but—"

The farmer reached up, took Galvan by the shoulders. "My father was a healer, Jess. A brujo. I see things in people. Maybe that sounds crazy to you."

"No, it—"

The farmer shook him off. "And you—you have a good soul. I see your struggle. The conflict in you. But, Jess"—Louis tightened his grip on Galvan's shoulders—"you will triumph. It is your destiny."

Galvan had no words. Louis didn't seem willing to release his grip until he said something. And so they just stood there, an unbroken circuit of belief and dismay, until Manuel trudged over.

Louis read the look on his son's face and turned. "What? What is it?"

"There's a man here," he said, voice low and inflectionless. "For him."

With a speed Galvan wouldn't have guessed the old man had in him, Louis grabbed the boy by the wrist.

"What have you done?" he hissed.

Manuel tried to jerk his arm free, but he could not.

"Nothing! He just— He knew. He's by himself. Says he wants to talk."

"Don't lie to me!" Louis applied more pressure. "Who did you call?"

Manuel winced, but he wouldn't give.

"I'm not! No one!"

"It's okay," said Galvan. "I'll go find out what he has to say." He patted Louis on the back. Reluctantly, the farmer released his son's arm. Manuel folded it to his chest like a broken wing, rubbed at the reddened wrist.

"He's at the front door," the kid mumbled and started to lead the way.

"I'll go alone," Galvan said and broke into a jog. He figured he'd flank the visitor—check out his vehicle, make sure he was really solo, then decide whether to speak with his mouth or his hands.

The car was unassuming, a mud-spattered Ford compact that had once been white. No sign of anybody lurking, no whiff of a trap. Just a lanky young dude standing before the closed front door, hands in the pockets of his jeans, close-shorn head bent toward the ground.

"Looking for me?" Galvan barked, striding toward him.

The guy spun, and Galvan stopped short.

"You gotta be fuckin' kidding me."

It was Bosco. He raised his hands, showing Galvan they were empty, then lifted his oversized T-shirt high enough to reveal a strip of belly, and the lack of a weapon on his waistline.

Galvan crossed his arms over his chest. "Really. They sent you. Over here. To talk to me."

Bosco shrugged and shoved his hands back in his pockets. "It was either me or twenty guys with guns."

"How'd you find me?"

Bosco pawed at the ground with a sneaker.

"I followed you back last night."

"The hell you did. I would have noticed."

"Guess you didn't, though."

Galvan came closer, got in Bosco's face.

"I should choke you to death right now for lying to me. You cost thirty men their lives, you know that?"

Another shrug. He was a cool customer. You had to give Bosco that.

"Better theirs than ours."

He blinked and fixed Galvan with a pair of eyes as cool and calm as dawn lakes. "Besides, it don't make no difference to you, does it? You just wanna kill, ain't that right?"

Galvan's fingers twitched with violence.

"What I want is all you miserable bastards out of this town," he said in a low growl.

Either Bosco had a death wish, or his heart pumped ice.

"That's not gonna happen," he replied. "If you want peace in Rosales, one side or the other has gotta win. That's why I'm here."

He took a step back and pulled a manicured, banded brick of fifty-dollar bills from his back pocket.

"My boss, he wanted to put a price on your head. I said fuck that, he's more valuable to us alive than dead." Bosco waved the money. "This is twenty-five grand. You already earned it, when you put in that work last night. Once we win this war, you'll get a hundred more. A *hundred*. How's that sound?"

The kid grinned. Maybe he wasn't so cool after all, Galvan mused. Perhaps he simply lived in a world where saying no to that kind of money was unthinkable, and the possibility that Galvan might refuse, emphatically, had simply not occurred to him.

He plucked the wad from Bosco's hand. "I'll take this as a down payment on all the damage you've already done. But I'm not for sale."

He turned on his heel and started to walk away. For show, mostly. He knew he wouldn't get far.

Sure enough: "What about your friends here?" Bosco called, and Galvan spun back.

"What about them?" he growled.

Just give me one reason. One fucking word.

And for the second time in twenty-four hours, Galvan couldn't tell whose thought it was.

Cucuy didn't really curse, though.

Guess that makes it mine.

Bosco shifted from foot to foot. "I'm saying, carnal. We know where you live now. My boys are already—"

He never finished the threat. Galvan's arm shot out, and his hand clamped around the base of Bosco's neck. A moment later, the kid was aloft, legs kicking wildly, face turning red, purple, finally blue.

CHAPTER 24

Galvan released his grip, and Bosco dropped like a sack of rice. He turned and found Louis and Manuel standing a pace away, eyes darting between Galvan and the corpse.

"Get Concepción and the kids, pack up what you need, and go someplace else," Galvan told them, walking over. "It's not safe here." He stopped before the farmer and added, "I'm sorry."

Louis shook his head. "This is my home. I'm not going anywhere."

Galvan studied him, found nothing in Louis's face that suggested he was to be swayed.

"Me neither," Manuel said, puffing up his chest. "I can fight."

"No, Manuel." Louis put a hand on his shoulder. "I need you to look after your mother and your brothers. Take them to the basement. Lock yourselves in."

"But—"

Louis cut off his objection. "He was from Sinaloa?" he asked, pointing at Bosco.

"Yeah. Thought he could buy me off."

"They will come," the farmer said quietly, and Galvan could see the gears turning. "They may be on their way already."

"So I'll take the fight to them," Galvan said. "Where can I find the cocksuckers?"

But the farmer had already made up his mind. "It is too late. Manuel!" he called. "Bring me my rifle. And all the ammunition you can find." He paused a moment, sighed, and called again. "And your own, if you are sure."

Manuel nodded and broke into a sprint.

"Louis . . ." Galvan could barely speak. "It's . . . You don't have to . . ."

The old man shook his head. "Even an avenging angel needs a little cover fire." He pointed to a small triangular window, set at the highest point of the barn's peaked frame. "I'll be up there."

THE SINALOANS TOOK their time, and with each anticipatory minute that ticked by, Galvan hated himself more. He should have forced Louis to evacuate, instead of watching as he and Manuel made a sniper's nest of their hayloft, standing idly by as Concepción herded the younger boys into the unfinished, dirt-floored basement. They could have been hours away by now, whizzing toward safety in that dirty Ford.

He should have surprised Sinaloa in their lair, like he had Azteca. Mowed them down and given Rosales a breather, a respite from death and terror.

Inasmuch as killing everybody could be considered a respite from death and terror, anyway.

Instead, he sat on the hood of Bosco's car, watching fat flies browse the kid's body and trying to ignore the mounting giddiness that coursed through him despite everything he had to feel terrible about—the danger he'd brought to his friend's doorstep, the imminent arrival of a convoy of armed murderers, the fundamental unsustainability of constant war as a strategy for psychic survival.

Sure was quiet, though. Outside and in.

Galvan felt himself drift, internal and external chaos canceling each other out, and a kind of equilibrium moved in to fill the void.

The sensation was delicious. He'd forgotten what a moment of peace felt like.

"Incoming!" Manuel hissed from his perch, and Galvan snapped out of it.

A line of armored Jeeps approached on the main road, across the field. Galvan tracked their progress until they disappeared around the bend, and braced himself for attack. If it was Sinaloa, they'd shoulder off the highway and onto the dirt road that led to Louis's front door.

The front door that led to Louis's family.

Galvan jumped down from the car and sprinted toward the road on the dead run.

If the men in the convoy's lead vehicle saw the blur speeding toward them from the driver's side, they didn't have time to react. Galvan, on the other hand, had a full seven seconds to wonder if he was overestimating his own strength, thinking he could knock a goddamn military Jeep doing twenty-five an hour on its ass merely by throwing himself at it. More than likely, he'd bounce right off. Or throw it into an easily corrected fishtail and shatter a shoulder in the bargain.

The speculation was inconclusive.

Some shit, you just had to learn by doing.

So fuck it.

He kicked it into the highest gear he had, built up a head of steam, and cut a path straight at his chosen point of convergence, a few yards past the turnoff. They'd have to slow down to accommodate the curve, which was a good thing impact-wise, though bad in terms of the follow cars' increased ability to brake and swerve, avoid a pileup.

Oh well. It was a start, anyway.

And his timing was perfect.

Galvan was in midair and still unseen when he noticed that the dude driving the lead Jeep preferred the gentle caress of a summer breeze to the security afforded by bulletproof, shatter-resistant Plexiglas.

So there was that.

He slammed against the side of the car, feet finding purchase on the running board, yanked the driver toward him with one hand, and knocked him the fuck out with the other.

That got their attention.

The body slumped over the wheel, and the dude in the passenger seat pulled a gun, trained it at Galvan. Mighta said some shit, too, "don't move" or the like, but the cacophony was deafening, the other six or seven dudes crammed into the back all screaming threats and instructions of their own, and it was indistinct.

In any case, dude would have been better off grabbing the wheel.

Galvan got there first, fisted it hard right, two and a half rotations, and the Jeep spun a hundred and eighty degrees, tires protesting, front seat gunslinger thrown hard against his door, unconscious driver's foot now heavy on the gas, the speed ratcheted from twenty-five to a double nickel. They were barreling straight at the vehicle in front of them now, the reversal too sudden for the driver to evade and no place for him to go anyway.

The Jeeps smashed into each other, head-on, grille meeting grille with a sound Galvan found deeply satisfying. He leaped to the ground, watched his front seat gunman and the other vehicle's driver and front passenger fly forward in a synchronized ballet of pain and smash into their respective windshields, leaving three matching smears of blood.

That's why you should always wear your seat belt, boys.

The last Jeep skidded to a halt, inches from the accident, and Galvan raced toward it. He figured the most immediate threat was from the dudes who didn't have to shake off the impact. In a second they'd have the doors jacked open and pour out from both sides, locked and loaded. They'd have the Jeep to use for cover. It would be a shit show.

The answer to most of life's problems, Galvan realized in that instant, involved flipping large vehicles upside down. He reached the Jeep just as the rear driver's-side door opened, and the first guy began to clamber out. Galvan threw his body hard against it, jammed the guy between the door and the jamb, and pressed for all he was worth until he heard a ragged cry of agony, the sharp snap of small bones. A hand, probably. The gun, an M16, dropped from the man's grip and got tangled up in his legs.

Galvan bent, pressed the flats of his palms to the Jeep's undercarriage, and strained against the weight. Every muscle in his body was on fire. The tendons of his neck bulged and throbbed; the veins of his arms engorged with blood, wriggled beneath the skin like snakes. His thighs trembled like leaves in the wind.

And slowly, inch by inch, the Jeep rose. The left-side tires came off the ground; gravity shut the open doors, and sent the men sliding the other way, out the right-hand doors and onto the ground in a jumble of limbs and guns. They scrambled to get away before the metal carcass came down atop them, but it was too late—a final roaring effort, and the Jeep was on its side, the men who'd spilled out crushed beneath, the men still trapped inside staring up at the clear blue sky, with nothing to shoot their weapons at but clouds.

It had taken all of three seconds, but that was enough time for the soldiers in the other Jeeps to shake off the crash and pile out onto the road.

Fourteen minus the guys riding up front left ten.

He could work with that.

If he worked fast.

Galvan climbed the upturned Jeep in two steps, came down hard with both feet on the bodies trapped inside. He scanned the twisted mass, decided nobody was a threat; one guy was trying to crawl toward the back, escape through the rear doors, but he was unarmed, hand-over-handing it across the leather terrain. Galvan threw a couple kicks, freed up a semiautomatic, made sure it was racked and ready. His breath was loud, raspy inside the close space.

There were a lot of bullets waiting for him out there. Maybe it was time for a little subterfuge.

Don't start getting cute now, he told himself.

The guy scrabbling for the back door had almost made it. Galvan shot a hand out, grabbed him by the ankle, pulled him back.

Time for a little test run. See where the shooters were.

He pulled the dude to him. "You want out, huh?"

"Fuck you," the guy responded, through a busted lip, and reared back a few inches to spit in Galvan's face.

Or try to. By the time the saliva crossed his lips, Galvan had tossed him straight up, through the open window. The sound of gunfire was sudden, deafening, and shockingly long, as the troops arrayed around the car dumped all their terror and most of their clips into the man they thought was Galvan.

By the time they'd determined the dude's identity, Galvan had kicked open the back door, circled around the side of the Jeep. He added his own staccato burst to the chorus, and five of the soldiers dropped dead.

The other five decided it was time to rethink their career paths and ran—dropped their guns, raised their hands in surrender, and fled down the road in mindless, abject terror, and, Galvan guessed, a good measure of disbelief.

He watched them go and allowed himself a deep sigh of relief. It was over. The violence hadn't spilled onto Louis's property, had not touched his brood. The cartels were in retreat and disarray. Maybe Rosales would have a respite. Perhaps Galvan had done some good in the world. And maybe—

The crack of a rifle cut the thought short. Galvan ducked and spun, gun at the ready, and his eyes widened.

A body hung halfway out of the Jeep, doubled over, arms dangling. A pistol slipped out of the man's lifeless grip, clanged against the hood, fell to the ground.

He'd been lining up his shot.

Silently.

From five feet away.

A shooter didn't miss at that range. A man didn't survive.

Galvan stared across the field, at the barn. He could barely make out the smoking rifle, much less the farmer who had saved his life.

CHAPTER 25

Herman Rubacalo was not a drinker, and thus Herman Rubacalo was drunk. That wasn't part of the plan, but maybe it was for the best. He melted into the buttery leather of his limousine, cracked open a bottle of water, and took a few deep, calming breaths.

He pressed a button on the console beneath his elbow, spoke through the intercom.

"They're still behind us?"

A burst of static preceded the driver's answer. A bad connection to six feet away.

"Yes, jefe."

"Good," Herman muttered, without bothering to hit the button again.

He checked his watch. Rosales was less than an hour off. He was closing in on the most important, least predictable rendezvous of his life, and he was traveling with less security than typically accompanied him on a dinner date with his wife.

Two guards, and two strangers.

Plus the straggling remains of Azteca's Rosales detachment, the men skilled or lucky or disloyal enough to have survived last night's one-man siege. Somehow, Rubacalo doubted any of them would make it to the farm on the outskirts of town where his intelligence said Galvan was hunkered down. He'd have been worried about them tipping off Sinaloa to his approach, but the other cartel's forces were as decimated as his own.

The sheriff seemed all right, Rubacalo mused. A reasonable man thrust into crisis by the vastness of his own confusion—but strong-willed enough to face it, instead of pretending he had not seen what he had. Nichols's vulnerability had turned him into a moral relativist, and this Rubacalo valued above all. If a man lacked the capacity to embrace the reprehensible, he was of little worth.

By that rubric, Herman's own worth was limitless.

He stared out the window, and forced himself to appreciate the view, the sky, the land, the furious contradictions of the world—its teeming desolation, its brutal equanimity. Through the heavy tint of the glass, he could stare directly at the low-slung sun, blazing its well-worn path across the sky.

If he had miscalculated in any way, Herman would not live to see it rise again.

"WHEN THIS IS over," Nichols said with a certainty he didn't feel, a certainty that had flat-out vanished from the world at large, "I'm gonna fucking kill you."

He scowled over at Fuentes, found his eyes glued to the road. "Where the fuck do you think you get off, setting me up like that? You hear me talking to you, asshole?"

"Like you said, hermano, you got bigger things to worry about right now."

"That's not what I said," Nichols snapped back, but goddamn, was it ever true.

Look on the bright side, Nichols. Galvan'll probably kill you before you get the first sentence out. Seems to be his M.O. these days.

Time flew when you were apoplectic with fear and reeling with incomprehensible new facts. Next thing Nichols knew, the sun was grazing the horizon, and the limo in front of them was pulling off the highway, onto a dirt road.

It didn't get far.

Three Jeeps in various states of wreckage blocked the way.

And then there were the bodies.

Nichols leaned forward, goggled through the windshield.

It had been a slaughter.

At least they'd come to the right address.

The limo's front doors opened and out stepped Rubacalo's goons. They made a slow tour of the carnage, frowned pointlessly at corpses and automotive detritus, bent to gather up the small arms strewn across the killing field.

"Might as well get on with it," Nichols said and heaved his bulk out of the car.

Fuentes stayed put.

"You comin' or what?"

The cop shrugged. "Think I'll stay here."

"The fuck you will. Get your ass on out, or I'll shoot you myself."

Nichols strode to the limo, rapped on Rubacalo's window. The cartel don buzzed it open, and Nichols stared down at him.

"What's the matter, Cortador? Cold feet?"

He turned away before Rubacalo could answer and trudged in the direction of the small clapboard house, across a broad field planted with some kind of vines that snaked their way up wooden stakes.

"Yo!" Nichols bellowed at the top of his lungs. Last thing he wanted to do was catch Galvan unaware. "Jess! You in there? It's me, Nichols. Hey! Jess!"

He crossed the field slowly, shouting through cupped hands all the way.

"Jess? Bob Nichols. If you're in there, come out and talk, man. I came a long way."

At last, when Nichols was close enough that shouting felt ridiculous, the door creaked open, and out stepped Galvan.

He was unarmed. That was a plus.

But the two men who emerged behind him both held shotguns.

"Hey, Jess. How you doing, buddy?" He gave the other two a hearty wave. "Howdy. Bob Nichols. Me and Jess, we're old friends."

Galvan's face could've been chiseled from stone. "How'd you find me?" he intoned, voice flat and low, as if the answer didn't interest him. As if the real question was not *how,* but *why.*

Nichols spread his arms, tried out a laugh. It went over like a turd in a punch bowl.

"Well, you been calling a little bit of attention to yourself, Jess. Know what I mean?"

Galvan raised his chin. "Who the fuck are they?"

Nichols twisted at the waist. Cortador, Fuentes, and the bodyguards stood twenty paces behind him, arrayed in a loose horseshoe.

"You remember my buddy Fuentes. Helped save our asses a few months back?"

Galvan took that in. "And who are they?"

Cortador strode up to Nichols's side.

"My name is Herman Rubacalo, Mr. Galvan. I am the CEO of Barrio Azteca. But that is not why I am here."

Galvan looked from Nichols to Rubacalo, then back to Nichols.

"What the fuck is going on?" he demanded. And then, before Nichols could answer, he pointed a finger at Cortador.

"Give me one reason not to rip out his throat right now." Galvan's face twitched—spasmed, almost. "What are you doing with him, Nichols? You know what he's done to this town?"

The goons didn't cotton to that kind of talk about the boss. They were ready to flex. Cortador shot them a stand-down look and took another step toward Galvan.

"I have no doubt that you could, Mr. Galvan. I do not even dispute that you would be justified. But please, hear us out first. Listen to your friend the sheriff. That is all I ask." He folded his palms behind his back. "My life is in your hands."

Galvan's furious, perplexed gaze jumped back to Nichols.

"Start talking."

If he'd been wearing a necktie, Nichols would have loosened it. "Okay. Look. I know what's going on. You don't have to hide anymore."

Galvan just stood there, seething, so Nichols faltered on.

"Cucuy," he stammered. "I know about Cucuy. He got inside you, and you're fighting him. Every minute since you ate that heart, he's been trying to take over. Isn't that right?"

Galvan's chest heaved. His eyes twitched, and he squeezed them shut, shook his head violently. All of a sudden, Nichols could see it, clear as day: the torment, the struggle, the insane amount of energy his friend burned to keep the demon inside him at bay.

And the inevitability of Galvan's failure.

"He's talking to you right now, isn't he?" Nichols went on, his voice just above a whisper. "What's he saying, Jess? He telling you to kill me?" Nichols gestured behind him, in the direction of the bodies, as if Jess could see him. "Did he tell you to kill them, too?"

Galvan's eyes fluttered open. Sweat had popped out on his brow, and he spoke through gritted teeth. "I did that myself."

His breath was coming in quick, shallow snorts. "I'm *fighting* him," he said, and the ferocious intensity of the words sent a chill down Nichols's spine.

"I believe you," Rubacalo declared, walking another pace toward Galvan. It was all Nichols could do not to turn tail and sprint away, or dig himself a hole to hide in. Now that he knew what it was, bearing witness to Jess's moment-by-moment battle to contain himself was horrific, grotesque in a way he could barely wrap his mind around.

"And because I believe you," the cartel boss continued, "I'm going to tell you something that has been hidden from Cucuy for generations. Something that puts my life, my family, at risk. Cards on the table time."

Galvan's eyes were locked on him now.

Or were they Cucuy's eyes, Nichols wondered. How much of his friend had the monster colonized? How tenuous was Galvan's control, how sapped his resistance?

"My forefather was Izel Notchi Icnoyotl. Does that name mean anything to you?"

Galvan shook his head. His hands flexed at his sides, as if in search of a weapon, or a neck. Nichols clenched his own fists and watched, transfixed, helpless.

Rubacalo stepped directly in front of Galvan and looked into his eyes as if peering into the recesses of a murky lake.

"What about you, Cualli? Remember your old friend Izel? What about Chacanza? Do you remember her?"

A glazed and distant look came over Galvan's face, and his mouth dropped open.

"He does," he whispered.

The color rose in Rubacalo's cheeks. "Then let me tell him this. Izel did not die in your purges, Cualli. He and his line survived. We have watched you from the shadows and kept guard over the final wisdom the gods gave to man before they left this place."

He smiled, as if imagining the impact of his words on his enemy. Nichols didn't like it one bit. Speaking directly to Cucuy or Cualli or whoever he was couldn't be a good idea.

Say the devil's name and he appears.

"The immortals were not so quick to abandon man as you thought," Rubacalo breathed. He had probably waited his entire life for this moment, Nichols reflected. To reveal himself, his family's existence, to Cucuy.

"Izel offered them a sacred sacrifice. And do you know what they gave him in return?"

He searched Galvan's eyes, gone blank and liquid, then pulled himself up to his full height.

"The secret of your undoing."

Rubacalo paused.

"I can feel his fear. Do you feel it too, Mr. Galvan?"

Jess ground his teeth so that his jaw flared, and he gave a tiny, almost imperceptible nod.

Nichols realized he wasn't breathing and huffed a draught of air into his lungs.

"Will you help us to destroy him?" Rubacalo pressed. "To eradicate the power of Tezcatlipoca from the world forever?"

Galvan was silent for a moment. When he spoke, his voice was a rasp, as dry and bleached as corn husk.

"What's he asking me to do, Nichols? He asking me to die?"

The sheriff dropped his hands to his waist and grimaced at his friend.

"Yeah, Jess. Something like that. But the good news is, it gets to mean something."

Galvan stared at him for a long moment, and then his gaze flickered over to Rubacalo. "Cucuy told me that if I died, Tezcatlipoca would be freed."

"That depends on how you die. Perhaps you know of the Virgin Army."

"I'm pretty goddamn familiar, yeah."

"Their queen. His wife."

Something changed in Galvan's face—the scowl softening, something Nichols couldn't identify moving in to take its place.

"The woman in yellow," Galvan muttered, and Nichols knew what it was.

Apparently, Galvan was not yet beyond shock.

Nor was Rubacalo.

"You have *seen* her?" he asked, incredulous.

"Only in my dreams. Or his dreams. I dunno which." The scowl was back in place. "What about her?"

"You must die at her hands," Rubacalo said simply. "It is the only way."

A sound like a low growl buzzed in Galvan's throat, and his eyes darted over to Nichols.

"You trust this motherfucker?"

Nichols sighed. "On one hand, he's the biggest narco trafficker in Mexico. On the other, he's been right about everything so far."

Rubacalo shifted his weight. "It is remarkable that you have resisted for so long," he told Galvan. "But you cannot do it forever. You know this."

He raised his eyebrows, waited for Galvan to concede the point.

It didn't take long.

"My life's unbearable," he said, mouth barely moving around the words. "I'd have ended it already if I wasn't afraid of what might . . ."

He trailed off, took a backward glance at the two men standing by the door, shotguns dangling from their slack hands. Nichols wondered how much they were able to follow.

"This fuckin' plan," Galvan said abruptly. "You're sure it'll work?"

"For five centuries, Mr. Galvan, my family has—"

"Yeah, you said that already. Seems like your fuckin' family found plenty of time to get rich off other people's misery, though."

"A means to an end, Mr. Galvan. It was the only way to get close to Cualli. Or so we thought—we never came near. He was too careful." Rubacalo spread his arms. "It's now or never, Mr. Galvan, and the choice is yours. I cannot force you."

"Yeah, I get that a lot." Galvan scratched at a stubbled cheek. "And if I say yes—if I give up my fuckin' life—what are you prepared to do, Rubacalo?"

The cartel chief opened his arms wider, the posture of entreaty transformed into one of beneficence.

"Anything you ask, Mr. Galvan. I give you my word."

"Your word don't mean shit to me. The shit I want you to do, I'm gonna watch you do it myself. And once I'm satisfied, well . . ." Galvan threw up his own arms. "Then I'll take one for the fuckin' team."

Rubacalo could barely contain his excitement. "Let us waste no time," he said. "What is it you—"

"I'm getting to that." Galvan unfolded a finger. "Number one, you get the fuck out of Rosales. You pay to rebuild it. And you do right by the families of the dead."

"Consider it done."

Galvan unfolded another finger. It was clear he was making this up as he went along, thought Nichols, wondering how far a man with bottomless leverage and zero fucks to give might take things.

"Number two. You're out of the drug business, as of right now."

Rubacalo nodded vigorously. "You have no idea how happy it will make me to comply, Mr. Galvan. This entire—"

"I'm not finished. You're in a new business now, Rubacalo. Barrio Azteca's new job is destroying Federacíon Sinaloa. One cartel is one too many. They've gotta both be gone."

Rubacalo was momentarily speechless. "That . . . will not be easy," he said at last.

Galvan shrugged. "Yeah, well, that's your fuckin' problem. Why bother to save the world from Cucuy if a bunch of scumbags are just gonna fuck it up again?"

"What you're talking about could take years, Mr. Galvan. And you do not have years. You may not have weeks."

The stalemate lasted fifteen of the longest seconds of Nichols's life, and then Galvan said, "Well, we'll see what you can get done in a couple weeks then, chief. Good-faith-effort-type shit. After that, you'll be responsible to these men." He pointed at Nichols and Fuentes. "I trust them."

"You shouldn't trust Fuentes," Nichols muttered.

"Okay then, fuck Fuentes," Galvan amended, not missing a beat. "We're gonna set it up so that if you renege on anything, my buddy Nichols here has enough dirt on you to lock your ass in jail for life."

"Agreed."

Rubacalo waited.

Galvan unfolded another finger.

"Number three. I got a daughter. I want her provided for."

"Oh, she's been provided for," called a voice, loud and far away.

Nichols spun, and his heart sank.

Crossing the field, with guns to their heads and an army at their backs, were Sherry Richards and Ruth Cantwell.

CHAPTER 26

"That's far enough," Domingo Valentine declared, and the procession came to a halt, a hundred feet from Galvan and the men to whom he spoke.

One of them, Valentine noted with surprise, was none other than Herman Rubacalo.

What in hell was the leader of Barrio Azteca doing here? he wondered. But it was irrelevant. Domingo Valentine's entire life had led to this moment. He would save his god, free the Ancient One from this crude prison of flesh and blood, sinew and bone, or he would die trying.

They all would.

What Valentine lacked in detailed knowledge of the esoteric, the mystical, the sacred, he made up for in instinct, and in will. If Cucuy was trapped inside the body of a man who refused to relinquish his own humanity, then Valentine would strip the humanity from him by force.

It would not be the first time. If Valentine's tenure as the Great One's procurer had taught him anything, it was that humanity could not withstand atrocity. Force a man to act like a savage beast—hell, *allow* him to—and he would be a man no more.

That had been Valentine's plan, until a greater inspiration struck.

Force a man to act like a god, and how could he oppose one?

"Send over the girls," Domingo Valentine commanded, and the ranks of his contingent—half a dozen True Natives, a dozen Ojos Negros guards—cleaved open, to reveal four of the finest specimens the procurer had ever culled, their wrists and ankles bound with chains.

Their purity was breathtaking; their very skin glowed with the health of youth.

And the fear of death.

The bikers prodded the girls, and they began a halting march. If they felt hope at parting company with the men who had kidnapped and imprisoned them, it did not show.

Valentine squared off with Galvan and beckoned Knowles to bring Sherry closer. The biker prodded her, gun to her back, and the girl stumbled to his side. Valentine could smell her hair. He made a show of grabbing a handful and lifted the soft tresses to his nose, never breaking eye contact with Galvan.

"Hello, Galvan," he said, volleying his voice across the distance between them. All this would have played better at greater proximity, but that was not an option. Even at this remove, he was well within the usurper's kill zone.

Or he would be, if not for the leverage he had.

"As you can see, I've got your daughter here. And her friend. I assume you'd like them to go on living, is that right?"

Galvan's only answer was a piercing stare, a seething look of rage. Valentine could see the Ancient One's power radiating from him—lighting Galvan up from the inside, somehow. He felt his resolve strengthen and added his own gun to Knowles's, pressing it to Sherry's temple. His knuckles whitened around the grip, and Valentine's whole body vibrated with adrenaline.

"I know how strong you are," he said. "And how fast. But you're not going to reach me faster than these bullets reach your daughter's brain. I think we can agree on that, yes?"

"What the fuck do you want?"

"To see how much you love your daughter. It's simple. Follow my instructions, and she lives. Disobey me, and she dies."

Galvan spread his arms wide, showed Valentine his palms. A gesture of surrender, Valentine knew, but somehow it read like a display of power. As if all that lay between his outstretched hands—Valentine and Knowles, the bikers and the guards—might be crushed within them.

"I'll do whatever you want."

Yes, I believe you will.

The girls had crossed the field. They stood before Galvan, shivering in terror, and Valentine felt a surge of sexual excitement as he anticipated what he was about to say. The way the drug-dulled fear on their faces would transform itself to vivid, pink-cheeked panic.

But it was Rubacalo whose voice rang out next.

"Aren't you going to introduce yourself, Domingo?" the cartel chief sneered. "Tell him who you are?"

He turned to Galvan and pointed a finger toward Valentine.

"He was Cucuy's errand boy. His job was girls. Leading the lambs to the slaughter." The cartel chief stepped closer to Galvan's side. "Whatever he asks you to do, it's a trick. A trap. It's what Cualli wants. You cannot—"

"My conditions could not be simpler. If your daughter's life is precious to you, then these girls must die in her place."

Rubacalo looked stricken. "He wants you to—"

Valentine cut him off, pleased at the chance to put that arrogant son of a bitch in his place. He would have mowed them all down, given the order and watched the bullets fly until only Galvan remained standing, if not for the possibility that the Timeless One might have some need for one of them.

"I am perfectly capable of telling him what I want," he snapped, and he felt a cruel smile bloom across his face. He had not expected to find joy in these fraught moments, tranquility in the eye of this all-consuming storm.

They waited.

Valentine pulled himself up to his full height.

"The Great One sustained himself on the hearts of virgins. I know he is inside you. We must feed him."

THE DAMS WERE broken. The firewalls, breached. Flood and flame filled Galvan, pounded and burned until he thought he might burst open like a geyser or explode into white-hot shrapnel.

Cucuy had broken loose inside. Galvan could feel, hear, sense him in every pore. Every fiber. Every cell. This was it. The push. The stand. The reckoning.

Kill them eat them devour ravish be a GOD.

Galvan wanted to fight, to sever and shut down whatever chamber of himself Cucuy was darting through, but he could not.

It wasn't that Cucuy was everywhere.

It was that Cucuy was right.

Everything Galvan had ever done had been for Sherry.

He could not let her die.

You cannot let her die.

His thoughts were blurring, merging with Cucuy's, the outlines of the world fuzzy now; *there is no other way.*

There is no other way.

Kill devour ravish feast. Embrace your power. Accept your glory.

Galvan's body thrummed, as if a low electrical charge ran through it. Every muscle seemed to vibrate. It was excruciating and exhilarating at once.

He stepped toward the girls. One turned and ran, only to trip over her shackles and fall headlong to the ground.

Another dropped to her knees and closed her eyes, lips moving rapidly in prayer.

The other two stood, rooted to their spots, eyes wide and full, their bodies racked with tremors.

"I will make it quick," he told them, saliva pooling in his mouth, throat burning in anticipation of warm, throbbing muscle, blood.

Devour ravish feast or let your daughter die. Become a god. Save her. Save her.

Galvan saw his arm rise, his hand tense into a claw—watched it happen as if from a great remove. And yet, at the same time, he had never felt more at one with his body. The strength coursing through it was more than he could contain, or control.

To crush this girl's fragile breastbone and withdraw the delicate organ within seemed the easiest thing in the world.

The easiest, and the most natural. The most just. He would do it with reverence, with dispassion. He would do what he had to, and so would she.

And she. And she. And she.

Galvan drew back his hand, felt it pulse with energy, a cobra about to strike.

Kill devour ravish feast. Embrace your power. Save your daughter.

Yes. If Sherry did not live, then all his agony, all his silence, had been in vain.

"I have to," Galvan whispered. And then, "I'm sorry."

Somewhere far off, he heard a cry, a desperate "No!" and knew it was Sherry.

But it didn't matter. It only proved that she was worth saving.

Galvan's hand shot forward, his eyes squeezed shut, and the girl shrieked. A flash of hot wet pain tore through his body.

He opened his eyes and found a Bowie knife embedded three inches deep in his forearm.

Bob Nichols's fist was wrapped around the handle. His anguished face floated an inch from Galvan's.

"I can't let you do this," he panted. "Snap out of it, Jess. We'll find another way."

For a moment, everything froze. Not just the scene, but Galvan's body. The pain ceased. The ability to move went with it. He was ice. A sculpture of a man, melting in the sun. There was no sound, no air. A lacuna of vacancy. A suspension of time.

Then it was over and the world was an inferno, a roiling pit of fire. Red noise filled Galvan's head. There were no more words—just a hissing, a crackling like the sound of devouring flame.

And there were no more thoughts.

Only obstacles and actions.

Sacrifices.

He grabbed the sheriff's hand, fisted around the knife, and crushed it in his own. Pulled the blade free from his arm, whipped it backhand through the air.

A broad sluice of crimson flew from Nichols's throat. He dropped to his knees, grasping at the wound. In an instant, his hands were covered in blood.

Eyes frantic.

Frantic.

Glassy.

He fell sideways into the dust.

Screams pierced the air, but Galvan was beyond hearing them.

It had to be done.

No way of knowing whether the sentiment was his own or the other's, whether it referred to the act he'd just committed or the one he was about to.

Maybe it was all the same. Time and intention collapsed, the world a giant sinkhole, swallowing everything down, vomiting it back up and swallowing it again.

Galvan reached the girl.

And reached inside.

It was as easy as he'd imagined. His hand was like steel; her body soft, yielding, complicit. It shuddered and twitched, the death rattle orgasmic.

Galvan looked down at the heart in his hand.

It was beautiful and delicate, soft and tough and vulnerable.

The vessel of the gods.

Life itself.

He threw back his head and watched the stars wheel above him.

Opened wide and felt the organ throb as it slid down his throat.

Once.

Twice.

Three times.

Gone.

He closed his eyes in ecstasy and the past and future vanished, the world of symbols and memories and possibilities incinerated by an eternal, never-ending, fearless *now*.

The world is a banquet. You are a god.

I am a god.

"Galvan!"

The shout punctured his reverie. Galvan turned and found Louis and Manuel advancing on him slowly, with rifles trained, backs hunched, knees bent—as if he were a deer they'd snuck up on and hoped to plug before he bucked.

"Galvan," the old farmer said again, as he duck-stepped closer.

"Come back, man. Come on. Don't make me shoot."

Galvan stared at him. At the road map of lines etched into his face, the sweat pouring down it, the thick vein pulsing in his neck.

He had nurtured some feeling for this man. But that sentiment was distant now, impossible to access no matter how he wrung his brain.

All he saw before him was an insect. A beetle. Earthbound and impudent. Blind, deaf, and dumb.

He spread his arms.

"Shoot all you want."

The farmer's brow furrowed, but he aimed his weapon. Galvan inhaled deep and waited. Eager. The spatter of buckshot would feel like rain against his skin. He would soak in the shower and then push it back out of his body, listen as it clattered to the ground, watch the shooter's jaw drop.

Grab that jaw and rip it clean off. Feel the bone's weight in his hand. Pitch it like a horseshoe, far away.

Then have himself another snack.

The very thought sent Galvan into an eyelid-fluttering paroxysm of bliss.

"Do it!" he bellowed, and two shots rang out, biting at his words.

Galvan looked down at his torso. He'd felt nothing.

And for good reason. Louis and Manuel had not squeezed their triggers.

Rubacalo had squeezed his, and they lay dead on the ground.

Galvan stared down at their bodies.

At Nichols.

At the girl.

The yawing, open cavity of her chest.

He blinked, and for an instant the fog of madness lifted.

What have I done?

The answer came from within.

You have failed.

He felt his eyes close, like twin curtains descending on the stage play of his life.

Good-bye, Jess Galvan.

And then he was gone.

CHAPTER 27

"Galvan!" Rubacalo shouted.

No response. The man was swaying, head tossed back, eyelids twitching, a cruel smile creeping gradually across his bloody face.

Not good.

Not good at all.

The cartel chief took a hard step forward, the pistol smoking in his hand.

"Galvan," he said again, and the eyes popped open, the head whipped toward him, a cruel new intelligence shining from eyes that were oil black and bottomless. Rubacalo's breath caught in his throat.

"Not anymore," the man said, and Rubacalo knew he had failed.

That he would die.

"Cualli," he whispered, the word out of his mouth before he could stop it.

The monster sauntered toward him, all swaggering hips and flicking tongue.

Looking into his eyes was like falling down a mineshaft, but Rubacalo forced himself.

Five hundred years, and it had come to this.

He could still die nobly. With the truth on his lips.

"You are no god. Only an impostor. Your very existence is unholy."

The look on Cualli's face was curious. Indulgent. As if he had forgotten what the foibles of men were like and was taking perverse delight in rediscovering them.

Or as if he welcomed the chance to explore the vastness of his nascent power.

"Your mistake is thinking that there is any such thing as holy." Cualli looked him up and down. "Izel's failure is now complete."

It was then that Rubacalo realized the knife was still in the monster's hand.

He steeled himself for pain and then oblivion, or for whatever lay beyond this world. Perhaps in death, the gods grant attentions they denied the living; perhaps they had not abandoned humankind as thoroughly as Izel had taught. Rubacalo had always dared to hope as much—and to believe that the purity of his purpose would wash away his multitude of sins when he crossed over. That he would be received with honor in whatever realm came next. Rewarded, rather than punished.

Suddenly, he wasn't so sure.

"Make it quick," he growled.

That brought a smile to Cualli's lips.

"Nothing is quick," he said, and he looked past Rubacalo at Valentine and his forces. At the shrieking girls, Galvan's daughter and Nichols's sweetheart, both of them hysterical, flailing against their captors, crazed with shock and rage.

"Dile a tus cuates que chinguen a esos pinches motociclistas," he commanded.

Tell your men to kill those biker assholes.

Valentine blinked, as if struggling to comprehend, to accept whose words that voice was speaking. Then he nodded, turned, repeated the command.

If the True Natives had understood any Spanish, they might have lived a little longer. But being a racist fuckwad carried a price.

Valentine's men—Cualli's men, now—had the drop. And they had the numbers.

Twelve guns. Six bikers.

Most of them had been killed twice before they hit the ground.

Valentine dispatched the big one, the leader, himself: head shot from point-blank range, the effluvia of blood and brain geysering from the side of his melon head and splattering itself across Galvan's daughter's neck, torso.

The girl was too far gone to even scream.

Valentine dropped his gun arm, turned to his men.

"Quién hubiera pensado que este cabrón tuviera tanta carne en esa cabeza hueca?" he cracked.

Who would have thought that son of a bitch had so much meat in that empty head?

Rubacalo studied the soldiers' faces. Their smiles were forced. They had no idea what the fuck was going on. Perhaps he could exploit that, somehow. Buy himself another chance.

His eyes flickered, and his mind took stock. He still had two bodyguards. A pistol in his hand. Fuentes was still breathing. The limousine was armored, and less than a hundred feet away, and secreted away inside was the only weapon Rubacalo had left.

Though perhaps the weapon was a weapon no more. Perhaps it had never been one.

Even as he tabulated the vectors, handicapped the chances, Rubacalo knew survival was a fantasy. Darkness had fallen.

On him, and on the world.

Death.

For those who could die, anyway.

More suffering for those who could not.

Five hundred years.

"I am at your disposal," Valentine called across the field, that sniveling coward. "Command me, Great One, and it shall be done."

Perhaps he could save his bodyguards, Rubacalo thought deliriously. Commit one final act of decency.

He had spent his life treating men like pawns on a chessboard, spoiling for an endgame that would never come.

The world was an infinitely worse place for his having lived.

Rubacalo tossed his pistol into the dirt and gestured at his men.

"These two are guns for hire," he told Valentine. "Better they work for you than die with me."

A smile spread across the procurer's face. "But how could I trust them?" he said. "If only there were some way they could demonstrate their loyalty."

Rubacalo spread his arms to crucifix height. "Do it already," he said. "I'm tired of waiting around."

The bodyguards stood mute, waiting for an order. One gave Rubacalo a tiny, tight nod of gratitude.

Perhaps my name will find honor among his children, Rubacalo thought. But he could not even remember the man's surname.

"Have you finished with him, my lord?" Valentine simpered. "Shall I—"

"No, I have not," Cualli thundered. "Take your men. Search the premises. There are two boys hidden, and a woman. I want no loose ends here. Leave Galvan's daughter and her friend with me."

Valentine's guards fanned out, eager to escape the monster's scrutiny. Rubacalo's followed, without risking so much as a backward glance at their former boss.

Valentine himself dragged the girl and the woman across the field and deposited them at the monster's feet. He passed within a few feet of Rubacalo, the pungent waft of his cologne cutting through the stench of sweat and blood that filled the air.

Close enough to kill, thought Rubacalo, and he imagined lashing out, snapping that skinny neck before Cualli could stop it. But his limbs felt leaden, immovable. His will was evaporating, pushing its way out through his pores like sweat, and before Rubacalo could muster the resolve, the procurer and the opportunity were gone.

"You," Cualli snapped, his voice like the crack of an icicle, and Rubacalo's heart fluttered.

But no. The Timeless One stepped around the heap of female flesh, Sherry, and the sobbing Cantwell woman, took three quick strides, and came to a stop in front of Fuentes.

The lawman quaked, and a dark stain spread across the front of his trousers. Rubacalo braced to watch him die, beginning to appreciate the deliberateness of Cualli, the utter lack of worry in him. It did not seem to cross this creature's mind that any of them—not the virgin girls sobbing pathetically in the high grass, not the billionaire drug lord, not the daughter of the man whose very body he had just colonized—might exercise the slightest vestige of will. Their actions, their motivations, were of no concern or consequence. Did not even exist for him.

Worse yet, Cualli's reality eradicated any other, in the minds of those in his presence. Became theirs, too. Through the sheer force of his being, Cualli leached away resistance.

He had all the time in the world.

All of it.

It belonged to him.

Rubacalo was through the looking glass: already dead, and watching with a kind of detached horror—or was it admiration—as Cualli set his house in order.

"What is your rank?" he asked Fuentes.

The man could barely speak. "Re-regional supervisor of police intelligence," he managed to get out.

The Ancient One mused on that a moment, as the piss stain on Fuentes's pants continued its inexorable expansion. It had become a symbol to Rubacalo in these last, unbearable moments. It represented corruption. Fear. Evil.

Soon it would be everywhere.

"Yes or no," Cualli snapped. "Are you for sale?"

"Yes," Fuentes answered, immediately.

"Then consider yourself bought."

The Ancient One spun away. "Get out of here."

"Yes, sir."

The cop sprinted for his car, assiduously avoiding even a stray glance at his dead friend's wife, or his dead friend. A moment later the engine revved to life, and he peeled the hell out of Rosales for all he was worth.

A bought man. A minion in the devil's army. A turncoat. A spy.

But he was still breathing.

Then again, so am I.

That was a cruelty. Cualli forcing him to savor the taste of death, the fullness of his failure. It was no surprise when the monster stalked back to Galvan's daughter and Nichols's woman.

"Rise," he commanded.

The girl pulled herself to her feet, her tear-streaked, dirt-begrimed face rigid and planar, old beyond its years. There was something of her father in her, Rubacalo thought.

It was more than could be said of the thing that stood before her, wearing her father's skin.

The other woman did not respond. She was a puddle, rippling with quiet sobs, writhing and clutching at her stomach.

Cualli did not seem to care. He addressed himself to the Galvan girl. "You are of my blood," he intoned. "Just as your father was. That is not a thing to be taken lightly."

She stared back at him, her eyes as hard as diamonds. "Where is he?"

Cualli licked a fleck of blood from his lip. "Gone. Never to return."

"You killed him."

"I wish, for his sake, that it was so simple. For although he was my enemy, I owe Jess Galvan a debt."

Sherry glared at him for a long moment. How could that feel? Rubacalo wondered. To look into her father's face and see a monster. That alone would drive a weak man insane.

But this was no weak man.

"If he's not dead, where the fuck is he?" she demanded.

"The Dominio Gris," Cualli said, his voice tinged with a dreamy quality. "A prison for those whose bodies have been severed from their souls. Forged by the gods themselves, and inescapable."

He leaned forward, until they were face-to-face. The girl didn't flinch.

"Out of respect for your father, and your blood, I will give you a choice, Sherry Galvan. You can live, you can die, or you can join him."

Rubacalo's mouth fell open in shock. Surely, this could not be mercy. The word was not in Cualli's vocabulary. Perhaps he was thinking of the propagation of his bloodline—that in a few hundred more years, some descendant of this girl's might provide his next home. Perhaps he hoped to multiply the trickle of DNA he shared with Galvan and with Sherry—to breed himself a more easily dominated victim. The notion unspooled from Rubacalo's mind, messy and speculative. There was only one thing he knew for certain.

If Cualli offered you life, you were better off choosing death.

"I want to live," said Sherry Richards, with all the conviction in the world and not an ounce of gratitude.

"So be it," the monster replied.

"And my friend, too." She reached down, pulled the other woman to her feet.

Cualli flicked his eyes down her length, and his lip curled in dismissal.

"Leave now," he ordered.

And at last, he looked at Rubacalo.

"He will not be needing his vehicle," the monster said.

A moment later, the ground beneath Herman Rubacalo's feet disappeared.

As did the air in his lungs.

Cualli held him aloft, squeezing ever so slowly. Ever so carefully.

Exquisite asphyxiation.

"Your sons and your daughter shall also die," the Ancient One whispered, as Rubacalo felt his head engorge with blood, watched the sky flicker, and a final, uncompromising darkness curled toward him. "Izel's line is at an end."

Speech was beyond him, but there was time for one last thought.

Rubacalo died with a tiny smile on his purple-black lips. Cualli was wrong about that much, at least.

Izel's line will never end.

CHAPTER 28

At least they weren't living on borrowed time anymore, Sherry Richards thought grimly as she crouched beside Ruth; she threw the woman's spaghetti-limp arm over her own shoulder, straightened her knees, and lifted the dead weight that was her shell-shocked friend.

For months, she'd been waiting for disaster to strike. The other shoe to fall. The devil to tally up the bill and demand payment. The dead, leaden sensation that filled her now was familiar. Welcome, even. It was horrible—a state beyond sorrow, a state of having cried yourself out, stared despair in the face until your eyes went dry and you wanted to drop to the ground and fall asleep—but it was where she lived. Who she was. The natural order of things.

And it was better than waiting. Better than dread.

Better than captivity. Better than listening to a gang of bikers openly discuss when, where, and how they were going to rape her.

But that was easy for Sherry to say. She hadn't lost what Ruth had. Her father was already gone—had been gone for months, even if she hadn't known it until now.

But Nichols? Nichols had been a good man, and very much alive. It was a good fucking thing Ruth was catatonic right now, because if she was in control of her senses, Sherry would not have been able to lead her past her beloved's body, twisted in the dust, and load her into the backseat of the limousine parked thirty yards past, its glossy black satin finish mottled by a thick layer of grime.

Best Sherry could do for a silver lining.

"We've got to get out of here," she told Ruth, voice resonant in the cushy, soundproofed chamber.

No response.

"Okay, just hang on a sec," Sherry chattered, knowing it was pointless, doing it anyway. Where she was getting her energy, she had no idea. It had to be pure adrenaline; she'd only slept in snatches since the True Natives had taken them: a twenty-minute nod on the back of a motorcycle, a couple of hours in the backseat of Valentine's car.

"I'm going to go look for the keys," she told Ruth, "and then we'll be on our way."

Or we won't.

But apparently when God closed a door, he opened a window. Or, more accurately, when he fucked you bloody, he left a nickel on the pillow. The keys were behind the visor; Sherry pulled it down, and they fell into her lap. The engine purred to life, an obedient tiger. She spun the wheel, kicked up a scrim, and drove right through it. The absurd taffy-stretched car of the dead kingpin shouldered onto the pavement a few seconds later. Within minutes she was banging a hard left onto the highway, and a few after that Sherry had mastered the wheel and memorized the unchanging road well enough to start dashboard-hunting for the nonessentials: air-conditioning, seat adjustment, the switch that brought down the smoked-glass partition cutting her off from Ruth.

That last one was an essential, actually. Sherry had been where Ruth was now, gaping into the maw of the abyss, and it wouldn't do to leave her friend alone there for any longer than absolutely necessary. Sherry thought back on the room she'd built inside herself—the padded isolation chamber to which she'd learned to retreat in the face of abuse, hopelessness, the incomprehensible.

That place outside of space and time had saved her life, but it was dangerous, too. Getting out was never as easy as getting in. Sunlight could not penetrate the walls; the voices of the people who loved you were inaudible. You risked losing yourself entirely.

And Ruth wasn't in there alone.

There was the baby to think about.

The fierce rush of protectiveness she felt for that kid brought tears to Sherry's eyes. Everything was simple now, she thought, backhanding the moisture away. No more divided allegiances, no more being pulled in two directions at once. The only people she had left were in this car right now. Sherry, Ruth, and the baby against the world.

The world.

Apparently, that thing was in some jeopardy. Unstoppable Aztec psychopath inhabiting her father's body and all that.

There was only one thing to do: get as far away as possible. Drive until the road ended, and get on a fucking boat. Get off the boat and get in a car and drive until that road ended.

Wash, rinse, repeat.

By the time she got the window down, Rosales was a memory, a speck in the rearview.

Sherry didn't trust mirrors, so she threw her arm over the seat back, twisted to check on Ruth.

The backseat was empty. For a split second, Sherry panicked. Then the sound of Ruth's ragged in-breath fluttered up from the floor, weak and labored.

"Ruth? You okay?"

No response. Sherry eased her foot down on the brakes, pulled onto the shoulder, parked, threw open the door.

The air outside was thick and muggy, the sun low in the sky and the ground practically pulsating with the day's heat. It was loud in that quiet way, or quiet in that loud way—the smallest movements of brush and bird and snake amplified, seeming to tear through the stagnant air.

Stopping at all went against Sherry's every impulse, even if there was nothing around for miles, but she had one job now, and she intended to do it. Cantwell could mourn all she wanted, but no way was she getting dehydrated on Sherry's watch. If tears came out, water was damn well going in. There had to be a wet bar or something in the limo. You

ADAM MANSBACH

couldn't expect a cartel chief to enjoy his satellite TV and butter-soft leather without a beverage in hand, could you?

She opened the door, found Ruth curled fetal on the floor—a far wider expanse than the seat, Sherry had to admit—her back expanding and contracting like an accordion with each deep, shuddery breath.

Sherry climbed inside, crouched over Ruth, and splayed a hand across her shoulder. She started at the touch, jerked away. That was good, Sherry told herself; she was responsive.

"Ruth, I need you to drink something. Can you sit up for me?"

Keep it simple, Sherry told herself. *Don't overload her circuits.*

But even as she thought it, Sherry became aware of what loomed on the periphery of her mind, a mushroom cloud of despair that billowed toward the heavens. The moment her laser focus on Ruth waned, it would engulf her. All this was a ruse, her brain's best attempt to distract her, lest she be blubbering on the floor beside her friend.

Well, she thought grimly, *thank God for that.* And pushed it all away.

"Come on, Ruth. Sit up." Sherry took her by the shoulders, pulled gently but insistently until Cantwell's body got the gist of it and decided that resistance would be harder than compliance. She leaned against the seat and blinked through her tears at Sherry; the world seemed to come back into focus.

"Good," Sherry said and squeezed her hand. "We're going to get through this, Ruth. But we've got to take care of you, okay? Keep your strength up. Make sure you eat and drink. Now, let's see. There's got to be a minibar or something in here."

She ran her hands over the leather upholstery, looking for a button, a switch, a keypad that might control the chunky, wood-grained console built between the backseat and the wall of the driver's cabin. It looked big enough to house a minibar of epic proportions. Hell, there could practically be a restaurant in there.

Before long, Sherry found what she was looking for. On the door panel, right beside the window controls, was a switch with four positions. She flicked it from left to left-center, and the panels of the console slid open.

Inside, resting on red velvet pedestals, were a pair of gleaming gold .45s. Sherry goggled at them for a moment—*good to know*—and flicked the switch to center-right.

Another velvet-lined cabinet, this one stocked with an array of decanters, full of clear and amber liquids. Beneath it was another, filled with bottled water, and a third, artfully lined with a range of snacks: chocolate bars and packets of tea cookies and all sorts of mouthwatering shit.

"Bingo." She cracked a water bottle, gave it to Ruth. "Drink." Tore open a chocolate bar, broke off a square, popped it in her mouth, and passed it over.

Ruth stared at the objects in her hands for a moment, as if unsure what they were. Then—haltingly, experimentally—she lifted the bottle to her lips, tipped it back. As soon as the water passed her lips, she seemed to realize how thirsty she'd been. Three gulps and the bottle was empty, the plastic crackling and caving from the force of her pull. She cast it aside, crammed half the chocolate bar into her mouth, and closed her eyes. If it wasn't ecstasy, at least it was relief.

It wasn't nutrition, though. Not the kind a growing baby needed. They hadn't had a proper meal in two days, if Sherry stopped to think about it, just the occasional apple or strip of beef jerky from the True Natives' saddle pouches. The stomach-churning fear had kept the hunger at bay, but now Sherry was ravenous—which must mean Ruth was doubly so.

For a moment, she considered heading back to Rosales to lay in some supplies. Who knew where the next town might be? To say nothing of how they'd get back into the States, passportless and driving a car that could only belong to a movie star or a successful killer.

But no. Put as much distance between themselves and the battlefield as possible. Drive until the road ended. That was the plan, shitty or not.

Sherry's hand wandered back to the switch she'd used to open the bar. She flicked it again, from center to right.

The console spun, and the plan went out the window.

The plan, and what little Sherry thought she knew about the world.

CHAPTER 29

I t was like looking into a diorama.

A miniature room, rendered in precise and loving detail.

A bed. A desk. A lamp. A chair.

And in the chair, a doll. He was meant to be an old man, Sherry thought, dropping to her knees and peering closely; the oddness of the tableau did not quite register because she was so taken, so transported, by the craftsmanship.

It was stunning. The doll was tiny—no larger than a small mouse, or a large cricket—but the desiccation of his face, the deep wrinkles lining his arms and neck where they sprouted from a loose white tunic, had been wrought with impossible care.

She stared, blinked, and stared some more. Ruth was by her side now, face a blank slate as she, too, stared in awed perplexity at the toy or the totem or whatever it was.

Cucuy did say that Rubacalo had a daughter, Sherry mused. *But what kind of little girl would want a doll like this?*

She peered still closer. There was something spooky about the doll—an intensity to the energy that surrounded it. Maybe it was a voodoo weapon, and somewhere a real man winced in pain every time Rubacalo plucked one of the doll's long white hairs.

But then why the furniture?

Sherry turned to examine the miniature bed more closely, and then startled at a tiny movement in the periphery of her vision. She could have sworn the doll had blinked.

I must be more exhausted than I thought.

Then he unfolded himself from his chair, walked slowly to the threshold of his three-sided room, and said, "Where is Herman?"

His voice was brittle and crackly, like sticks snapping in a fire. But it was clear. And sad. As if he knew the answer. Sherry looked into his tiny face, aged beyond age, and felt her heart swell with strange sympathy for this creature, whatever he was.

"He's dead," she said softly. And then, without thinking, she added, "I'm sorry."

He blinked his clear brown eyes—they shone within his shrunken face like minute jewels, the only part of him that had not been utterly ravaged—and a heavy sigh rattled through his sticklike body. "Then Cualli has won."

Sherry nodded. "I'm afraid he has." Something in her wanted to comfort him, and so she said, "For now, anyway."

His eyes, locked to hers, pulsed with a kind of energy. "Brave words," he said. "Who are you, child?"

"My name is Sherry. Sherry Richards. This is my friend Ruth."

He lifted a bony, withered hand, and smoothed down the few strands of pure white hair that grew atop his liverspot-mottled head. Something about his movements, his physique, reminded Sherry of a grasshopper, or a praying mantis: the large eyes in the small head, the thin, folded arms and legs.

"You are his daughter. The man Cualli took. Herman told me of you."

Sherry nodded.

"Then I am sorry for your loss. I felt his soul and body cleave apart. I have become attuned to such things, over time."

"What *are* you?"

"My name is Izel."

"And you're . . ."

"I am a man, child. A man, in a body that was never meant to last this long."

A shudder passed through her. "How long?"

"Five hundred and twenty-seven years. Cualli was my fellow priest. My closest friend. I watched him become the abomination you have seen today. And before the gods renounced this world and left us to destroy ourselves, I begged them to tell me how he could be unmade. Do you know what the First Oath is, Sherry Richards?"

She shook her head slowly. "I didn't even know there were gods. I mean, I thought there was only one. And that he was fake. Or dead."

"It is we who are dead to them. I am the last man ever to lay eyes on one." His eyes welled with tears. "In that moment, I understood how blessed we had been, and how far from grace we were about to fall. Do you know what hell is, Sherry Richards?"

"This," she said simply, without thinking.

Izel nodded his ancient head. "Yes. The absence of the divine."

"I meant more like the presence of monsters. Especially when they take over your father's body."

It was hard to read Izel's face; it was so small, so racked by time. But Sherry thought she saw him wince.

"The First Oath," she prompted.

"Yes," he nodded. "Yes. It is the oldest prayer. From a time when we knew nothing of the gods but fear. It is a promise to forsake, to sacrifice, that which is most precious." He closed his eyes, remembering, and two more tears leaked out, disappeared into the deep ravines lining his cheeks. "I believed that was my nephew. The only other member of my family to survive Cualli's purge. But I was wrong."

Izel opened his eyes. "The most precious thing was death," he whispered. "That is what Chimalma took from me that day."

"So the gods answered your prayer," Sherry said and felt her face flush as something like hope suffused her.

Or purpose.

Yes. Purpose was what she felt.

"That means you know how to kill him," she went on, keeping the question out of her voice, willing the sentence to be fact.

"I do. But for all the long years of my life, no such opportunity has emerged. Cualli is too smart. Too cautious. He does not take risks unless he has to—and now he will not have to for a very long time."

"No," Sherry heard herself say, as the flush spread through her and the world unblurred and a new fist of resolve clenched tight inside.

She was Jess Galvan's daughter, and that meant more than it ever had.

"No," she said again, steel in her voice now. "The time is now. He thinks he's invulnerable. That he's won. He's going to be overconfident. And ambitious. He'll stick his neck out. I'm sure of it."

"Perhaps," Izel said. "But we cannot unmake him. There is only one who can do that."

"Now we're getting somewhere," Sherry said. "Who?"

"The one he made," the ancient priest replied, and Sherry felt her jaw tighten.

"I'm not really a big fan of riddles. You got a name?"

Izel shut his eyes, his withered body going perfectly, uncannily still.

"His wife," he said at last. "My sister. Chacanza."

"Wife?" Sherry repeated, dumbfounded. "This fuckin' guy is married?"

To her surprise, it was Cantwell who answered. The doctor's eyes were red and wet, but they were clear. She'd come a long way in a short time, Sherry thought. From despair to determination. From mourning what she'd lost to defending what she had.

"The Queen of the Virgin Army," she said, in a voice both choked and hollow. "That's who you mean, isn't it?"

"I'm afraid so."

"I've studied the legend," Cantwell told him. "Tezcatlipoca stole her away from him, right?"

"In a sense," Izel replied. "Her soul resides with his, trapped in the Dominio Gris. But her body remains here on earth, her will set against her great love, her great betrayer. All those sacrifices became a part of her, an extension of that will."

"Can we talk to her?" asked Sherry. "I mean, is she still a *person*?"

"I do not know. She is hidden, as I have been. Herman put vast resources into finding her, as did his father before him, but their efforts bore no fruit. She is said to walk the desert by night, and to feed on the flesh of men. But these may be nothing more than peasants' tales, invented to frighten children into behaving. The layering of one legend atop another."

"Does she know what she's capable of?" Cantwell asked. "Does she know she can kill him?"

Izel shook his head. "Almost certainly, she does not—though she may understand that they are bound together. That she can never rest while he lives."

They were quiet for a moment. Izel fell back into the state of stillness he seemed to occupy with such ease, and the women mulled his words.

"So basically," said Sherry, cracking her knuckles, hand-heel popping against each one in turn, an old habit of her father's, "we've got to find a cursed, undead, body-without-a-soul cannibal with an army at her beck and call. Who's managed to stay hidden for hundreds of years, despite all the time and money that generations of rich drug lords have spent trying to get a bead on her. And if we do track her down, we have to hope she's capable of listening to us, although it's just as likely that she decides we'd make a delicious afternoon snack. And then we convince her that she's the only one who can kill Cualli, and . . . then what? She hops in the car and we go knock on his door? Pretend we're the Girl Scouts, maybe?"

She bent low over Izel. Face-to-face with him, she realized she must look like a giant to the wizened priest. "After five hundred fuckin' years, is that seriously the best you got?"

A loud rap on the window of the open car door made Sherry jump and spin.

"I can help you," declared a raggedy figure, backlit by the setting sun.

For a moment, Sherry thought it was a ghost. A cloud of wispy, person-shaped smoke.

"You want the queen, I'm your man."

He stepped closer, became more real. Sherry saw cracked lips and raw sunbaked skin, and she dove toward the console button, pushing it until Izel spun out of sight and was replaced by Rubacalo's shining artillery.

She snatched up a .45. The gold was legit; it felt heavy in her grip. She heaved out of the car and squared her shoulders to his, the gun loose at her side.

"Who the fuck are you?"

"Your dad, he was a friend of mine. They call me Gum."

He took a step toward her, and Sherry filled the space between them with arm, fist, and weapon.

"Funny, he never mentioned you."

But as she said it, Sherry felt a surge of recognition and realized who this man was. The knowledge appeared in her brain—not like something she'd remembered, but like something she'd just been given.

She felt something else, too.

An abstract, unmistakable sense that her father was near.

Thanks, Dad.

And then, just as suddenly, he was gone.

"Gum," she said to the wastrel before her, naming him the way you named a stray dog, to tame whatever flex he had left in him. "Yeah. My father told me about you. Start talking."

He rested an elbow on the top of the car door and relaxed against it. The way his bony hands dangled from his wrists reminded Sherry of perched vultures, waiting to swoop.

"I can feel her," he said, voice low and gruff. "She and I, we're both in two places at once, see. Only, I ain't dead like everybody else there. I— I did like your father. Ate somethin' I wasn't supposed to, know what I mean?"

Sherry lowered the .45 and shuffled aside a pace, as Cantwell clambered out of the car and stood beside her.

"You're in the Dominio Gris," Ruth said, matter-of-factly.

"A part of me is."

"Is my father there?" Sherry demanded.

Gum nodded. "But I ain't seen him yet. I dunno if I will."

"And why's that?"

"Dunno what the god will do to him."

"Tezcatlipoca," said Ruth.

"He don't like that name no more."

"Why the fuck should I trust you?" Sherry asked, and she jerked the car door back so that Gum's elbow slid off and he fell back a pace. "For all I know, you wanna feed us to Queen Whatshername."

"Chacanza," he said, supplying the name with a kind of breathy reverence. And then, "I don't." He shook his head. "I don't."

Sherry stared at him. "That's it? That's your entire argument?

Gum dropped him arms and his voice and stepped closer.

Sherry let him.

"I know her *there*," he said. "She's kind. She does what she can to help people. Here . . ." He shrugged. "Here she's pretty fucked up, seems like to me."

"Yeah, you think so?"

Gum shrugged again. "I'll take my chances with her. And with y'all. Things can't get no worse for me than they already are."

"That's comforting."

Sherry sized him up again. He was beyond the point of hiding, she thought. Too divided against himself, too torn apart by the limbo he was in, to pull off major acts of subterfuge.

She'd take her chances with him, too.

Not like there was a plethora of options.

She was about to open her mouth when the console spun again, and Izel regarded them from his chair.

From this angle, it looked distinctly like a throne.

"Give me a few words with this creature," he said. "Alone."

CHAPTER 30

What have I done?
Good-bye, Jess Galvan.

And then he was falling through blackness—flailing, bracing to hit bottom any second and pancake, the world growing colder with each passing moment until breathing hurt, the lungs too tender for the harsh air.

At least I still have lungs.

From the depths came a fast-rushing sound, and then bats were everywhere, thousands of them shooting past, their stink and screams filling the emptiness, the bright yellow malevolent streaks of their eyes all Galvan could see.

He fell past them, and everything slowed. The air grew warmer, thicker, turned gelatinous. Instead of falling, he slid through it more slowly and then not at all. It oozed into every orifice, filled his nose and ears and asshole, his mouth and eyes, invasive and unpleasant, inescapable. He could hear his teeth grinding, loud and brittle in the silence.

The silence.

Galvan probed it, cautious and fearful.

Yes. It was real.

Whatever dimension he'd been banished to, whatever had been stripped from him, whatever atrocities he'd committed and whatever punishment awaited, Galvan was alone in his body again.

Alone in his mind.

No Cucuy. No fight.

He was whole, and it was glorious.

For a few moments, that was enough. The ocean of violence and terror inside had receded; it was unreachable now, a fading memory. He knew he should be on fire, crazed with remorse and ravenous for revenge, but he wasn't. Perhaps that *was* the punishment. Perhaps he was a ghost, and everything would fade away, memory and passion, hate and love, until humanity itself was just a dream.

Beneath his feet: ground. Apparently, he'd never stopped falling, just stopped being able to perceive his own movement. Galvan wrenched free of the squelchy substance that encased him, protected him. In the last few seconds it had hardened into a Galvan-shaped mold, and extrication proved simple, as if the stuff understood its job was over and wanted to set him loose.

He was in a kind of bubble—Galvan flashed on a photograph he'd seen once, a raindrop with a tiny insect floating inside—and he pushed forward, the jelly giving way, and birthed himself into the world that lay outside.

The landscape was entirely alien. He cast about for some detail he might use to orient himself—ground, sky, horizon—and reaped only dizziness for his efforts.

Light suffused this place, but it seemed to have no source; there was no sun, no moon, no vale of stars. Instead, the land itself—the sand-that-was-not-sand beneath his feet, the rolling hills or dunes in the distance—glowed from within, the colors changing slowly in a kind of rolling visual symphony of lush sunset shades: salmon and magenta and blush pink, deep purple and shallow purple and ochre, on and on.

It all changed together, which was why distinguishing the land from the sky was so difficult—and why it took Galvan a pocket eternity to realize he was standing at the shore of a lake or an ocean. There was no tide, no shimmer to the water, nothing to shimmer upon it. Only when he walked a few paces away from the melted cocoon that had brought him there and felt warm wetness envelop his bare foot did he understand that before him lay a body of water.

He drew back his leg, shocked, and noticed he was naked. The scars that defined him were gone; his skin was smooth and perfect, like a newborn's.

"Hello?" he said, and the word echoed in the tropical air—as if the vault of the sky were low and tight against the land, the visible world smaller than it appeared, a cavern of sorts.

No response. Galvan turned in a slow circle, refamiliarizing himself with his body and weighing his options in this still and lifeless place.

It was the water that called to him, that seemed to offer solace. He found a whisper of passion again, in the simple desire to submerge himself, and so he indulged it.

One step. Two. Calf deep. Waist. Chest. But was this liquid even water? It seemed to have no density, no substance of its own. He wondered if it would support his weight, or if he would fall right through it like empty space. Nor did its temperature give it form; the water was no warmer or colder than the air. Or perhaps it was no warmer or colder than his body. It was impossible to tell. Just as the unity of form and color blurred the sky, land, and water, the sameness of temperature complicated any distinction between Galvan and not-Galvan, made him wonder where he began and ended.

If life on earth had been asserting and policing those lines of demarcation, then perhaps life here—if this was life, and if *here* was somewhere—was about letting them go.

It was a theory, anyway.

Galvan took another step and felt the water ring his neck.

Perhaps he could breathe underwater, he thought. He'd been able to inside that jelly-bubble, when by all rights he should have suffocated, so why not? And besides, maybe the action was underwater around here. There certainly wasn't much going on up top.

Or maybe you're alone here. For all eternity.

It was a theory, anyway.

He hedged his bets and filled his lungs, then dove beneath the surface and frog-kicked toward the depths. The light was unchanging, grew no darker as Galvan forced himself deeper. Nor did the water grow colder.

The temptation to risk a breath mounted with each stroke, but he resisted—relished both the feeling of wanting and the feeling of denying himself. The lines distinguishing Galvan from not-Galvan were sharpening.

He shot through the water, knew he'd burned through more than half his store of oxygen, passed the point of no return. The water turned from tangerine to lemon by degrees and then began to shade toward fuchsia. Galvan could see clearly, no salt to brine his eyeballs, but there was nothing to look at. The ocean was as featureless as the land, and as bereft of life.

His chest burned, and he put on a final burst of speed, told himself some destination lay ahead. That it had to. That he would not have been drawn to the water without reason, that he had not come all this way simply to perish.

Yeah, because your life's been so full of purpose until now?

Could he die here? Galvan imagined his limbs going limp as water filled his lungs. His corpse drifting through this barren ocean forever, like an astronaut's through deep black space.

Then he breached the surface and plunged, limbs akimbo, through open air and sky. A cassock of soft purple moss softened his landing, but did nothing to cushion his consciousness.

What the fuck?

He blinked away the stars, got his legs beneath him, sucked in a huge gust of humid air, and staggered to his feet.

Sure enough, the ocean was high overhead—vast and wide, like an endless color-shifting cloud bank, suspended and self-contained, a big fat middle finger in the face of earthly physics. Whatever meniscus he'd broken to escape it and fall to the ground had repaired itself instantly.

He tore his eyes away and looked around.

There was only one word for this place.

Insane.

To start with, there were the colors. It looked like a four-year-old with a jumbo box of fluorescent crayons had run roughshod over a drawing of a magical kingdom—as conceived and penciled by her nine-year-old sister. The ground cover was a mishmash of high grasses and low mosses, in every color but green. Creeping vines of scarlet kudzu twined around blue cacti in a marriage of climatic opposites; trees bearing an array of fruit Galvan had never seen dotted the vast, gardenlike landscape— gardenlike except where giant pits of sand interrupted, or clusters of massive, steaming icicles sprouted from the ground.

But it wasn't the flora.

It was the fauna.

The ocean might have been empty, but this place teemed with life.

Human life.

Female human life.

There must be hundreds of them, Galvan thought, eyes darting from one vista to the next, distant to near, the garden unending.

No, thousands.

They slept, strolled, and sprawled. Some wore simple clothing, fabric fashioned from plant fibers, but most were naked.

And all of them were young.

Innocent.

Pure.

The words flashed through his mind, as Galvan put it all together, remembered what Cucuy had told him.

For every body buried in a shallow grave out *there,* every heartless virgin the Ancient One had sacrificed and discarded, there was a girl here. Cucuy had built a harem for the god.

Starting with his own wife.

A cold chill ran through Galvan.

She was here somewhere.

The woman in yellow. The seductress who had filled his dreams.

Or had they been Cucuy's dreams, and Galvan merely an interloper, an eavesdropper on her siren call to the man who had betrayed her unto hell or purgatory or limbo or whatever this place was?

But even as he thought it, Galvan knew it was none of those. He was mapping Christian ideas on to it, but those concepts were foreign, imposed, after the fact. The Dominio Gris was the Dominio Gris. A prison turned playground, if Cucuy was to be believed. And there was no reason to doubt him. He might have been a monster, but he hadn't lied yet.

All that explained why homegirl napping against the closest Day-Glo palm tree looked so familiar. He'd probably laid eyes on her a few months back, when he'd made his border run and every Virgin Army conscript close enough to sense the presence of the heart had done her damnedest to stop him.

He'd probably laid more than eyes on her, actually. Probably driven a station wagon over her or swung a machete at her neck. Maybe she was among those who'd swarmed and devoured his buddy Payaso, or ripped the strongman Gutierrez limb from limb.

If so, she looked no worse for wear—or for the violence Cucuy had perpetrated either. No more than Galvan himself did. Apparently, the travails of the body were erased here.

As no doubt befit the pleasures of the god whose garden this was.

The garden, and every piece of fruit it bore.

Galvan walked a few paces, until he stood directly before a girl with dark eyes, whose flowing raven-black tresses covered her small breasts. She looked old, he thought; not *old* old, barely sixteen, but old like she'd been born a few hundred years back, before the gene pool diversified. Thoroughbreds like her didn't exist anymore.

She peeled a large fruit with her teeth, a cross between a kiwi and a mango, green pulpy flesh beneath silky ribbon-thin skin. She took no notice of Galvan whatsoever.

"Howdy," he tried, with a halfhearted little wave. "I'm, uh . . . new here."

She blinked at him, lower half of her face invisible behind the fruit, then spun on her heel and walked away.

Tough crowd.

"They can't talk to you."

It was Galvan's turn to spin on his heel.

He found himself face-to-face with a lean, handsome young man, sandy haired, with piercing green eyes. A piece of fabric, tied around his waist like a skirt, was his only nod to modesty.

The dude smiled. "Don't recognize me, huh?" He shifted his weight, from one foot to the other. "It's me, Gum. I look a little different here."

"Gum. Jesus Christ. You clean up good." Galvan looked him up and down, grimaced. "I could use one of those. Feels kinda wrong to be walking around with my dick swinging in the breeze."

Gum unwrapped the cloth from his torso, ripped it cleanly in half, and offered Galvan a strip just wide enough to do the job.

"Thanks. So we're . . . dead, or . . . what the fuck, man?"

Gum shook his head. "Nah." He jutted his chin at the garden, the girls. "They're dead. Or—more dead. Undead. You and me, we're different. We didn't die. But me, I'm still out there. And you, you're not."

Galvan mulled that over for a few moments. "So you've got a foot in each world."

Gum's baleful stare confirmed it.

"How the fuck you manage that? I mean, right now, we're here, having this conversation. But somehow you're also, like . . ." He trailed off, unable to find a way to balance the idea atop the teetering stack that already filled his mind.

Gum pawed the ground with his bare foot and winced. "It feels like being torn apart," he said quietly.

The gears of Galvan's mind were turning. Slowly, grimed with rust. But turning.

"Find my daughter." He reached out, grabbed Gum's shoulder. "Please. I've gotta know if she's alive."

Gum's eyes flitted left-right-left, like he was reading type off Galvan's forehead.

Or deciding whether to lie.

"She is," he said at last. "I'm with her."

Galvan felt the sweat burst from his pores. All was not lost. He could still reach out to Sherry. The questions poured out of him, each one erasing the last.

"Where is she? Who's she with? Is she safe?"

"For now," Gum said, but something had shifted. His eyes, his posture. A new caginess. Or, more accurately, the old caginess.

"Tell her to get as far away as she can," Galvan said. "Tell her run and don't look back. And that I love her. And that I'm sorry. And that I'm gonna—"

Gum's face was a brick wall, and it brought Galvan up short. "What?"

"She's with Izel. They're going to find Chacanza."

"I don't know who either of those people are," Galvan said, but his stomach dropped as he said it.

He knew. Her name, her face, her very essence had echoed, rattled, and floated through Galvan for as long as Cucuy had colonized his body. She was the ghost in the machine, the fist of regret and love, fear and hatred that clutched at the monster's heart.

The last vestige of his humanity.

The final threat.

"Why?" he breathed, bracing himself for the answer. "They got a plan?"

It was Gum's turn to grimace. "Not much of one."

Galvan clenched his fists. "You've gotta stop her."

One look at Gum's face, and Galvan knew that wasn't gonna happen. Sherry was too willful, too reckless, too headstrong.

Too much his daughter.

"I gotta get out of here."

"Nobody gets outta here, man. It's—"

"Then I'll be the first."

"Yeah?" Gum crossed his arms. "How you plan to do that, guy who just got here five minutes ago?"

Galvan mulled that over. "I'm gonna make Tezcatlipoca an offer," he said at last, the germ of an idea taking root. "You know where I can find him?"

"Why you think I'm here?" Gum countered. "He sent me to come get you, boss. Only I wouldn't be so eager, if I was you."

CHAPTER 31

Ojos Negros loomed before him, huge, squat, and menacing. Finally Domingo Valentine had something to stare at besides the man sitting across from him in the limousine's spacious rear chamber.

Man.

It was a term he used loosely.

The change that had come over the former Jess Galvan was subtle but unmistakable, and for the journey's duration Valentine had toyed deliciously with the paradox, as if it were a wiggly tooth.

It was almost too much to hold in his mind, the way his companion both was and was not the Ancient One. Valentine remembered an interview he'd heard on the radio, decades ago. Some scientist, talking about a made-up experiment where you replaced each part of a man, one after the next, until nothing of him remained. A new heart, a new lung. Cornea transplants. Artificial legs. Finally, the brain. At what point, the scientist had asked—or maybe he had been a philosopher—was the man no longer himself, but someone else?

This was different, of course. No surgery, and no question. Jess

Galvan had been obliterated. There was a god inside the man. That was what the Great One had always been.

It is of no more significance than a new suit of clothes, Valentine thought.

But that wasn't exactly true either. This body was stronger. Much stronger. Valentine thrilled at the possibilities. The power. Only now, seeing Cucuy enshrined within this new form, did he understand how enfeebled the Ancient One had been in the previous one. How limitless his reach was now.

And yet, Valentine mused, the Timeless One might walk undetected in this new skin. The very prisoners who had slept and eaten alongside Jess Galvan a few months earlier would merely assume he had returned to Ojos, as so many did, and take him back into the fold with nary a second glance.

But that was only because, as the Great One had taught Valentine, the human brain refused to process anything that lay outside its understanding of the world. Like any animal, man relied on filters. Blinders. Ignorance was survival, except when it was death. A frog recognized a fly when the fly flew. Surround it with live flies hanging from strings, and the creature would starve to death.

Of course, only a cruel god, a force outside of nature, would present a frog with such a scenario.

And under closer scrutiny, the Great One would not be able to disguise his glory—not that Valentine imagined he intended to live undetected among inmates.

Galvan's eyes had been brown or green or hazel; now, they were a black beyond black, and possessed of an intense magnetism, so circuit scrambling that Valentine could not be sure whether they attracted or repelled. They were Cucuy's eyes; Valentine had watched in jubilant disbelief as Galvan's had dulled, like spent lightbulbs. An instant later the Timeless One's glowed, brighter than Valentine had ever seen them.

His whole body glowed, in fact. As if his heart pumped molten lava through his veins instead of blood.

That was new.

"Everything is new," Cucuy declared, reading his mind. Valentine startled and nodded. The voice was hardest to get used to; it was

Galvan's through and through, no matter how closely Valentine listened for some subsonic growl, some hint of his master's vicious rasp.

"The world is remade," Cucuy continued. "And it is time to work. Are you ready to work, Domingo?"

Valentine drew himself up, his back arching away from the leather seat. "I have never stopped."

Until he said it, Valentine had not known how deeply he pined for his master's recognition, for the Timeless One to credit him with orchestrating this triumph—and now, he castigated himself for being weak, petty.

Everything might have changed, but some things never would. To clamor for Cucuy's praise was to invite its opposite.

But the Great One had not noticed his petulance or else chose to ignore it. Either way, Valentine was grateful.

"Tell me what you need," he said.

Cucuy stretched his legs in front of him, locked his elbows, fisted his hands, and turned his arms left and right, as if turning a pair of spigots.

Acclimating to his new dimensions, Valentine thought.

He unclenched his right hand, finger by finger, counting off a list.

"Girls. My appetite for girls remains the same." He said it slowly, as if realizing it as he spoke or surprised that it was so. Another finger unfurled from the thick, muscular palm, and a toothy grin spread across the Great One's face. "And fruit. I have a need for fruit."

"Fruit?" Valentine repeated, incredulous, before he could stop himself. *What am I, a caterer?*

Thankfully, Cucuy was half lost in reverie.

"Yes. The fruits of my young days. I cannot remember their names."

"I will look into it, my lord," Valentine assured him, growing more anxious by the moment. Had the Timeless One lost some part of himself, trapped in that incorporeal netherland? Had his lust for—

"And now, to more important matters."

Ah. Okay.

Cucuy gestured at the prison. "How many men?"

"About eighty-five hundred."

"Assemble them. Now."

The sweat seeped from Valentine's brow, and the air conditioner converted it into a salty residue, tight on his skin. The only place the entire population of Ojos Negros could conceivably fit was in the yard, and no more than a tenth of the inmates were permitted to congregate there at once. A quarter might overwhelm the guards; en masse, they would be fools not to look around, do the math, and realize how simply collective exodus could be achieved.

These men might be cutthroats, but they were far from fools.

"If I may make a suggestion, Great One . . . in the past you have controlled them from a distance. Through guards. Intermediaries. The leaders of the cartels. To bring together so many men at once might be . . . unwieldy."

Cucuy's smile was icy.

Icy, and unprecedented.

"You doubt I can control them, Valentine?"

The procurer gulped down the lump rising in his throat. "Of course not, master. I was only—"

"Go, then."

Valentine reached for the door, threw it open, stepped into the late-afternoon heat. A shaft of sunlight fell into the car, and Cucuy slid across the seat to bathe in it, catlike.

Valentine hesitated, just long enough to banish a thought from his mind.

"Something else?"

Valentine's pulse pounded in his temples, so hard he wondered if his head was vibrating like a bass woofer. He turned, sucked in a breath of air, bent to look at Cucuy and found himself caught in those oil-well eyes.

"It's just . . . in your absence, I . . . I had to manage the cartels as best I could. I hope I didn't—"

At first, Valentine didn't know what to make of the sound that emanated from the Ancient One, low and syncopated, dastardly, like a man falling down a flight of stairs.

Then he realized it was laughter.

"They are of no consequence. You have done well, Domingo Valentine. There is a place for you in the New World."

He crossed his legs at the knee and folded his hands, the pose oddly aristocratic, and for the hundredth time today the procurer reflected that he knew nothing, must assume nothing. The habits, the manners, the concerns of the master he had served were no more. A new master sat before him, and his own survival depended on learning how to become indispensable to him.

Who he was, and what he wanted.

Both questions had the same answer, Valentine thought abruptly. *Everything.*

"Thank you," he whispered and hurried off to do his master's bidding.

THE GUARDS WERE nervous. Trigger happy. They'd refused to stand among the inmate population, and for the sake of expedience, Valentine had agreed to put them all on the roof and in the watchtowers, safe from the riot they seemed to think was inevitable the moment you asked Azteca and Sinaloa to share the yard.

He had invoked Cucuy's name—as if they didn't know for whom he spoke—but, over the last few months, the power of that invocation had waned considerably due to overuse, invisibility. His grip on power had been far more tenuous than he had realized, Valentine reflected. But he had completed his task. *Done well.*

The steward had worn the crown until the king's return. It had not touched the ground.

And now, he thought, as he stood by the Great One's side and watched the men emerge from their cells and shuffle down the five stacked tiers, trickle out of the cafeteria, the laundry, the workshops—streams and rivers of humanity fusing into a vast ocean that flowed toward the open, dusty yard at the prison's center—*the kingdom would be set right.*

He hadn't the foggiest notion what that meant.

The only Great One Valentine had ever known had been intent on survival, stealth and shadow, manipulation and puppetry. The biding of time. The gathering of strength. He had never spoken of what came afterward, and it had never occurred to Valentine to wonder, much less ask.

But here they were.

That word flashed through the procurer's mind again. *Everything.*

At last, the cells were empty, the yard full. The smell, the energy, the sheer jittery malevolence of so many men accustomed to being treated like animals was overwhelming. The yard was a rippling ocean, yes—and at the center of it was an island, a small circumference of space upon which the water did not dare encroach.

Alone on that island, like a single palm tree, stood the Great One, his hands clasped behind his back as his terrible eyes moved across the crowd, the subtle glow of his body brightening as the light failed.

Valentine watched the men watch him. The silence was absolute. They didn't know what they were looking at, but they felt its power, knew they had never seen its like before.

The Timeless One luxuriated in their attention for a full minute, and Valentine sensed the fear, the wonder, the excitement cresting. Becoming a wave.

When Cucuy finally spoke, a low current of electricity ran beneath his words—a subsonic vibration that buzzed against some pleasure center in the brain, splitting the difference between seduction and hypnosis.

"You may think you know me," he said, softly enough that they had to strain to hear him, and it dawned on Valentine that this was no public address, but rather eight thousand private conversations.

"But you do not. You may recognize the body of a man named Jess Galvan who was once a prisoner here. But I am not Jess Galvan. This, you already know."

He dropped his head to his chest, walked forward a pace.

"You have heard my name whispered all your lives."

He looked up, met the collective gaze.

"I am the one they call Cucuy."

Valentine scanned the sea of faces, expecting shock, skepticism.

All he found was silence.

"I was once a priest," the Ancient One went on. "My god was the god of your forefathers. The god of your true nature, before that nature was buried under lies.

"Mercy." He spread his arms and spat the word. "Have you found mercy in the world? In your own hearts?"

He glared at them, long and hard. Waited. Let them mull it over.

Silence, awestruck and fearful.

Thoughtful.

"Answer me!" he thundered, and they jolted out of it.

"No," a thousand voices mumbled and shouted, plaintive and choked, furious and reverent.

"Redemption." Cucuy turned left and right. "Forgiveness. 'The lamb who goes not to the slaughter.' These are the lies on which your world is built. And when you reject them and embrace your nature, what then? Are you given mercy? No." He stamped his foot, raising a cloud of dust that swirled as high as his waist. "Prison!"

A murmur of agreement rippled through the yard. Of possibility.

He has offered them nothing, Valentine mused. Demonstrated no power. Made no promises, no threats. Merely claimed a name out of some ancient, collective nightmare and spun a world around it.

"The old gods are gone," Cucuy went on. "But I am here. Their power is mine." He made a fist and shook it in the air. "Because I *took* it. I took it, and I waited. Until the time was right. Until falsehood and delusion had crippled the world, made it ripe for collapse. That time is now."

Valentine took stock again. Something had shifted, by a hair. The rhetoric was too abstract for men like these. They knew they'd been wronged; they felt the boot of the world on their necks. But their world was within these walls, and there was no falsehood here, no delusion. Authority wasn't abstract. Authority could have you raped in the showers or shanked to death in your bunk.

No sooner had Valentine thought it than the Great One pivoted, gave them his terms, exploded their world.

"Today this is a prison. Five hundred years ago, it was a temple. And tomorrow it will be a fortress. The first of many. And you, all of you, will be an army. *My* army."

He paused, to let that ripple through the crowd and settle, and then his mouth cleaved into a vicious grin.

"Unless you prefer to remain shackled and powerless."

Valentine reeled with the genius of it, even as he tensed for the inmates' response.

Every prison a fortress.

Every prisoner a soldier.

They were already vicious and disciplined, regimented and organized. If there was a swifter way to recalibrate the balance of power in
the world, he couldn't bring it to mind.

"I already got a boss," somebody said, from deep within the dense
thicket of bodies, and a nervous ripple of guttural agreement spread
from that unseen point.

Cucuy nodded. "Yes. Of course. Azteca. Sinaloa. Those organiza-
tions have raised you, no? Taught you the meaning of loyalty. But the
new war must bring the old war to an end."

He glanced over his shoulder at Valentine. "The bosses," he said.
"The top men here. Who are they?"

"Milagros," Valentine replied, thrilled to have the information at his
fingertips. "And El Sastre."

The Great One nodded, raised a hand, and beckoned with two fingers. "Milagros. El Sastre. Step forward."

The sea parted, and two men walked the corridor of bodies until
they stood before him, square shouldered and resolute.

El Sastre was white haired and lanky, Azteca's capo since long before
Valentine's time, the brother-in-law of the man who ran shipping for
the cartel on the outside. An aristocrat, of sorts. The stereo system in
his suite of cells was worth more than the guards made in a year, and he
favored violin concertos.

Milagros was young and squat, an enforcer who had climbed the
ranks through a combination of brutality and cunning and would likely
meet his end at the hands of a younger version of himself.

Cucuy looked at each of them in turn. Appraising. Sizing up. The
men stood with their chins raised, waiting for the opening salvo in a
business meeting, a truce negotiation.

Instead, the Ancient One's arms shot out and seized hold of both
men's faces, jerking their heads sideways until their necks snapped with
a pair of *criks* that echoed through the yard.

He let go, and the bodies dropped into the dust.

"That way of life is over."

He pointed at the crowd with both hands, fingers sweeping across
the wide-eyed prisoners.

"You are no longer Barrio Azteca. You are no longer Federacíon Sinaloa. As of this moment, those words mean nothing."

The silence was charged with dread, and with excitement. Here was liberation from all they had ever known—replaced by allegiance to a being, a cause, they might never understand.

"As of this moment, you are mine."

CHAPTER 32

He had betrayed her. Traded love for power, light for darkness. The future for the past. Humanity for godhood.

She had watched her heart beat for the last time, glimpsed the fear, anguish, and excitement fighting for control of her lover's face, and then passed out of space and time into the Great Void. Ceased to exist.

But oblivion had not wanted her. The void spit her back out. She was reborn in darkness, terrified and ravenous, gasping for breath, suffocating beneath the weight of the earth.

Until she realized that she did not need to breathe. The soil held her, rich and loamy, teeming with life. She could hear each wriggling worm and creeping blind insect, sense the thin roots of the grass questing for nutrients and the penetrating warmth of the sun. Slowly, the panic subsided—and the hunger moved in swiftly, to fill the empty space.

She clawed at the cakey earth and felt it crumble toward her, fall into her nose and eyes and mouth. There was only so much space—a thin bubble, a tiny cavern her body had hollowed out, and Chacanza's task was to change its location, move it upward inch by inch until it broke against the meniscus of the world.

The grave was deep. The hunger gnawed. But Chacanza felt her strength returning.

No—not *her* strength. A new strength, cold and unflagging, unlike any she'd possessed in life. As if mercury filled her veins instead of blood.

But now it was hers, and she would use it—all of it. Empty the reservoir of her powers. Nothing was bottomless.

Not her strength, and not his.

What she was, she did not know. But what she was meant to do, why the Great Void had sent her back, could not have been clearer.

When at last she breached the surface, the process of learning about herself commenced. Lesson one: the sun and the breeze were lost to her; Chacanza's body was insensate to their embrace. She found herself unsurprised and unconcerned; she was something else now, something new.

A creature of different pleasures. Of pure appetite.

As befit one who had been severed from her soul.

Her hunger focused at the thought of him, contracted into a fist of intention. Cualli had fed on her virtue, her innocence and love. Now the abomination he had created would return the favor. Destroy the vile, corrupt thing he had become. Unmake them both.

A monster for a monster.

And yet.

Here she stood, atop the Mount of Sacred Grace. The man who had defiled her body had buried it with the greatest of honor, in accordance with every ancient ritual; she had been transported nearly sixty miles from the capital and lain to rest on the peaceful, desolate plateau of a site holy to Chimalma, Shepherdess of Life, Chacanza's patron goddess.

She could not make sense of it and soon ceased trying. There were more important things to discern. She did not know how long she had been gone; perhaps time had moved on without her. Perhaps it was a day since her death, or a year, or a thousand. She knew only that Cualli was alive—and that the gods were dead. Whether they had vanished from the world or were merely absent from whatever blighted shadow version of it she now inhabited, Chacanza could not be sure. But she felt the void. The loss. It was part of the ache inside.

There was no help for her, not from the divine and not from the living. No prayer would be heard, and even if her family still existed—and what reason was there to believe Cualli had spared any who might pursue vengeance on her behalf?—she was unfit to be seen by them. Were this mountain still a holy site, she would defile it. But Chimalma was gone. This mountain was no longer her temple, but her funeral mound. Yet another blasphemy Cualli had wrought.

And so Chacanza walked down toward the capital, to destroy him.

To destroy them both.

LIKE ANY DAUGHTER of the empire, no matter how poor or prosperous, Chacanza was raised to know what nourishment the desert yielded: how to tap its hidden water, pluck its edible vegetation.

But none of that mattered now. She was a creature of blood. She knew it before she made her first kill. The sun could no longer warm her, but the rich liquid of life still had power.

A rabbit.

A mountain cat.

On the third sleepless day of her journey, with the city looming on the horizon, a man.

A peasant, out hunting too, slingshot in hand. It was no different to kill and drain a man, provoked no feeling beyond satiation. She left his body where it lay, walked on.

Chacanza reached the capital at nightfall, disguised herself with a stolen scarf and headed for the temple of Tezcatlipoca, keeping to the narrowest roads.

But one did not simply approach the temple.

Not when the entire population of the capital was assembled before its steps, united in a frenzy of worship.

Not when a new god had supplanted the old, declared the site his seat of worship and government, and dispatched his personal army to eviscerate whatever infidels refused to bow before him.

And certainly not when the new god's nightly sacrifice was being presented, atop the same temple steps where only days before he had been a man, a priest, humble, beloved.

Now he was transformed.

All-powerful, the people whispered, on Chacanza's left and right, with reverence and with terror. Single-handedly, he had vanquished the old gods, the cruel gods. Taken their powers for himself—and for them. For humanity. He was both man and god, and the world was made anew. How miraculous, that a man could become a god! How liberating, to no longer labor beneath the yoke of those distant, unknowable beings, accessible only via the swollen, debauched ranks of the sundry priesthoods! Truly, this was mankind's finest hour—to worship one of their own! To look upon him in the flesh, to know his appetites and supplicate him without confusion, or misgiving, or intercession—to have the veil finally lifted, and the truth revealed!

Suddenly, the crowd roared as one, and Chacanza watched as a dozen soldiers marched up the long sweep of glimmering quartz stairs and took up positions behind an empty throne.

The noise of the crowd resolved into a chant.

Cu-cuy! Cu-cuy!

So. He had taken a new name.

Chacanza scanned the rippling multitude and realized she did not recognize a single face. These were peasants. Newcomers from the provinces. It was as she had surmised: no one with any power, any lineage, had been left alive.

Cu-cuy! Cu-cuy!

But the man who took the stage was not her defiler. He was old and withered, dressed in the raiment of a priest.

What was a god without a priest?

By his side stood a young girl in a white tunic. Her bare legs trembled, and terror danced in her eyes.

What was a god without a sacrifice?

Chacanza turned on her heel, began to push her way through the throng and out of the square. There was no chance of getting to him now; she needed to retreat and reconsider. It had been foolish to come without a plan. Her enemy was the lord and master of all he surveyed; she could sense his strength in the air, feel it without even laying eyes on him. She would not bear witness as some innocent girl suffered the same death she had—would not add her eyes to the thousands eager to watch red soak the virgin-white tunic and tell themselves the monster who consumed the girl's beating heart was worthy of their worship.

Chacanza missed her mountain.

Missed her grave.

At the outskirts of the capital, she broke into a run. Cucuy had his empire. His army. If she was to destroy him, perhaps she needed her own.

Why had she not thought to run before? The desert blurred, flew by, her legs pumping faster, the stride lengthening, the night purpling, the sun rising and peaking and disappearing behind cloud banks. Emerging in decline. Setting.

She reached Sacred Grace in the middle of the night, having broken stride only to hunt and eat. Time slipped away from her slowly, like a language she no longer understood. Its passage might still compel her to hunger or exhaustion—she felt her eyelids growing heavy even now, as she climbed the thistle-laden hillside, and wondered if she would sleep, if she *could* sleep, what sleep meant for a being like her—but the clock of mortality had stopped ticking.

Life was a countdown, driven by all the fear and urgency the lessening of days implied. But this, this was not life. It could only end in triumph, for its end would mean his end. This, Chacanza knew. The knowledge resided deep in her bones, unassailable, rigid.

The rest she would have to figure out. She had nothing but time.

She reached the flat plateau, lay down beside the hole in the ground, the mound of churned black earth, and learned that sleep was not among the many pleasures she had been denied.

CHACANZA OPENED HER eyes. She was lying naked on the banks of a drab, colorless ocean. A low sky leached of any hue loomed overhead. There was no sun in sight, nor any clouds to hide one. No horizon line separated the indistinct mass of the water from the equally featureless sky.

The sand against her body was gritty, unpleasant, but otherwise indescribable, lacking in qualities. It was as if everything here was unfinished, lightly sketched. Form without content. Form almost without form.

The air was still, unbroken by birdsong or the buzz of insects. Breezeless. Not even the water moved.

She stood, turned in a circle, tried to find some point on which to focus. Was this a dream? Or had she awakened from a long, vivid nightmare, into an anodyne realm beyond death?

A flash of white light crackled across the sky, as if in answer, and Chacanza started. She wanted to hide, but that was impossible.

The water rippled and a tiny wave licked its way up the shore, turned the sand a slightly darker shade of colorlessness. Chacanza squinted into the distance, tracing the disruption to its source, and saw a shape cutting through the water at tremendous speed, the ocean cleaving before it, splitting in two, great walls of water furling on either side.

The shape grew closer, more distinct, and Chacanza gasped, felt her body go rubbery, and her legs give out. She fell to her knees, eyes pinned to the form as it grew closer.

Closer.

Brighter.

Golden.

Stunning. Unbearably beautiful—so beautiful that it was somehow cruel. She could not look away, though the luminescence of this creature seemed to be inside her now, lighting her own body from within, glowing from her mouth, her eyes, her womanhood.

Especially her womanhood.

There was no doubt in Chacanza's mind or flesh. She was gazing upon a god.

Beneath her, the sand moved, rose. She felt caressed, lifted. It was becoming a new form, taking on new qualities. The granularity gave way to soft, smooth seamlessness—to something like the silk of the gowns she'd once worn. She felt her limbs being rearranged, configured, supported.

And still the light, beaming into her, beaming out of her, connecting her to the approaching god as he came to rest before her, magnificent and terrible.

"Hello, my queen. And welcome to hell."

Only then did Chacanza realize that she was sitting on a throne.

The god spread his arms, and his golden light shot in both directions, freezing the faceless landscape in glory.

"But I shall make a heaven of this hell."

He held out his hand, and Chacanza reached for it.

When her palm touched his, the spasm of pleasure that tore through her body was like nothing she had ever known.

THE BLOODCURDLING SHRIEK that rent the air, cut short the dream, might well have been Chacanza's own. To be yanked back to reality was worse than death—just as the world she and Tezcatlipoca had created, *were creating,* was better, sweeter, than life had ever been.

The two of them, alone in the void, turning thoughts to matter, an abyss into a paradise. She had only to describe a fruit, a color, a nuance in the landscape, and he willed it into existence.

Her suffering had been worth it. A rite of passage, Tezcatlipoca explained. The only way he could guide her into the void. They were one being, one organism, two halves, one whole, and this was forever. Eternal. Unchanging, except through her suggestion and his artistry.

But it was just a dream.

She woke in a lather of panic and confusion. The memory of fruit lingered on her tongue, the indescribable pleasures of Tezcatlipoca still reverberated through her body, the perfect warmth of the sun he had made still danced on her skin.

She was a creature of blood again. An abomination.

The sun could not touch her.

But she was not alone.

Climbing her way out of the grave—Chacanza's grave—was another.

Another, but also a part of herself. An extension of her consciousness. Subsumed by it, immediately and forever, the moment Chacanza turned her focus toward the creature.

It was the girl. The virgin she'd refused to watch sacrificed. Her shriek cut off abruptly, as the key to Chacanza's will slid cleanly into the lock of her mind.

And turned. And clicked.

Total control.

I have my first soldier. My second set of eyes.

I am a queen here, too.

My numbers will grow.

I shall contain multitudes.

CHAPTER 33

I t was amazing what you could accomplish with eight thousand men working in shifts around the clock.

Less than twenty-four hours had passed since the Great One's announcement broke the grip of the cartels, declared the prisoners an army and the prison a fortress.

Already, it was more than that.

They were more than that.

Ojos Negros was a temple, filled with warrior-acolytes. The men were loyal and eager, boundless in their energy. Valentine didn't know if Cucuy had worked some kind of spell on them, or if the power—the illusion—of their newfound self-determination was what drove them. Regardless, they worked as if the lash were at their backs.

But no, Valentine corrected, that wasn't it—rather, they worked as if fealty to the Timeless One were a form of liberty. Toiling in his service was not like working for the cartels, with their revolving-door midlevel leadership and grotesque campaigns of intimidation, and the men sensed that. His authority was of a different magnitude. A higher order. They didn't need words like *deity* or discourses on the hypocrisy of religion to respond accordingly, any more than a horse needed to know the pedigree of its rider.

The hand that gripped the reins was firm. That was all that mattered.

Valentine stood in the middle of the yard, let the activity flow around him. The level of coordination and cooperation was astounding; he felt as if he were inside a beehive, or an ant colony. Was it possible that Cucuy orchestrated all this? That in a few short hours, he had molded them into a hive mind? Or was this simply what men looked like when they no longer labored under the weight of uncertainty, individuality, untethered ambition?

Valentine looked up, squinting in the noonday sun, at what had been a guard's tower and was now a command center. Cucuy sat motionless, surveying the landscape from atop a massive golden throne.

But no, not golden.

Gold.

It had taken six men two hours to carry it up from the catacombs. Valentine had never seen it before, never even known about the room from which it came, but the message it embodied was clear.

A new reign had begun.

The procurer glanced at his timepiece—a Philippe Patek model for which Herman Rubacalo no longer had any use—and saw that it was time.

As if on cue, a mechanized grinding filled the air, and Valentine turned to see the prison's intake gate, through which prisoner transport vehicles delivered the newly unfree into bondage, slowly open.

A long line of identical white vans rumbled out of the prison's belly, kicking up a scrim of dust. Valentine counted as they passed, double-checking his math.

Thirty vans at sixteen men per was four hundred and eighty.

That left sixty men unarmed, and four hundred and twenty equipped with a cache of assault weapons Valentine had laid in three weeks earlier, for distribution to whichever client's inexhaustible thirst for artillery manifested first.

Those numbers would do just fine.

He glanced again at the guard tower, found the throne abandoned, and turned his gaze back to the vehicle bay just in time to see his master's limousine roll out into the sunlight.

Domingo Valentine scurried around the back, yanked on the door's still-cool chrome handle, and joined the Timeless One inside. Not until the last of the convoy disappeared over the horizon did they follow.

Better to give the soldiers a head start.

BARRANCO BLANCO WAS a forty-five-mile drive from Ojos Negros. It housed twelve thousand men, their crimes ranging from fraud to murder, separated into ten tiers and two buildings according to the seriousness of their infractions. Barrio Azteca was the dominant power, with control of six tiers to Sinaloa's three; the last one was a ragtag collection of foreigners and head cases, men not worth controlling.

The men who sat atop the infrastructure knew what was coming, had been informed the previous evening via cell phone, told to ready their people. The guards in their pockets knew, too: they had been told to stand up or duck down.

By the time the first white van pulled up at the intake gate, Valentine guessed, word would have reached as much as 70 percent of the prison's population. And if Barranco Blanco was anything like Ojos, that meant tension floated through the air like clouds of mustard gas—that every jaw was clenched in anticipation of action, that small fights had broken out since breakfast, that whatever information had come down from the bosses on the top tiers had been diluted, muddled as it spread through the general population, and the only thing the rank-and-file scumbags knew for sure was that something was going to jump bad.

They'd assume it was the usual: widespread chaos as a cover for some specific act of retribution. Thousands set in violent motion so that one disloyal man, one snitch or rat or stoolie—or hell, one dude whose cousin on the outside had tried to steal a shipment, whose sister had rebuffed a boss's advance, whose father-in-law had refused to pay protection— might meet a suitably gruesome and instructive end.

The prisoners were used to that. A riot served a general purpose, the alleviation of boredom, as well as myriad specific ones: under the blanket of tumult, a hundred other acts of vengeance might be committed unseen and without repercussion. The grudge burning a hole in your stomach, the shank burning a hole in your pocket—now was the time to find relief.

But this was no riot, Valentine thought, as the limousine crested a final hill and bore down on the long straightaway that terminated at the gate.

This was regime change, and it was well under way.

The white vans had disappeared into an underground garage, and a legion of men with fresh-out-of-the-crates AK-47s marched back out. By the time Valentine traded the cool confines of his own car for the hot sun, the prison was already under new management—or, at least, the old management was lined up on their knees in the yard, surrounded by a sea of stunned, jostling prisoners held at bay by some of Ojos's finest.

They knelt upright, backs straight, hands clasped behind their heads, sweat stains beneath their arms. A long, snaking row of unbought, out-gunned guards, speckled with the occasional prison doctor, nurse, or warden.

The Ojos contingent was thorough, Valentine mused as he strode toward them at Cucuy's side, the Ancient One's pace measured and stately. They'd left no stone unturned, flushed out anybody wearing a uniform or getting a paycheck. And they'd done it with a stunning, bloodless efficiency.

Sure, a few hundred assault weapons lent anybody a certain authority—but that was just it. The control. The discipline. Cucuy had deemed them an army worthy of his name, and here they were, acting like it. No cowboy shit, no murder for the fuck of it.

That lesson was not lost on the new recruits. The Barranco boys were eerily quiet. No calls for mercy or blood, just a breathless anticipation, a million unasked questions thickening the air.

Valentine fell back as the Great One strode to the front of the crowd. With a sweep of his hand, he brushed away the soldiers cordoning off the inmates; they dispersed and he turned to stroll down the row of prostrate prison employees with long, slow strides.

"Today, you shall have justice," he said, and stopped before the warden. The man was six two and hatchet faced, his small, deep-set eyes electric with fear.

"Rise."

He stood on shaky legs, lowered his arms slowly to his sides.

"Your fates have been placed in this man's hands," the Terrible One said, his voice bouncing off the high walls of the tight-packed, silent yard. "Now, I place his fate in yours. Does he live or die?"

Valentine braced for a cacophony of voices, but instead a low, nervous murmur spread through the yard. Perhaps they feared it was a trick question.

Or that once the killing began, it would not end.

Cucuy waited, his gaze surfing the crowd.

"Die!" the shout came at last. A single man, a single word. A verdict rendered.

"Die!" someone else repeated, and then the cries began, as ragged and staggered as seagulls' caws at first and then coalescing into a chant. A rhythm.

"Die! Die! Die!"

Cucuy raised a hand, and they fell silent.

Then that hand gripped the warden by the neck. The other grabbed him between the legs.

And in one fluid motion, the Great One sent him flying through the air. The prisoners gasped in disbelief, twelve thousand faces rising and turning to track the dark blur framed against the azure sky, hear the fading scream of terror.

The warden cleared the prison's outer wall by several feet and passed out of all knowing.

That wall, Valentine guessed, was a good thirty-five feet high.

"Who wants to join my army?" Cucuy asked, and every convict raised his hand.

He'd streamlined his recruitment speech nicely, Valentine thought.

AN HOUR LATER, they were back in the car, bound for Ojos. Valentine was working both his satellite and cell phones, laptop open before him, familiar hat back on his head.

He was a procurer. He reached his long arms into the world and retrieved whatever was needed.

Right now, that meant weapons. Vehicles. Materiel. All of it in quantities that staggered the mind.

There was an army to outfit. Today, it was twenty thousand men. By week's end, it would be ten times that size. The strike teams in the white vans would not return to Ojos; they would continue on to the next prison. Barranco Blanco had vans of its own. Guns of its own, too, once the guards' room had been pillaged and a portion of the AKs handed off.

The Great One's presence was no longer needed; his legend would reach the prisons long before the vans did.

Valentine glanced up at him, found Cucuy's eyes closed, his breathing heavy.

"Master?" he ventured. He was loath to probe for information, but his ability to do his job faltered without it.

"What," the Ancient One replied, without opening his eyelids.

"How many prisons do—did—the cartels control? That is, how many are you planning to . . ."

Cucuy sat up, and Valentine looked into the swirling black whirlpools that were his eyes.

"All of them. In this country and the other."

He rolled down the window, let the air caress his face, whip through his hair.

"It's brilliant," Valentine said, half to himself, as massive reams of data scrolled furiously through his mind.

Supply chains.

The routing of payments and trucks, drugs and airplanes.

The unfathomable merger necessitated by the collapse of the cartels. The staggering manpower involved.

It was enough to make him dizzy.

But it was also what Domingo Valentine did better than any man on earth.

"You will be unstoppable," he whispered.

"That is only the beginning," the Terrible One said and closed his eyes.

Valentine thought about that, and an involuntary shudder went through him. Whether it was excitement or fear, he could not be sure.

CHAPTER 34

The passage of centuries had not blunted Izel Notchi Icnoyotl's faculties, and sometimes he thought this was the cruelest punishment of all. He forgot nothing, felt pain and loss, regret and foreboding with a searing, undiminished acuity. And as his body withered, became an affront to the laws of life and death, his mind seemed to expand—to travel as he could not—and sense the presence, the movement, the agony of other anomalies, other disruptions to the natural order.

Other abominations like himself.

A white-hot jolt had passed through him when Galvan ate the heart that became his doom. This Gum fellow's wanderings were like faint lines traced onto the map of his consciousness. And Cualli's very existence was a boulder that never stopped weighing on Izel's soul.

But his sister was beyond detection.

Izel felt only her absence. The ache of it, almost indistinguishable from the absence of the divine. The soul-deep chill that had enveloped this forsaken world and wrapped itself around whatever was left of him.

Not even the desert heat could touch it, but it was good to feel the sun beat down on him again—to feel a sense of purpose, a glimmer of hope. For too long he had hidden, counseled Herman from secret compartments, and told himself that survival was victory enough, that patience would pay off, that the world turned like a wheel and opportunity would come around.

That Cucuy would falter and they would pounce.

That the means justified the end, and no money was too dirty if it bought revenge.

For too long, Izel had believed it.

But no more. The wheel had indeed turned—and then, swift and brutal, it had turned again. The moment had come and gone.

Unless the girl was right.

Unless this wastrel Gum, this walker in two worlds, could do what he claimed. Succeed where generations of Izel's family had failed.

Though if he did, their problems were just beginning.

The priest looked up at Sherry Richards. Her face was caked with grime, streaked with sweat.

Then, he looked down at Sherry Richards. Her strides were long and sure, legs pumping like pistons. She walked as if the destination lay just around the next bend.

He was sitting on her bare shoulder; he could not remember the last time his skin had touched skin, and the warmth was a revelation.

The fact that she and the pregnant doctor and this Gum creature had left Herman's limousine behind three hours earlier and were striding across parched, unmapped wilderness was less reassuring.

Gum claimed they were close, that they would reach her citadel within the hour and the border of her domain any minute.

What happened after that was anybody's guess. Izel didn't anticipate a warm reception.

Much less an offer of liquid refreshment.

The contents of Herman Rubacalo's minibar skewed heavily toward the alcoholic. Two bottles of tonic water separated them from dehydration.

For Izel's part, a thimbleful was enough to slake thirst, and Gum didn't appear to require much of anything in the way of sustenance. But the other two—the other three, Izel corrected himself, glancing at the

Cantwell woman's stomach, the life inside too small to be visible but the way she splayed her hands over her belly giving everything away—the other three would need to keep up their strength.

A chill went through Izel, banished all thought from his mind. He clutched a hand to Sherry's shoulder to alert her, squeezed with all the strength his brittle fingers had left. She drew up short, with a sharp intake of breath, and the others followed suit.

What Izel sensed, they saw for themselves an instant later. A tremor in the earth, directly ahead. And then another and another. They had passed the invisible borderline of Chacanza's domain, and Izel sensed her minions. She was undetectable, but these tendrils of her will were not. Some hundred and fifty years ago, Izel and Herman's great-grandfather had tried to interrogate them as a way to find her. He flashed on those pointless, misguided months of torture and felt a profound shame at the brutal stupidity of it all.

The memory dissipated, as a sextet of girls emerged from the ground, hands flowering first, elbows pushing their way free, arms leveraging heads, necks, and torsos into being. Legs scissoring their way out of the grave as if the earth were a swimming pool. Knees flexing, calves going taut as they regained their feet.

For a moment they stood motionless, slack jawed and loose limbed, as if awaiting orders. Izel felt drawn to the closest one, a girl with waist-length raven hair, wearing the dirt-stained tatters of a dress that had once been white.

She was of his time, he thought. She had not died in secret, stolen away from her family, but with ceremony and fanfare, before throngs of sweat-drenched zealots.

Somehow, that made it worse.

Izel looked into her eyes. Looked through them and tried to imagine his sister on the other side, watching him back.

The girl took a step forward.

Izel nearly fell to the ground as Sherry Richards reached behind her back, pulled the gun from the rear of her waistband, and squeezed off half the clip.

"No!" Izel screamed, but his voice didn't have a chance.

The first bullet hit her in the shoulder, spun her ninety degrees, and pitched her backward, arms flailing at the air. The second impacted just above the right temple—and at this range, from a gun that big, there was little left of the girl's face by the time she collapsed in a cloud of dust, and even less after the next two rounds tore through her chest. Her legs still scrabbled at the ground, like a dog having a dream about running, but she wasn't going anywhere.

"What the fuck are you doing?" Gum shouted, beating Izel to the question. The other five girls hadn't moved, but Sherry's gun was trained on the next-closest one, fist clenched so hard the knuckles were bone white.

Izel knew what she was thinking: not enough bullets.

"Put it down, Sherry," he said into her ear—and for an instant, an absurd image flitted through Izel's mind: another him, perched on her other shoulder, egging her on to shoot, the proverbial devil to his angel.

Stay alive long enough, and the imagery of religions you hate saturates your thinking.

"She made a move!" Sherry yelled, swinging the weapon from one girl to the next as if these drones might spook.

"Listen, girlie, if she'd made a move, you'd know it," Gum shot back.

"Sherry. Please. I must speak through them to my sister," Izel intoned, in the most authoritative voice he could muster.

In the moment it took Sherry to relent and lower the weapon by halting degrees, Izel reflected on how pathetic it was that after five hundred years, he still had to strain to project authority.

"Thank you," he said to her, and then he locked eyes with the closest remaining girl, a long-limbed, T-shirt-clad specimen who'd most likely met her end in the filthy bowels of Ojos Negros, perhaps so recently that her family still held out hope for her return.

"Chacanza," he said, and something in her visage changed. The eyes dilated; the brow furrowed in consternation.

"This is your brother, Izel. I must see you. The gods have turned me into the wretch you see before you, but they have kept me alive. I have but one purpose, sister, and it is the same as yours."

He paused without breaking eye contact and summoned all the conviction, all the persuasion, he had in him. "I know how to kill him, Chacanza. I failed you once. I will not do so again."

For a moment, the girls stood stock-still. Izel could hear Sherry's pulse throbbing in her neck; he felt his own heart race and knew that whatever minute trickle of adrenaline his body could still produce was swirling its way into his bloodstream.

Abruptly, the five girls turned on their heels and began to walk.

It took no prodding from Izel for Sherry to fall into step behind them.

THE GIRLS DIDN'T look back. Not once, in the hour it took them to lead the way to Chacanza's keep.

That she had no doubt the supplicants would follow, Izel understood. That she didn't want to take even one more look at the grotesquely transformed brother she hadn't seen in five hundred years, he found a little more troubling.

I failed you once. The admission, which had tripped so easily off his tongue, might well have doomed him—doomed them all. He'd had centuries to lament his actions on the day of her death and agonize over whether his sister had guessed at his complicity. He'd once fantasized about begging her forgiveness, but long ago dismissed the notion as selfish. What mattered was destroying Cualli, not salving his own conscience. Anything that complicated that goal had to be put aside.

And yet, what had he done within seconds?

You are weak, old man.

All the long days of your life come down to this.

Don't fuck it up.

"Almost there, boss," Gum said, lengthening his stride and pulling up alongside Sherry. And indeed, Izel could sense a kind of mounting density, a hum of life.

But no, not life.

A hum of undeath.

At its center, its hub, there was nothingness. A void in his sensory map so profound, it had to be Chacanza.

Izel looked up and found himself staring at the slope of a tall hill, the only incline of note between here and the horizon. Something fired in his memory: this was a place he had known once, in the days before the fall.

A holy site.

One that Cualli, in his manic erasure of the old ways, had forgotten to raze.

Or one that he had left alone.

The Mount of Sacred Grace. Holy to Chimalma, the last of the gods. Whose blessing, whose curse, kept Izel's heart beating in his chest even now.

If his sister had died with a prayer on her lips, it was Chimalma's deaf ears upon which it had fallen.

But the girls did not lead them toward the summit, where worship and burial had once taken place. They marched instead to the base of the hill, where an enormous boulder rested against its sharply inclined side.

Together they grabbed hold and pushed it aside. Izel was astonished that the five of them could manage such a feat, until the passageway behind the boulder was revealed, and he saw that another half-dozen of Chacanza's minions stood inside, assisting in the task.

The smell of earth, damp and fetid, wafted from the mouth of the cavern. Torchlights flickered in the far distance, throwing light that failed to reach the high ceiling or the well-trodden floor. Pinpricks of light filtered in from tiny holes, just large enough to vent the meager smoke of the torches.

This is her work, Izel marveled. *He buried her here, and she turned her grave into this. Hollowed out an entire mountain. Made it a crypt.*

Though not without help.

Sherry stepped across the threshold, and Izel felt the cool air envelop him.

The girls fell away, joining countless others in the dim recesses of the cavern.

They were on their own.

"This way," breathed Gum. "She's over here."

"How do you know that?" Cantwell asked, in the same hushed mausoleum tone.

"I feel her."

The girls they passed on the trek through the yawing cavern ignored them utterly. Izel watched one, naked and statuesque, carry a lit torch to a wall niche where its predecessor had burned out and swap the one for the other.

This is her staff, he thought. *Warriors out there, elect in here.* Another girl, equally alluring and unclothed, passed in front of them, and Izel wondered what other duties the staff might perform for their master. Whether her legendary appetite for flesh might extend beyond protein, and into pleasure.

Gum led them up a long, twisting stairway, carved from the bedrock of the mountain; it hugged the contour of the main chamber for some hundred feet, then broke off and climbed at a steeper angle, toward a pale yellow light seemingly siphoned from the world above.

Sherry stepped inside, and the timeline of Izel's life collapsed on itself, five hundred years of misery blowing away like dust in the breeze as he gazed across the long room at his sister.

For a split second he was young again—as radiant as she was—and the gods had not forsaken the earth. He *felt* them: ghostly and dilute, mere shadows flitting across a wall, but it was more than he had ever hoped to feel again.

She rose from her stone chair and strode toward him so swiftly that her long raven hair fanned out behind her like a veil. And then the hard, shimmering emeralds of Chacanza's eyes filled Izel's visage, and the hard grip of her hand encircled his fragile torso.

The heat of Sherry Richards's body faded away, replaced by the shocking, bone-deep chill of Chacanza's flesh.

The world in which she lived, he understood abruptly, was devoid of warmth.

She brought him close, inspected him. Izel did the same. She looked exactly as she had the day she'd stood atop the temple steps and pledged her body and soul to Cualli.

The smell of her breath put the lie to that. Her mouth was closed, her lips pressed together in a tight, pinched look of appraisal, but the stench of rotten flesh behind them was almost unbearable.

As if it filled her, Izel thought. *As if it occupied the vacant space where her soul ought to be.*

"Sister," he said, and her clasp tightened, became a vise.

"I am no one's sister. No one's daughter. No one's wife."

"Chacanza," he managed, with the last of his air. If she squeezed any harder, the brittle bones of his rib cage would shatter, become dust.

"I do not answer to that name." But her grip loosened. For the first time, she looked past him, eyes flickering up and down the lengths of his companions. Whether in curiosity or contempt, Izel could not be sure.

Or it might have been hunger.

"Cualli is born anew," he said, and the searing bright green eyes flashed back to him. "You know this. You have felt it."

"I have," she said, but something else had captured her attention; Izel felt the slip, the drift, and tried to follow its vector, to imagine what could possibly be of more interest to her than this.

"We can destroy him, but we must act now," he said. "We can—"

But she was not listening. She returned him to his perch on Sherry's shoulder and strode over to Gum, until they stood an inch apart.

She leaned in close and inhaled. Smelled him deep and long.

He did not flinch.

"My queen," he said when she pulled back to regard him from a slightly greater remove, and he gave a small, graceless bow.

"What are you?"

"Your loyal servant always, my most merciful queen."

Her brow furrowed, and she cocked her head.

"Queen of what?"

He raised his eyes, met hers.

"Of the Dominio Gris."

Her arm shot out, hand striking Gum's neck like a viper. She lifted him effortlessly into the air, and Izel felt his own throat constrict in sympathy.

"How do you know my dreams?" she demanded.

Gum's arms hung limp at his sides; either he understood the futility of fighting back, or he saw another way through this.

"They aren't dreams, my queen. The Dominio Gris is real. You created it. You and Tez—"

She jerked her hand back as if it had touched flame, and Gum fell, crumpled to the ground. She stared down at him, wild-eyed, watched, waited as Gum brought a hand gingerly to his throat. Finally, he looked up at her.

"It's real," he said again. "I'm there right now, and so are you." He jerked his head at the cavern below. "And all of them. The only difference is, I know it. It's not a dream. That's your soul trying to communicate with your body, or something."

Gum planted an arm against the floor, pushed off, regained his feet.

"I *know* you there," he said. "You made it all. The ocean in the sky. The blue mountains. All of it. That was his gift to you when—" Gum broke off and winced, Adam's apple lolloping in his throat. "When things were better," he finished softly.

They stared at each other for a long moment, and then Gum said, "It could work, what he's talking about. There's a guy there, Galvan—"

Her eyes pulsed, so hot they seemed to light up the room.

"You've seen him," Gum surmised. "Maybe you've . . . had dreams about him?"

The queen only nodded.

"That's whose body Cualli took. But he's— Well, he's a fighter. He kept Cualli at bay for longer than I woulda thought possible. And to hear him tell it, he ain't done with this world yet."

"That's my father," Sherry declared, stepping forward, bringing Izel with her. Neither of them paid her the slightest mind.

Izel took the opportunity to rejoin the conversation. "He's at the temple," he told his sister. "Where it all started. He's gathering his strength. Building his army. We need to march on him now, before it's too late. Let your girls do what they were meant—"

She whirled toward him.

"The temple," Chacanza repeated, snatching Izel from his perch again. "Where you betrayed me, *brother*."

It is justice, Izel thought to himself.

He closed his eyes and said a silent prayer to the gods beyond the vale—the gods he knew could hear him still, hard as they might try not to listen.

He was completely at peace by the time Chacanza dashed his brains against the cold stone wall of the cavern.

CHAPTER 35

Galvan craned his neck to gaze at their destination and realized that contrary to his initial impression, Tezcatlipoca's palace didn't sit atop the looming mountain; the mountain simply became the palace. It was all one.

Of course it was. There was no carpentry here. No labor. No grafting of one form onto another. The god had thought it into being, and if tomorrow he wanted to dwell underwater, or reside in a floating mansion among the clouds, then this mountaintop keep might disappear entirely or sit abandoned.

Word made flesh.

Except, not flesh.

According to Gum, that was the one power Tezcatlipoca had been unable to conjure in this purgatory turned playground.

Every last soul had been imported.

"What the fuck," huffed Galvan, short of breath, thighs aching, and unaccustomed to both these human shortcomings. "Why doesn't he just teleport me up there or some shit?"

Gum shrugged. "Dunno. He could."

"What else can you tell me?" Galvan asked. "I'm flying blind here. I mean, is he . . . am I gonna be talking to a man, or a six-headed eagle, or, I dunno, a giant glass of orange juice, or what?"

Gum pulled up short, and Galvan almost ran into him.

"There's only one thing I can tell you." He glanced up at the citadel and lowered his voice. "He's a sick fuckin' insane lunatic."

"Okey dokey, then," said Galvan. "Thanks. That's helpful." And he trudged on.

Voicing it seemed to open the floodgates, turn Gum from reticent to chatty. "I mean, imagine you're all-powerful. You can make anything, do anything. But you're trapped. There's nobody to bump against, nobody who even comes close to being on your level; it's just you and your big fuckin' divine brain and all these luscious chicks keep on pouring in— these virgins who stay virgins no matter how many times you fuck 'em. What's there to do, after the first hundred, two hundred years except figure out more cruel and depraved shit to do with your time, right?"

"Could take up needlepoint," said Galvan, and he put one foot in front of the other again. He had a feeling he'd be dead of exhaustion before he ever reached the top and found out for himself.

"You'd fuckin' lose it, man. Everybody needs boundaries, know what I mean? Or, like, goals. Shit, even me. I was a low-life fuckin' dope fiend half my life, but I had that next high to chase, and that kept me connected to something. Tez—he goes by Tez, that's another thing you oughta know—it's like he's high all the time. His body or whatever, it can *handle* that. No such thing as an OD for him, boss, lemme tell you. Shit, he can fuck for a month straight if he wants to. Or have a fuckin' daylong orgasm. There's a girl here who—"

"I get it," Galvan interrupted. "I get it." He glared up at the peak one more time. "You know what? Fuck this shit." He cupped his hands around his mouth like a bullhorn.

"Hey! Yo! Tez! You wanna see me, I could use a little help down here!"

He glanced at Gum, found him pale with trepidation.

Galvan shrugged. "Nothing ventured, nothing gained, right?"

No sooner had he said it than the ground beneath them disappeared, and Galvan found himself tumbling upward at tremendous speed, head over heels, ears popping, the mountainside a blur beside him, and then gone, pink sky in its place, an open vista—

And then he was falling, the polarity reverse. Gum's flailing form followed the same trajectory a few feet away, both of them overshooting the mountaintop and slamming toward it now—

Galvan came down hard, side first, his hip and rib cage connecting with a springy green mosslike ground cover.

He rolled onto his back and looked up. He was in a kind of open-air parlor of vast proportions, vegetation creeping and climbing over regal stone furniture, all of it jarringly—comfortingly?—earthlike compared to the rest of what he'd seen: no wild colors, no outlandish formations. Even the trees bore familiar fruit.

He stood and turned to take it all in. There was something familiar about this place.

Perhaps, he thought dizzily, he'd seen it in a dream. Glimpsed it during one of his encounters with the woman in yellow, the prize Tezcatlipoca had wrested from Cucuy and built this empire around. Perhaps this place was her attempt to re-create some semblance, some shadow, of the life she'd had.

Where was she, then?

He narrowed his eyes, as if she might be hiding in plain sight—then startled as a shrill, piercing cry cut through the heavy air, and spun to locate its source.

It took him a moment to realize that it came from above. Galvan looked up and understood for the first time the limits of his own imagination.

Hovering in midair, some thirty feet above, was a huge, muscled human form that could only be Tezcatlipoca. He spun like a centrifuge, or a tornado, and in his clutches was a woman—no, there were two women, both shrieking, both splayed flat, one in front of him and one in back, one faceup and one facedown, the three of them forming a six-pointed star. His glistening torso pumped in either direction as he fucked them with two enormous organs, faster and faster, spinning all the while.

And then suddenly, the spinning stopped, and both girls flew away from him. Tezcatlipoca roared, and both his cocks grew longer and gave chase. They were the length of spears when, at precisely the same moment, they reached the girls and entered them. The girls screamed, as the god forced himself deeper inside.

He'll break them, Galvan thought in disbelief and horror. *He'll split them apart.*

And indeed, a moment later, with a guttural moan that shook the treetops, Tezcatlipoca climaxed and his organs tore through their torsos from inside, emerged covered in viscera just below their rib cages. He spun again and sloughed their bodies to the ground. They came down hard, one to the left of Galvan and the other to the right, lifeless, bloodied and broken.

He stared down at them, unable to fathom what he'd just seen, and missed Tezcatlipoca's landing.

His transformation.

The being Galvan saw when he looked up was tall and slight, almost elfin in the delicacy of his features, with arms that seemed too long for his body and a flat, hairless chest. The monstrous cocks were gone; he appeared asexual now, almost prepubescent. The only points of continuity were a golden glow that emanated from within his chest, and the utter blackness of his eyes.

He stepped toward Galvan without so much as a glance at the bodies lying between them and wiped a trace of perspiration from his thin upper lip.

"Never fear, Jess Galvan," he said, in a voice that seemed to come from everywhere, a voice that was neither high nor low, resonant nor flinty, but all those things at once. "It is a deathless realm."

He gestured to the girls, and Galvan glanced down and saw that their wounds had healed. Their eyes were closed and they were breathing deeply, regularly, as if sound asleep.

"Isn't that right, my queen?"

Chacanza was walking toward them, her eyes fixed on the prostrate girls, her face a husk of silent hatred. She didn't look up at Tezcatlipoca to acknowledge his question and didn't appear to notice Jess. She knelt before the closer girl, brushed a lock of bloody hair off her forehead, then raised her head and nodded into the distance.

Four more girls approached on silent feet, clad in identical tunics made of a burlaplike plant fiber. They bent before the sleeping girls, lifted them expertly beneath the knees and arms, and carried them away.

"So," Tezcatlipoca continued, "you are the one from whom Cualli reaped new life." He looked Galvan up and down and then glanced at Gum, who hovered by the parlor's periphery as if hoping to go unseen. "And I am told that you resisted for some time. That must have caused him no end of misery."

He strolled closer and fixed his bottomless eyes on Galvan. "This pleases me. I may allow you some enjoyment here."

He opened his palm and offered Galvan a glinting, marble-sized bit of matter; it looked like a clump of earth, or a globule of resin.

"An intoxicant of my creation. Based loosely on the fruit of the poppy, but infinitely stronger. It may kill you, for a while."

Galvan stepped closer.

"I'm not interested in that. I've got a deal for you."

Tezcatlipoca regarded him with curiosity and popped the drug into his own mouth.

"There is nothing I want."

Whatever the hell he'd just ingested was taking effect fast. A ripple of iridescence streamed down the god's body like a gentle wind; in its wake his limbs took on a new lugubriousness.

Tezcatlipoca crossed his arms behind his head, his body rising slightly off the ground as he reclined on an invisible bed.

"Speak your mind," he slurred, looking up at the sky. "If I don't like it, I'll tear out your liver twice a day for the next hundred years."

"Fair enough." Galvan took a deep breath and wondered whether Tezcatlipoca's state would make him more receptive to the pitch or less. He sensed movement in the periphery of his vision and looked over to see Chacanza striding toward him, slow and stately. He caught her eye, hoping for some hint of recognition, of confederacy. But there was nothing.

"Put me back in my body and let me kill Cucuy. The right way. Once and for all."

Tezcatlipoca's body swung vertical, and he leaned toward Galvan.

"Why would I want that?"

"Because if he dies any other way, you lose all this. No more virgin fucktoys, no more drugs, no more conjuring shit into being. Just seven billion assholes busy destroying the planet all by themselves."

Tezcatlipoca was quiet for a moment. Whether he was weighing the words or simply too zooted to listen, Galvan didn't know. But he continued.

"I dunno, maybe that sounds like fun to you. Pop back up, surprise-surprise, hey, wow, it's Tezcatlipoca, the Divine Sorcerer, Most Fearsome and Beloved. Bam, he's blowin' shit up, he's real, boom, fall the fuck in line, humanity. Except here's the thing: three-quarters of them would rather die than turn their backs on Jesus or Allah or fuckin' Vishnu. And even if you do convert them all or kill off the heathens, then what? Spend twenty years waiting for a bunch of slaves to build you a castle you could've snapped your fingers and created here? Float around double-dicking chicks to death Dominio Gris style, except out there they got wills of their own, plus you gotta find 'em and replace 'em cuz they won't just heal up afterward?"

Galvan paused, trying to gauge how this was going over, but Tezcatlipoca was inscrutable.

"Bottom line, there's not a single reason for you to trade this for that, so let me unmake that fucker. Because believe me, if I don't kill him right, sooner or later somebody else is sure as hell gonna do it wrong."

He realized he'd reached the end of his sales pitch, shut his mouth, and waited for a response. Tezcatlipoca was undulating in a slow, hypnotic rhythm now. The outlines of his body blurred, became indistinct and wavy. As if he were fading into the ether, becoming one with the air.

That was some fuckin' drug, all right.

"Do you know how to do it?"

Galvan's head snapped toward the voice.

It was Chacanza. Her hands were folded, her shoulders squared to his.

Her face was seared into Galvan's memory in a wide range of states: seduction and aggression, determination and abandon. But this expression, Galvan could not read.

It took him several moments to understand that it was hope.

"Think so," he said.

"Then allow me to remove all doubt."

A stalactite of lightning crackled through the sky, and Galvan spun in time to see it hit Tezcatlipoca square in the middle of the chest.

Where his heart was, assuming that the god had one.

And precisely where you'd slam a junkie with a syringe of adrenaline to bring him out of a nod.

His body shuddered and Tezcatlipoca groaned in ecstasy as the surge of electricity crackled through him, blue sparks shooting in all directions.

His feet found the firmament.

His body found form.

The bottomless black eyes found Galvan.

"I have renounced the earth. This realm is my only home."

He raised a hand, and Galvan watched as the fingers grew together, turned metallic, became a reaper's sickle. "But if I were forced to return, it would not be to wage petty war. It would be to finish the job my brothers and sisters abandoned, and destroy that world entirely."

"All the more reason for me to do it right." Galvan clenched his teeth, felt his jaw flare. "He stole from you. Kept what wasn't his to keep. You landing on your feet here doesn't change that."

Galvan spread his arms. "Make me your weapon of vengeance."

For the first time, the full weight of Tezcatlipoca's attention came to rest on him. The pressure seemed to begin inside Galvan's head, as if the god were probing the very folds of his brain. He winced, as the pain ratcheted up to excruciating and the world beyond went fuzzy.

"It is not a decision to be made on faith," Tezcatlipoca intoned. "You must prove yourself worthy to be my sword."

Galvan felt the ground beneath him drop away, and then everything went black.

CHAPTER 36

Miguel Fuentes had lost track.
Of time.
His present physical location.
His place in the world.
The basic rules by which the universe was governed.
All he knew was that he was very, very drunk.
And hundreds of miles from anywhere he ought to be.
And totally, permanently, royally fucked.
Consider yourself bought.

For days now, he'd tried to blot out those words. How many, he couldn't be sure. Beer didn't help, so he'd switched to tequila. When that proved ineffective, he'd tried sex; the roadhouse bar he'd stumbled into rented rooms by the hour, and a handful of working girls trickled through when the sun went down. He had a go at one the first night, and out of embarrassment at how that had gone, he swapped the booze for coffee a few hours before dusk the second night and took a different one upstairs.

But sobriety only unleashed the black-eyed monster inside.

As far as work knew—work and his wife—Fuentes was on the clock. Working a contact, trying to flip a disgruntled lieutenant and roll him up at his Barrio Azteca superiors. Just another badass workweek for the pride and joy of Intelligence Ops.

And when he rolled back into town with Herman Rubacalo's corpse in his trunk and some kind of heroic story about how it had gotten there—a story he was currently too drunk to devise, since the inspiration to double back and collect the body was the last sober-headed thing Fuentes had done—well, shit. The sky was the limit. Awards and promotions out the asshole.

Cucuy was gonna own himself one high-ranking son of a bitch.

If Fuentes managed to sack up and go home before the body rotted beyond recognition, anyway.

The odds on that were maybe three to one.

He leaned forward until his forehead touched the bar, and he raised a finger for more tequila.

When he looked up, he was staring at a basket of steaming tortillas instead.

"You should eat something," the barkeep said.

"Fuck you," Fuentes mumbled, already tearing into the hot morsels.

Before he could swallow, his phone chirped in his pocket and Fuentes nearly toppled off his stool. He fumbled for it, filled with dread, anticipating the flash of Marisol's name across the screen. But when he wrestled the device free, there was no name on the screen at all.

In its place was the word *Unknown*.

As if it was his future calling, Fuentes thought as he stared at it, trying to bring the word into focus, obscurely proud of the sentiment's poetry.

"Fuentes," said Fuentes.

"Do you know who this is?" The voice was low, even, almost a purr. And yet, it made every hair on his body stand.

"How did you get this number?" he blurted, without thinking.

The empty air on the other end of the line was answer enough.

"Valentine," Fuentes capitulated at last. "It's Valentine."

"Tomorrow between three and four P.M., a cargo plane will land at a hidden airfield fifteen miles outside Gómez Palacio. You will meet it. You will unload it. And you will transport the contents to Ojos Negros. This will require three or four large vehicles. Police vehicles. I will transmit exact coordinates when I hang up. You will be paid upon delivery. Is all that clear?"

Fuentes's stomach plummeted, as a host of impossibilities swarmed around his head like flies. He could not put hands on that many vehicles, or that many men. Questions would be asked. Getting from here to home to there in time also posed difficulties. Particularly in his current state of shitfacedness.

And then there was the plane's cargo.

Guns or drugs if he was lucky. Fucking surface-to-air missiles if he was not.

"I don't think—"

"Do not think. Do as you are told."

"I'd like to, Mr. Valentine, of course." He could feel the sloppiness of the words as they rolled off his tongue, the inadvisability of each one. But Fuentes couldn't stop himself. "It's just that right now isn't really the—"

"Your wife's name is Marisol," the procurer said, as if he were informing Fuentes of the weather. "She's thirty-nine years old, too pretty for you, and wants another child. The ones you already have are Javier, Jacinta, and fat little Federico. Shall I go on?"

Fuentes's spine went rigid, and a bead of sweat rolled down his back.

In a flash, he was stone-cold sober.

"That won't be necessary," he said, rubbing his eyelids with a thumb knuckle and forefinger. "I'll be there. I'll figure it out."

"I'm sure you will."

The line went dead.

Fuentes could hardly breathe. He slapped open the bar's saloon doors, staggered into the stifling heat, and sucked down a huge helping of dusty air.

His lungs burned as he scrolled through his contacts, looking for Marisol's cell number. Fuentes pressed the phone to his sweaty ear and prayed his wife would pick up.

His heart played over the ringtone in triplicate. Just as he was about to hang up, she answered.

"Miguel?"

"Where are you? Are you at home?"

The panic in his voice was unmistakable, and that was all it took for Marisol's to jump into the same register.

"What's wrong? What's happened?"

"You've got to leave town, Marisol. Take the kids and go, right now."

"Go where? Miguel, you're scaring me. What's happened?"

"Go to your parents. No— Go to the airport. To Alberto's."

"In California? Miguel, please, what are you talking about? What kind of trouble are you in?"

Fuentes heaved a sigh, stared past the meager parking lot and into the sun-blighted desert beyond.

His eyes widened, and his arm dropped to his side. The phone slipped from his slack hand, dropped soundlessly to the ground.

"Miguel? Hello?"

"Mother of Christ," Fuentes whispered.

Perhaps he was hallucinating. He blinked, rubbed his eyes, hauled off and slapped himself hard in the face like some kind of goddamn Loony Tunes character.

Nothing doing. They were still there.

Thousands of them, streaming over a hill in the distance, and down across the flat plain.

Swarming like ants. The entire landscape suddenly dark with bodies.

And those bodies were headed straight toward him. Toward the town, as if it represented no impediment whatsoever to their progress. As if they didn't even notice it, any more than a tsunami noticed land.

Fuentes felt the bile rise in his throat. He bent double, hands on his knees, waiting for his insides to knot and rebel, but still he craned his neck up at the approaching storm. The coming plague.

It didn't matter that they were young, female, dressed in rags or sundresses or nothing at all.

Fuentes knew an army when he saw one.

He could smell the stench of death in the air.

The closest ones had left the hill behind now, halved the distance to him in the scant, frozen minutes he'd been watching.

Fuentes's phone rang—Marisol trying to figure out what was

going on—but he couldn't process the sound. It entered his mind as a death knell.

Run, he thought, but could barely stand.

A gush of vomit poured from him, splashed hot against the ground. He gagged, spat, squinted back up at the advancing army.

And found the ground erupting, giving birth to more.

There and *there* and *there.*

The new recruits fell seamlessly into step with their sisters, joined a progression that was swift and wordless, chillingly efficient, silent except for the cacophony of footfalls.

It was loud enough to bring the rest of the bar's patrons spilling outside. A dozen others joined Fuentes in the next few seconds—first with the boozy joviality of men finding distraction in an unexpected spectacle, and then with the quiet terror of men gazing upon a scene out of some ancient, communal nightmare.

Since Fuentes had gotten there first—or maybe because he comported himself like a man who'd looked into the devil's eyes—they all deferred to him.

"The fuck is that, cabrón?" the man closest to him asked in a guttural whisper. He was a rangy dude, none too steady on his feet, and as he spoke he gestured with an almost-empty beer bottle.

"The Virgin Army," Fuentes heard himself say. The words sounded far off and hollow, as if his mouth were a cave. There was a bitter taste on his tongue, a taste like ash.

The guy elbowed him in the shoulder, like Fuentes had made a joke. "Yeah, right," he said. "Tell me another one, Grandpa."

Then he looked for himself—really looked—and shut the fuck up.

Dozens of people were standing in the street now; every business on the strip that comprised this town's commercial district had emptied out. Women with their hair in curlers stood crossing themselves in front of the salon across the street; old men stood gape jawed before the bodega on the corner.

No one ran; no one even spoke. It was as if they'd all, somehow, been waiting their whole lives for this moment. And now that it was here, there was nothing left to fear, no illusion that they had any agency in the face of it.

The girls were almost upon them now—crossing out of the desert and into the town by the score. The great river of bodies cleaved in half to stream around the back of the bar and then re-formed, whole again.

They never once broke stride. And they paid absolutely no mind to the living.

Fuentes stood still and let the endless wave of girls wash over him, and everybody else did exactly the same. They were all inside the same spell, he thought, the watchers and the walkers—or no, the opposite, it was like they occupied two entirely different worlds and one just so happened to be passing in front of the other at that moment, gliding over the face of it like the moon eclipsing the sun.

For the first minute, he didn't even breathe. At any instant, half a dozen of them were close enough to touch.

All that young, supple flesh.

Young, supple, cold, and dead.

Fuentes didn't know whether to pop a boner or drop dead from fear. But the stampede went on, thousands of them passing by as thick and swift as driven cattle, and kicking up just as much dust. And like anything, it became normal after a while.

Maybe not *normal.*

Fuentes was breathing again, though.

This too shall pass.

Wait it out, man. Just wait it out.

Rest of your problems are gonna look a whole lot better afterward, cuz as fucked up as your life is, it ain't half as fucked up as a billion undead bitches headed who knows where to do who knows what to who knows who.

Even as he thought it, Fuentes realized he knew.

Cucuy.

Who else could it be?

Either they'd been summoned, or they were on the warpath. Hell, maybe the Virgin Army was his fucking salvation. The enemy of his enemy.

The monster's monster.

A man could dream, couldn't he?

The stream of girls was thinning; a second battalion was crossing the hill, but they weren't here yet. Fuentes and his fellow witnesses stood in the eye of the hurricane.

That was when he saw the palanquin.

It was a word he knew from reading King Arthur stories to his sons—not something he'd ever had the opportunity to use in conversation, much less lay eyes on in the real world.

Twelve girls gripped the ends of the long wood beams that supported it, three walking on each of the four sides, their pace stately, their footfalls synchronized, so as not to jostle whoever was inside the long, curtained box that sat atop the beams.

The queen, thought Fuentes, and his throat constricted. Did one bow? Kneel? Avert his eyes? Run back inside and hide behind the bar?

No, you fuckshit. Just be cool. This too shall pass.

The porters' bearing was regal: backs straight, chins level with the ground, eyes thousand-yard staring into a future Fuentes couldn't even fathom.

The palanquin drew closer, the curtains billowing in a sudden, slight breeze, and Fuentes braced himself.

He had to look. Lay eyes on the one whose will had set these beings in motion.

The conveyance drew parallel now. Fuentes mopped the sweat pouring into his eyes and bent forward to peer inside.

There were four people seated against the straight wooden walls. Three women and a man. But Fuentes only had eyes for one.

She was cold and radiant as the moon, with jet-black hair and skin as pale as alabaster.

When her emerald eyes met his, Fuentes felt a jolt of electricity surge through his body and knew he was in the presence of unfathomable power.

"Command me," he heard himself say, voice husky with a desire he couldn't begin to understand. "Tell me what to do, my queen, and I am yours."

The bearers stopped on a dime, and the entire army halted with them.

But it was not the queen's voice that rang through the air. It was the girl by her side, face smudged with grime, eyes blazing with hatred.

All at once, Fuentes realized who she was.

"He needs to die," Jess Galvan's daughter said. "He needs to die right fucking now."

The queen blinked.

The bearers resumed their inexorable march.

The Virgin Army fell into step ahead, next to, and behind.

Except for the six girls closest to Fuentes. They turned their heads toward him as one and saw a man where before there had been only scenery.

They fell on him together, and a moment later the arc of blood spurting from Miguel Fuentes's jugular vein painted a final monument to his life on the ground of the bar's parking lot.

CHAPTER 37

Math had never been her forte, but right now Sherry Richards
was running through calculations like her life depended on
the results.

Maybe because it did.

One girl a week? One girl a day?

If it was only one a week—and even that number was staggering, if
you stopped to remember that it wasn't a number but a life, snuffed out
in panic and agony long before its time—that added up to fifty-two a
year. Round it down to fifty, multiply it by five centuries, and you got
twenty-five thousand girls.

Subtract a few thou from that number, on the assumption that not
every one of them remained an able-bodied warrior. Certainly, men
like her father must have cut some down over the years, and perhaps
Chacanza had chosen not to roust others from their slumber to join
this siege; maybe she even had favorites who were exempt from combat. There had definitely been some kind of lesbo vibe going on back
at the cave.

A conservative reckoning of the force sweeping toward Ojos Negros, then, would fall somewhere in the range of twenty thousand.

That was a lot of fucking girls.

Sherry lifted her eyes and threw a furtive look across the palanquin at Chacanza, who sat rigid backed against the opposite wall.

The queen's eyes were closed, not that Sherry would have dared speak to her anyway. Her sole words to Chacanza had come untold miles back, when they'd run across Fuentes in that little shitstain of a town.

Don't get it twisted, she told herself, watching Chacanza's eyes dart back and forth beneath their closed lids, her smooth unlined face more expressive in repose than in waking life. *Don't let looks deceive. She's not human, any more than that thing was my father.*

Sherry's eyes drifted to the sleeping Gum, and she silently repeated the warning.

Surrounded by monsters.

What else was new?

She flashed on Cucuy and the offer he had made.

You can live, you can die, or you can join him.

It took her several moments to realize that the sound filling the makeshift room came from Cantwell, and another few to process the noise and realize her friend was sobbing.

Had been sobbing for some time.

"What's wrong?" Sherry asked, and instantly felt idiotic, given the circumstances of the conversation.

What wasn't?

Cantwell's hands cradled her belly. "I don't wanna lose him," she whispered, voice ragged and hoarse.

"Oh, so it's a boy now?" Sherry said, trying for levity. The kid was Tic Tac sized, after all.

Cantwell didn't seem to get the joke. "Yes," she said, nodding her head gravely, and then seeming to forget how to stop.

Sherry peeled away one of Ruth's hands and clasped it between her own. It was clammy, despite the overwhelming heat.

"Look at me."

Cantwell blinked out a few more tears, then complied.

"I'm not gonna let anything happen to either one of you, okay? That's a promise."

How the fuck she intended to make good on that, Sherry had no idea. But she felt her spine stiffen and knew she believed it.

From the look on her face, so did Cantwell.

That was something, anyway.

Just then the smoothness of the ride gave way to a rhythmic bumpiness, as if the bearers had stepped onto a more even, less forgiving surface. Sherry pulled back the curtains and saw asphalt below. She craned her neck to look forward, and there it was.

Ojos Negros. Squat and giant, shimmering in the midday sun, and by all appearances blissfully unaware of the approaching hell.

The gates stood partway open, and even from a quarter mile's remove, through the moving scrim of female bodies, the place bustled with industry. The sliver of yard Sherry could see afforded a glimpse of a line of men unloading parcels from what looked like a large military truck, and another group assembling some kind of contraption made from gleaming metal parts. The guard towers looming above all stood vacant, as if no further supervision was needed—and indeed, the yard looked like a factory floor operating at peak efficiency.

What it looked nothing like, Sherry realized, was a prison.

Nor did these men look like prisoners.

Prisoners didn't carry guns.

They didn't build cannons.

Chacanza was awake now, her energy like a frigid blast of air on Sherry's neck.

She turned and found herself eye to eye with the queen. Sherry fell back and watched as Chacanza took in the scene, the prison.

The army.

Any second, one of those men would look up, see their approach, and sound an alarm.

The battle would begin.

And sooner or later, the monster shaped like her father would appear.

The mere thought made Sherry feel like her heart was about to explode inside her chest.

"It's a trap," she heard herself say. "We're too late. He's already got an army."

Chacanza didn't seem to hear. She murmured something under her breath, craned her neck to the sky. Her eyes zagged wildly across the landscape, memorizing it.

Or, perhaps, remembering.

"What'd you say?" Sherry asked.

All at once, the soldiers came to a halt. Twenty thousand girls stood motionless, and the air seemed to throb with silence. The absence of footfalls.

"This was a temple once," the queen repeated, still gazing beyond her—beyond everything, it seemed to Sherry. Into a past far realer than any danger the present had to offer.

Something like a smile touched the corner of her lip.

"And a temple it shall be again."

DOMINGO VALENTINE STOOD beneath the flickering candlelight of the Ancient One's library, nestled along the deepest corridor of Ojos Negros's many warrens. His attention was in high demand elsewhere; there were takeoffs and landings to schedule, prison uprisings to coordinate in Arizona, Florida, Chiapas, and Guadalajara, monies to be couriered to various overseas accounts, cartel operations to be scheduled and consolidated, redundant personnel to be retired.

Corporate restructuring was a bitch.

His weapons of choice beckoned: the satellite phone lying atop his desk and the triple-encrypted, military-issue laptop that sat next to it. But until the Great One dismissed him, Valentine would stand right here, watching Cucuy pore through the blood-burgundy pages of his sacred book, and marvel at all that the Great One had wrought and all that was to come.

It was in this very room that he'd discovered the master's putrefying body. But had he doubted? Abandoned his belief or his post? Not for an instant. His faith had been unstinting, his work dogged.

He had prepared the way—just as John the Baptist had done for Jesus, according to the boy-fucking priests of his youth. Without Valentine, the master might not sit before him now, resplendent and reborn, ready to rise up from the depths in which he had been mired and retake the world.

His strength was a rising tide that would lift all ships.

Especially the S.S. *Valentine*.

It was time to think big, to envision his place in the new world that was coming. And in whatever spare moments he could find, the pro-curer found himself remembering the countless childhood hours he'd spent watching the ocean. Reading the surf as if it held the secret of his future. Gazing out at the distant ships sitting so placidly atop the clam-oring, crashing waves, their bellies full of cargo, monuments to both freedom and service.

Valentine pictured himself standing on the top deck of a massive yacht, its prow jutting through turquoise waters, the ship simultane-ously tranquil and perpetually in motion.

He would be the ruler of all he surveyed, his reach second only to Cucuy himself. And perhaps, just perhaps, in gratitude for all he had done to turn adversity to triumph—perhaps a door could be opened for him and Valentine could become more than a man himself. The sorcery of the Timeless One knew no bounds, now that he had cast off his weakened form as the wasp did the chrysalis. Surely there must be some way to—

With a dry slap of parchment on parchment, Cucuy shut the book and raised his head. The black of his eyes seemed to swirl, to suck the meager light toward themselves like twin black holes. He stood, the faint luminescence of his body intensifying, turned on his heel, and strode into the corridor.

Valentine scurried after, the Terrible One's light filling what had been a pitch-black passageway, the question out of his mouth before he could stop it.

"Is something wrong, master?"

Cucuy spun toward him, and Valentine instinctively threw up his arms in fear.

As if that would do anything, in the event that the master chose to strike him.

But it was not anger that played on his lips.

It was a smile.

Cruel and wide.

"She is close by," he said, and stalked down the hall.

Valentine panted as he sprinted to keep up. Cucuy appeared to be walking but moved at a phenomenal speed, as if the Timeless One existed in some sped-up version of reality, the glow of his body streaming out behind him like the phosphorescent tentacles of a jellyfish.

Cucuy took the steepest, most direct path, the grade forcing Valentine to walk nearly doubled over, thighs burning with the effort. The temperature rose as they left the cool, damp underground for the parched, scorching surface.

The sound so overwhelmed at first that it didn't register in the procurer's mind—the clamor filled the whole auditory spectrum, canceling itself out like the crash of surf or the blare of traffic.

And then, as the sunlight penetrated the wide mouth of the tunnel, it hit him all at once.

The bloodcurdling screams of killers, and the moans and prayers of dying men.

The staccato report of thousands of guns, the cacophony as dense and oppressive as the acrid clouds of smoke floating toward him.

He turned the final corner and braced himself, knowing he was about to look upon the face of war.

But nothing could have prepared Valentine for what he saw when he stepped into the light.

This wasn't just war.

This was Armageddon.

The besieging army poured into the prison yard unchecked—their numbers unfathomable, the desert black with their bodies. The men had commandeered the guard towers, were spraying barrages of AK-47 fire into the oncoming horde. But it made no difference; they might as well have been firing into the ocean.

The wave swept on.

And all at once, Valentine understood who the enemy was.

That they could not be killed, because they were already dead.

Each and every one of them, at Cucuy's hands.

Already, they swarmed over the men, like some time-lapse nature film showing how piranhas turned a cow into a skeleton. Their teeth were lethal weapons; their numbers overwhelming. The elaborate weaponry of the prisoners was useless at close quarters, obsolete in a battle that seemed torn from mankind's most ancient, terrifying past.

Valentine's head darted from left to right. Everywhere he looked, a tableau of utter carnage unfolded.

Two blood-spattered girls pinned down a man, his handgun firing uselessly into the sky as a third found his carotid artery and a geyser of blood arced through the air. They were up in a flash, swarming their next victim.

A pair of prisoners stood back-to-back, their faces contorted in wide-eyed, last-stand roars as they spun and fired, heedless of the comrades they might take down. The girls converged on them from all sides, as if by telepathic consensus, absorbed the shelling until they were close enough to pounce. The men disappeared in a writhing frenzy of arms, legs, hair, tits, ass.

The will of the men was at its breaking point. Utter derangement hit some full on; they tried to scrabble their way up the prison yard's unscalable walls, or turned tail and fled toward the tiered cell blocks—though even in the blind flush of their panic, not a single prisoner headed for the tunnels; either they were unaware of the netherworld of chambers that lay below the prison, or they feared it more than death.

The girls chased them down, triangulating and herding, lions after antelope. The iron scent of blood was everywhere, mingling with the gun smoke and the spreading stench of shit as doomed men's bowels voided in a last act of release.

Valentine stepped back into the corridor, the protection of shadows. He might be a killer, but he was not a soldier. This death was not for him.

The thought cleared his mind, like a sudden gust of wind dispersing clouds, and Valentine realized that the Timeless One had disappeared—charged out of this very tunnel moments before—and was nowhere to be seen upon the battlefield. His heart surged with new confidence, and he castigated himself for his momentary lapse in faith.

What were these abominations to the master?

A moment later, Domingo Valentine had his answer.

A thunderclap boomed across the sky, so sharp and deafening it felt like a slap across the eardrum. The procurer rushed forward, reached the mouth of the tunnel just as the sky went dark.

The sun had been snuffed out, abruptly and completely, casting the prison yard into a midnight blackness.

For an instant, everything stopped, as if both commanders—Cucuy and the unseen consciousness masterminding the invasion, the *she* who had brought that wicked smile to the master's lips—had agreed on a time-out, their forces frozen like the warriors adorning the frieze of some Greek temple.

And then, slowly at first, light returned to the world.

The sun had changed shape.

The sun was a man now.

He stood atop the prison wall, legs spread and arms raised to the sky. The glow emanated from his heart; Valentine could see it pulse, grow hotter.

Orange red.

Pale blue.

Pure white.

And then, as if the proper conditions for combustion had been achieved, the heat began to spread, to flow like magma through the intricate, filigreed system of his veins, each one becoming visible as it spread.

Valentine dropped to his knees.

I will never doubt you again, Great One.

The light or heat or energy or whatever the fuck it was reached his fingertips, and Cucuy's raised arms shot downward, like a pianist sounding a concert's first notes.

The light cut through the darkness, ten blinding high beams forked and divided in midair, branched and rebranched.

By the time they reached the combatants on the ground, there were hundreds of them.

Each one found the chest of a Virgin Army soldier and lit her up like a paper lantern. They thrashed, tried to escape, but the light was like a tractor beam; it held them immobile, penetrated their bodies until they, too, glowed from within.

The scent of burning flesh rose from them, and Valentine flashed on childhood afternoons spent immolating ants with a magnifying glass.

But this was something else.

A moment later, in perfect synchronicity, every last girl caught in Cucuy's clutch exploded into a fountain of charred flesh and black blood.

They spattered the ground like tiny storms of hail, and Valentine released the breath he hadn't realized he was holding.

The sun was back in the sky now, shining down on a very different war. Cucuy raised his arms toward it again, and Valentine understood, with a rush of elation, that he was reloading.

SHERRY WATCHED FROM the palanquin, perched high atop a hill that afforded a perfect sight line into the prison yard.

Chacanza had startled when the beams hit, and she twitched when the girls went down, wrenched as if she could feel their pain.

By the time the monster destroyed a second cadre of warriors, the queen's face was a mask of dismay and hatred. Her army was in disarray; some of them sprinted away from Ojos Negros and others fought on, flailing at the rejuvenated prisoners as if the goal was to savage as many as possible before their own inevitable demise. But their coordination was off, the hive mind ruptured; they no longer moved in orchestrated collaboration.

The mind controlling them was divided against itself, Sherry thought. She glanced over at Chacanza, but the queen was gone.

Cucuy's third strike took down as many as the first two combined. The sun blinked like a loose lightbulb in the sky, and Sherry braced herself for more, wondered how far his reach extended, where the limits of his power lay.

If there were any.

She found Chacanza standing just outside the conveyance, staring straight at him. Sherry couldn't begin to fathom the look on her face. How long had the queen lain in wait, in secrecy, building her strength, spoiling for war?

The answer, it seemed, was *too long*.

And now she was exposed. Routed. Hemorrhaging soldiers, forced to watch as the enemy's tentacles began their insidious creep across the face of the world.

Sherry had been wrong. He did not *think* he was invulnerable. He *was* invulnerable.

And if she was to keep her promise to Cantwell, they had to get the fuck out of there right now.

Sherry wasn't afraid to say so.

She stepped before the queen to block her view. "Hey. We gotta go. Now. Before it's too late. Before he sees you."

"He cannot kill me," Chacanza answered, but her voice was hollow, flat. "He cannot even see me, unless I allow it to be so." She moved a step to her right, reestablished her vigil.

Sherry stepped in front of her again.

"Yeah, well, he can kill me. And my friend. We've gotta fall back. Make another plan."

"No."

The voice came from behind her. Sherry turned. Gum was hauling himself out of the palanquin, rubbing the crust from his eyes.

"We've gotta stay the course."

Sherry felt her sap rise. "Are you out of your fucking mind?" She jabbed a finger toward Ojos. "Take a look. While you've been sleeping, we've been getting slaughtered."

Gum's lank body vibrated with urgency, the man suddenly a tuning fork. He wrapped one clammy hand around Sherry's forearm, then reached out, grabbed Chacanza with the other, spun her toward him.

"Galvan," he said. "I seen him. And Tezcatlipoca. I was with 'em both." He found Chacanza's eyes. "I seen you too."

"What did you see?" Sherry demanded. "What's happening?"

Another web of light flashed down from Cucuy's hands, and Chacanza buckled at the knees as hundreds more of her followers were obliterated.

Gum watched it happen, then turned back to them and swallowed hard.

"We've gotta buy him more time."

CHAPTER 38

Galvan plummeted through the void, arms and legs pinwheeling. He clawed at the empty air, opened his mouth to scream—

Wait.

Hold on, motherfucker.

Calm your stupid ass down.

Breathe.

This wasn't free fall. This was a holding pattern. A waiting room. Tezcatlipoca was stitching together a world, building a crucible in which to drop him. Best thing to do was center himself, face whatever was coming with an empty mind, loose limbs, a total lack of expectations.

Strip himself down to reflex and muscle.

Luckily, a lifetime of being an impulsive knucklehead and three months of tamping down the Aztec priest trying to colonize his body had prepared Galvan nicely for this contingency.

Wasn't much point in trying to anticipate what a crazy, sadistic, drug-addled deity might dream up anyway.

There was ground beneath him now, a landscape of red clay dirt and scrub brush that spread across the nothingness like spilled water.

Galvan felt his velocity diminish as he fell toward it. When his feet touched the earth, he came down gently, as if he wore a parachute.

At least Tezcatlipoca wasn't trying to handicap the match.

Galvan got into a ready crouch and did a slow three-sixty, scanning this barren, horizonless world for whoever or whatever it was he was supposed to fight.

You must prove yourself worthy to be my sword.

With his feet under him and his senses coming back online, the god's words took on new shades of possibility.

Put another way, that shit could mean anything.

There was no reason to assume he'd have to vanquish some fuckin' mythical beast. Maybe Tezcatlipoca wanted to see if he had the mental toughness to endure a hundred years of isolation.

Or a hundred years of torture.

Or, hell, put together a million-piece jigsaw puzzle.

What was time to an immortal?

It was hard to know where the three-sixty was supposed to end; nothing in this hastily created world provided Galvan with a landmark. He made two full rotations before he found what he was looking for.

And even then, it was the last thing he expected to see.

Standing fifteen feet away from Galvan, as if he had just sprouted from the earth—

Was Galvan.

It was like looking in a mirror. The man staring back at him was identical in every way, down to the loincloth wrapped around his waist, the furrowed brow, the look of heated confusion flashing in his eyes.

The large stone in his right hand.

Galvan broke off staring and looked down the length of his own arm.

Sure enough, he was clutching the same stone.

The same weapon.

What else could it be? What else could *this* be? It made sense—as much sense as anything else Tezcatlipoca could have thrown at him, anyway.

What better way to prove your worthiness, your will, your mettle, than by vanquishing yourself?

In that fucker's mind, anyway. What Tezcatlipoca didn't know about Galvan could fill a fucking warehouse.

Killing himself was nothing new.

He planted his back leg, cocked back his arm, and hurled the rock at the other Galvan's head with all his might.

Halfway to its target, it collided with the rock Galvan's enemy had hurled at him, and both projectiles fell to the ground.

Galvan looked down at his empty hand and willed a gun to appear.

By the time he raised and fired, the enemy had done the same. The bullets met in midair, just as the rocks had, lead meeting lead, the tips crushing each other and the deformed lumps jumping slightly apart as they, too, fell uselessly to the ground.

Galvan's mind raced.

He doesn't just look like me, he thinks like me. Moves like me.

Is me.

I've gotta go outside myself. Do some shit I'd never think of.

Before he does the same.

Galvan threw himself sideways, squeezed off three shots before he hit the ground shoulder first, and watched in consternation as the enemy executed precisely the same move, the bullets canceling each other out.

He scrabbled to his feet, cast the weapon aside, and charged at the other Galvan, full speed ahead.

It wasn't an original idea.

The right cross Galvan threw never met the jaw for which it was intended. Instead, with a sickening bone-on-bone crunch, it met its mirror-image blow, and Galvan's fist learned how those bullets must have felt.

He howled in agony and spun away, cradled his shattered hand, the sound and action doubled.

They regarded each other warily now, twin lions pacing invisible cages, Galvan trying to think through the pain. Whatever deathless-realm quick-healing shit applied to Tezcatlipoca's fuck buddies definitely wasn't in effect here; at least three of his knuckles were broken, the hand mangled and useless.

You're real, Galvan thought feverishly, clenching and unclenching his good fist, his fury mounting as the enemy did the same. *He's not.*

Even if his fuckin' brain is an exact replica of yours, your pain still runs deeper and your anger burns hotter. You been through hell and you got shit to fight for. All he's got is what you give him.

And all you've gotta be is one heartbeat quicker. Get close enough that copycat shit won't cut it, and break that motherfucker's neck.

Do it for the world.

For Nichols.

For Sherry.

Take all the rage and suffering you've ever felt and turn that shit into a grenade, pull the pin, and cram it down his throat.

Galvan didn't know he was running until he saw the other Galvan doing the same. They collided like opposing tackles at the line of scrimmage, and a half phrase Galvan had picked up in high school physics flashed through his mind.

Something about equal and opposite forces.

He couldn't remember the rest, but he knew this much: he didn't have one iota more strength than this guy. He was putting everything he had into gaining the slightest advantage—calves and thighs, chest and arms straining, blood pounding in his veins—and anybody watching would have thought they were a goddamn statue.

So give. Drop your knees and flip him up and over. Use his own momentum against him.

The instant he did it, so did the other—matching Galvan's precise reduction of torque, the exact bend of his legs. They fell to their knees together, still locked in a stalemate.

Galvan wrested his left hand free, raised it to the sky, called down a sword, a knife, some kind of fucking blade. A moment later, he felt the cool hilt in his hand and brought it slicing toward the enemy's vein-engorged neck.

It clanged against metal instead, and suddenly Galvan's head filled with an echo, a memory, a rebroadcast of Cucuy's voice.

The very voice that had done him in.

You cannot outrun me, Jess Galvan.

He sprang backward, escaped from the grappling deadlock; it would have been impossible had his opponent not matched the action.

Again, they regarded each other from across a chasm of inches.

The man and the shadow.

This time, Galvan had a new thought.

What is it that makes me human?

Until I know that, I cannot win.

STAY CLOSE TO me if you want to survive.

There was so much Sherry didn't understand about those words.

Why Chacanza gave a fuck whether she lived or died, for one.

How proximity to the undead woman currently charging into battle against her ancient, all-powerful lover and sure to command his complete attention the moment he saw her was any kind of recipe for personal well-being, for another.

But here was Sherry, scurrying along in Chacanza's wake as the queen entered the gates of the prison, Cantwell by her side, the three of them flanked by an honor guard of girls, the palanquin and whatever safety or anonymity it afforded abandoned at the top of the hill.

Apparently, buying her father more time—another phrase Sherry was sure she didn't understand—translated to Chacanza as a full frontal assault on Cucuy's stronghold. There he stood, even now, arms raised to the sun, unfathomable power roiling through him and all of it, every last ounce, focused on destruction.

And yet, when she looked at him, all Sherry could see was her father. His poor, colonized body, enslaved by the monster's invisible yoke and driven by its invisible whip.

For her.

Wherever you are, Dad, hurry the fuck back.

Cucuy's gaze dropped from the heavens to the earth, his black eyes flashing.

A current of electricity rattled through her body, and Sherry knew he had seen her.

She prayed it would not hurt.

The beams shot from his hands. Forked and divided into hundreds of tendrils that crackled through the air.

An instant before they found their marks, Chacanza raised her eyes to his, and her voice cut through the air with as much force as his weaponry.

"Cualli!"

The beams froze in midair.

And then, like tributaries emptying into the ocean, they flowed backward, unbranched, became a single spear of energy.

He sees her, Sherry thought, dumbstruck.

And then, *That can't be good.*

Cucuy smiled.

If you could call it that.

Then the beam shot forward and hit Chacanza square in the chest.

Sherry heard herself scream. She grabbed Ruth and ran for cover, all that *stay close to me* shit out the window now that the one who'd said it was nanoseconds from bursting like a water balloon.

Her eyes darted frantically across the yard, in search of safe haven. Chacanza's troops were frozen, as immobile as their commander, useless as marionettes without the puppeteer. Some of the Ojos Negros prisoners took the opportunity to drop them with head shots from point-blank range—walking up to them in disbelief and on tiptoe, as if approaching some wild animal that had wandered onto their lawn. Others closed in on the girls with hideous leers spread across their faces; it was dawning on the true scumbags in the crowd that there were other things that could be done to these suddenly oblivious girls.

Most of them, though, stared up at Cucuy, transfixed, waiting. They must have sensed that the battle hinged on these next few moments, on the stunning green-eyed beauty on whom their master's focus rested.

Sherry darted through their ranks, Ruth's hand in hers, until she reached the mouth of a tunnel at the edge of the yard. They stepped inside, and darkness enveloped them. Sherry pressed against the cool wall, her heavy breath echoing against the low ceiling, and peered back out at the battlefield.

Chacanza was still standing.

Still alive.

Still dead.

Whatever the fuck.

And whatever Cucuy threw at her, the queen absorbed.

Or stole. Her body pulsed with the same energy as his now.

But it was more than that, Sherry realized with a surge of hope. She was holding him at bay. Locking him down. That beam might as well have been a rope, and Chacanza was holding on tight.

Buying them time.

No sooner had she thought it than a cool hand encircled her wrist, and Sherry heard the soft click of a pistol's hammer at her ear.

"Nice to see you again," intoned Domingo Valentine.

GALVAN BROUGHT THE blade to rest at his side and shut his eyes, trusting his shadow would do the same—and that what they'd see would be different.

He was staking everything on a concept that had never made a lick of fucking sense to him.

What makes me human?

Faith.

Try to feel some.

Ask and ye shall receive, or whatever the fuck.

With that, Galvan reached out, projected his mind and soul into the cold dark universe, through realms and dimensions unseen and unknown, in search of anything resembling a friend of mankind.

Pinpricks of light shot past him in the darkness, Galvan traveling at the speed of light or thought or who knew what and finding only emptiness, desolation, the very cosmos he'd always envisioned as a cynical kid, a jaded adult, life on this planet just a one-in-a-zillion coincidence and nothing else out there but rock, gas, and crushing sadness.

Then one point of light glowed brighter than the rest, and everything slowed until Galvan felt a sense of absolute stillness.

The point of light grew larger, brighter, until it seemed to scour his insides and burn his soul clean.

Until it had a face.

A name.

Chimalma.

He didn't know who or what that was, but Chimalma was the source of the buzz that filled his mind. He felt enveloped, subsumed into the womb of the feminine divine, a pulse of wisdom passing into him as if through an umbilical cord.

To call the sense of love he felt for Chimalma overwhelming wouldn't do it justice. He was not evolved enough to hold or understand love of that magnitude—could feel his consciousness push outward simply to make room for the feeling—and knew that if and when the connection was severed, a new order of misery, of desolation, would move in and fill it.

Knew with a sudden, fleeting clarity that it was precisely this desolation that afflicted and defined the world.

And then it happened. The light receded. The warmth drew back into itself, and Galvan was more alone than he had ever been.

Forsaken.

But he knew what he had to do.

The test Tezcatlipoca had set before him was not a question of physical prowess. One did not conquer the self through aggression, any more than a sword was capable of cutting through shadow.

Or, to put it in fortune cookie terms, *Man who fights himself will always lose.*

Galvan opened his eyes, and stared into the enemy's.

Which were, of course, his own.

He dropped the blade.

Fell to his knees.

And for the first time since he had materialized, Galvan's double did not respond in kind.

He simply stared.

Galvan knew the look on his face.

Utter incomprehension.

Exactly.

He took a step toward Galvan, the blade fisted in his hand.

Galvan spread his arms, threw his head back to the sky, the lack of sky, the unformed nothingness of this hastily sketched arena, and offered his neck to the blade.

I must look, he thought, *like Jesus on the cross.*

The very lie, the exact perversion that had steered mankind's ship through an ocean of desolation.

God does not die for man.

Man dies for god.

But not today.

He heard another footstep, and then a third, but Galvan didn't move.

Sometimes you gotta lose to win, he told himself, blinking up at the formless void above.

Thesis, antithesis, synthesis.

Or whatever the fuck.

The footfalls stopped, and for a moment there was silence. He could hear his own breathing, but not the other's. Either it was so synchronized as to be indistinguishable, or this motherfucker didn't need oxygen.

Galvan held out as long as he could before he lowered his head and looked.

When their eyes met, the being before him smiled. And then, like water streaming down the face of rock, his form melted away and Galvan was staring up at Tezcatlipoca, the Divine Sorcerer, Bringer of Glory, Most Fearsome and Beloved, Supreme Fuckwad.

The enemy of my enemy . . .

Galvan's knees creaked as he stood.

"So," he said. "Do I get the job, or what?"

Tezcatlipoca blinked.

And once again, the world fell away.

CHAPTER 39

"He told me you'd come back," Valentine hissed, jerking Sherry's arm behind her back with such force it brought tears to her eyes. "You're in his plans, girlie."

He spun, pointed the gun at Cantwell.

"You, not so much."

The moment Valentine took his eyes off her, Sherry made him pay. She turned her free hand into a fist, the fist into a mallet, and swung it backward at the procurer's balls with all the strength she had.

He yelped and doubled over in pain, his gun hand falling instinctively to his crotch, the grip on Sherry's arm slackening. She jerked free, turned, and kneed him in the face. The gun clattered to the ground, and Sherry grabbed it as he staggered, off balance, only the wall behind him preventing Valentine from going down.

"I've got my own plans," she panted, and pressed the barrel to his forehead.

Ruth stepped toward her. "Sherry. Don't."

She scowled. "Why the fuck not?"

Ruth's hand found her wrist, exactly as Valentine's had.

"Because," she said softly. "We might need the bullets."

She lifted Sherry's hand, the gun with it, and slammed the butt of the pistol against the back of Valentine's head. He collapsed into a heap at their feet. The two of them stepped over him and peered out into the light.

At Cucuy and Chacanza.

The unstoppable force and the immovable object, locked in an unbreakable stalemate, that beam of savage energy suspended between them like a bridge to heaven or a slide to hell.

"Something's gotta give," Ruth muttered, without taking her eyes off them. "And we've gotta get out of here before it does. And fuck those tunnels."

A burst of gunfire punctuated the sentiment. They both fell silent and surveyed the yard. The men roamed across it now with the swagger of Old West sheriffs, some of them still potshot-dropping the motionless girls, but most busy tensing for what came next.

Saving their bullets, just like Ruth was saving hers.

They just happened to have about ten thousand more of them.

"You're crazy if you think we're getting through there," Sherry said, gesturing with the gun. Its weight felt good in her hand. Natural, like an extension of her fist, her will.

But it didn't solve a goddamn thing.

"Well, we can't st—"

Sherry raised her arm. Ruth saw the look on her face and shut up.

Something was happening out there. A new instability, a growing imbalance between the combatants. Sherry could sense it even if she couldn't pinpoint it.

Much less handicap it.

Something was about to give.

And sure enough, a moment later Cucuy's body spasmed atop the high wall of the prison, the beams lifting off Chacanza, becoming long whips, flailing uselessly against the sky. It was as if she'd pulled that old kids' tug-of-war trick, where you released your hold and let your opponent's own sudden lack of static equilibrium topple him over backward

For several heart-stopping seconds he teetered there, arms pinwheeling, torso spinning an invisible hula hoop.

Then two things happened at once, as Sherry watched breathlessly from below.

The black drained from Cucuy's eyes.

And he plummeted thirty-five feet, to the hard-packed ground below.

BLACKNESS. THEN CHAOS—THE sunlight blinding, the power too much to control, Ojos and the girls and the queen, and *what the fuck is going on*, Galvan's soul or whatever slamming back into a flesh-and-blood body and realizing upon impact that what he'd inhabited in the Dominio Gris was only the rumor of one, a sensation like stepping out of weightlessness and into gravity.

And then the fall.

Blackness again.

Blackness and pain, searing and sharp. His legs tingled, but he didn't dare find out if he could make them move. Drawing breath into his lungs was challenging enough, each rib like a jagged piece of glass, stabbing him from inside.

Out of the blackness came a voice. Terrible, furious, and everywhere at once.

How can this be? The laws of the universe do not allow it!

Jess Galvan couldn't move, but he could damn well smile. As Cucuy's outrage spread through Galvan's body, inflaming every cell, he felt the old strength, the old resilience, course through him as well.

His broken bones fused back together. The air moved in and out of him with greater ease until all traces of pain were gone. His eyes fluttered open, and Galvan got his legs beneath him, pressed his right palm to the warm, blood-spattered ground, and stood.

He had the sensation of having awakened into a world in which time had stopped; of the thousands of men and women arrayed before him—alive, dead, undead, dying—not a soul moved more than a pair of eyeballs.

Inside his head, Cucuy railed.

However you have done this, your return is insignificant. You cannot contain me, Jess Galvan. Not before and not now. Your mind is weak. It is only a matter of time.

"Maybe so, but you ain't got time. I know how to kill you now, you piece of shit."

It took Galvan a moment to realize he'd said it out loud, and another to realize that the words had set the world back in motion. Two women were striding toward him from opposite directions, each one cutting a swath through the bodies that cluttered the battlefield.

One was his reason for being.

The other was his destiny.

Chacanza walked at a stately clip, a pace befitting a queen. She had waited this long to confront Cucuy; a few seconds more or less didn't appear to matter.

Sherry broke into a run, beat her there, and leaped into her father's arms the way she had when she was six years old. He lowered his head, pressed his cheek to hers, and inhaled the scent of her hair.

It smelled like sweat and dust and fire, with hints of kerosene and blood. Which was different from when she was six, but he'd take it.

You can't kill me, Cucuy sneered. *And when you fail, Jess Galvan, everyone and everything you love will pay. Take a good look around you. Because every last man you see here will have his way with your precious daughter.*

"Dad." Sherry buried her face in his neck. Whatever she said next was muffled by flesh and tears, but it didn't matter. Galvan was caught between the ecstasy of her embrace and the torment of once again being occupied, colonized. Cucuy slithered through him at blinding speed, a desperate and vicious snake.

He wasn't going to play the long game this time around.

Then again, neither was Galvan—and the knowledge that all this was fleeting, that he had made his deal with the devil and was only here to carry it out, was almost more than he could bear.

Sherry was still glued to him, as if she knew. She'd lost him so many times already, Galvan reflected. To divorce. To prison. To Cucuy. To the Dominio Gris.

Something hard was digging into his back, and all at once he realized that Sherry was clutching a gun. He wondered if she'd use it.

If she'd have to.

He raised his eyes and found Chacanza standing before him. Sherry sensed her too, broke the embrace, and came to stand beside him.

"Dad, this—"

"I know who she is."

He stepped forward, clasped his hands before him. "You helped me get back here," he told her. "Whether you know it or not."

Whatever you have seen of her, I have shown you, Cucuy raged. *She is not what you think. She will destroy you.*

The Ancient One's fear thudded through Galvan's veins; it was intoxicating, and he savored it.

"We must—" he began, then stopped short as he realized that thousands of eyes were boring into him; Cucuy's men were utterly at a loss, and still at his command. Galvan turned away from Chacanza and uttered a proclamation that rang out across the yard.

"Put down your weapons. This fight is done."

The men looked dubious, but they complied. The consensus slapped across their faces read *you'd have to be crazy to fuck with Cucuy.*

But there was one in every crowd.

And significantly more than that if that crowd happened to comprise a who's who of the region's biggest scumbags, who had spent the last few hours indulging their basest bloodlust and sensed the sudden waning of their leader's strength.

A jumbo-sized asshole toting an assault rifle was the first to pull a Chuck Heston and decide the gun would have to be pried from his cold, dead hands. He threw a defiant grin at the guys closest to him, then lifted the weapon and squeezed off a few rounds at the closest of Chacanza's minions. Kept riddling her even after she lay facedown in the dirt.

Galvan gave the queen a bow.

"Excuse me for a moment."

He was on the dude in a flash, relishing his renewed speed. Another fleeting pleasure.

Your taste is for blood. Do not be a fool. We are the same.

A moment later, he held both the dude's hands in his own, having ripped the dumb fucking meathead's arms off at the shoulders. He threw them into the dust and raised his eyes to the crowd.

"Anybody else forget how to follow orders?"

Nobody raised a hand.

"Now get the fuck out of here. Go to your cells. Go home to your families. I don't care. We're done."

He strode back to Chacanza, to Sherry. To Ruth Cantwell, now standing by his daughter's side.

The men began to drift away, this way and that, like so much flotsam and jetsam. There was a downtrodden, meandering quality to them; they had been given freedom, but it was a poor substitute for the purpose that had been so cruelly snatched away.

"Yours too," Galvan said to the queen. "You don't need them anymore."

Chacanza nodded. "So it must be," she said, and like a single organism, the girls began to stream toward the prison gate.

He wondered if they were happier here or there: as Chacanza's slaves, or Tezcatlipoca's. Given an equal measure of dominion, was the queen of the Virgin Army any better than the king of the Grey Realm?

Then again, perhaps happiness was beyond their capacity. Perhaps suffering was, as well.

Lucky them.

"He speaks to you, does he not?" Chacanza asked.

"He does."

She came closer. Closer. Stopped a foot away from Galvan and stared into his eyes, her gaze no less hypnotic than in his dreams, visions, the Dominio Gris. Only the smell of her breath was different: rotten where it had been sweet. But Galvan noted it without revulsion; somehow, the tinge of suffering made her all the more alluring.

"What is he saying now?"

Galvan felt as if his spirit was pulling away from his body and floating toward hers. He couldn't separate his desire from her magnetism, cause from effect, and maybe such distinctions were pointless.

"He's quiet," Galvan told her. "It's . . . I've never felt it before. It's like he's paralyzed or something."

"He is in conflict," Chacanza said. "He feels both love and hate. As do I."

She stepped even closer, took Galvan's face in her hands, stared through his eyes, into whatever cavern or crevice in which Cucuy lurked.

Her voice was lush, low, but the edges of her words were razor sharp. "Cualli. Listen to me now, and listen well. I do not blame you for betraying me. You were a man who served a god. You knew not what you did. But this ends now."

She let go of Galvan's face, stepped back a pace. "Say your good-byes and follow me. There is somewhere we must go."

The moment she turned away, Cucuy swelled, his presence flooding every pore of Galvan's consciousness. His panic was wordless, but unbearably loud—a screeching, seething, fulminating protest that filled every register with notes of terror and rage, resistance and persuasion. Galvan wanted to scream, to tear at his hair, to beat his brains out against the nearest wall.

Instead he squared his shoulders and staggered to Sherry, found tears streaming freely down her cheeks.

"Don't leave me."

He had to read the words off her lips, the buzzsaw wail in his head was so loud.

"I gotta go, baby," Galvan said, or thought he did.

"Then take me with you."

But he knew Sherry understood that was impossible. They were just words. Galvan took her in his arms, put his lips to her ear, told Sherry he loved her and assumed she said the same.

The blood in his veins felt as if it were boiling now. He pulled back, looked his daughter in the eye, memorized every last beautiful detail.

"Who knows," he said, and tried to smile. "I came back once, right? Maybe I can do it again."

He didn't believe it for a goddamn second, but it looked like maybe, just maybe, she did. Sherry gulped and nodded, and Galvan squeezed her hand one final time and trudged away, toward the waiting Chacanza, crying himself now. He threw his daughter one mournful over-the-shoulder glance after another until the darkness of the tunnel fell over him like an executioner's hood, and the world of sun and tears and people became a thing of memory.

SHE HAD NOT traveled this system of tunnels in five hundred years— not since the world was alive with promise and the presence of the gods filled it with grace. Not since she was a radiant young bride, and this cobwebbed labyrinth of misery a monument to divine and ever-lasting glory.

But Chacanza knew exactly where she was going.

Nothing was ever lost. Not while memory lived on.

And here, at the end of her days, time had become a serpent, eating its own tail.

She was leading her husband to their wedding chamber. The sacred place of transformation. Where one life was meant to end, as a new one began.

Now, as ever, it was where Chacanza would find peace.

The tunnels wound, branched, and spiraled, leading downward and onward, but Chacanza never hesitated. The path was imprinted on her consciousness. She could have walked it blind.

The man, the vessel, followed behind, a torch in his hand. Before long they were so deep that the earth muffled all sound, and there was nothing to hear but his labored breath and both their footfalls, nothing to see but their own deformed shadows, bobbing against the walls. She wondered what Cualli was thinking as he floated in his prison, what poisonous bile or honeyed words spewed from him at this very moment.

Whether a part of him craved this. Longed for sweet obliteration, as she did.

The answer depended on how much of him remained. Whether some spark of the sweet and noble man she'd once known had managed to sustain itself inside the corrupted, blackened thing that was Cucuy.

You will never know, she told herself. *Soon all you have seen and done will be as ash in the wind, and the world will be cleansed of abomination. Perhaps the gods will feel a ripple in the fabric of the cosmos. Perhaps they will return.*

Chacanza smiled.

She was ready. And they had arrived.

DO NOT ENTER that room if you value your life. Not even I have dared set foot there since—

The blare of Cucuy's voice cut off abruptly, like a radio losing its signal, as Galvan followed Chacanza across the threshold.

There was nothing inside but a wooden platform covered in disintegrating, mildewed linens.

The marriage bed.

Galvan leaned the torch against a wall. Chacanza stared down at the bed, and Galvan followed her gaze, saw the stains. Burgundy.

And lying atop it, covered in rust, the sacred knife.

It hit him with the force of revelation, though he had known it all along.

"This is where you died."

"Yes."

She met him at the foot of the bed. "Tell me what I must do."

You know not what you do! Cucuy bellowed, so suddenly that Galvan startled. *Destroy me and you loose Tezcatlipoca on this world! Let us rule it together instead! Use my strength, Jess Galvan. Make yourself a god. Rule them with wisdom. Show them justice. I wanted those things too once. When I last stood in this room. I give you my word, I will not interfere.*

For a split second, a vision flashed through Galvan's mind.

Himself atop a golden throne, munificent and all-knowing.

Nice try, motherfucker.

Galvan shook it off.

"You've got to kill me," he told Chacanza, stepping around the bed so that they stood only inches apart. "The same way he killed you. Rip out my heart. Eat it."

All that you know will be torn asunder. Do not do as I have. Do not dabble in the arts of the gods.

Chacanza's eyes were wide and earnest.

"That will unmake him? Unmake us both?"

Galvan nodded. "But there's one more thing. We've got to be . . ."

She waited for him to tell her.

He waited for her to get it.

Expel me from this realm and I shall avenge myself against you with a fury you cannot begin to fathom.

"Fucking," Galvan blurted, when Cucuy's rant had run its course. "We've got to be fucking."

The word meant nothing to her. It was not of Chacanza's world.

"You know . . ." Galvan rifled through his mind for the phrase his compadre Brittanica had used, three months and what seemed like an entire lifetime ago, when the convict had first told Galvan the tragic story of Cualli and Chacanza.

For a long moment, the only thing that came to mind was an awful pun, *talk about going out with a bang,* Galvan's brain determined to spend its final minutes deploying the same laugh-to-keep-from-breaking dumbassery that had gotten him this far.

At least he was consistent.

"Joined as one," Galvan remembered at last.

That, Chacanza understood.

"It is the only way," she said. It was not a question but a statement, and Galvan didn't bother to reply.

Instead, with trembling hands and a heart gone hummingbird inside his chest, Galvan unclasped his belt and let his pants drop to the floor.

He'd been trying not to think about this part.

Chacanza watched him, somber, her green eyes like shimmering pools, and then lifted her dress over her head and stood naked before him.

"I'm ready," she said, and she climbed onto what remained of the bed.

Galvan looked over at her, and then down at himself.

"I'm, uh . . . not," he said.

Your children. Your children's children. All your issue, until the end of time. I will drive them mad, one after the next, until your name becomes a curse that men and gods alike despise to utter.

That wasn't helping either.

He closed his eyes and ground his teeth together, tried to concentrate. To cut through the blaring cacophony, subdue the terror.

Master himself.

You've come this far.

You ain't leaving this room alive.

So get it up and save the world, motherfucker.

But it was as if he'd already begun the process of abandoning his body. Only the thinnest filament of sensation connected him and his mind to his sex.

He groped with a hand, but neither part felt like it was his own. A cold sweat broke out across his brow, beneath his arms. He felt nauseated, feverish, as if his body was already breaking down, crumbling, returning to the earth.

And then, all of a sudden, Galvan felt her hands on him. Her mouth. His body came back into focus. He opened his eyes, looked down, and saw the sculpted porcelain curve of her back as she bent over him, and every vision he'd ever had of Chacanza came flooding into his mind, as if the dam holding them back had broken.

Cucuy was loose inside him, frenzied and desperate but also confused. Conflicted.

Excited.

Those haunting dreams of the woman in yellow had not been Galvan's alone; for five hundred years, the Terrible One had dreamed of his bride. They had called out to each other, beckoned across the vast reaches of space and time.

They were one being. They completed each other. And though he railed against it, recoiled from it, unfurled a litany of threats and pleas and lies, a part of Cucuy wanted this.

Wanted her, even if having her destroyed him.

If he hadn't, Galvan's body could not have cooperated.

As it was doing now.

Lust filled him, and he reached down and took Chacanza's face in his hands. She took her mouth off his cock, stared up at him, spoke in a throaty whisper.

"Take me, Cualli. Let us bring each other peace."

She took his hand, led Galvan to the bed. He eased inside her and heard himself moan, guttural and low, starbursts of color filling his field of vision. Cucuy's presence was a subsonic rumble inside him now, like a cat's purr, bespeaking some incomprehensible mixture of pleasure and violence, a precise fault line separating abandon and defeat.

She began to move beneath him, hips undulating, one hand pressed to his chest and the other wrapped around the hilt of the knife.

"Don't do it yet," he grunted. "Wait a little while."

Chacanza's legs were like a vise grip, locked around his back. She nodded.

"Yes. I will enjoy you first, my love."

Galvan closed his eyes. He didn't want to know when it was coming. Endorphins he'd never known existed saturated his body; he was experiencing heights of sensation he'd never dreamed possible, as far beyond normal human experience as the strength, the speed with which Cualli's presence had endowed him.

I should have done more of this.

He felt his release building, mounting inside him, and Galvan's eyes popped open.

Chacanza stared back, emerald eyes blazing like some otherworldly fire, and Galvan knew it was time.

His scream was pain and ecstasy at once, as Galvan came and the knife tore through his chest. Chacanza's hand plunged inside him, wrapped itself around the beating muscle, ripped it from its mooring of tissue and vein.

She shoved it in her mouth, and they died staring into each other's eyes.

Again.

EPILOGUE

No blackness this time.

No flurry of bats, no half-formed waiting room, no colorless ocean in the sky.

Those histrionics, he guessed, were reserved for the new arrivals.

Not the motherfuckers with the frequent customer punch cards.

Galvan awakened as if from a nap, naked and unscarred, heart beating quietly inside his chest. He was in a garden, strange and familiar at once. The place had changed in the time he'd been gone, but there was no mistaking it.

When the soul and body are severed from each other in a manner that is unnatural . . .

Galvan rose and looked around. There was a pall over the realm, somehow; the once-vibrant colors seemed muted, drained, as if Tezcatlipoca's kingdom were in mourning.

Which, it dawned on him now, was precisely the case.

The Dominio Gris had lost a queen. He felt it suddenly, acutely. Chacanza had been unmade. Her soul and body reunited and passed blissfully out of existence. She was at rest.

That was the price Tezcatlipoca had paid to know that he was safe, that he could not be summoned back from this land of invention and depravity. He'd given up his queen, just as he'd forced Cucuy to do.

Cucuy.

Galvan felt his heartbeat accelerate as he considered the priest's fate.

Let us bring each other peace, Cualli.

Chacanza had believed it. Mercy had guided her hand. What she had done, she had done for them both. To rejoin what had been torn asunder, rid the universe of the twinned abominations Tezcatlipoca had brought into being.

But perhaps Tezcatlipoca had other ideas. Perhaps his gambit had been about more than securing the borders of his land, eliminating any challenge to his timeless reign.

Perhaps his own capacity for cruelty bored him. Perhaps the beings who populated this realm, with their limitless capacity to endure it, did too.

Just then, a voice broke the silence.

"Maybe you're wondering where everybody is."

Galvan turned to see Gum picking his way across a vast, empty expanse of light pink sand.

And indeed, just as he said, the place was utterly devoid of life.

"Yes," he heard himself say, in a voice sludgy with disuse.

"Come with me." Gum beckoned, and Galvan followed.

In the distance, beyond a sweeping hill, a sound like thunder boomed. They walked toward it.

"So," Gum said, "how was that shit, anyway?"

Galvan scowled at him.

"You know. The queen."

And Gum made the finger-in-the-hole gesture, like some third-grade punk. Without thinking, Galvan swung a fist and knocked him on his ass.

"Whoa, whoa. Take it easy." Gum raised his palms in surrender, and Galvan shook his head, extended a hand, hauled him back up.

"She died a hero," he said. "Heroine. Whatever. That's all you need to know."

Gum shut the fuck up, and they walked on.

"Well, shit's been crazy here, boss. When she died, Tezcatlipoca shut everything down. I'm talking no light, no water, no fucking *atmosphere*. It was like being a bug stuck in amber. Total sensory deprivation, except for *that*." Gum gestured at the hill, the sound. "His screams. Seemed like it lasted forever."

Galvan furrowed his brow. "How long's it been since—" he started to ask, but it didn't matter. Time didn't work the same here anyway.

He'd have to get used to that.

"And it's only gonna get crazier," Gum concluded, as they reached the top of the hill. "See what I mean?"

Galvan looked, and his jaw dropped.

Sitting low above the valley was the ocean in the sky. It churned with pregnant fury, a swirl of pastel hues.

Below, the girls swarmed the field—all twenty-some-odd thousand of them. They stared up at the sky, rapt and expectant, as the ocean shaped itself into a funnel, a tornado.

Tezcatlipoca floated above them, his form massive, his golden glow filling the air. And as the funnel deepened, his booming cries of anguish changed.

Grew deeper.

Became a maniacal laugh more terrifying than any wail of sorrow.

The tornado disgorged what was contained within in, and the god's laughter reached a crescendo.

A young man, clad in robes of pure white, spun through the air in what seemed like slow motion and then crashed to the ground.

Silence, sudden and absolute.

Tezcatlipoca alighted a few paces away, strode to the supine newcomer as the girls crowded around, jostling for position.

The man lifted his head an instant before the god grabbed his mane of jet-black hair and jerked him to his feet.

It was Cualli.

Cualli, tall and fresh and beautiful.

Cualli as he must have looked when the world was young and uncorrupted.

Cualli, gazing at the women he had doomed.

The god he had served.

The god he had betrayed.

The very beings at whose eternal mercy he now found himself.

Though *mercy* was a word that had no place here.

For some reason he could not explain, Galvan felt a sudden, uncontrollable urge to help him, an inexplicable sense that even in this land beyond all reckoning, their fates were still intertwined.

"Welcome," Tezcatlipoca said. "You have no idea how badly I have wanted to see you again, Cualli."

And the god's laughter boomed across his kingdom.

ABOUT THE AUTHOR

ADAM MANSBACH is the author of the instant *New York Times* bestsellers *Go the F**k to Sleep* and *You Have to F**king Eat*, as well as the novels *The Dead Run, Rage is Back, Angry Black White Boy*, and *The End of the Jews*, the winner of the California Book Award. He was the 2009–2011 New Voices Professor of Fiction at Rutgers University, a 2012 Sundance Screenwriting Lab Fellow, a 2013 Berkeley Repertory Theater Writing Fellow, and a 2015 Artist in Residence at Stanford University's Institute for Diversity in the Arts. His work has appeared in *The New Yorker,* the *New York Times Book Review, Esquire,* and *The Believer,* and on National Public Radio's *All Things Considered.* He lives in Berkeley, California.